$15.95

D

PENGUIN  CLASSICS

TWO TUDOR TRAGEDIES

THOMAS NORTON, son of a well-to-do London citizen, was born in 1532. Educated at Cambridge and married to a daughter of the martyred Archbishop Thomas Cranmer, in 1555 he entered the Inner Temple in London and in 1561 published Calvin's *Institution of Christian Religion* in English translation. He also served as an MP on several occasions. The savagery he exhibited in interrogating English Catholics later earned him the nickname of 'Rackmaster General', but his criticism of Anglican bishops eventually led to his own imprisonment in the Tower of London for treason. His period in prison appears to have broken his health, and he died in March 1584.

THOMAS SACKVILLE was born in Sussex in 1536 and died as Baron Buckhurst and Earl of Dorset. Son of a prosperous lawyer and government official, he studied at Oxford as well as at the Inner Temple, where Thomas Norton was a fellow-student. Like Norton, he entered Parliament in 1558, becoming a favourite of Queen Elizabeth and a member of various diplomatic missions abroad. He was ennobled in 1567 and made a Privy Councillor in 1571, served as Lord Treasurer of England from 1599 and was created an Earl in 1604. His literary work included the *Induction* to the 1563 edition of *A Mirror for Magistrates*. He died during a meeting of the Privy Council at Whitehall in April 1608.

THOMAS KYD, the son of a prosperous London scrivener, was born in 1558; he attended the Merchant Taylors' School in the City but did not proceed to university, probably following his father's trade for some years before adopting literature as his profession. His name is first associated with that of a leading theatrical company, the Queen's Men; in 1591 he was sharing rooms with his fellow-playwright Christopher Marlowe. In 1593 both Kyd and Marlowe were arrested, and Kyd was imprisoned and possibly tortured. Despite the publication in 1594 of *Cornelia*, a version of Robert Garnier's French neo-classical tragedy, Kyd's career seems never to have recovered, and he died, impoverished, in August 1594.

WILLIAM TYDEMAN, educated at Maidstone Grammar School and University College, Oxford, is currently Professor of English at the University of Wales, Bangor, and Head of the School of English and Linguistics there. His publications include *The Theatre in the Middle Ages* (1978) and *English Medieval Theatre 1400–1500* (1986); he edited *Four Tudor Comedies* in the Penguin Classics series and in 1987 contributed a study of *Henry V* to Penguin Critical Studies.

Two Tudor Tragedies

GORBODUC
THOMAS NORTON AND THOMAS SACKVILLE

THE SPANISH TRAGEDY
THOMAS KYD

Edited with an Introduction and Notes by
WILLIAM TYDEMAN

PENGUIN BOOKS

To Peter Bayley, Dennis Burden, John Buxton +

My very noble and approv'd good masters

PENGUIN BOOKS

Published by the Penguin Group

Penguin Books Ltd, 27 Wrights Lane, London w8 5tz, England

Penguin Books USA Inc., 375 Hudson Street, New York, New York 10014, USA

Penguin Books Australia Ltd, Ringwood, Victoria, Australia

Penguin Books Canada Ltd, 10 Alcorn Avenue, Toronto, Ontario, Canada m4v 3b2

Penguin Books (NZ) Ltd, 182–190 Wairau Road, Auckland 10, New Zealand

Penguin Books Ltd, Registered Offices: Harmondsworth, Middlesex, England

This edition first published 1992

1 3 5 7 9 10 8 6 4 2

Printed in England by Clays Ltd, St Ives plc

CONTENTS

INTRODUCTION

I

No one could seriously assert that *Gorboduc* offers a more satisfying theatrical experience than *King Lear* or pretend that *The Spanish Tragedy* can ever hold a place in our imaginations comparable to that assigned to *Hamlet*. Two mature law-students collaborating on a resolute exercise in classical pastiche, and a playwright inventing a saga of intrigue, courtship and bloodshed, could scarcely be expected to add a *Dr Faustus*, a *Macbeth*, a *Duchess of Malfi* to the stock of national masterpieces overnight. Yet so rapidly did English tragedy develop in fluency and sophistication during the 1590s that we may easily underestimate the achievements of those who blazed an experimental Anglo-Saxon trail into territories often regarded as sacred to the ancient Greeks. Few literary genres can have had such unlikely begetters as English Renaissance tragedy, and it is one of literature's stranger success stories that from a union between the heavy Latin chamber-dramas of Seneca and the homiletic narratives of medieval Christianity sprang a dramatic hybrid in whose image Marlowe, Shakespeare, Webster and their contemporaries would create some of their finest work. Whatever the shortcomings of the earliest English tragedies, we cannot help being aware as we read them (or very rarely watch them) that they anticipate the signal excellence of dramas then unwritten. Aged Gorboduc summoning a council to witness the parcelling-out of his kingdom to rival offspring, old

Hieronimo desperately clinging to his sanity while seeking a means by which to exact revenge, may not exhibit the universal appeal of a Lear or a Hamlet, but the resemblances are there. Later Elizabethan and Jacobean tragedy might have developed very differently had it not been for the turn taken by the pioneering spirits of Sackville, Norton and Kyd.

Their inheritance was complex. Artistic presentations of physical and emotional suffering were not unknown in literature during the Middle Ages, but the mental framework of the late medieval period gave to its tragedy a very different orientation from that of the Elizabethans. In medieval writing one senses little resistance to the notion that sorrow and pain are the unavoidable lot of human beings while on earth, and small belief that mortal existence offers the opportunity for achieving a sense of enduring personal fulfilment. Human experience seems merely to demonstrate the deceptive allure of temporal glory, the fragility of fortune's favours, the inevitability of mortality, and the general instability and transience of life in an inimical universe:

> Wynter wakeneth al my care,
> Nou this leves waxeth bare;
> Ofte I sike [sigh] ant mourne sare [sore]
> When hit cometh in my thoht
> Of this worldes joie, hou hit goth al to noht.

In these and in similar terms the medieval concept of tragedy usually defines itself, focusing on the unwisdom of reposing faith in life's capacity to sustain our deepest needs and desires.

The Middle Ages did not reserve the term 'tragedy' exclusively for drama: Chaucer in completing his poem of love and war, *Troilus and Criseyde*, refers to it as 'litel myn tragedye' (V. 1786), and his use of the word is instructive. His radical reworking of Boccaccio's *Il Filostrato* locates the tragic experience in the Trojan warrior Troilus's doomed love-affair with the widowed daughter of the traitor Calchas, a heady but vulnerable relationship unable to withstand the pressures of wartime so that it ends with Criseyde's defection to the Greeks and Troilus's death in battle. While the loss of an ardent young life is regretted, Chaucer shies away from placing the emphasis where an Elizabethan might lay it, namely on the tragedy of youthful innocence caught in the grip of forces beyond its control (as might be claimed of Romeo and Juliet), stressing rather the callow understanding of a lover who had entrusted all his hopes to the durability of an emotional bond certain to prove fragile and evanescent. To fall in love was not itself culpable; the fatal error was to believe that such an experience was stable enough to meet that longing for permanence for which there was only one true satisfaction:

> O yonge, fresshe folkes, he or she,
> In which that love up groweth with youre age,
> Repeyreth hom fro worldly vanyte,
> And of youre herte up casteth the visage
> To thilke God that after his ymage
> Yow made, and thynketh al nys but a faire
> This world, that passeth soone as floures faire.
>
> (V. 1835–41)

What appears initially to be a vindication of the Right to Love or a lament that 'Nobody Understands Young People' turns out to demonstrate the traditional moral that this unsatisfactory and transitory world is to be despised and mistrusted, a sermon on the perils of laying up treasure on earth.

Another *locus classicus* of medieval tragedy is found in *The Canterbury Tales* at the point where the normally jovial Monk decides to contribute to the proceedings a number of 'tragedies' whose subjects range from Lucifer to Julius Caesar, but which prove too tediously gloomy for his fellow-pilgrims to suffer for long. Yet the premise behind these potted biographies is by

medieval standards immaculate; the Monk speaks by the book
when he announces his intentions:

> Tragedie is to seyn a certeyn storie,
> As olde bookes maken us memorie,
> Of hym that stood in greet prosperitee,
> And is yfallen out of heigh degree
> Into myserie, and endeth wrecchedly.
> (*The Canterbury Tales*, B² 3163–7)

For this diagnosis and the Monk's method of illustrating it,
Boccaccio was once more Chaucer's inspiration; his *De Casibus
Virorum Illustrium* ('Of the Falls of Famous Men') (*c.* 1360–74)
set a fashion for narrative accounts of the unhappy case-histories
of celebrated figures from legend and chronicle, whose worldly
success culminated in downfall and disaster. Boccaccio was
clearly influenced by the belief that human beings cannot
control their own destinies, and while aware that tragedy is not
totally arbitrary in its operation, since it tends to visit those
whose temperaments incite them to heroic action, he refuses to
link it causally to any kind of character flaw or weakness of
personality. Tragedy can visit both the just and the unjust; it is
the price paid by those whose nature or social standing inspires
them to undertake strenuous tasks. As Jean Anouilh was to
observe later, 'tragedy is for kings', a vehicle in which plebeians
cannot aspire to star. To attain tragic stature one must have
attained eminence, even that bad eminence to which Lucifer
was exalted, in order to plunge downwards with sufficient
momentum to attract attention.

For Boccaccio tragedy resides less in the individual's responsibility for his or her fate, and more in the contrast between
one's status and contentment when Fortune smiled, and one's
wretchedness now she frowns. Since her behaviour is arbitrary
one must learn not to 'trust on blynde prosperitee', which is
fickle: the two imposters Triumph and Disaster are to be

accepted with equanimity as equally untrustworthy. Best of all attitudes is to regard this earth as an unsatisfactory vale of sorrows to be endured rather than enjoyed, and to focus one's thoughts on that celestial happiness which lies beyond the grave and will last for ever. As a result, to the committed Christian believer human existence could never be utterly tragic, since for the virtuous at least the consolation of an after-life must balance out mundane disappointments. A Christian universe must be held in abeyance to be compatible with the notion of tragic finality; the assurance of a life after death must negate whatever is suffered submissively here below.

As the Middle Ages approached the transition to the Renaissance, however, the blows Fortune dealt out to the unwary were explained less as arbitrary penalties likely to be exacted from innocent and culpable alike, and more as a retributive punishment divinely imposed on those guilty of vice and moral error. During the fifteenth century such writers as John Lydgate in his monumentally protracted *Fall of Princes* (*c.* 1431–9) showed tragedy not so much as the fortuitous reversal of good luck as the result of heavenly chastisement for sins committed. Such a shift in thinking is less apparent in the religious drama of the period, where the morality plays in particular continue to depict Christian salvation as the guaranteed reward of every repentant transgressor against God's laws who chooses to turn from his wickedness and live. Guilty of folly and moral blindness, the morality heroes of the fifteenth and early sixteenth centuries foreshadow the thoughtless or feckless conduct of their counterparts in Elizabethan tragedy, but with this difference, that they are reprieved at the last moment by the intervention of spiritual mentors who steer them away from utter damnation. Yet as the sixteenth century advances, moral plays demonstrate increasingly that failure to reform and repent can have but one end, a conclusion which an orthodoxly Christian reading of Marlowe's *Faustus* would confirm.

This is clearly brought out in the celebrated Elizabethan

continuation of Lydgate's lengthy compilation, an extension first published in 1559 and undergoing several revisions. *A Mirror for Magistrates* utilizes examples from British myth and history to illustrate the same process that lies behind the original *De Casibus* narratives of Boccaccio and Lydgate. Following the latter's example, the authors of the poetic monologues which comprise the *Mirror* stress that misfortunes are rarely random assaults on the innocent but generally plague those whose wicked conduct or faulty judgement renders them liable to succumb. Viciousness is not always the cause of downfall; more often inordinate ambition or unreasonable aspiration is to blame, and the message becomes increasingly admonitory as new editions appear: learn wisdom from examples before you, and worldly prosperity may still be attained and enjoyed in serenity of mind. No longer is the warning heard that *all* worldly endeavour is vain travail and not worth the struggle; the aim is rather to avoid 'the just punishment of God in revenge of a vicious and evil life' (George Puttenham). Kings, princes and governors (the 'magistrates' of the title) should exercise restraint and discretion in their dealings, which are more essential than practising a by-now-discredited asceticism. Herein lay the foundations for a native approach to the creation of tragic drama.

The idea that there was a correlation between a person's personality, conduct and ultimate fate did not develop spontaneously, nor did it inform every specimen of sixteenth-century tragedy; some might argue that the concept of an arbitrary Fortune still prevails in Marlowe's *Tamburlaine* and in *Romeo and Juliet*. But in general the nexus perceived between character, behaviour and destiny was vital in making possible the great tragedies composed in the years 1590–1620: acceptance of Fortune's arbitrary transformations had to give way to a keener awareness of humanity's capacity to take independent decisions and exercise moral choices before the world could be viewed as something other than

> a Chequer-board of Nights and Days
> Where Destiny with Men for Pieces plays . . .

A greater freedom to speculate on the ultimate purpose of human life on earth became apparent, and the traditional medieval doctrine that the world should be held in contempt was replaced by the belief that mortal life did not have to be dismissed as a mere painful prelude to a glorious recompense in some Celestial City. Renaissance thinkers were in the main optimistic about the human potential for terrestrial happiness and fulfilment: it is notable that the heroes and heroines of great tragedy are inclined to demand too much of the universe, not too little; they gain our pity in part from their capacity to be betrayed by a world in which they had some justification for placing their trust.

The climate was right for dramatic tragedy to emerge, but the final impetus was supplied from a curious quarter. Lucius Annaeus Seneca (*c.* 4 B.C.–A.D. 65), a Roman writer of treatises on Stoic philosophy and of memorable letters, was also the composer of nine or ten tragedies in verse, rendering into somewhat unrelievedly formalized Latin the familiar Greek stories of Oedipus, Medea, Phaedra, Thyestes, Agamemnon and others. Seneca's dramas are pallid beside those of his Athenian models, but for the neo-classical aspirants of the Renaissance his insistent moralizing, his aphorisms, his doom-laden settings, his contrivedly striking flights of rhetoric, his horrifying climaxes (such as that in which Thyestes is tricked by his brother Atreus into consuming the remains of his sons baked in a pie), made a profound appeal. Seneca provided a safe route to the riches of the classical heritage as well as an accessible precedent for those European authors eager to emulate the literary achievements of the ancient world.

Perhaps too much was made early in this century of Seneca's influence on the development of English tragedy, and certainly the *De Casibus* tradition continued to act as a powerful and popular inspiration. Yet the vogue for Seneca in both schools and universities cannot be ignored; the plays were first published in Italy in 1474, the earliest English stage production recorded dates from 1551, and between 1559 and 1561 Jasper Heywood started a fashion by making English versions of the *Troas, Thyestes* and *Hercules Furens* which formed the nucleus of a collection entitled *Seneca His Ten Tragedies translated into English*, compiled by Thomas Newton (1581). These translations, though fairly accurate, often expand liberally on Seneca's already verbose originals, and employ fourteen-syllable lines arranged in rhymed couplets, neither feature being destined, one feels, to increase the circle of Seneca's English admirers appreciably. Yet T. S. Eliot has accorded these versions 'considerable poetic charm' and even 'occasional flashes of real beauty', and their quality as well as their importance must be admitted. Seneca was well-known to many in both translation and in the original, and numerous playwrights capitalized on that familiarity by sprinkling their dramas with stylistic features which the Roman writer had made his own, most notably the *sententia* or pithy aphorism which encapsulated some piece of generalized gnomic wisdom. While the centrality of ghostly visitants and ghastly violence to the Senecan convention has been over-exaggerated – only two ghosts appear in the nine tragedies indisputedly his and violence is more often reported than seen – his distinctive mode of discourse – vehement, frenzied, self-questioning, colourfully mythological, hyperbolic, indicative of extreme states of physical and emotional stress – is a pervasive presence in early Elizabethan tragic drama.

As Eliot admitted, 'In the plays of Seneca the drama is all in the word,' and dramatic value lies in its manner of delivery rather than in what is delivered. Moreover, little attempt is made to give the characters distinct modes of speech by which they can be identified, or to employ language in order to create personality. The deleterious effect that this has on the evolution of vibrant and dynamic drama can be seen in *Gorboduc*, yet it seems reasonable to accept that this could reflect Seneca's lack of interest in seeing his tragedies publicly presented, and to attribute to his influence at least the genesis of a style of stage oratory which in the hands of abler craftsmen became one of the most glorious achievements of the Elizabethan stage.

Seneca offered his disciples more than this. He supplied them with a sense of structure, which native precedent signally failed to do. True, his organization is imposed from without, rather than being organic, but it is there. Whether it is to him or to the Roman comic dramatist Terence that we owe the 'five-act structure' of the majority of Elizabethan plays is not clear, but the increasingly logical and integrated construction of English plays after *c.* 1560 owed much to a writer who had demonstrated how to build a carefully shaped dramatic whole through a series of sequential steps. Seneca's plots were notably uncomplex, and men like Kyd had to depart from their model if they were to find room for all the heterogeneous materials they chose to include. Yet the Roman playwright supplied a stringent touch of dramatic discipline when the development of English tragic drama had need of it.

II

Gorboduc, which had its first performance at London's Inner Temple during the Christmas celebrations of 1561, may have come into being largely as a result of the Senecan cult, but it is clear that it owes its existence to something more than an urge to produce a colourless imitation of a Latin tragedy. Faithful as they were to their mentor in dividing the dramatic action into five phases, in introducing choric commentators at the close of each act, in lavishly lacing their verse with *sententiae*, and in banishing physical violence to the wings, Sackville and Norton succeeded in avoiding servile pastiche. Sir Philip Sidney in his *Apology for Poetry* (1595) was quick to reprehend the authors for ignoring the ancient recommendations concerning the handling of time and place:

> . . . it is faulty in both place and time, the two necessary
> companions of all corporal actions. For where the stage
> should always represent but one place, and the uttermost
> time presupposed in it should be, both by Aristotle's
> precept and common reason, but one day, there is both
> many days, and many places, inartificially [inartistically]
> imagined.

Yet the choice of a diffuse subject inevitably dictated straying
outside the narrow limits of Gorboduc's palace, while the
story-line necessarily demanded a longer time-span than the
single day advocated in Aristotle's *Poetics*. Medieval tradition
sanctioned an elastic time-scale and the establishment of several
different locations successively and sometimes simultaneously.
Sidney, who waxes scornful at the primitive crudity of multiple
settings, might have complimented his authors on the relative
modesty of their demands on their audience's credibility, and
commended them on avoiding any notion of a sub-plot (particularly a comic one) which would have threatened the singleness
of the action and the homogeneity of the tragic diction.

Gorboduc's modified classicism is compromised in other ways;
while ostensibly a tragedy of familial passion and internecine
strife, its inspiration through British pseudo-history accentuates
its national and political concerns. John Bale, in his Protestant
polemic based on the idealized figure of King John (*c.* 1538),
had already employed for the purposes of topical propaganda
thirteenth-century events and personalities, much as Sackville
and Norton were to use the figures of Geoffrey of Monmouth
for similar ends. In the same way, the play's strong political
concern for the welfare of the realm relates it to such works as
John Skelton's *Magnificence* (*c.* 1520) and Nicholas Udall's *Respub-
lica* (*c.* 1553), which not only allegorize the nation's problems,
but virtually make the fate of the kingdom their overriding
theme. But perhaps the most significant deviations from the
Senecan model occur where the genre of the religious morality

play is laid most heavily under debt. While Sackville and Norton eschew the presentation of graphic personifications of abstract qualities, the Greek-derived names of several of the leading figures remind us of the moralities by conveying to educated spectators the psychological calibre of the characters concerned. Thus Arostus is 'weak', Philander 'seeks to please', Eubulus exercises 'prudent judgement'. Moreover, the highly patterned complementary nature of many of the exchanges testifies to the pervasive influence of the religious morality, which specializes in similarly antithetical dialogue in which conflicting forces strive for mastery over the conduct of a central vacillating figure. The structure of many scenes may owe something to the forensic bias of their authors' professional training, but the battles between the forces of good and evil for mastery over the spiritual destination of a Mankind figure are certainly called to mind as parasite and sage combat verbally for the attention of a Ferrex or a Porrex torn between two courses of action very much as the hero of the Christian drama teeters between salvation and damnation.

The play thus partakes of several conventions, but it was doubtless the *De Casibus* tradition which accounts for the choice of subject-matter. The principal source was almost certainly the *Historia Regum Britanniae* (The History of Kings of Britain), composed by the twelfth-century chronicler Geoffrey of Monmouth, who completed his blend of fact, fiction and fancy in 1136. His literary importance lies less in the accuracy of his statements than in his appeal to the creative imagination; in his pages we not only discover a seminal account of the legendary warrior-king Arthur, but also the first allusion to events said to have taken place during and after the reign of King Leir or Lear.

On the face of it Geoffrey's account of occurrences involving Gorboduc and his progeny is not particularly remarkable; it is printed in full in the Appendix to this edition so that readers may judge the matter themselves. What is immediately notable is that into Geoffrey's outline Sackville and Norton incorporated features which potentially at least increased its theatrical possibilities. Gorboduc, instead of being senile, is introduced in Act I Scene 2 as a vigorous old man still in command of his faculties, seeking justification from his counsellors for an already determined act of abdication which will divide his realm between his two sons. As a result their rivalry has its origins in Gorboduc's own action; by concentrating on the monarch's personal responsibility for his decision to abdicate and ignore the laws of primogeniture, Sackville and Norton make Gorboduc one of that breed of men indicted in *A Mirror for Magistrates* for acts of folly and inept judgement, while the chronicler merely saw him as innocent victim. The disasters which befall his house and his kingdom are in some measure self-generated, and Gorboduc pays the price.

What the authors obviously found appealing in Geoffrey's account and in any other versions they may have read was the close affinity between the blood-feuds within the royal household – jealous brothers, partial mother, fratricide, filicide – and those crimes of ambition and revenge which formed a central aspect of Seneca's revampings of Greek tragedy which they so admired. The gruesome blights which disfigure the family trees of Agamemnon, Oedipus and Atreus conditioned those who sought to emulate the Roman tragedian to adopt a story-line from British history which offered them similar scope for exploiting aspiration and vengeance, passion and lamentation, crime and punishment, within a single household.

Other changes are of equal significance: clearly it was not in keeping with even the loosest interpretation of the classical 'rules' that Norton and Sackville should allow themselves scope to represent Ferrex's expedition to seek aid from the King of the Franks, and this aspect of Geoffrey's chronicle is not alluded to. However, it was astute to link to the deaths of Gorboduc and Videna the popular rising which precipitates the period of civil war, even if the former's murder deprives the final act of the play's central character, a deficiency open to objection not merely from doctrinaire Aristotelians, but also from those who prefer tragedies to culminate in some climactic crisis rather than to peter out in political platitudes, however motivated by concern for the commonwealth. The danger is that our interest, sustained by concern for the plight of Gorboduc, not that of his disturbed kingdom, tends to wane.

However, we must attempt to see this aspect of the action through Elizabethan eyes, and not lose sight of the topical impulse behind the Inner Temple enterprise. A comparison between Geoffrey of Monmouth's narrative and the argument of the play highlights one further difference between them: the Elizabethan writers' removal of Gorboduc before the end of the tragedy which bears his name reveals that dynastic propaganda and issues of national welfare were more important to them than the creation of a personal tragedy. To the sixteenth century the events of history had a peculiar status second only to that of Holy Writ as a potent source of precedents and examples on which the present generation could draw for guidance, inspiration or admonition. This was after all the premise upon which the success of *A Mirror for Magistrates* relied, and that it was never far from the minds of the authors of *Gorboduc* seems explicitly acknowledged in the conclusion of the chorus to Act I:

And this great King, that doth divide his land,
And change the course of his descending crown,
And yields the rein into his children's hand,
From blissful state of joy and great renown,
A mirror shall become to princes all,
To learn to shun the cause of such a fall.

(lines 457–62)

The application of the play's political didacticism to the England of Elizabeth I may not appear obvious at first sight:

Elizabeth was unlikely either to abdicate in 1562 or to divide her realm between two offspring which she did not have, but Sackville and his partner did not conceive their message in quite such unsubtle terms. It is often forgotten, in the light of the so-called glories of her later years on the throne, that Elizabeth's grip on the reins of government was never a secure one. It could never be guaranteed that some over-mighty subject, a Spanish assault-force or a Catholic assassin would be permanently frustrated in the attempt to remove her from her high office. Should she die through natural cause or unnatural crime, moreover, the line of succession was more than likely to be contested, and there was no shortage of king-makers who might plunge the court and the nation into a long spell of conflict. While it was vital that Parliament should be associated with any decision taken on naming a suitable successor for the Queen, it was felt to be even more important that Elizabeth should marry and set about providing the country with an undisputed heir. It is this lesson which *Gorboduc* appears to have been composed to teach in as tactful but firm a manner as possible, by pointing up the horrors which had befallen the ancient kingdom of Britain because of the unnecessary creation of harrowing dynastic convulsions.

That the Queen herself felt impelled to demand a command performance in her palace of Whitehall on 18 January 1561-2 may be an indication of the importance she attached to *Gorboduc*'s use of the drama as a vehicle for patriotic sentiment, but it does not automatically follow. The Queen's curiosity may have been as much inspired by her diligence as a student of the classics and as a reader of Seneca herself as by her sensitivity as a politician. Sackville was after all a kinsman, his father being cousin to her mother Anne Boleyn, and glowing accounts of her clever relative's prowess as an author may have persuaded her to receive the players at Whitehall, rather than any concern to see that the Inns of Court men were not over-stepping the mark by discussing issues affecting the royal prerogative.

Gorboduc was a new departure from theatrical precedent, and Elizabeth could well have wished to inspect such a novelty for herself.

It is a pity that one of its novelties was that it was apparently the first major work for the English stage to be written in blank-verse. So accustomed are most readers of *Gorboduc* to approach it only after developing at least a nodding acquaintance with Shakespeare's fluent and dynamic iambic pentameters that they are apt to dismiss the verse of Sackville and Norton as stiff, frigid and monotonous by contrast. For their time, however, the metrics of *Gorboduc* are in fact surprisingly accomplished, given that blank-verse itself can hardly have been much practised prior to 1547, when its 'inventor', Henry Howard Earl of Surrey, was beheaded by Henry VIII. Admittedly, there is more end-stopping of the lines than we can now approve of, but there is also a greater degree of *enjambement* than we might anticipate; the regular positioning of the caesura is all too easy to forecast, but there is still an unexpectedly large amount of variation within lines, and an assurance and polish which, while lacking a few artful irregularities to supply variety, is still welcome beside the clumsy thump of the 'fourteeners' beloved of the Senecan translators. *Gorboduc* is a conscious attempt to equip the stateliest literary form known to the pioneers of 1561 with a verse medium dignified enough to allow weighty and illustrious characters to speak without incongruity.

What one misses most obviously is the full range of a rich and copious vocabulary deployed to lend the diction colour as well as sonority. There is a costive quality about the language, a clinical and antiseptic chill pervades it, and the absence of alluring figures such as simile and metaphor is felt the more acutely because of the brilliance with which the grand masters of the English tongue were to employ them some decades later. The vocabulary is frequently repetitive, the vast array of synonyms and variants which Marlowe and Shakespeare fling about so liberally is missing, and even when figurative features raise their heads, they seem tame and obvious. Yet there is a compensatory unity about the play's verbal texture; just as kings and clowns are not permitted to mingle on the neo-classical stage, so the diction of *Gorboduc* does not require us to reconcile or make constant adjustments between the dialogue of those who dominate throne-rooms and those who frequent taverns. The restless modulations of *Henry IV* lay some thirty years or more in the future: *Gorboduc* is conceived of as a single monochrome tapestry, not an extravagantly multi-coloured patchwork quilt.

As drama *Gorboduc* consists of a mixture of effective stage moments and a plethora of lengthy static set-speeches. How-ever, to judge the work objectively we must bear in mind Wolfgang Clemen's shrewd remark that 'Speech is the lifeblood of *Gorboduc*, the almost exclusive medium by which it is given the character of a play.' As spectators brought up with an entirely different set of criteria for theatrical excellence, we may become restive when confronting a work whose vitality seems stifled by the stiff brocade of formal oratory, yet in 1561 tragedy was in its infancy, and had to be protected from the contaminating touch of colloquial laxity. Sceptical of the regis-ter in which so much of the boisterous business of the Tudor interlude was conducted, Sackville and Norton may have delib-erately decided to avoid anything smacking of native unsophisti-cation, aware of Seneca's blend of lofty rhetoric and visual stasis, and perhaps lacking the inventiveness to balance out their linguistic austerity with sufficiently exciting stage action.

Not that the abstinence from theatrical satisfactions is total: the dumb-shows could well prove effective in production, and there are moments of genuine tension and conflict scattered throughout the tragedy, however little characterization contrib-utes to the effect. The first scene between Ferrex and his mother is brief but promises well, fraught as it is with sup-pressed hatred and the undertones of an incestuous love, yet the long scene which follows is disappointingly tame, given the competing views advanced. Norton (if the scene is his) lacks the skill to convey temperament through traits of speech, so that a stereotyped sameness informs the rival counsellors' speeches, which does little to relieve the prolixity of their replies to Gorboduc's request for advice. It is also unfortunate that the King, having allowed them their say, decides not to arbitrate between his advisors' views, but proceeds to announce his plans almost as if his advisors had never spoken.

Act II is considerably stronger in dramatic interest: the figures of Ferrex and Porrex are economically drawn, and one senses a greater degree of vacillation in the characters as they are pulled this way and that by opposing forces. Norton here reveals a shrewder grasp of theatrical dynamics: Hermon, in suggesting that Ferrex would be wise to get his blow in first, is credibly irresponsible, and there is a nice touch of tactical disbelief in Dordan's shocked response, and a perennial irony in Ferrex's bland assertion that, although he will never be the aggressor, it may be as well to prepare armaments in case Porrex is tempted to steal a march on him. Act II Scene 2, though more terse, follows the pattern of its predecessor, Tyndar neatly echoing Hermon by inciting Porrex to action on the strength of his brother's military preparations, in whose defensive nature he clearly does not believe.

Act III contains fewer dramatic rewards: although Philander's arrival with news of the outbreak of hostilities between the brothers bodes well, the tension is soon dissolved in debate until the Messenger appears to report the death of Ferrex. The poignancy is weakened by the generalized manner in which Gorboduc expresses his grief, and although the act would not prove impossible to stage in a slightly abstract sense, the pathos of the protagonist seems curiously deficient. More powerful is Videna's eighty-line soliloquy in Act IV in which she keys herself up by means of some highly Senecan rhetoric replete with garish imagery in order to avenge the murder of her favourite son, but where she still manages to convey something of her own sentiments into the bargain. Some effort is expended here to develop the suggestion of a sentient personality behind the words, but the dominant impression is still of an oratorical set-piece being adapted to fit the rhetorical needs of the situation, rather than convey its theatrical and psychological implications. In the scene which follows (IV.2), another excellent potential conflict, this time between Gorboduc and Porrex, gets bogged down in discourse, although Porrex's defence of his own actions and description of what he regards as his brother's treacherous machinations form a striking passage (lines 1088–127). The action terminates with Marcella's impassioned account of Videna's murder of her younger son, which momentarily lifts the finale of the act.

It is hard to resist the notion that Act V constitutes an anticlimax, however hard one maintains that the kingdom not the King is by now the true subject of the tragedy. The only characters to arouse our interest are dead, and we are left with a residue of faceless nobles and counsellors whose functions have previously been subordinate ones. Now they are thrust forward without the needful dramatic authority to hold our attention. Little of Geoffrey's account remains for development and although Fergus might have commanded some belated curiosity, perhaps by being accorded some of the engaging traits of the morality Vice figure, he lacks the charisma or dynamism of personality and speech that were to make Shakespeare's usurping schemer, Richard Duke of Gloucester, such an outstandingly attractive and entertaining stage villain. Not only does Fergus arrive on the scene too late to involve us in his plans, but we are never privileged to see the nakedness of his ambitions in a context provided by other contenders for or defenders of the crown. Dramatic inventiveness appears to be at a low ebb by now, and Act V Scene 2, though long on political wisdom and national fervour, is distinctly short on theatrical drive and linguistic pith, and the action has ceased to engross us well before Eubulus's lengthy speech concludes the tragedy with a dark vision of political anarchy which lightens only in the last few lines.

Gorboduc has been variously criticized as being defective in imitating the best features of classical tragedy, as belonging more to antiquarianism than to live drama, as cold and unrelieved, and even as being 'a pretty sorry piece of work'. However, to judge it fairly we must adopt the standards of its own age, in which context its chaste and majestic austerity, its rejection of secondary interests, its consistency of register, its carefully evolving development, its harmonious blend of native and classical elements, all offset the lack of conventional theatrical stimuli. Given imaginative direction and a tolerant audience aware of its historical significance, *Gorboduc* might still be brought to life in the theatre today. Despite obvious weaknesses, there is a kind of classical purity and marmoreal strength about the first English tragedy.

III

The Spanish Tragedy seized the public imagination in the decade between 1580 and 1590 when the permanent playhouses of Elizabethan London were becoming leading components of the capital's leisure scene, and young writers of ambition and talent were jostling each other aside in their attempts to establish themselves in this challenging new industry. Many, like John Lyly, Robert Greene, George Peele, Christopher Marlowe and Thomas Nashe, former students of Oxford and Cambridge Universities, were attracted to the theatre much as their bright young successors of the 1950s and 1960s were to be fascinated by the world of television, and part of the jealousy aroused by Shakespeare no doubt stemmed from his provincial grammar-school background and lack of an honours degree. The famous attack on the 'upstart crow' by Robert Greene accused the man from Stratford of cribbing from his intellectual and educational superiors.

Thomas Kyd too seems to have won the disapproval of his competitors for theatrical acclaim; an attack by Thomas Nashe published as part of his preface to Greene's *Menaphon* in 1589 pours scorn on Kyd's intellectual pretensions and lack of academic qualifications. In it he argues that Kyd followed his father's trade as a scrivener before adopting the profession of playwright, and that he pillaged Seneca for some of his best aphorisms, an ephemeral fashion of which the public would soon grow tired. He concludes by sneering that Kyd and others of his ilk have a faulty command of metre so that they need 'to bodge up a blank verse with ifs and ands', while their knowledge of classical mythology is so garbled that they locate the Elysian Fields within the boundaries of Hell, which admittedly is what Kyd does in the first scene of *The Spanish Tragedy*. Most intriguingly, Nashe seems to suggest that Kyd was also the author of a play featuring Hamlet, a pre-Shakespearean tragedy on the Prince of Denmark now lost to sight. The thrust of Nashe's satire is not always clear, but the applicability of his jeers to Kyd seems at times irresistible. Kyd's father Francis was a London scrivener (like Milton's father); he attended the Merchant Taylors' School in the City, though not apparently either of the universities. Though his Latin is not notably worse than that of his contemporaries, his one certain tragedy does borrow tags from Seneca, while from the fact that in it we have a father called upon to revenge his son, it is not impossible that Kyd also wrote a tragedy in which a son is urged by his father's ghost to revenge 'his foul and most unnatural murder'. That a pre-Shakespearean *Hamlet* did exist we have independent evidence in Thomas Lodge's *Wit's Misery* (1596), where he alludes to the 'visard [mask] of the ghost which cried so miserably at the Theatre [i.e. the Theatre playhouse in Shoreditch] like an oyster wife, "Hamlet, revenge"'. Of this last version Harold Jenkins, editor of the Arden edition of *Hamlet* (1982), argues that 'We cannot regard Kyd's authorship . . . as less than highly probable.'

Of other works a version of Tasso's *Padre di Famiglia*, entitled *The Householder's Philosophy*, published in 1588 and no doubt the reason for Nashe's sneer at Kyd having 'to intermeddle with Italian translations', can be assigned to him, along with an English rendering of Robert Garnier's Senecan tragedy, *Cornélie*, which appeared as *Cornelia* in 1594, the year Kyd died. Possibly he should also be credited with the anonymous play *Soliman and Perseda* (1592), since its principal source has close links with the entertainment staged in the last scene of *The Spanish Tragedy*. But it is unlikely that this meagre harvest represents Kyd's complete literary output: born in 1558, he probably had some years of authorship behind him when he sold his one undisputed masterpiece to an Elizabethan acting company for its initial presentation.

The date on which this occurred is still open to dispute. The first performance for which records exist was at the Rose Theatre on Bankside, noted in the 'diary' or day-book of the impresario Philip Henslowe for 23 February 1591–2, but how long the piece had been in the repertory is unknown. It probably cannot be dated earlier than 1582, for in that year appeared Thomas Watson's *Hecatompathia* from which Lorenzo and Balthazar quote in Act II Scene 1, although, as J. R. Mulryne points out, Kyd could have read Watson's manuscript. However, it seems wise to assume a composition-date between 1582 and 1592; within that span it is impossible to pinpoint a more precise date, scholars arguing vigorously for different years. The handling of the Spaniards in the drama might result from enmity occasioned by the sending of the Armada in 1588, but the play's tenor scarcely assists us in deciding whether the invasion crisis was past or yet to come. Many assign the piece to 1587. Nashe's attack suggests that Kyd progressed from *The Spanish Tragedy* to Italian translation, which supports a date prior to publication of *The Householder's Philosophy* in 1588; commentators such as Philip Edwards favour 1590–91, though the parallels Edwards cites are, as he admits, no more than suggestive.

One additional complication is the existence of what purports to be a forerunner, but may well be a sequel, to Kyd's tragedy; *The First Part of Hieronimo*, published in 1605, is considerably shorter than its more accomplished counterpart, and few consider it sufficiently fluent or coherent as it stands to be by Kyd himself. Fewer still believe that it pre-dates his better-known play, but it has been argued by Andrew S. Cairncross in his edition of 1967 that both the manifold imperfections and the brevity are accounted for by its being a 'memorial reconstruction' by actors who had once performed it and then sought to commit it to paper (not very accurately) from memory in order to sell it to a printer. Certainly there are precedents for *1 Hieronimo* having served as Part One of a two-part play – such pairings are not uncommon on the Elizabethan stage – and there is little doubt that its existence does enable us to flesh out the events which precede the action of *The Spanish Tragedy*, including the vexed question of the manner in which Don Andrea died in battle. However, there is some scepticism as to the likelihood of the play's composition pre-dating Kyd's indubitable work. Yet the complex intrigue plot of *1 Hieronimo* is not unworthy of Kyd in its ingenuity, and there is a faint outside possibility that the 'spanes comodye' (as Henslowe terms the inferior piece) represents the surviving form of a garbled version of a Kydian original dating back to a period when he was also at work on *The Spanish Tragedy*.

Kyd has been dubbed the father of the Elizabethan revenge play and even of English tragedy, and neither tribute is extravagant. Tragedies there had been before, *Gorboduc* among them, but the Elizabethan article could never have developed in power and range had it followed the Senecan path laid down by the Inns of Court venturers. Revenge had also played a role in such important earlier dramas as John Pickering's *Horestes* (1567), which took as theme the classical myth of Orestes' vengeance on his mother Clytemnestra for the murder of her husband Agamemnon following the Trojan campaign. *Horestes* blends Aeschylean characters and medieval personifications, but it remains cumbersome and uncertain in focus, deficient in the decorum and discipline which *Gorboduc* observes so meticulously. Kyd's achievement was to take the Senecan model which Norton and his colleague had striven to adapt for the esoteric stage, and to assimilate the bolder demands made by popular audiences, to free the theme of revenge from the grip of moral didacticism, and make it a dynamic force in its own right, so creating a drama which offered the public not only food for thought but theatrical situations which satisfied the senses of eye and ear as well.

Kyd naturalizes Seneca by combining those features of his art which intrigued Sackville and Norton with other aspects which their fastidious tastes rejected. Hence he exploits the ghostly visitant from Hell whose quest motivates and whose presence frames the action; he treats crime and retribution as no longer incidental but fundamental to the dramatic narrative; powerfully patterned rhetoric now complements the theatrical images rather than displacing them; the horrific descriptions of physical cruelty and mental anguish are not so much decorative accompaniments to the decorous personalities of the protagonists as vibrant verbal equivalents to the intensity of feelings generated by strong passionate natures. In short, Kyd extracted from his Latin author all those ingredients which appealed to his theatrical instincts, and rejected those which smacked of formality and frigidity.

Like his predecessors, Kyd was no slavish follower of the Senecan letter, but worked in its spirit transformed by a powerful awareness that a play for the public arena had to entertain and excite before it could instruct and inform. Kyd did not scruple to jettison the un-English chorus; he integrated the masques and dumb-shows of tradition into his stage texture rather than using them as punctuation-marks; bloody deeds were not now merely reported by a distraught nurse or breathless messenger but staged in full view as living testimony to

Fortune's fickleness or the instability of life at princely courts. And perhaps most importantly, Kyd exhibits a superior ability to create a blend of linguistic registers and methods sufficiently wide-ranging to accompany his multi-levelled plot, whose inventiveness was in itself his single most vital contribution to the refinement of English dramatic art.

Nor is *The Spanish Tragedy* devoid of intellectual subtlety, however crude some critics profess to find it as tragedy. Kyd's play was an appropriate trend-setter in that it embodied something of the conflict of attitudes towards revenge which many Elizabethans may have experienced in daily life. Retribution plays a role in *Gorboduc* but the ethics of vengeance are not touched on, except in so far as Videna's unmaternal depravity is condemned. But in Kyd's play Hieronimo's dilemma is highlighted, in that the Christian code of conduct that vengeance is best left to God conflicts with an acute concern for family honour emphasized by the Knight Marshal's powerlessness to strike at his son's murderers while they enjoy the immunity of the nobly-born. Kyd again reveals his independence from Senecan influence by setting his tragedy of sin and punishment in a contemporary context where the Roman edict of 'an eye for an eye' has no authority, and where Hieronimo's doubts as to the justification for taking the law into his own hands can be graphically presented, notably in Act III Scene 13, where juxtaposed quotations from the scriptures and from Seneca emphasize his mental conflict. Hieronimo's uncertainty reflects a controversy current in late Elizabethan society; Francis Bacon's essay on the subject of private vengeance begins by stating that 'Revenge is a wild kind of justice' since it makes the law impotent, yet even the circumspect jurist admits that 'The most tolerable sort of revenge is for those wrongs which there is no law to remedy,' which precisely reflects Hieronimo's position, since his access to those who should redress *his* wrongs is blocked by the Machiavellian Lorenzo. Even then some might contend that the Marshal's attitude should have remained that expressed by John of Gaunt in *Richard II*:

> But since correction lieth in those hands
> Which made the fault that we cannot correct,
> Put we our quarrel to the will of heaven,
> Who, when they see the hours ripe on earth,
> Will rain hot vengeance on offenders' heads.
>
> (I. 2. 4–8)

Hence it is impossible to re-create the multiple responses engendered in a typical Elizabethan audience by Hieronimo's conduct – later commentators have certainly winced at his apparent relish in accomplishing his revenge – but Kyd opened a fruitful vein for further exploration when he developed the character of a just man called upon to avenge a crime for which there seemed to be no redress but by committing further wrong.

How did Kyd set about realizing the full theatrical potential of his theme? Not, one feels, through the possession of deep insight into the springs of human conduct, nor the exercise of that lyrical expressiveness or forensic skill with words that some of his successors enjoyed in abundance. Kyd's rhetorical tactics are not despicable, but they hardly propel him towards those timeless felicities of utterance for which the creators of Faustus or Othello are renowned. Kyd's linguistic powers are more homely and earth-bound, often betraying the fact that, although the building has been completed, the scaffolding has yet to be dismantled, so that we are all too aware that a special rhetorical effect has been deliberately engineered:

> There met our armies in their proud array,
> Both furnish'd well, both full of hope and fear:
> Both menacing alike with daring shows,
> Both vaunting sundry colours of device,
> Both cheerly sounding trumpets, drums and fifes,
> Both raising dreadful clamours to the sky . . .
>
> (lines 115–20)

or

> First in his hand he brandished a sword,
> And with that sword he fiercely waged war,
> And in that war he gave me dangerous wounds,
> And by those wounds he forced me to yield,
> And by my yielding I became his slave . . .
>
> (lines 690–94)

or again

> Here lay my hope, and here my hope hath end;
> Here lay my heart, and here my heart was slain;
> Here lay my treasure, here my treasure lost;
> Here lay my bliss, and here my bliss bereft;
> But hope, heart, treasure, joy, and bliss,
> All fled, fail'd, died, yea, all decay'd with this.
>
> (lines 2564–9)

Yet the somewhat blatant construction methods employed are not entirely to Kyd's discredit. Dramatic speech was still struggling to free itself not only from the pernicious effects of the jog-trot beat of remorselessly applied rhythmic principles, but from the anarchy of no structural principles at all as far as syntactic practice went. The allure of anadiplosis and anaphora may have been unduly seductive, but such devices helped to salvage many a long speech from shapeless and shameless prolixity by imposing definition on it, and although, just as in the field of comedy Lyly's thick-clustering images needed pruning, Kyd's stylistic obviousness also required to be curbed, yet without their excesses dramatic language might never have reached maturity in the hands of Marlowe and Shakespeare.

What commends Kyd's style is its sheer virtuosity and flexibility. He can modulate from the rhetorical blatancies already characterized to speeches of an easy and assured colloquialism, such as the terse prose scene (Act III Scene 5) in which the Page discovers to his horrified delight and ours that the box in which Pedringano's pardon supposedly rests secure is empty. Nor can anyone who enjoys the cut-and-thrust of good dialogue fail to take pleasure in the accomplished battle of Senecan one-line exchanges known as *stichomythia*, by which Kyd establishes the relative roles in the game of courtship and rebuff played in Act I Scene 4 by Bel-imperia, Balthazar and Lorenzo. A figure which appears occasionally in *Gorboduc* as little more than a dutiful echo becomes in the hands of a natural playwright a device charged with dramatic potential.

This technical skill with language is more than matched by a non-Senecan dexterity at manipulating plot-materials which even Ben Jonson might have envied. If the main action reaches its climax in Andrea's long-awaited vengeance on Balthazar and Lorenzo for their treachery in battle, we (like Andrea himself) suffer for much of the action from a sense of frustration as the apparently clean-cut issues are soon convincingly complicated by the love-affair between Horatio and Bel-imperia, the Machi-avellian ruthlessness of Lorenzo, the murder of Serberine and the comic villainy of Pedringano, Hieronimo's madness and qualms of conscience, the successful blocking of his attempts to obtain justice through official channels. Kyd thinks up device after device in order to delay the *dénouement* in such a way that we are rarely led (as some critics of *Hamlet* have been led) to protest that weak contrivances are prolonging the duration of the action to the play's detriment. It is a testimony to Kyd's sense of theatre that he can build the tension so plausibly that suspense increases as revenge recedes further into the future. How is the final act of justice promised to Andrea to be accomplished when the action appears to be tending in an entirely opposite direction? Our excitement in suffering the uncertainties encountered *en route* to the agreed destination constitutes a major part of the pleasure.

Kyd's demonstration that forces outside human jurisdiction

achieve their ends by indirect means and remote control represents in some measure a reversion to classical notions of transgression and divine jurisdiction. The play may be set in Christian Spain and refer to Christian concepts, but it offers few indications that its world-picture is even nominally Christian. The action seems governed by the same spirit of Senecan fatalism as we discover in *Gorboduc*, and which is quite at odds with the Christian view of a heavenly after-life. The imagery of the classical vision of Hell where souls writhe in pain and suffer the torments of the damned is so powerfully invoked that the minimal allusions to heavenly bliss for the righteous count for little, entangled as they become with pagan visions of the Elysian Fields. There is an overwhelming sense of powers at work in the world whose superiority cannot be challenged: while human beings blunder about attempting to fulfil their own petty ambitions, they are in actuality serving not their own ends, but those of forces of whose purposes they guess nothing. This irony is strongly reinforced by the continuing presence on the fringes of the action of the Ghost of the slain Andrea and his mentor and agent Revenge. Characters may delude themselves that they possess free will, but like the figures of the classical tradition they all seem puppets manipulated by fate or fortune, destiny or the gods, to some predetermined end.

This sense that nothing occurs casually or by chance is echoed in Kyd's densely concentrated plot. The time has long since lapsed when he was dismissed loftily as a mere crude sensationalist who packed every conceivable lurid ingredient into his work merely to achieve a *pot-pourri* of heterogeneous horrors. By skilfully orchestrating his materials, he provides for variations on a unified theme while exploiting every opportunity for vivid dramatic contrast. The episodes set at the Portuguese court, for example, may strike one initially as serving little purpose except as a respite from exclusive concentration on Spanish affairs, yet the rivalry between Villuppo and Alexandro serves to stress the corruption and intrigue common to all courts, while in the complacent gullibility of the Viceroy we see foreshadowed the bland attitude adopted towards Hieronimo's pleas by the Spanish King and the Duke of Castile. Alexandro's search for justice in Portugal nearly ends in disaster, just as Hieronimo's quest does; just as Alexandro is saved from the flames only in the nick of time, so Hieronimo obtains his goal only at the eleventh hour.

Kyd is equally astute in weaving into his tragedy the black comedy surrounding Lorenzo's trouble-shooter Pedringano, whose exploits divert spectators from the central issues for a time, but still contribute to the main purpose. Not only do Pedringano's activities help to reinforce the theme of justice subverted, but in his confident defiance of the law and attempt to cheat the gallows we sense human powerlessness in the face of superior intelligences, in this case that of Lorenzo, the archperverter of legality and probably the prototypical Machiavellian villain in English drama, unless Marlowe's Ferneze in *The Jew of Malta* preceded him by a year or two. Moreover, even this semi-comic diversion is tied in ingeniously with the plot: from Pedringano's pocket comes the fatal letter placed in Hieronimo's hand by the crestfallen executioner, which convinces him of the truth of Bel-imperia's note, and of the implication of Lorenzo and Balthazar in Horatio's murder. From the manner in which Kyd makes every detail contribute to the onward thrust of the action we receive the welcome impression of an artist in control of his art.

The Spanish Tragedy is unlikely to appeal to those who prefer their plays streamlined and monolithic, but as G. K. Hunter has observed, 'its complex, ironic, multi-layered structure, its subtle mixture of divergent tonalities, offered Shakespeare his prime tragic model' (not that the piece would be any less impressive if Shakespeare had admired it and done otherwise). It is not a succinct drama, and in the latter years of the sixteenth century five passages were either added to or substituted for the original text of 1592; they were first printed in 1602. These additions testify to the continuing popularity of the piece, amounting as they do to over 300 lines of text. Most of them are devoted to embellishing the portrayal of Hieronimo as an aged father grieving over his dead son, and one of them – the so-called 'painter episode' inserted between Act III Scenes 12 and 13 – is generally agreed to be masterly, even if it adds little to what we already know of Hieronimo's disturbed state of mind, and has little real relation to overall plot development. We know that in September 1601 and again in June 1602 Ben Jonson was paid for making 'new adicyons for Jeronymo' and it is not impossible, despite arguments based on grounds of style and the late date, that Jonson indeed composed the interpolations printed in the 1602 edition. On the other hand, it is just possible that the additional passages were Kyd's own, though if they are, they are somewhat garbled, since they do not bear his characteristic hallmarks. However, as editors point out, they are in a corrupt condition much like parts of the main text, and may have been 'memorially reconstructed' in a manner which might also explain the state of the later parts of the 1592 version, and suggest that the so-called 'additions' may be no more than original or early matter recovered and incorporated into the play at the first opportunity. What is at any rate clear is that *The Spanish Tragedy* retained its popularity into the 1600s, despite the rapid changes in taste among the *avant-garde* which led Jonson and others to mock at its excesses.

Kyd did not outlive his major theatrical triumph by many years. His association with that stormy petrel of Elizabethan drama, Christopher Marlowe, with whom he shared rooms in 1591, may have hastened his end. By June 1593, following Marlowe's death in the notorious tavern brawl in Deptford, Kyd was desperately seeking to disassociate himself from Marlowe's heretical and racialist opinions and denying involvement in a blasphemous 'disputation' found in the room he had shared with his colleague. Kyd may well have undergone torture at this time; by mid-August 1594 he was dead at the age of 35. With the departure of Greene, Marlowe and Kyd within the space of two years, the only 'famous gracer of Tragedians' of note to survive was the 'upstart crow' from Stratford who was not so steeped in arrogance that he was inhibited from profiting from the theatrical genius of men like Thomas Kyd. By the time Kyd died Shakespeare's only tragedies were *Titus Andronicus* and perhaps *Romeo and Juliet*. The quantum leap in artistic quality between these early ventures and *Hamlet* may owe at least something to the influence of *The Spanish Tragedy*.

IV

While *The Spanish Tragedy* offers armchair directors ample scope for fruitful speculations on its original staging, few have shown much interest in the initial *mise-en-scène* of *Gorboduc*. This is partly because its authors delicately avoid a great deal of stage action, partly because their text lacks the kind of stage-directions which can set the imagination to work, but partly because Inns of Court productions fail to stimulate the response that performances at the great playhouses of Elizabethan London tend to do. The almost nationwide interest taken in the discovery and excavation in 1989 of the foundations of the Rose playhouse, venue for early presentations of *The Spanish Tragedy*, demonstrated the degree to which the Elizabethan theatre can still appeal to the British sense of heritage in a way that the Inns of Court stages can never do.

If further knowledge of the way in which *Gorboduc* was presented came to light, it might well convince sceptics that this tragedy in performance may have proved something other than 'a certain number of lines recited with just gesture and elegant modulation', Dr Johnson's frigid description of drama in general. Static as certain aspects of its realization must have been, *Gorboduc* was almost certainly enlivened with a good deal of sumptuousness and ceremonial which must have provided its first audiences (including a young queen celebrated for her love of colour and display) with some concept of primitive splendour. In an era when royalty looked the part, the bringing of kings, queens and princes on to the stage offered opportunities which even the most ascetic Elizabethan is unlikely to have resisted, and if we allow for the influence of court masques and disguisings, street pageants and the *intermedii* of Italian court entertainments, not to mention the still potent influence of the morality play, the first performances of Sackville and Norton's tragedy could hardly have turned out to be the drab ordeals sometimes assumed.

The precise techniques employed on the production are elusive to recover or reconstruct. Its chief antecedents would no doubt have been the banquet-hall presentations of the late Middle Ages and early Renaissance, in which the accent was as much on honouring the assembled guests as on the aesthetic perfection of the dramatic fare offered to them. *Gorboduc* at its initial performance took its place as part of a sequence of Christmas revels designed not only to celebrate the festive season but to reinforce the Inn's sense of communal purpose and achievement, even if it also set out to dramatize a political issue of some interest and concern to its auditors. Thus the occasion was not exclusively a theatrical one, as with *The Spanish Tragedy* some thirty years later, when the political resonances were far less explicit. Kyd had a commercial dramatist's approach to his task, which was primarily to entertain; *Gorboduc* formed part of a celebration of corporate identity and an expression of national sentiment.

Its physical realization is unlikely to have been simple or crude. While performers in such early Tudor interludes as *Fulgens and Lucres* played their roles in the spaces between the dining-tables of the hall (possibly that of Lambeth Palace), for *Gorboduc* a scaffold or platform would almost certainly have been erected at one end or on one side of the hall of the Inner

Temple, possibly built up over the customary dais where the high table stood. Such a procedure seems to have been followed at the Palace of Whitehall for the command performance on 18 January 1561–2, since Henry Machyn's diary which records the date speaks of the erection of 'a great scaffold' for the royal presentation. Such a platform must have been sufficiently elevated for the three Furies of the dumb-show preceding Act IV to have been concealed beneath it, although it is not axiomatic that they emerged through a trap-door in the stage floor. They could have appeared through curtains concealing the area below the base of the platform, much as hangings did on the pageant-waggons on which the civic cycle performances were staged at some centres. The Inner Temple platform presumably was large enough to accommodate a dozen or so players at any one time, but there would probably have been little scenery to occupy valuable space, although whether the pointed reference to the provision of a 'chair of estate' for the dumb-show to Act II means that Gorboduc had no such throne to sit on during *his* scenes is unclear. Elaborate sets are certainly unlikely, given that the conditions must have been too restricted for major changes of setting. Tables in the main part of the hall may have been cleared away to increase sitting- or standing-space for spectators, but the usual accoutrements of a Tudor banqueting-hall may well have remained in place.

The text itself, apart from the instructions for staging the dumb-shows, offers us little guidance in establishing the nature of the physical action. The chosen medium was more verbal than visual, and while the script of *Gorboduc* presents a blank cheque to anyone anxious to speculate on its staging, support for one's conjectures is not easy to find. What seems clear is that Sackville and Norton generally severed all links with the earlier tradition of overtly recognizing the presence of spectators by means of asides, direct address, and the cultivation of spectator participation in the action. Rarely is it acknowledged that an audience is present, or that they may have come with certain expectations of having their theatrical desires met. Indeed, the authors are so eager to conform to the supposed demands of classical precept that they ignore the histrionic possibilities of their new-found genre. However, one of the few devices they allow themselves, that of 'marching about the stage' which occurs in the dumb-shows to Acts III, IV and V, anticipates its use on the public stage later in Elizabeth's reign, and was to prove a useful method of maximizing the use of a body of figures whose numbers were too meagre to create an impact in themselves.

If Sackville and Norton left few indications in their text that their tragedy was intended for the theatre, Kyd or the company who bought *The Spanish Tragedy* bequeathed copious and enlightening details of stage business to posterity. Not that everything is quite as clear-cut as we might wish: whether or not the Ghost and Revenge watched the action from the playhouse galleries is still controversial, as is the question of the placement of the royal party as it sits to watch the final masque-and-mayhem in Act IV. The cutting-down of the arbour by Isabella in Act IV Scene 2 also presents a problem, as does the issue of Bel-imperia's awareness of the identities of her lover's murderers in Act II Scene 4. What is evident, however, is that Kyd was a master-manipulator of theatrical space, and saw to it that his action was deployed over the entire range of available playing locations, or incorporated several separate areas such as the gallery, the mainstage and the rear façade simultaneously. Throughout the action Revenge and Andrea's Ghost apparently spectate from either the stage platform itself or from one of the tiered galleries to the rear or the side of the stage; Lorenzo and Balthazar eavesdrop in a similar manner from 'above' on the amorous dalliance of Horatio and Bel-imperia in Act II Scene 2; Hieronimo's triple masque in the first banquet scene (Act I Scene 4) and the celebrated 'play-within-a-play' in the last act require both a site for their presentation and a location from which they can be viewed. Indeed, the entire tragedy might have been composed as an exercise in metadrama, in that here a theatre audience watches a pair of stage characters looking on at the spectacle of other stage figures performing various kinds of play, from Pedringano's virtuoso charade on the scaffold to Hieronimo's grisly device for dispatching his enemies as they act out their passions in seeming pretence. To realize his aim of presenting the world as a stage, Kyd orchestrates his use of theatrical space in an expert manner, exploiting to the full the resources which the playhouse offered.

Where the text of *Gorboduc* is tacit on most matters affecting stage movement and gesture, *The Spanish Tragedy* is generously endowed with frequent hints and clues as well as hard evidence. One may consider, for example, the significance Kyd attaches to physical contact in a play built on images of violent death, illicit love, overt and concealed cruelty. Characters therefore kiss, embrace, threaten, assault, execute one another; people fall to the ground, drop gloves, whisper confidences, give each other chains, letters, papers, gold; they enter bearing a book or a halter and poniard; they fix up curtains, sit down to banquets and run mad. In studying the text one must also be struck by the comprehensive list of concrete objects its successful realization requires, from the scarf given to Horatio by Bel-imperia (which may well be the same 'handkercher' with which Hieronimo seeks to staunch his son's blood and which later serves him as a reminder of his vow of vengeance) to the box with which the Page maliciously induces Pedringano to jest away his last moments on earth. Kyd again reveals himself as a pioneer in the inventive use of stage properties.

Not that his theatrical inheritance was primitive; the use of daggers, halters and other devices can be traced to the moralities. Kyd also owed a debt to the set-piece tableaux so typical of medieval pageant-masters and those responsible for devising the lavish spectacles which enlivened the streets and squares of Renaissance towns and cities, and carried their legacy into the elaborate fêtes and masquerades beloved of even the sober

Francis Bacon. Just as the dumb-shows of *Gorboduc* partly rely on this fertile tradition by making their points in symbolic form, so Kyd embodies the highlights of his tragedy in telling stage images, nowhere more so than at the opening of the drama where the allegorical personification of Revenge is shown to be the guiding spirit of the ensuing action. Hieronimo's prowess as a deviser and director of masques is in perfect keeping with the nature of a tragedy which abounds in opportunities for display and ceremonial, pomp and parading, ritual and pageantry of every kind.

Yet these are insufficient in themselves to create for Kyd's play its high level of visual impact. What gives the piece its ultimate theatrical distinction is its constant recourse to strikingly memorable stage pictures which capture in a single emblematic device the intellectual and emotional connotations of a situation, and so exact the appropriate response from the spectator. Even mere readers cannot easily erase from their minds the mental picture of the aged Hieronimo aroused from sleep, staggering out into his darkened garden to brush against the punctured corpse of his only son dangling from the leafy arbour. Few can forget the moment when Andrea, indignant at seeing his dreams of vengeance frustrated perhaps irrevocably, yells frantically at the sardonic figure peacefully slumbering at his side, that its elaborate stratagem has gone out of control. The macabre spectator-sport provided by Pedringano's breezy cross-talk act with the Hangman; the brief vignette of sexual arousal between Bel-imperia and Horatio prior to their hideous severance; the pathetically comic pursuit of Hieronimo by his frenzied clients; all denote a dramatist whose knowledge of what would work in the playhouse more than compensates for the limitations of his stage rhetoric. By exploring to the utmost the range of possibilities latent in the conditions of the stage on which he worked, Kyd created a tragedy by no means inferior in purely theatrical terms to those masterpieces soon to be produced by his more sophisticated successors.

A GUIDE TO FURTHER READING

Works dealing with Elizabethan drama in general, and Elizabethan tragedy in particular, are already legion, and it has been
necessary to scale down this list of complementary reading-
matter to reasonable proportions, in the hope that the reader
will feel able to embark on a review of at least those aspects of
the subject which will enhance *Gorboduc* and *The Spanish Tragedy*.
Those anxious for more comprehensive coverage are referred
to the large-scale bibliographies cited below. Details of other
editions of the two plays are given in the introduction to each.
Place of publication is London unless otherwise indicated.

BIBLIOGRAPHIES AND REFERENCE WORKS

W. W. GREG, ed., *A Bibliography of English Printed Drama to the
Restoration*, 4 vols., 1939–59.

Alfred HARBAGE, ed., *The Annals of English Drama, 975–1700*,
Philadelphia, 1940; third edn, ed. Sylvia Stoler Wagonheim,
1990.

George WATSON, ed., *The New Cambridge Bibliography of English
Literature: I, 600–1600*, Cambridge, 1974.

GENERAL WORKS ON TRAGEDY

Geoffrey BRERETON, *Principles of Tragedy: A Rational Examination of the Tragic Concept in Life and Literature*, Coral Gables, Florida, 1968.

Robert W. CORRIGAN, ed., *Tragedy, Vision and Form*, Chandler, San Francisco, 1965.

R. P. DRAPER, ed., *Tragedy: Developments in Criticism: A Casebook*, 1980.

Northrop FRYE, *Anatomy of Criticism*, Princeton, 1957.

T. R. HENN, *The Harvest of Tragedy*, 1956.

Clifford LEECH, *Tragedy*, 1969.

H. A. MASON, *The Tragic Plane*, Oxford, 1986.

Richard B. SEWALL, *The Vision of Tragedy*, New Haven and London, 1959.

George STEINER, *The Death of Tragedy*, 1961.

Raymond WILLIAMS, *Modern Tragedy*, 1966.

SENECA AND HIS INFLUENCE

M. J. ANDERSON, *Classical Drama and Its Influence*, 1965.

Gordon BRADEN, *Renaissance Tragedy and the Senecan Tradition: Anger's Privilege*, New Haven and London, 1985.

H. B. CHARLTON, *The Senecan Tradition*, Manchester, 1946.

Hardin CRAIG, 'The Shackling of Accidents: A Study of Elizabethan Tragedy', *Philological Quarterly* 19 (1940), pp. 1–19.

J. W. CUNLIFFE, *The Influence of Seneca on Elizabethan Tragedy*, 1893.

T. S. ELIOT, 'Seneca in Elizabethan Translation' (1927) and 'Shakespeare and the Stoicism of Seneca' (1927), in *Selected Essays*, 1932.

Gareth Lloyd EVANS, 'Shakespeare, Seneca and the Kingdom of Violence', in T. A. Dorey and Donald R. Dudley, eds., *Roman Drama*, 1965, pp. 123–59.

G. K. HUNTER, 'Seneca and the Elizabethans: A Case Study in "Influence"', *Shakespeare Survey* 20 (1969), pp. 17–26.

Jean JACQUOT and Marcel ODDON, eds., *Les Tragédies de Sénèque et le théâtre de la renaissance*, Paris, 1964.

F. L. LUCAS, *Seneca and Elizabethan Tragedy*, 1933.

E. M. SPEARING, *The Elizabethan Translations of Seneca's Tragedies*, Cambridge, 1912.

Peter URE, 'On Some Differences between Seneca and Elizabethan Tragedy', in J. C. Maxwell, ed., *Elizabethan and Jacobean Drama*, Liverpool, 1974, pp. 63–74.

Henry W. WELLS, 'Senecan Influence on Elizabethan Tragedy: A Re-Estimation', *Shakespeare Association Bulletin* 19 (1944), pp. 71–84.

EARLY ELIZABETHAN TRAGEDY

Howard BAKER, *Induction to Tragedy*, Baton Rouge, 1939; New York, 1965.

Fredson BOWERS, *Elizabethan Revenge Tragedy 1587–1642*, Princeton, 1940.

M. C. BRADBROOK, *Themes and Conventions of Elizabethan Tragedy*, Cambridge, 1935.

Wolfgang CLEMEN, *English Tragedy before Shakespeare*, Heidelberg, 1955; translated 1961.

Willard FARNHAM, *The Medieval Heritage of Elizabethan Tragedy*, Berkeley, 1936.

Charles A. HALLETT and Elaine S. HALLETT, *The Revenger's Madness: A Study of Revenge Tragedy Motifs*, Lincoln, Nebraska, 1980.

G. K. HUNTER, 'Shakespeare and the Tradition of Tragedy', in Stanley Wells, ed., *The New Cambridge Companion to Shakespeare Studies*, Cambridge, 1986, pp. 123–41.

Emrys JONES, *The Origins of Shakespeare*, Oxford, 1977.

J. M. R. MARGESON, *The Origins of English Tragedy*, Oxford, 1967.

Moody E. PRIOR, *The Language of Tragedy*, New York, 1947.

A. P. ROSSITER, *English Drama from Early Times to the Eliza-bethans*, 1950.

Norman SANDERS et al., *The Revels History of Drama in English*, II *1500–1576*, 1980; J. L. BARROLL et al., III *1576–1613*, 1975.

Percy SIMPSON, 'The Theme of Revenge in Elizabethan Tragedy', in *Proceedings of the British Academy* 1935, pp. 101–36; repr. in *Studies in Elizabethan Drama*, Oxford, 1955.

F. P. WILSON, *The English Drama 1485–1585* (*Oxford History of English Literature*, IV, 1), Oxford, 1969.

GORBODUC

Marie AXTON, *The Queen's Two Bodies: Drama and the Elizabethan Succession*, Royal Historical Society, 1971.

Normand BERLIN, *Thomas Sackville*, New York, 1974 (especially chapter 6).

David M. BEVINGTON, *Tudor Drama and Politics: A Critical Approach to Topical Meaning*, Cambridge, Mass., 1968.

Marvin T. HERRICK, 'Senecan Influence in *Gorboduc*', in *Studies in Speech and Drama in Honor of Alexander M. Drummond*, Ithaca, 1944, pp. 78–104.

Barbara H. C. de MENDONCA, 'The Influence of *Gorboduc* on *King Lear*', *Shakespeare Survey* 13 (1960), pp. 41–8.

Jacobus SWART, *Thomas Sackville*, Groningen, 1949.

Ernest W. TALBERT, 'The Political Import and the First Two Audiences of *Gorboduc*', in *Studies in Honor of DeWitt T. Starnes*, Austin, 1967, pp. 87–115.

Robert Y. TURNER, 'Pathos and the *Gorboduc* Tradition, 1560–1590', *Huntington Library Quarterly* 25 (1961–2), pp. 97–120.

Sarah R. WATSON, '*Gorboduc* and the Theory of Tyrannicide', *Modern Language Review*, 34 (1939), pp. 355–66.

THE SPANISH TRAGEDY

Barry B. ADAMS, 'The Audiences of *The Spanish Tragedy*', *Journal of English and Germanic Philology* 68 (1969), pp. 221–36.

Frank ARDOLINO, '*Corrida* of Blood in *The Spanish Tragedy*: Kyd's Use of Revenge as National Destiny', *Medieval and Renaissance Drama in England* 1 (1984), pp. 37–49.

Howard BAKER, 'Ghosts and Guides: Kyd's *Spanish Tragedy* and the Medieval Tragedy', *Modern Philology* 33 (1935), pp. 27–36.

Jonas A. BARISH, '*The Spanish Tragedy*, or the Pleasures and Perils of Rhetoric', in J. R. Brown and B. Harris, eds., *Elizabethan Theatre*, Stratford-upon-Avon Studies 9 (1966), pp. 59–86.

A. R. BRAUNMULLER, 'Early Shakespearian Tragedy and its Contemporary Context', in M. Bradbury and D. Palmer, eds., *Shakespearian Tragedy*, Stratford-upon-Avon Studies 20 (1984), pp. 97–128.

Ronald BROUDE, 'Time, Truth and Right in *The Spanish Tragedy*', *Studies in Philology* 68 (1971), pp. 130–45.

John S. COLLEY, '*The Spanish Tragedy* and the Theatre of God's Judgements', *Papers on Language and Literature* 10 (1974), pp. 241–53.

Ernest DE CHICKERA, 'Divine Justice and Private Revenge in *The Spanish Tragedy*', *Modern Language Review* 57 (1962), pp. 228–32.

Philip EDWARDS, *Thomas Kyd and Early Elizabethan Tragedy*, 1966.

William EMPSON, '*The Spanish Tragedy*', *Nimbus* 3 (Summer 1956), pp. 16–29; repr. in R. J. Kaufmann, ed., *Elizabethan Drama: Modern Essays in Criticism*, 1961, pp. 60–80.

Arthur FREEMAN, *Thomas Kyd, Facts and Problems*, Oxford, 1967.

Jean FUZIER, '"La Tragédie espagnole" en Angleterre', in

Jean Jacquot, ed., *Dramaturgie et Société*, 2 vols., Paris, 1968, II, pp. 589–606.

Michael HATTAWAY, *Elizabethan Popular Theatre*, 1982 (especially pp. 101–28).

G. K. HUNTER, 'Ironies of Justice in *The Spanish Tragedy*', *Renaissance Drama* 8 (1965), pp. 89–104.

G. K. HUNTER, 'Tyrant and Martyr: Religious Heroisms in Elizabethan Tragedy', in Maynard Mack and George deForest Lord, eds., *Poetic Traditions of the English Renaissance*, New Haven and London, 1982, pp. 85–102.

Ejner J. JENSEN, 'Kyd's *Spanish Tragedy*: The Play Explains Itself', *Journal of English and Germanic Philology* 64 (1965), pp. 7–16.

S. F. JOHNSON, '*The Spanish Tragedy*, or Babylon Revisited', in Richard Hosley, ed., *Essays on Shakespeare and Elizabethan Dramatists in Honor of Hardin Craig*, Columbia, 1962, pp. 23–36.

Carol M. KAY, 'Deception Through Words: A Reading of *The Spanish Tragedy*', *Studies in Philology* 74 (1977), pp. 20–38.

Richard C. KOHLER, 'Kyd's Ordered Spectacle: "Behold . . ./ What 'tis to be subject to destiny"', *Medieval and Renaissance Drama in English* 3 (1986), pp. 27–49.

David LAIRD, 'Hieronimo's Dilemma', *Studies in Philology* 62 (1965), pp. 137–46.

Scott McMILLIN, 'The Figure of Silence in *The Spanish Tragedy*', *Journal of English Literary History* 39 (1972), pp. 27–48.

Peter B. MURRAY, *Thomas Kyd*, New York, 1969.

J. D. RATCLIFFE, 'Hieronimo Explains Himself', *Studies in Philology* 54 (1957), pp. 112–18.

Anne RIGHTER, *Shakespeare and the Idea of the Play*, 1962 (especially pp. 71–8).

D. F. ROWAN, 'The Staging of *The Spanish Tragedy*', in G. R. Hibbard, ed., *The Elizabethan Theatre* 5 (1975), Hamden, Conn., pp. 112–23.

Eleanor M. TWEEDIE, '"Action is Eloquence": The Staging of Thomas Kyd's *Spanish Tragedy*', *Studies in English Literature 1500–1900*, 16 (1976), pp. 223–39.

S. VISWANATHAN, 'The Seating of Andrea's Ghost and Revenge in *The Spanish Tragedy*', *Theatre Survey* 15 (1974), pp. 171–6.

William H. WIATT, 'The Dramatic Function of the Alexandra–Villuppo Episode in *The Spanish Tragedie*', *Notes and Queries* 203 (1958), pp. 327–9.

THE ELIZABETHAN STAGE

E. K. CHAMBERS, *The Elizabethan Stage*, 4 vols., Oxford, 1923.

T. W. CRAIK, *The Tudor Interlude*, Leicester, 1958.

Andrew GURR, *The Shakespearean Stage, 1574–1642*, Cambridge, 1970; second revised edn, 1980.

Richard SOUTHERN, *The Staging of Plays before Shakespeare*, 1973.

Peter THOMSON, 'Playhouses and Players in the Time of Shakespeare', in Stanley Wells, ed., *The New Cambridge Companion to Shakespeare Studies*, 1986, pp. 67–83.

TRANSLATIONS

GEOFFREY OF MONMOUTH, *The History of the Kings of Britain*, translated by Lewis Thorpe, Harmondsworth, 1966.

SENECA, *Four Tragedies and Octavia*, translated by E. F. Watling, Harmondsworth, 1966.

Seneca His Tenne Tragedies, Translated into English, edited by Thomas Newton (1581), The Tudor Translations Second Series, XI, XII, ed. Charles Whibley, 2 vols., 1927.

A NOTE ON THE TEXTS

I have tried to make the plays accessible to the student and the general reader without any special knowledge of, or training in understanding, Elizabethan texts in their original spelling, by modernizing all old and inconsistent spellings of words still in current use. I have, however, retained obsolete forms of words where to modernize would affect the meaning for a modern reader. I have also adopted certain conventions of presentation, departure from which might cause confusion or irritation. In the Notes I have usually modernized illustrative quotations except for lines from Chaucer, from Tudor translations of Seneca, and from *The Faerie Queene*.

I have regularized and expanded cast-names and speech-prefixes, and converted them to roman type in dialogue or capital letters in the stage-directions and speech-headings according to modern usage. Stage-directions are now printed in italic; the black-letter type in which *Gorboduc* was set forth in 1570 has been replaced by roman or italic as appropriate. Numerals both arabic and roman are spelt out, as are such abbreviations as '&'. Capital letters and divisions between words are silently made to conform with modern preferences in such matters.

Punctuation presents a problem, in that a number of respected scholars believe that to modernize punctuation in editing material of this vintage is to ignore indications of the rhetorical effects aimed for and to obliterate subtleties of nuance and meaning. I still remain sceptical as to the degree of authorial authority to be attached to punctuation in printed texts of the period, particularly where the semi-ephemeral genre of drama is concerned, but more importantly, feel that to reproduce Elizabethan punctuation exactly in an edition such as this would seriously impair its usefulness for all but the most scholarly expert. I have therefore adjusted the punctuation of the original texts to suit modern needs, but hope to have been sparing with my interventions.

I have taken it upon myself to expand or interpolate stage-directions and scene-locations wherever those of the original seem to be lacking or insufficiently explicit to make clear what one assumes to be occurring on stage; occasionally I have found it necessary to adjust a stage-direction's position to provide a more accurate notion of the apparent situation. In these and similar cases, as in instances of editorial adjustments to the dialogue, interpolations can be easily recognized by their placement within square brackets; however, obvious errors are corrected without comment or specific indication, and quotations from Latin and European languages have been brought into line with modern practice.

Unfamiliar words or phrases have been glossed at the foot of each text-page; definitions are repeated where necessary, but a complete glossary appears at the end of the book. More detailed explanations and fuller comments are reserved for the Notes, some of which deal with technical points of interest primarily to the textual scholar. A short discussion of the printing history of each tragedy forms the introduction to the text of the play itself.

ACKNOWLEDGEMENTS

My thanks are due to the General Editor of the Penguin Classics series for his willingness to commission this edition, and for his patience in awaiting its eventual completion. I must also thank my colleague, Christopher Jones, for harnessing twentieth-century technology to cope with the vagaries of sixteenth-century vocabulary, and Joyce Williams and Gail Kincaid for accomplishing one more onerous secretarial task in the midst of so many others.

GORBODUC

THOMAS NORTON AND THOMAS SACKVILLE

¶ The Tragidie of Ferrex
and Porrex,

set forth without addition or alteration but altogether as the same was shewed
on stage before the Queenes Maiestie,
about nine yeares past, *vz.* the
xviij. day of Ianuarie. 1561.
by the gentlemen of the
Inner Temple.

Seen and allowed. &c.

⚜ Imprinted at London by
Iohn Daye, dwelling ouer
Aldersgate.

The relationship between the two earliest extant editions of *Gorboduc* appears relatively simple. The first text to be published was apparently that dated 22 September 1565 and printed by one William Griffith who sold his wares 'at the Signe of the Faucon' situated in the churchyard of St Dunstan's-in-the-West on the north side of Fleet Street. A unique copy of this first edition, now in the Henry E. Huntington Library in San Marino, California, provides the following information:

THE / TRAGEDIE OF GORBODVC; / whereof three Actes were wrytten by / *Thomas Nortone*, and the two laste by / *Thomas Sackuyle.* / Sett forthe as the same was shewed before the / QVENES most excellent Maiestie, in her highnes / Court of Whitehall, the xviii. day of January, / *Anno Domini.* 1561. By the Gentlemen / of Thynner Temple in London.

However, subsequent statements suggest that the text supplied to William Griffith and published in 1565 was issued without the authors being consulted, or a careful check being made for possible errors; at least this is the impression which John Day or Daye was anxious to convey in his address to the Reader which preceded his version of the play, published in 1570:

one W.G. getting a copie therof at some yong man's hand that lacked a litle money and much discretion, in the last great plage, an[no] 1565, about v. yeares past, while the said Lord [i.e. Sackville] was out of England, and T. Norton farre out of London, and neither of them both made privie, put it forth excedingly corrupted . . . They, the authors I meane, though they were very much displeased that she [i.e. their play-text] so ranne abroad without leave, whereby she caught her shame, as many wantons do, yet seing the case as it is remedilesse, have for common honestie and shamefastnesse new apparelled, trimmed, and attired her in such forme as she was before. In which better forme since she hath come to me, I have harbored her for her frendes' sake and her owne, and I do not dout her parentes the authors will not now be discontent that she goe abroad among you good readers, so it be in honest companie.

Thus it was ostensibly under the claim that he was righting the wrongs done to Norton and Sackville by their first printer that John Day 'dwelling over Aldersgate' in the city of London 'imprinted' his edition of the tragedy which he entitled:

The Tragidie of Ferrex / and Porrex, / set forth without addition or alte-/ration but altogether as the same was shewed / on stage before the Queenes Maiestie, / about nine yeares past, *vz.* the / xviij. day of Ianuarie. 1561. / by the gentlemen of the / Inner Temple.

However, it has been established beyond reasonable doubt that Day thought Griffith's edition, despite its many errors, was still accurate enough for his own version to be set up and printed from a corrected copy of the pirated edition with which so much dissatisfaction had been expressed. It was corrected

perhaps by Thomas Norton himself, yet although the quarto of
1570 contains a large number of superior readings to those of
1565, there are occasions when the 1565 reading is to be
preferred, even if the version of 1570 is generally the more
satisfactory text on which to base a modern edition of the
tragedy. Copies of John Day's edition are not true bibliographi-
cal rarities: there are at least seven copies extant, including one
in the British Library (shelfmark C. 34.a.6), and one in the
Malone Collection at the Bodleian Library, Oxford (shelfmark
Malone 257). The present edition is based on the British
Library copy and on the excellent facsimile version of the
Bodleian copy, produced by the Scolar Press in 1968 and cited
below. It is also indebted to the texts edited by Irby B. Cauthen
and by T. W. Craik.

The principal modern editions of the play are:

J. W. CUNLIFFE, ed., *Early English Classical Tragedies*, Oxford,
1912.

A. K. McILWRAITH, ed., *Five Elizabethan Tragedies*, World's
Classics, Oxford, 1938.

Thomas SACKVILLE and Thomas NORTON, *Gorboduc [1570]
The Tragedy of Ferrex and Porrex*, A Scolar Press Facsimile,
Menston, Yorks, 1968.

Irby B. CAUTHEN Jr, ed., *Gorboduc or Ferrex and Porrex*,
Regents Renaissance Drama Series, Lincoln, Nebraska, and
London, 1970.

T. W. CRAIK, ed., *Minor Elizabethan Drama: Tragedy*, Everyman's University Library, London, 1974.

THE ARGUMENT OF THE TRAGEDY

Gorboduc, King of Britain, divided his realm in his lifetime to his sons, Ferrex and Porrex. The sons fell to dissension. The younger killed the elder. The mother, that more dearly loved the elder, for revenge killed the younger. The people, moved with the cruelty of the fact, rose in rebellion and slew both father and mother. The nobility assembled and most terribly destroyed the rebels. And afterwards for want of issue of the Prince, whereby the succession of the crown became uncertain, they fell to civil war in which both they and many of their issues were slain, and the land for a long time almost desolate and miserably wasted.

fact: crime, deed

THE P[RINTER]. TO THE READER

Where this tragedy was for furniture of part of the grand
Christmas in the Inner Temple, first written about nine years
ago by the Right Honourable Thomas now Lord Buckhurst,
and by T. Norton, and after showed before her Majesty, and
never intended by the authors thereof to be published: yet one
W.G., getting a copy thereof at some young man's hand that
lacked a little money and much discretion, in the last great
plague, an[no]. 1565, about five years past, while the said Lord
was out of England, and T. Norton far out of London, and
neither of them both made privy, put it forth exceedingly
corrupted: even as if by means of a broker for hire, he should
have enticed into his house a fair maid and done her villainy,
and after all to-bescratched her face, torn her apparel, berayed
and disfigured her, and then thrust her out of doors dishon-
ested. In such plight after long wandering she came at length
home to the sight of her friends, who scant knew her but by a
few tokens and marks remaining. They, the authors I mean,
though they were very much displeased that she so ran abroad
without leave, whereby she caught her shame, as many wantons

---

for furniture: as an adornment or
'attraction'
grand Christmas: splendid Christmas
celebrations
by means of a broker: through the agency
of a pimp

all to-bescratched: very badly scratched
berayed: defiled, dirtied
ran abroad: circulated freely
wantons: people of loose behaviour

do, yet seeing the case as it is remediless, have for common honesty and shamefastness new apparelled, trimmed, and attired her in such form as she was before. In which better form since she hath come to me, I have harboured her for her friends' sake and her own, and I do not doubt her parents, the authors, will not now be discontent that she go abroad among you good readers, so it be in honest company. For she is by my encouragement and others' somewhat less ashamed of the dishonesty done to her because it was by fraud and force. If she be welcome among you and gently entertained, in favour of the house from whence she is descended, and of her own nature courteously disposed to offend no man, her friends will thank you for it. If not, but that she shall be still reproached with her former mishap, or quarrelled at by envious persons, she (poor gentlewoman) will surely play Lucrece's part, and of herself die for shame, and I shall wish that she had tarried still at home with me, where she was welcome: for she did never put me to more charge, but this one poor black gown lined with white that I have now given her to go abroad among you withal.

shamefastness: modesty, decency

THE NAMES OF THE SPEAKERS

GORBODUC, *King of Great Britain*
VIDENA, *Queen and wife to King Gorboduc*
FERREX, *elder son to King Gorboduc*
PORREX, *younger son to King Gorboduc*
CLOTYN, *Duke of Cornwall*
FERGUS, *Duke of Albany*
MANDUD, *Duke of Loegris*
GWENARD, *Duke of [Camberland]*
EUBULUS, *Secretary to the King*
AROSTUS, *a counsellor to the King*
DORDAN, *a counsellor assigned by the King to his eldest son Ferrex*
PHILANDER, *a counsellor assigned by the King to his younger son*
   Porrex (Both being of the old King's council before)
HERMON, *a parasite remaining with Ferrex*
TYNDAR, *a parasite remaining with Porrex*
NUNTIUS, *a messenger of the elder brother's death*

Duke of Cornwall: see note
Albany: Scotland; but see note
Loegris: England (see note)
[Camberland]: Cambria, or Wales (see note)
Eubulus: from the Greek, meaning 'prudent'
Secretary: an official entrusted with secret or private business

Arostus: from the Greek, signifying 'weak'
Philander: derived from the Greek for 'benign, pleasing'
parasite: a 'sponger' who lives off the bounty of others, usually by flattering them (see note)

NUNTIUS, *a messenger of Duke Fergus rising in arms*
MARCELLA, *a lady of the Queen's privy chamber*
CHORUS, *four ancient and sage men of Britain*
[SOLDIERS, ATTENDANTS, SERVANTS, etc.]
[The figures in the dumb-shows]

[The play is set in ancient Britain]

THE TRAGEDY OF GORBODUC

First the music of violins began to play, during which came in upon the stage six wild men clothed in leaves. Of whom the first bare in his neck a faggot of small sticks, which they all both severally and together assayed with all their strengths to break, but it could not be broken by them. At the length one of them plucked out one of the sticks and brake it. And the rest, plucking out all the other sticks one after another, did easily break them, the same being severed, which being conjoined they had before attempted in vain. After they had this done, they departed the stage, and the music ceased. Hereby was signified that a state knit in unity doth continue strong against all force, but being divided is easily destroyed. As befell upon Duke Gorboduc, dividing his land to his two sons which he before held in monarchy, and upon the dissension of the brethren to whom it was divided.

in his neck: on his shoulders   *Duke:* leader (see note)
faggot: bundle (see note)

ACT I SCENE I

[*Enter* VIDENA *and* FERREX.]

VIDENA: The silent night, that brings the quiet pause
  From painful travails of the weary day,
  Prolongs my carefull thoughts, and makes me blame
  The slow Aurore, that so for love or shame
  Doth long delay to show her blushing face:
  And now the day renews my griefull plaint.

FERREX: My gracious lady and my mother dear,
  Pardon my grief for your so grieved mind,
  To ask what cause tormenteth so your heart.

10 VIDENA: So great a wrong, and so unjust despite,
  Without all cause, against all course of kind!

FERREX: Such causeless wrong and so unjust despite
  May have redress, or at the least, revenge.

VIDENA: Neither, my son: such is the froward will,
  The person such, such my mishap and thine.

FERREX: Mine know I none, but grief for your distress.

VIDENA: Yes; mine for thine, my son. A father? No.
  In kind a father, not in kindliness.

FERREX: My father? Why? I know nothing at all,
20 Wherein I have misdone unto his grace.

VIDENA: Therefore the more unkind to thee and me.
  For, knowing well, my son, the tender love
  That I have ever borne and bear to thee,
  He, griev'd thereat, is not content alone
  To spoil me of thy sight, my chiefest joy,
  But thee of thy birthright and heritage

---

2   *travails:* labours
3   *carefull:* full of anxiety
4   *Aurore:* the dawn (see note)
6   *griefull:* full of sorrow
10 *despite:* insult, contempt
11 *kind:* what is natural, normal (see note)
14 *froward:* perverse
20 *misdone:* acted wrongfully
25 *spoil:* deprive

Causeless, unkindly, and in wrongful wise,
Against all law and right, he will bereave.
Half of his kingdom he will give away.
FERREX: To whom?
VIDENA: Even to Porrex, his younger son,   30
Whose growing pride I do so sore suspect,
That, being rais'd to equal rule with thee,
Methinks I see his envious heart to swell,
Fill'd with disdain and with ambitious hope.
The end the gods do know, whose altars I
Full oft have made in vain of cattle slain
To send the sacred smoke to Heaven's throne,
For thee, my son, if things do so succeed,
As now my jealous mind misdeemeth sore.
FERREX: Madam, leave care and carefull plaint for me: 40
Just hath my father been to every wight.
His first unjustice he will not extend
To me, I trust, that give no cause thereof:
My brother's pride shall hurt himself, not me.
VIDENA: So grant the gods! But yet thy father so
Hath firmly fixed his unmoved mind
That plaints and prayers can no whit avail,
For those have I assay'd, but even this day
He will endeavour to procure assent
Of all his council to his fond device.   50
FERREX: Their ancestors from race to race have borne
True faith to my forefathers and their seed:
I trust they eke will bear the like to me.

27	*unkindly:* in an unnatural manner	41 *wight:* human being, person
28	*bereave:* rob, dispossess	50 *fond device:* foolish scheme
34	*disdain:* contempt	53 *eke:* also
38	*succeed:* come to pass, turn out	
39	*jealous:* zealous, suspicious	
	misdeemeth: suspects, greatly fears	

VIDENA: There resteth all. But if they fail thereof,
And if the end bring forth an ill success,
On them and theirs the mischief shall befall,
And so I pray the gods requite it them,
And so they will, for so is wont to be!
When lords, and trusted rulers under kings,
60   To please the present fancy of the prince
With wrong transpose the course of governance,
Murders, mischief, or civil sword at length,
Or mutual treason, or a just revenge,
When right succeeding line returns again,
By Jove's just judgement and deserved wrath,
Brings them to cruel and reproachful death,
And roots their names and kindreds from the earth.
FERREX: Mother, content you; you shall see the end.
VIDENA: The end? Thy end I fear: Jove end me first!
                                        [*Exeunt.*]

ACT I SCENE 2

[*Gorboduc's court*]
[*Enter* GORBODUC, AROSTUS, PHILANDER, EUBULUS,
CHORUS, ATTENDANTS *etc.*]
70   GORBODUC: My lords, whose grave advice and faithful aid
Have long upheld my honour and my realm,
And brought me to this age from tender years,
Guiding so great estate with great renown,
Now more importeth me than erst to use
Your faith and wisdom, whereby yet I reign:

---

55   *success:* outcome, result
57   *requite:* pay back, avenge
61   *transpose:* pervert, corrupt
62   *mischief:* disaster
66   *reproachful:* shameful

67   *roots:* uproots, extirpates
74   *Now more importeth* etc.: now it
signifies more to me than formerly, to make use of

That when my death my life and rule shall cease,
The kingdom yet may with unbroken course
Have certain prince, by whose undoubted right
Your wealth and peace may stand in quiet stay;
And eke that they whom nature hath prepar'd   80
In time to take my place in princely seat –
While in their father's time their pliant youth
Yields to the frame of skilful governance –
May so be taught and train'd in noble arts,
As what their fathers which have reigned before
Have with great fame derived down to them,
With honour they may leave unto their seed
And not be thought for their unworthy life,
And for their lawless swerving out of kind,
Worthy to lose what law and kind them gave;   90
But that they may preserve the common peace,
The cause that first began and still maintains
The lineal course of kings' inheritance.
For me, for mine, for you, and for the state,
Whereof both I and you have charge and care,
Thus do I mean to use your wonted faith
To me and mine, and to your native land.
My lords, be plain without all wry respect
Or poisonous craft to speak in pleasing wise,
Lest as the blame of ill-succeeding things   100
Shall light on you, so light the harms also.
AROSTUS: Your good acceptance so, most noble King,

79	*stay:* equilibrium, rest	90	*kind:* nature
85	*As:* so that	98	*wry:* perverted, unjust
	fathers: ancestors, forefathers		*respect:* partiality, deference
86	*derived down:* handed down, bequeathed	100	*ill-succeeding:* turning out badly
89	*swerving:* deviating		
	kind: natural conduct		

Of such our faithfulness as heretofore
We have employed in duties to your grace
And to this realm, whose worthy head you are,
Well proves that neither you mistrust at all,
Nor we shall need in boasting wise to show
Our truth to you, nor yet our wakeful care
For you, for yours, and for our native land.
110 Wherefore, O King, I speak as one for all —
Sith all as one do bear you equal faith —
Doubt not to use our counsels and our aids,
Whose honours, goods and lives are whole avow'd
To serve, to aid, and to defend your grace.
GORBODUC: My lords, I thank you all. This is the case:
Ye know the gods, who have the sovereign care
For kings, for kingdoms, and for commonweals,
Gave me two sons in my more lusty age,
Who now in my decaying years are grown
120 Well towards riper state of strength,
To take in hand some greater princely charge.
As yet they live and spend their hopeful days
With me and with their mother here in court.
Their age now asketh other place and trade,
And mine also doth ask another change,
Theirs to more travail, mine to greater ease.
When fatal death shall end my mortal life,
My purpose is to leave unto them twain
The realm divided into two sundry parts:
130 The one Ferrex, mine elder son, shall have;
The other shall the younger, Porrex, rule.
That both my purpose may more firmly stand,
And eke that they may better rule their charge,

---

111   *Sith:* since   124   *asketh:* demands, calls for
113   *avow'd:* sworn   *trade:* way of life
118   *lusty:* vigorous

I mean forthwith to place them in the same,
That in my life they may both learn to rule
And I may joy to see their ruling well.
This is in sum what I would have ye weigh:
First, whether ye allow my whole device
And think it good for me, for them, for you,
And for our country, mother of us all;   140
And if ye like it, and allow it well,
Then for their guiding and their governance,
Show forth such means of circumstance
As ye think meet to be both known and kept.
Lo, this is all; now tell me your advice.

AROSTUS: And this is much, and asketh great advice.
But for my part, my sovereign lord and King,
This do I think; your Majesty doth know
How under you in justice and in peace
Great wealth and honour long we have enjoy'd,   150
So as we cannot seem with greedy minds
To wish for change of prince or governance.
But if we like your purpose and device,
Our liking must be deemed to proceed
Of rightful reason and of heedful care,
Not for ourselves, but for the common state,
Sith our own state doth need no better change.
I think in all as erst your grace hath said:
First, when you shall unload your aged mind
Of heavy care and troubles manifold   160
And lay the same upon my lords your sons,
Whose growing years may bear the burden long
(And long I pray the gods to grant it so)

---

135 *life:* lifetime
137 *weigh:* consider, weigh up
138 *allow:* approve of, accept
     device: plan, scheme

143 *circumstance:* 'effecting it'
157 *better change:* no change to improve it
158 *erst:* previously

And in your life while you shall so behold
Their rule, their virtues, and their noble deeds,
Such as their kind behighteth to us all,
Great be the profits that shall grow thereof.
Your age in quiet shall the longer last;
Your lasting age shall be their longer stay,
170 For cares of kings, that rule as you have rul'd
For public wealth and not for private joy,
Do waste man's life and hasten crooked age,
With furrow'd face and with enfeebl'd limbs,
To draw on creeping death a swifter pace:
They two, yet young, shall bear the parted reign
With greater ease than one, now old, alone,
Can wield the whole, for whom much harder is
With lessen'd strength the double weight to bear.
Your eye, your counsel, and the grave regard
180 Of father, yea, of such a father's name –
Now at beginning of their sunder'd reign,
When is the hazard of their whole success,
Shall bridle so their force of youthful heats,
And so restrain the rage of insolence
Which most assails the young and noble minds,
And so shall guide and train in temper'd stay
Their yet green-bending wits with reverent awe,
As now inur'd with virtues at the first,
Custom, O King, shall bring delightfulness.
190 By use of virtue, vice shall grow in hate;
But if you so dispose it that the day

---

166 *kind behighteth:* nature promises, holds out hope of
169 *stay:* support
171 *wealth:* well-being, prosperity
175 *parted:* divided
177 *wield:* govern, rule
182 *hazard:* greatest risk, peril (see note)
184 *rage:* rashness, violence
     insolence: inexperience (see note)
186 *stay:* stability
188 *inur'd:* accustomed

Which ends your life shall first begin their reign,
Great is the peril what will be the end.
When such beginning of such liberties —
Void of such stays as in your life do lie —
Shall leave them free to random of their will,
An open prey to traitorous flattery,
The greatest pestilence of noble youth.
Which peril shall be past, if in your life
Their temper'd youth with aged father's awe   200
Be brought in ure of skilful stayedness,
And in your life their lives disposed so
Shall length your noble life in joyfulness.
Thus think I that your grace hath wisely thought,
And that your tender care of common weal
Hath bred this thought, so to divide your land,
And plant your sons to bear the present rule,
While you yet live to see their ruling well,
That you may longer live by joy therein.
What further means behoveful are and meet   210
At greater leisure may your grace devise,
When all have said, and when we be agreed
If this be best to part the realm in twain
And place your sons in present government,
Whereof, as I have plainly said my mind,
So would I hear the rest of all my lords.
PHILANDER: In part I think as hath been said before;
In part again my mind is otherwise.
As for dividing of this realm in twain,

---

195   *stays:* restraints
196   *random* etc.: deviate as they fancy
      (see note)
199   *life:* lifetime
201   *Be brought* etc.: become accus-
      tomed to firm and steadfast gov-
      ernment

203   *length:* lengthen
210   *What further* etc.: what further
      means are necessary and appropri-
      ate

220 And lotting out the same in equal parts
To either of my lords, your grace's sons,
That think I best for this your realm's behove,
For profit and advancement of your sons,
And for your comfort and your honour eke.
But so to place them while your life do last;
To yield to them your royal governance;
To be above them only in the name
Of father, not in kingly state also;
I think not good for you, for them, nor us.
230 This kingdom, since the bloody civil field
Where Morgan slain did yield his conquered part
Unto his cousin's sword in Camberland,
Containeth all that whilom did suffice
Three noble sons of your forefather Brute:
So your two sons it may suffice also,
The moe the stronger, if they gree in one.
The smaller compass that the realm doth hold,
The easier is the sway thereof to wield,
The nearer justice to the wronged poor,
240 The smaller charge, and yet enough for one.
And when the region is divided so,
That brethren be the lords of either part,
Such strength doth nature knit between them both,
In sundry bodies by conjoined love,
That not as two, but one of doubled force,
Each is to other as a sure defence.
The nobleness and glory of the one

220   *lotting:* apportioning (land)
222   *behove:* benefit
230   *civil:* communal (see note)
231   *conquered part:* see note
233   *whilom:* once, formerly
236   *moe:* more
      gree: agree

237   *compass:* extent
      hold: include
240   *charge:* burden, task, responsibility

Doth sharp the courage of the other's mind
With virtuous envy to contend for praise.
And such an equalness hath nature made   250
Between the brethren of one father's seed,
As an unkindly wrong it seems to be
To throw the brother-subject under feet
Of him whose peer he is by course of kind.
And Nature, that did make this equalness,
Oft so repineth at so great a wrong,
That oft she raiseth up a grudging grief
In younger brethren at the elder's state,
Whereby both towns and kingdoms have been raz'd
And famous stocks of royal blood destroy'd.   260
The brother, that should be the brother's aid
And have a wakeful care for his defence,
Gapes for his death, and blames the lingering years
That draw not forth his end with faster course;
And, oft impatient of so long delays,
With hateful slaughter he prevents the fates,
And heaps a just reward for brother's blood,
With endless vengence on his stock for aye.
Such mischiefs here are wisely met withal,
If equal state may nourish equal love,   270
Where none hath cause to grudge at other's good:
But now the head to stoop beneath them both,
Ne kind, ne reason, ne good order bears.
And oft it hath been seen, where Nature's course
Hath been perverted in disorder'd wise,
When fathers cease to know that they should rule,

248   *sharp the courage:* stimulate the
      vigour
252   *unkindly:* unnatural
254   *peer:* equal
263   *Gapes for:* eagerly desires (see
      note)

266   *prevents:* anticipates
268   *for aye:* for ever
269   *mischiefs:* calamities, evils
273   *Ne . . . ne:* neither . . . nor

The children cease to know they should obey,
And often overkindly tenderness
Is mother of unkindly stubbornness.
280   I speak not this in envy or reproach
As if I grudg'd the glory of your sons,
Whose honour I beseech the gods increase,
Nor yet as if I thought there did remain
So filthy cankers in their noble breasts,
Whom I esteem – which is their greatest praise –
Undoubted children of so good a King.
Only I mean to show by certain rules
Which kind hath graft within the mind of man
That Nature hath her order and her course,
290   Which, being broken, doth corrupt the state
Of minds and things, even in the best of all.
My lord, your sons may learn to rule of you;
Your own example in your noble court
Is fittest guider of their youthful years.
If you desire to see some present joy
By sight of their well ruling in your life,
See them obey, so shall you see them rule.
Whoso obeyeth not with humbleness
Will rule with outrage and with insolence.
300   Long may they rule, I do beseech the gods;
Long may they learn, ere they begin to rule!
If kind and fates would suffer, I would wish
Them aged princes and immortal kings.
Wherefore, most noble King, I well assent
Between your sons that you divide your realm,
And as in kind, so match them in degree;

278	*overkindly:* abnormally indulgent	288	*kind:* nature, commonsense
284	*cankers:* inward malice (see note)	302	*suffer:* allow it
287	*rules:* laws	306	*kind:* birth, heritage

But while the gods prolong your royal life,
Prolong your reign; for thereto live you here,
And therefore have the gods so long forborne
To join you to themselves that still you might   310
Be prince and father of our commonweal.
They, when they see your children ripe to rule,
Will make them room, and will remove you hence,
That yours, in right ensuing of your life,
May rightly honour your immortal name.
EUBULUS: Your wonted true regard of faithful hearts
Makes me, O King, the bolder to presume,
To speak what I conceive within my breast,
Although the same do not agree at all
With that which other here my lords have said,   320
Nor which yourself have seemed best to like.
Pardon I crave, and that my words be deem'd
To flow from hearty zeal unto your grace,
And to the safety of your commonweal.
To part your realm unto my lords, your sons,
I think not good for you, ne yet for them,
But worst of all for this our native land.
Within one land, one single rule is best:
Divided reigns do make divided hearts,
But peace preserves the country and the prince.   330
Such is in man the greedy mind to reign,
So great is his desire to climb aloft,
In worldly stage the stateliest parts to bear,
That faith and justice and all kindly love
Do yield unto desire of sovereignty,
Where equal state doth raise an equal hope

---

308 *thereto:* for that purpose   314 *right ensuing:* correctly following
311 *commonweal:* public good   325 *part . . . unto:* divide between
312 *They:* i.e. the gods   334 *kindly:* natural, familial

To win the thing that either would attain.
Your grace remembereth how in passed years
The mighty Brute, first prince of all this land,
340 Possess'd the same and rul'd it well in one;
He, thinking that the compass did suffice
For his three sons three kingdoms eke to make,
Cut it in three, as you would now in twain.
But how much British blood hath since been spilt
To join again the sunder'd unity!
What princes slain before their timely hour,
What waste of towns and people in the land,
What treasons heap'd on murders and on spoils
Whose just revenge even yet is scarcely ceas'd,
350 Ruthful remembrance is yet raw in mind –
The gods forbid the like to chance again!
And you, O King, give not the cause thereof:
My Lord Ferrex, your elder son, perhaps
(Whom kind and custom gives a rightful hope
To be your heir and to succeed your reign)
Shall think that he doth suffer greater wrong
Than he perchance will bear, if power serve;
Porrex, the younger, so uprais'd in state,
Perhaps in courage will be rais'd also.
360 If flattery, then, which fails not to assail
The tender minds of yet unskilful youth,
In one shall kindle and increase disdain
And envy in the other's heart inflame,
This fire shall waste their love, their lives, their land,
And ruthful ruin shall destroy them both.

---

340 *in one:* as a single kingdom
341 *compass:* bounds, extent
346 *timely hour:* appropriate time (of death)
348 *spoils:* pillagings

350 *Ruthful:* grievous, lamentable
      raw in mind: fresh in thought
357 *bear:* accept, put up with
359 *courage:* pride, ambitiousness
361 *unskilful:* inexpert, unaware

I wish not this, O King, so to befall,
But fear the thing that I do most abhor.
Give no beginning to so dreadful end;
Keep them in order and obedience,
And let them both by now obeying you   370
Learn such behaviour as beseems their state:
The elder, mildness in his governance,
The younger, a yielding contentedness.
And keep them near unto your presence still,
That they, restrained by the awe of you,
May live in compass of well-temper'd stay
And pass the perils of their youthful years.
Your aged life draws on to feebler time,
Wherein you shall less able be to bear
The travails that in youth you have sustain'd,   380
Both in your person's and your realm's defence;
If planting now your sons in further parts,
You send them further from your present reach,
Less shall you know how they themselves demean.
Traitorous corrupters of their pliant youth
Shall have unspied a much more free access;
And if ambition and inflam'd disdain
Shall arm the one, the other, or them both,
To civil war, or to usurping pride,
Late shall you rue, that you ne reck'd before.   390
Good is, I grant, of all to hope the best,
But not to live still dreadless of the worst;
So trust the one, that the other be foreseen.
Arm not unskilfulness with princely power,

371	*beseems:* is appropriate to	384	*demean:* behave
376	*in compass of:* within the bounds of	387	*disdain:* indignation
380	*travails:* labours, 'stress'	390	*ne reck'd:* took no notice of, did not foresee the result of
382	*further:* farther off	394	*unskilfulness:* inexperience

But you that long have wisely rul'd the reins
Of royalty within your noble realm,
So hold them, while the gods for our avails
Shall stretch the thread of your prolonged days:
Too soon he clamb into the flaming car,
400   Whose want of skill did set the earth on fire.
Time and example of your noble grace
Shall teach your sons both to obey and rule;
When time hath taught them, time shall make the place,
The place that now is full: and so, I pray,
Long it remain, to comfort of us all.
GORBODUC: I take your faithful hearts in thankful part,
But sith I see no cause to draw my mind
To fear the nature of my loving sons,
Or to misdeem that envy or disdain
410   Can there work hate where Nature planteth love,
In one self purpose do I still abide.
My love extendeth equally to both;
My land sufficeth for them both also.
Humber shall part the marches of their realms,
The southern part the elder shall possess,
The northern shall Porrex, the younger, rule;
In quiet I will pass my aged days,
Free from the travail and the painful cares
That hasten age upon the worthiest kings.
420   But lest the fraud (that ye do seem to fear)
Of flattering tongues corrupt their tender youth
And writhe them to the ways of youthful lust,

395   *rul'd:* controlled
397   *avails:* advantage, benefit
399   *Too soon* etc.: too soon he climbed
         into the fiery chariot (see note)
403   *make the place:* create the vacancy
411   *self:* integrated, single

414   *part the marches:* mark the bounda-
         ries
420   *fraud:* deceitfulness
422   *writhe:* twist, deflect
         lust: obsessive desire

To climbing pride, or to revenging hate,
Or to neglecting of their carefull charge,
Lewdly to live in wanton recklessness,
Or to oppressing of the rightful cause,
Or not to wreak the wrongs done to the poor,
To tread down truth, or favour false deceit,
I mean to join to either of my sons
Someone of those whose long approved faith   430
And wisdom tried may well assure my heart
That mining fraud shall find no way to creep
Into their fenced ears with grave advice.
This is the end, and so I pray you all
To bear my sons the love and loyalty
That I have found within your faithful breasts.
AROSTUS: You, nor your sons, our sovereign lord, shall want
 Our faith and service while our lives do last.
 [*Exeunt all but the* CHORUS.]
CHORUS: When settled stay doth hold the royal throne
 In steadfast place, by known and doubtless right,   440
 And chiefly when descent on one alone
 Makes single and unparted reign to light,
 Each change of course unjoints the whole estate,
 And yields it thrall to ruin by debate.

 The strength that, knit by fast accord in one
 Against all foreign power of mighty foes,
 Could of itself defend itself alone,
 Disjoined once, the former force doth lose:
 The sticks that sunder'd brake so soon in twain,

425	*lewdly:* wickedly, basely	
427	*wreak:* avenge	
432	*mining:* undermining	
433	*fenced:* fortified, protected	
437	*you:* i.e. neither you . . .	
	want: lack	
439	*stay:* stability	
440	*doubtless:* unquestionable	
444	*debate:* dissension	

450   In faggot bound attempted were in vain.

Oft tender mind that leads the partial eye
Of erring parents in their children's love
Destroys the wrongly loved child thereby:
This doth the proud son of Apollo prove,
Who, rashly set in chariot of his sire,
Inflam'd the parched earth with heaven's fire.

And this great King, that doth divide his land,
And change the course of his descending crown,
And yields the rein into his children's hand,
460   From blissful state of joy and great renown,
A mirror shall become to princes all,
To learn to shun the cause of such a fall.

THE ORDER AND SIGNIFICATION OF THE DUMB-SHOW
BEFORE THE SECOND ACT

First the music of cornets began to play, during which came in
upon the stage a king accompanied with a number of his
nobility and gentlemen. And after he had placed himself in a
chair of estate prepared for him, there came and kneeled before
him a grave and aged gentleman and offered up a cup unto him
of wine in a glass, which the king refused. After him comes a
brave and lusty young gentleman and presents the king with a
cup of gold filled with poison, which the king accepted, and,
drinking the same, immediately fell down dead upon the stage,
and so was carried thence away by his lords and gentlemen,

450   *faggot:* bundle
451   *partial:* biased
458   *descending:* hereditary

461   *A mirror:* a model or pattern
Dumb-show
      chair of estate: state chair, royal throne
      brave: 'smart', bold
      lusty: cheerful

and then the music ceased. Hereby was signified that as glass by nature holdeth no poison, but is clear and may easily be seen through, ne boweth by any art, so a faithful counsellor holdeth no treason, but is plain and open, ne yieldeth to any undiscreet affection, but giveth wholesome counsel, which the ill-advised prince refuseth. The delightful gold filled with poison betokeneth flattery, which under fair seeming of pleasant words beareth deadly poison, which destroyeth the prince that receiveth it, as befell in the two brethren Ferrex and Porrex, who, refusing the wholesome advice of grave counsellors, credited these young parasites and brought to themselves death and destruction thereby.

ACT II SCENE I

[*Ferrex's court*]

[*Enter* FERREX, HERMON *and* DORDAN.]

FERREX: I marvel much what reason led the King
My father, thus without all my desert,
To reave me half the kingdom, which by course
Of law and nature should remain to me.

HERMON: If you with stubborn and untamed pride
Had stood against him in rebelling wise,
Or if with grudging mind you had envied
So slow a sliding of his aged years,
Or sought before your time to haste the course
Of fatal death upon his royal head,
Or stain'd your stock with murder of your kin,
Some face of reason might perhaps have seem'd
To yield some likely cause to spoil ye thus.

470

---

holdeth: harbours
ne boweth: is not deflected
undiscreet: impudent
credited: believed

464 *desert:* deserving it
465 *reave me:* bereave, deprive me of
466 *remain:* continue to belong
475 *spoil:* deprive, rob

FERREX: The wreakful gods pour on my cursed head
Eternal plagues and never-dying woes;
The hellish prince adjudge my damned ghost
To Tantale's thirst, or proud Ixion's wheel,
480 Or cruel gripe to gnaw my growing heart,
To during torments and unquenched flames,
If ever I conceiv'd so foul a thought,
To wish his end of life, or yet of reign!
DORDAN: Ne yet your father, O most noble Prince,
Did ever think so foul a thing of you:
For he, with more than father's tender love,
While yet the fates do lend him life to rule
(Who long might live to see your ruling well),
To you, my lord, and to his other son,
490 Lo, he resigns his realm and royalty,
Which never would so wise a prince have done
If he had once misdeem'd that in your heart
There ever lodged so unkind a thought.
But tender love, my lord, and settled trust
Of your good nature and your noble mind
Made him to place you thus in royal throne,
And now to give you half his realm to guide –
Yea, and that half which in abounding store
Of things that serve to make a wealthy realm,
500 In stately cities, and in fruitful soil,
In temperate breathing of the milder Heaven,
In things of needful use, which friendly sea
Transports by traffic from the foreign parts,
In flowing wealth, in honour and in force,
Doth pass the double value of the part

476	*wreakful:* vengeful	492	*misdeem'd:* suspected
480	*gripe:* vulture (see note)	501	*breathing:* breath, breeze
481	*during:* lasting, enduring	505	*pass:* surpass

That Porrex hath allotted to his reign.
Such is your case, such is your father's love.
FERREX: Ah love, my friends? Love wrongs not whom he loves.
DORDAN: Ne yet he wrongeth you, that giveth you
So large a reign, ere that the course of time   510
Bring you to kingdom by descended right,
Which time perhaps might end your time before.
FERREX: Is this no wrong, say you, to reave from me
My native right of half so great a realm,
And thus to match his younger son with me
In equal power, and in as great degree?
Yea, and what son? The son whose swelling pride
Would never yield one point of reverence,
When I the elder and apparent heir
Stood in the likelihood to possess the whole;   520
Yea, and that son which from his childish age
Envieth mine honour and doth hate my life.
What will he now do, when his pride, his rage,
The mindful malice of his grudging heart,
Is arm'd with force, with wealth, and kingly state?
HERMON: Was this not wrong, yea, ill-advised wrong,
To give so mad a man so sharp a sword,
To so great peril of so great mishap,
Wide open thus to set so large a way?
DORDAN: Alas, my lord, what griefull thing is this,   530
That of your brother you can think so ill?
I never saw him utter likely sign
Whereby a man might see or once misdeem
Such hate of you, ne such unyielding pride.

510   *reign:* territory to rule? (see note)
511   *descended:* hereditary
512   *which time* etc.: during which period you might die yourself
513   *reave:* rob, plunder
519   *apparent:* evident, undoubted
521   *childish age:* youngest years
524   *mindful:* brooding, unforgetting
529   *to set* etc.: to provide so obvious an opportunity

Ill is their counsel, shameful be their end,
That, raising such mistrustful fear in you,
Sowing the seed of such unkindly hate,
Travail by treason to destroy you both.
Wise is your brother, and of noble hope,
540 Worthy to wield a large and mighty realm;
So much a stronger friend have you thereby,
Whose strength is your strength, if you gree in one.
HERMON: If nature and the gods had pinched so
Their flowing bounty, and their noble gifts
Of princely qualities, from you, my lord,
And pour'd them all at once in wasteful wise
Upon your father's younger son alone,
Perhaps there be that in your prejudice
Would say that birth should yield to worthiness.
550 But sith in each good gift and princely art
Ye are his match, and in the chief of all –
In mildness and in sober governance –
Ye far surmount; and sith there is in you
Sufficing skill, and hopeful towardness
To wield the whole, and match your elder's praise,
I see no cause why ye should lose the half.
Ne would I wish you yield to such a loss,
Lest your mild sufferance of so great a wrong
Be deemed cowardish and simple dread,
560 Which shall give courage to the fiery head
Of your young brother to invade the whole.
While yet, therefore, sticks in the people's mind
The loathed wrong of your disheritance;

540 *wield:* rule
542 *gree in one:* mutually agree, 'see eye to eye'
543 *pinched:* been niggardly with, stinted
548 *in your prejudice:* against your interests
554 *towardness:* aptitude, promise
560 *courage:* vigour, encouragement
561 *invade:* usurp, seize

And ere your brother have by settled power,
By guileful cloak of an alluring show,
Got him some force and favour in the realm;
And while the noble Queen your mother lives,
To work and practise all for your avail;
Attempt redress by arms, and wreak yourself
Upon his life, that gaineth by your loss   570
Who now to shame of you, and grief of us,
In your own kingdom triumphs over you.
Show now your courage meet for kingly state,
That they, which have avow'd to spend their goods,
Their lands, their lives and honours in your cause,
May be the bolder to maintain your part,
When they do see that coward fear in you
Shall not betray ne fail their faithful hearts.
If once the death of Porrex end the strife
And pay the price of his usurped reign,   580
Your mother shall persuade the angry King;
The lords your friends eke shall appease his rage;
For they be wise, and well they can foresee
That ere long time your aged father's death
Will bring a time when you shall well requite
Their friendly favour, or their hateful spite,
Yea, or their slackness to advance your cause.
'Wise men do not so hang on passing state
Of present princes, chiefly in their age,
But they will further cast their reaching eye   590
To view and weigh the times and reigns to come.'
Ne is it likely, though the King be wroth,

564 *settled:* established   581 *persuade:* win over
568 *practise:* scheme, plot   585 *requite:* repay
569 *wreak:* avenge   592 *wroth:* angry
574 *avow'd:* pledged
578 *fail:* let down, deceive (?); see
     note

That he yet will, or that the realm will, bear
Extreme revenge upon his only son;
Or if he would, what one is he that dare
Be minister to such an enterprise?
And here you be now placed in your own,
Amid your friends, your vassals, and your strength:
We shall defend and keep your person safe,
600   Till either counsel turn his tender mind,
Or age or sorrow end his weary days.
But if the fear of gods, and secret grudge
Of Nature's law, repining at the fact,
Withhold your courage from so great attempt,
Know ye that lust of kingdoms hath no law:
The gods do bear and well allow in kings
The things that they abhor in rascal routs.
'When kings on slender quarrels run to wars,
And then in cruel and unkindly wise
610   Command thefts, rapes, murders of innocents,
The spoil of towns, ruins of mighty realms,
Think you such princes do suppose themselves
Subject to laws of kind and fear of gods?'
Murders and violent thefts in private men
Are heinous crimes and full of foul reproach,
Yet none offence, but deck'd with glorious name
Of noble conquests, in the hands of kings!
But if you like not yet so hot device,
Ne list to take such vantage of the time,

596	*minister:* executant, agent	611	*spoil:* sacking
600	*tender:* easy-going	615	*heinous:* hateful, infamous
602	*grudge:* uneasiness, scruple	616	*none:* no
603	*Of:* concerning	618	*so hot device:* such a violent plan
	repining: fretting, 'whingeing'	619	*vantage:* advantage
	fact: deed, crime		
607	*rascal routs:* the common herd, rabble		

But, though with peril of your own estate,   620
  You will not be the first that shall invade,
  Assemble yet your force for your defence,
  And for your safety stand upon your guard.
DORDAN: O Heaven, was there ever heard or known
  So wicked counsel to a noble prince?
  Let me, my lord, disclose unto your grace
  This heinous tale, what mischief it contains:
  Your father's death, your brother's and your own,
  Your present murder and eternal shame.
  Hear me, O King, and suffer not to sink   630
  So high a treason in your princely breast!
FERREX: The mighty gods forbid that ever I
  Should once conceive such mischief in my heart!
  Although my brother hath bereft my realm,
  And bear perhaps to me an hateful mind,
  Shall I revenge it with his death therefore,
  Or shall I so destroy my father's life
  That gave me life? The gods forbid, I say!
  [To HERMON] Cease you to speak so any more to me.
  [To DORDAN] Ne you, my friend, with answer once repeat   640
  So foul a tale. In silence let it die.
  What lord or subject shall have hope at all
  That under me they safely shall enjoy
  Their goods, their honours, lands and liberties,
  With whom neither one only brother dear,
  Ne father dearer, could enjoy their lives?
  But sith I fear my younger brother's rage,
  And sith perhaps some other man may give
  Some like advice to move his grudging head
  At mine estate, which counsel may perchance   650

629   *present:* immediate (see note)   649   *grudging:* resentful

Take greater force with him than this with me,
I will in secret so prepare myself,
As if his malice or his lust to reign
Break forth in arms or sudden violence,
I may withstand his rage and keep mine own.

> [*Exeunt* FERREX *and* HERMON.]

DORDAN: I fear the fatal time now draweth on
When civil hate shall end the noble line
Of famous Brute and of his royal seed.
Great Jove defend the mischief now at hand!
660   Oh that the Secretary's wise advice
Had erst been heard when he besought the King
Not to divide his land, nor send his sons
To further parts from presence of his court,
Ne yet to yield to them his governance!
Lo, such are they now in the royal throne
As was rash Phaeton in Phoebus' car;
Ne then the fiery steeds did draw the flame
With wilder random through the kindled skies,
Than traitorous counsel now will whirl about
670   The youthful heads of these unskilful kings.
But I hereof their father will inform:
The reverence of him perhaps shall stay
The growing mischiefs, while they yet are green.
If this help not, then woe unto themselves,
The Prince, the people, the divided land! [*Exit.*]

ACT II SCENE 2
[*Porrex's court*]
[*Enter* PORREX, PHILANDER, *and* TYNDAR.]

651	*Take greater force:* make a more	660	*the Secretary's:* i.e. Eubulus's
	powerful impression	668	*random:* impetuosity
653	*As if:* so that if	670	*unskilful:* inexperienced, inexpert
657	*civil:* communal	672	*stay:* halt
659	*defend:* avert, ward off		

PORREX: And is it thus? And doth he so prepare
    Against his brother as his mortal foe?
    And now, while yet his aged father lives?
    Neither regards he him, nor fears he me?
    War would he have? And he shall have it so.   680

TYNDAR: I saw myself the great prepared store
    Of horse, of armour, and of weapon there;
    Ne bring I to my lord reported tales
    Without the ground of seen and searched truth.
    Lo, secret quarrels run about his court
    To bring the name of you, my lord, in hate:
    Each man almost can now debate the cause
    And ask a reason of so great a wrong,
    Why he, so noble and so wise a prince,
    Is as unworthy reft his heritage,   690
    And why the King, misled by crafty means,
    Divided thus his land from course of right?
    The wiser sort hold down their griefull heads;
    Each man withdraws from talk and company
    Of those that have been known to favour you.
    To hide the mischief of their meaning there,
    Rumours are spread of your preparing here;
    The rascal numbers of unskilful sort
    Are filled with monstrous tales of you and yours.
    In secret I was counsell'd by my friends   700
    To haste me thence, and brought you, as you know,
    Letters from those that both can truly tell
    And would not write unless they knew it well.

PHILANDER: My lord, yet ere you move unkindly war,
    Send to your brother to demand the cause:

---

684   *ground:* valid basis   689   *he:* i.e. Ferrex
688   *ask a reason of:* demand a reason   690   *as:* as if he were
      for   704   *unkindly:* cruel, unnatural

Perhaps some traitorous tales have fill'd his ears
With false reports against your noble grace,
Which, once disclos'd, shall end the growing strife,
That else not stay'd with wise foresight in time,
710   Shall hazard both your kingdoms and your lives.
Send to your father eke; he shall appease
Your kindled minds, and rid you of this fear.

PORREX: Rid me of fear? I fear him not at all,
Ne will to him ne to my father send!
If danger were for one to tarry there,
Think ye it safety to return again?
In mischiefs, such as Ferrex now intends,
The wonted courteous laws to messengers
Are not observ'd, which in just war they use.
720   Shall I so hazard any one of mine?
Shall I betray my trusty friends to him,
That have disclos'd his treason unto me?
Let him entreat that fears; I fear him not.
Or shall I to the King my father send?
Yea, and send now, while such a mother lives
That loves my brother and that hateth me?
Shall I give leisure, by my fond delays,
To Ferrex to oppress me all unware?
I will not, but I will invade his realm
730   And seek the traitor prince within his court!
Mischief for mischief is a due reward:
His wretched head shall pay the worthy price
Of this his treason and his hate to me.

710   *hazard:* imperil, expose to risk
(see note)
715   *If danger were:* if it were dangerous
717   *In mischiefs:* when trouble is
brewing, when evil's abroad
720   *of mine:* of my followers
727   *leisure:* 'a breathing space'
fond: stupidly diffident

Shall I abide, and treat, and send, and pray,
And hold my yielden throat to traitor's knife,
While I with valiant mind and conquering force
Might rid myself of foes and win a realm?
Yet rather, when I have the wretch's head,
Then to the King my father will I send.
The bootless case may yet appease his wrath;   740
If not, I will defend me as I may.
    [*Exeunt* PORREX *and* TYNDAR.]

PHILANDER: Lo, here the end of these two youthful kings,
    The father's death, the ruin of their realms.
    'O most unhappy state of counsellors
    That light on so unhappy lord and times,
    That neither can their good advice be heard
    Yet must they bear the blames of ill success.'
    But I will to the King, their father, haste,
    Ere this mischief come to the likely end;
    That if the mindful wrath of wreakful gods,   750
    Since mighty Ilion's fall not yet appeased
    With these poor remnants of the Trojan name,
    Have not determin'd by unmoved fate
    Out of this realm to rase the British line,
    By good advice, by awe of father's name,
    By force of wiser lords, this kindled hate
    May yet be quenched, ere it consume us all.
                          [*Exit.*]

CHORUS: When youth, not bridled with a guiding stay,
    Is left to random of their own delight,
    And wields whole realms by force of sovereign sway,   760

---

734 *treat:* negotiate (see note)
735 *yielden:* yielded, surrendered
740 *bootless case:* the situation he
     cannot remedy
750 *mindful:* unforgetting
     wreakful: vengeful
751 *Ilion's:* Troy's
754 *rase:* erase, eradicate
758 *stay:* check, restraint
759 *random:* stray at liberty

Great is the danger of unmaster'd might,
Lest skilless rage throw down with headlong fall
Their lands, their states, their lives, themselves and all.

When growing pride doth fill the swelling breast,
And greedy lust doth raise the climbing mind,
Oh, hardly may the peril be repress'd!
Ne fear of angry gods, ne laws [of] kind,
Ne country's care can fired hearts restrain,
When force hath armed envy and disdain;

770   When kings of foreset will neglect the rede
Of best advice, and yield to pleasing tales
That do their fancies noisome humour feed,
Ne reason nor regard of right avails;
Succeeding heaps of plagues shall teach too late
To learn the mischiefs of misguided state.

Foul fall the traitor false that undermines
The love of brethren to destroy them both!
Woe to the prince that pliant ear inclines,
And yields his mind to poisonous tale that floweth
780   From flattering mouth! And woe to wretched land
That wastes itself with civil sword in hand!
Lo, thus it is, poison in gold to take,
And wholesome drink in homely cup forsake.

761 *unmaster'd:* uncontrolled, un-
     tamed
762 *skilless:* inept, ignorant
767 *laws [of] kind:* laws relating to
     kindred (see note)
770 *of foreset:* intentionally
     rede: prudence (see note)
772 *noisome humour:* harmful fantasy

THE ORDER AND SIGNIFICATION OF THE DUMB-SHOW
BEFORE THE THIRD ACT

First the music of flutes began to play, during which came in upon the stage a company of mourners all clad in black, betokening death and sorrow to ensue upon the ill-advised misgovernment and dissension of brethren, as befell upon the murder of Ferrex by his younger brother. After the mourners had passed thrice about the stage, they departed, and then the music ceased.

ACT III SCENE I

[*Gorboduc's court*]
[*Enter* GORBODUC *with a letter,* EUBULUS, AROSTUS *and* ATTENDANTS *etc.*]

GORBODUC: O cruel fates! O mindful wrath of gods,
    Whose vengeance neither Simois' stained streams
    Flowing with blood of Trojan princes slain,
    Nor Phrygian fields made rank with corpses dead
    Of Asian kings and lords, can yet appease,
    Ne slaughter of unhappy Priam's race,
    Nor Ilion's fall made level with the soil,   790
    Can yet suffice, but still continu'd rage
    Pursues our line, and from the farthest seas
    Doth chase the issues of destroyed Troy.
    'Oh no man happy, till his end be seen!'
    If any flowing wealth and seeming joy
    In present years might make a happy wight,
    Happy was Hecuba, the woefullest wretch
    That ever liv'd to make a mirror of,
    And happy Priam with his noble sons,

787   *rank:* crowded, thick, foul
790   *Ilion's:* Troy's
796   *wight:* person, creature
798   *mirror:* model, example

800 And happy I, till now! Alas, I see
     And feel my most unhappy wretchedness:
     Behold, my lords, read ye this letter here.
     Lo, it contains the ruin of our realm,
     If timely speed provide not hasty help.
     Yet, O ye gods, if ever woeful king
     Might move ye, kings of kings, wreak it on me
     And on my sons, not on this guiltless realm!
     Send down your wasting flames from wrathful skies,
     To reave me and my sons the hatefull breath!
810 Read, read, my lords. This is the matter why
     I call'd ye now to have your good advice.

     The letter from DORDAN, *the counsellor of the elder prince.*
     EUBULUS *readeth the letter.*
     EUBULUS: 'My sovereign lord, what I am loath to write
     But loathest am to see, that I am forc'd
     By letters now to make you understand.
     My Lord Ferrex, your eldest son, misled
     By traitorous fraud of young untemper'd wits,
     Assembleth force against your younger son;
     Ne can my counsel yet withdraw the heat
     And furious pangs of his inflamed head.
820 Disdain, saith he, of his disheritance
     Arms him to wreak the great pretended wrong
     With civil sword upon his brother's life.
     If present help do not restrain this rage,
     This flame will waste your sons, your land, and you.

806 *wreak:* avenge
809 *reave me:* deprive me of
     hatefull: full of hatred
816 *fraud:* deception
     untemper'd: immoderate, uncon-
     trolled
819 *pangs:* anguish, keen emotion
820 *Disdain . . . of:* contempt at
     disheritance: being disinherited (of
     half the kingdom)
821 *wreak:* avenge
     pretended: proffered

      Your majesty's faithful and most
      humble subject, Dordan.'

AROSTUS: O King, appease your grief and stay your plaint;
  Great is the matter, and a woeful case,
  But timely knowledge may bring timely help.
  Send for them both unto your presence here;
  The reverence of your honour, age, and state,
  Your grave advice, the awe of father's name,   830
  Shall quickly knit again this broken peace.
  And if in either of my lords your sons
  Be such untamed and unyielding pride
  As will not bend unto your noble hests;
  If Ferrex, the elder son, can bear no peer,
  Or Porrex, not content, aspires to more
  Than you him gave above his native right,
  Join with the juster side. So shall you force
  Them to agree, and hold the land in stay.

EUBULUS [*looking offstage*]: What meaneth this? Lo, yonder
    comes in haste   840
  Philander from my lord, your younger son.
  [*Enter* PHILANDER.]

GORBODUC: The gods send joyful news!

PHILANDER: The mighty Jove
  Preserve your Majesty, O noble King.

GORBODUC: Philander, welcome. But how doth my son?

PHILANDER: Your son, sir, lives, and healthy I him left.
  But yet, O King, the want of lustful health
  Could not be half so griefull to your grace
  As these most wretched tidings that I bring.

GORBODUC: O Heavens, yet more? No end of woes to me?

PHILANDER: Tyndar, O King, came lately from the court   850

---

834 *hests:* bidding   846 *lustful:* vigorous, vital
839 *in stay:* steady, stable

Of Ferrex to my lord your younger son,
And made report of great prepared store
For war, and saith that it is wholly meant
Against Porrex, for high disdain that he
Lives now a king and equal in degree
With him that claimeth to succeed the whole,
As by due title of descending right.
Porrex is now so set on flaming fire,
Partly with kindled rage of cruel wrath,
860   Partly with hope to gain a realm thereby,
That he in haste prepareth to invade
His brother's land, and with unkindly war
Threatens the murder of your elder son;
Ne could I him persuade that first he should
Send to his brother to demand the cause,
Nor yet to you to stay this hateful strife.
Wherefore sith there no more I can be heard,
I come myself now to inform your grace,
And to beseech you, as you love the life
870   And safety of your children and your realm,
Now to employ your wisdom and your force
To stay this mischief ere it be too late.
GORBODUC: Are they in arms? Would he not send to me?
Is this the honour of a father's name?
In vain we travail to assuage their minds,
As if their hearts, whom neither brother's love,
Nor father's awe, nor kingdom's care can move,
Our counsels could withdraw from raging heat:
Jove slay them both, and end the cursed line!
880   For though perhaps fear of such mighty force
As I, my lords, joined with your noble aids,

856   *succeed:* inherit, succeed to   875   *assuage:* calm, appease
862   *unkindly:* unnatural, cruel

May yet raise, shall repress their present heat,
The secret grudge and malice will remain;
The fire not quench'd, but kept in close restraint,
Fed still within, breaks forth with double flame:
Their death and mine must pease the angry gods.
PHILANDER: Yield not, O King, so much to weak despair:
  Your sons yet live, and long, I trust, they shall.
  If fates had taken you from earthly life
  Before beginning of this civil strife,   890
  Perhaps your sons in their unmaster'd youth,
  Loose from regard of any living wight,
  Would run on headlong, with unbridled race,
  To their own death and ruin of this realm.
  But sith the gods, that have the care for kings,
  Of things and times dispose the order so
  That in your life this kindled flame breaks forth,
  While yet your life, your wisdom, and your power
  May stay the growing mischief, and repress
  The fiery blaze of their enkindled heat,   900
  It seems, and so ye ought to deem thereof,
  That loving Jove hath temper'd so the time
  Of this debate to happen in your days,
  That you yet living may the same appease,
  And add it to the glory of your latter age,
  And they your sons may learn to live in peace.
  Beware, O King, the greatest harm of all,
  Lest by your wailful plaints your hasten'd death
  Yield larger room unto their growing rage:
  Preserve your life, the only hope of stay.   910

882	*repress:* restrain, suppress	899	*mischief:* trouble, evil
886	*pease:* appease	900	*enkindled:* inflamed
891	*unmaster'd:* untamed, insubordinate	903	*debate:* strife
897	*life:* lifetime	910	*stay:* stability

And if your highness herein list to use
Wisdom or force, counsel or knightly aid,
Lo, we, our persons, powers and lives are yours;
Use us till death, O King; we are your own.

EUBULUS: Lo, here the peril that was erst foreseen
When you, O King, did first divide your land,
And yield your present reign unto your sons:
But now, O noble prince, now is no time
To wail and plain, and waste your woeful life.

920   Now is the time for present good advice:
Sorrow doth dark the judgement of the wit.
'The heart unbroken and the courage free
From feeble faintness of bootless despair
Doth either rise to safety or renown
By noble valure of unvanquish'd mind,
Or yet doth perish in more happy sort.'
Your grace may send to either of your sons
Some one both wise and noble personage,
Which with good counsel and with weighty name

930   Of father shall present before their eyes
Your hest, your life, your safety, and their own,
The present mischief of their deadly strife.
And in the while, assemble you the force
Which your commandment and the speedy haste
Of all my lords here present can prepare:
The terror of your mighty power shall stay
The rage of both, or yet of one at least.
       [*Enter* NUNTIUS.]

NUNTIUS: O King, the greatest grief that ever prince did hear,

---

911	*list:* chooses, wishes	925	*valure:* merit, worthiness
921	*dark:* darken	926	*sort:* kind of way, manner
	wit: intellect, mind	931	*hest:* command
923	*bootless:* incurable, lacking remedy	937	s.d. NUNTIUS: messenger

That ever woeful messenger did tell,
That ever wretched land hath seen before, 940
I bring to you: Porrex, your younger son,
With sudden force invaded hath the land
That you to Ferrex did allot to rule,
And with his own most bloody hand he hath
His brother slain, and doth possess his realm.
GORBODUC: O Heavens, send down the flames of your revenge!
Destroy, I say, with flash of wreakful fire
The traitor son, and then the wretched sire!
But let us go, that yet perhaps I may
Die with revenge, and pease the hatefull gods. 950
              [*Exeunt all but the* CHORUS.]
CHORUS: The lust of kingdom knows no sacred faith,
No rule of reason, no regard of right,
No kindly love, no fear of Heaven's wrath,
But with contempt of gods, and man's despite,
Through bloody slaughter doth prepare the ways
To fatal sceptre and accursed reign:
The son so loathes the father's lingering days,
Ne dreads his hand in brother's blood to stain.

O wretched prince, ne dost thou yet record
The yet fresh murders done within the land 960
Of thy forefathers, when the cruel sword
Bereft Morgan his life with cousin's hand?
Thus fatal plagues pursue the guilty race,
Whose murderous hand imbru'd with guiltless blood
Asks vengeance still before the Heavens' face,
With endless mischiefs on the cursed brood.

950	*hateful:* full of hate	959	*record:* recall
951	*lust of kingdom:* desire to rule	964	*imbru'd:* stained
954	*despite:* scornfulness	965	*Asks:* demands

The wicked child thus brings to woeful sire
The mournful plaints, to waste his very life;
Thus do the cruel flames of civil fire
970 Destroy the parted reign with hateful strife,
And hence doth spring the well from which doth flow
The dead black streams of mourning, plaints and woe.

THE ORDER AND SIGNIFICATION OF THE DUMB-SHOW
BEFORE THE FOURTH ACT.

First the music of hautboys began to play, during which there came from under the stage, as though out of Hell, three Furies — Alecto, Megera, and Tisiphone — clad in black garments sprinkled with blood and flames, their bodies girt with snakes, their heads spread with serpents instead of hair, the one bearing in her hand a snake, the other a whip, and the third a burning firebrand, each driving before them a king and a queen, which, moved by Furies, unnaturally had slain their own children. The names of the kings and queens were these: Tantalus, Medea, Athamas, Ino, Cambises, Althea. After that the Furies and these had passed about the stage thrice, they departed, and then the music ceased. Hereby was signified the unnatural murders to follow, that is to say, Porrex, slain by his own mother, and of King Gorboduc and Queen Videna, killed by their own subjects.

ACT IV SCENE I
[*Enter* VIDENA.]
VIDENA: Why should I live and linger forth my time
In longer life to double my distress?
O me, most woeful wight, whom no mishap

Dumb-show
   hautboys: oboes,   high-pitched
   wind instruments (see note)

Long ere this day could have bereaved hence!
Mought not these hands by fortune, or by fate,
Have pierc'd this breast, and life with iron reft?
Or in this palace here, where I so long
Have spent my days, could not that happy hour   980
Once, once, have happ'd in which these hugy frames
With death by fall might have oppressed me?
Or should not this most hard and cruel soil,
So oft where I have press'd my wretched steps,
Sometime had ruth of mine accursed life,
To rend in twain and swallow me therein?
So had my bones possessed now in peace
Their happy grave within the closed ground,
And greedy worms had gnawen this pined heart
Without my feeling pain. So should not now   990
This living breast remain the ruthful tomb,
Wherein my heart yielden to death is grav'd,
Nor dreary thoughts with pangs of pining grief
My doleful mind had not afflicted thus.
O my beloved son, O my sweet child,
My dear Ferrex, my joy, my life's delight!
Is my beloved son, is my sweet child,
My dear Ferrex, my joy, my life's delight,
Murder'd with cruel death? O hateful wretch!
O heinous traitor both to heaven and earth!   1000
Thou, Porrex, thou this damned deed hast wrought;
Thou, Porrex, thou shalt dearly bye the same;
Traitor to kin and kind, to sire and me,

976	*bereaved:* removed, torn away	985	*ruth of:* pity on
977	*Mought:* might	989	*pined:* wasted through suffering
978	*reft:* taken away	992	*yielden:* yielded
981	*hugy frames:* large timber struc-		*grav'd:* buried
	tures	993	*dreary:* gloomy
982	*oppressed:* crushed	1002	*bye:* pay for

To thine own flesh, and traitor to thyself!
The gods on thee in Hell shall wreak their wrath,
And here in earth this hand shall take revenge,
On thee, Porrex, thou false and caitiff wight!
If after blood so eager were thy thirst,
And murderous mind had so possessed thee;
1010   If such hard heart of rock and stony flint
Liv'd in thy breast, that nothing else could like
Thy cruel tyrant's thought but death and blood;
Wild savage beasts, mought not their slaughter serve
To feed thy greedy will, and in the midst
Of their entrails to stain thy deadly hands
With blood deserv'd, and drink thereof thy fill?
Or if nought else but death and blood of man
Might please thy lust, could none in Britain land,
Whose heart betorn out of his panting breast
1020   With thine own hand or work what death thou would'st –
Suffice to make a sacrifice to pease
That deadly mind and murderous thought in thee
But he who in the self-same womb was wrapp'd,
Where thou in dismal hour receivedst life?
Or if needs, needs, thy hand must slaughter make,
Mightest thou not have reach'd a mortal wound,
And with thy sword have pierc'd this cursed womb
That the accursed Porrex brought to light,
And given me a just reward therefore?
1030   So Ferrex yet sweet life mought have enjoy'd,
And to his aged father comfort brought,
With some young son in whom they both might live.

1007	*caitiff:* wretched, despicable	1021	*pease:* appease, pacify
1008	*eager:* fierce, keen	1023	*wrapp'd:* enclosed, concealed
1011	*like:* please, satisfy	1026	*reach'd:* struck, achieved
1016	*deserv'd:* justly shed	1028	*brought to light:* gave birth to
1018	*lust:* desire		

But whereunto waste I this ruthful speech
To thee that hast thy brother's blood thus shed?
Shall I still think that from this womb thou sprung?
That I thee bare? Or take thee for my son?
No, traitor, no! I thee refuse for mine:
Murderer, I thee renounce, thou art not mine!
Never, O wretch, this womb conceived thee,
Nor never bode I painful throes for thee;   1040
Changeling to me thou art, and not my child,
Nor to no wight that spark of pity knew.
Ruthless, unkind, monster of Nature's work,
Thou never suck'd the milk of woman's breast,
But from thy birth the cruel tiger's teats
Have nursed thee. Nor yet of flesh and blood
Form'd is thy heart, but of hard iron wrought,
And wild and desert woods bred thee to life.
But canst thou hope to scape my just revenge,
Or that these hands will not be wroke on thee?   1050
Doest thou not know that Ferrex' mother lives
That loved him more dearly than herself?
And doth she live, and is not veng'd on thee?
                                                    [*Exit.*]

ACT IV SCENE 2
[*Gorboduc's court*]
[*Enter* GORBODUC *and* AROSTUS.]
GORBODUC: We marvel much whereto this lingering stay
    Falls out so long: Porrex unto our court,
    By order of our letters, is return'd,

1040	*bode:* endured	1048	*desert:* desolate
1041	*changeling:* a child surreptitiously	1050	*wroke:* avenged
	substituted for another	1054	*whereto:* to what purpose
1043	*Ruthless:* merciless		*stay:* standstill, impasse

And Eubulus receiv'd from us by hest
At his arrival here to give him charge
Before our presence straight to make repair,
1060   And yet we have no word whereof he stays.

AROSTUS [*looking offstage*]: Lo, where he comes and Eubulus
    with him.
    [*Enter* PORREX *and* EUBULUS.]

EUBULUS: According to your highness' hest to me,
    Here have I Porrex brought, even in such sort
    As from his wearied horse he did alight,
    For that your grace did will such haste therein.

GORBODUC: We like and praise this speedy will in you
    To work the thing that to your charge we gave.
    Porrex, if we so far should swerve from kind
    And from those bounds which law of Nature sets,
1070   As thou hast done by vile and wretched deed,
    In cruel murder of thy brother's life,
    Our present hand could stay no longer time,
    But straight should bathe this blade in blood of thee
    As just revenge of thy detested crime.
    No, we should not offend the law of kind,
    If now this sword of ours did slay thee here,
    For thou hast murder'd him, whose heinous death
    Even Nature's force doth move us to revenge
    By blood again, and justice forceth us
1080   To measure death for death, thy due desert.
    Yet sithens thou art our child, and sith as yet
    In this hard case what word thou canst allege

1057   *hest:* order, command
1058   *give him charge:* order him
1059   *make repair:* appear
1060   *whereof:* why
1063   *in such sort:* in the very condi-
        tion

1068   *swerve from kind:* deviate from
        obligations of kinship
1081   *sithens:* since

For thy defence by us hath not been heard,
We are content to stay our will for that
Which justice bids us presently to work,
And give thee leave to use thy speech at full
If aught thou have to lay for thine excuse.

PORREX: Neither, O King, I can or will deny
But that this hand from Ferrex life hath reft,
Which fact how much my doleful heart doth wail;   1090
Oh would it might as full appear to sight
As inward grief doth pour it forth to me!
So yet perhaps if ever ruthful heart
Melting in tears within a manly breast
Through deep repentance of his bloody fact;
If ever grief, if ever woeful man,
Might move regrate with sorrow of his fault;
I think the torment of my mournful case,
Known to your grace, as I do feel the same,
Would force even Wrath herself to pity me.   1100
But as the water troubled with the mud
Shows not the face which else the eye should see,
Even so your ireful mind with stirred thought
Cannot so perfectly discern my cause.
But this unhap, amongst so many heaps,
I must content me with, most wretched man,
That to myself I must reserve my woe
In pining thoughts of mine accursed fact,
Since I may not show here my smallest grief
Such as it is, and as my breast endures,   1110

1085	*presently:* immediately	1103	*ireful:* angry
1086	*at full:* amply	1105	*unhap:* misfortune
1087	*aught:* anything		*so many heaps:* such a mess
1095	*fact:* deed, crime	1107	*reserve:* keep
1097	*regrate:* lament, compassion (see note)	1108	*pining:* tormenting

Which I esteem the greatest misery
Of all mishaps that fortune now can send.
Not that I rest in hope with plaint and tears
To purchase life, for to the gods I clepe
For true record of this my faithful speech;
Never this heart shall have the thoughtfull dread
To die the death that by your grace's doom
By just desert shall be pronounc'd to me:
Nor never shall this tongue once spend the speech
1120   Pardon to crave, or seek by suit to live.
I mean not this, as though I were not touch'd
With care of dreadful death, or that I held
Life in contempt, but that I know the mind
Stoops to no dread, although the flesh be frail;
And for my guilt, I yield the same so great
As in myself I find a fear to sue
For grant of life.

GORBODUC: In vain, O wretch, thou showest
A woeful heart: Ferrex now lies in grave,
Slain by thy hand.

PORREX: Yet this, O father, hear:
1130   And then I end. Your Majesty well knows
That when my brother Ferrex and myself
By your own hest were join'd in governance
Of this your grace's realm of Britain land,
I never sought nor travail'd for the same,
Nor by myself, nor by no friend I wrought,
But from your Highness' will alone it sprung,
Of your most gracious goodness bent to me.
But how my brother's heart even then repin'd

1114   *clepe:* call (to witness)
1115   *record:* testimony
1116   *thoughtfull:* anxious
1117   *doom:* sentence judgement

1134   *travail'd:* toiled
1137   *bent:* directed, applied
1138   *repin'd:* fretted, 'whinged'

With swollen disdain against mine equal rule,
Seeing that realm, which by descent should grow   1140
Wholly to him, allotted half to me!
Even in your Highness' court he now remains,
And with my brother then in nearest place,
Who can record what proof thereof was show'd,
And how my brother's envious heart appear'd?
Yet I that judged it my part to seek
His favour and good will, and loath to make
Your Highness know the thing which should have brought
Grief to your grace, and your offence to him,
Hoping my earnest suit should soon have won   1150
A loving heart within a brother's breast,
Wrought in that sort that for a pledge of love
And faithful heart, he gave to me his hand.
This made me think that he had banish'd quite
All rancour from his thought and bare to me
Such hearty love as I did owe to him;
But after once we left your grace's court,
And from your Highness' presence liv'd apart,
This equal rule still, still, did grudge him so
That now those envious sparks, which erst lay rak'd   1160
In living cinders of dissembling breast,
Kindled so far within his heart disdain,
That longer could he not refrain from proof
Of secret practice to deprive me life
By poison's force, and had bereft me so,
If mine own servant hired to this fact

1140   *descent:* heredity   1160   *rak'd:* covered up
1144   *record:* remember   1161   *living:* glowing, active
       proof: evidence   1163   *proof:* an attempt
1149   *offence:* displeasure   1164   *practice:* treachery, conspiracy
1150   *won:* secured   1166   *fact:* crime
1152   *Wrought in that sort:* acted in
       such a way that

And mov'd by truth with hate to work the same,
In time had not bewray'd it unto me.
When thus I saw the knot of love unknit,
All honest league and faithful promise broke,
The law of kind and truth thus rent in twain,
His heart on mischief set, and in his breast
Black treason hid, then, then, did I despair
That ever time could win him friend to me!
Then saw I how he smil'd with slaying knife
Wrapp'd under cloak; then saw I deep deceit
Lurk in his face and death prepar'd for me.
Even Nature mov'd me then to hold my life
More dear to me than his, and bade this hand
(Since by his life my death must needs ensue,
And by his death my life to be preserv'd)
To shed his blood, and seek my safety so:
And wisdom willed me without protract
In speedy wise to put the same in ure.
Thus have I told the cause that moved me
To work my brother's death, and so I yield
My life, my death, to judgement of your grace.

GORBODUC: O cruel wight, should any cause prevail
To make thee stain thy hands with brother's blood?
But what of thee we will resolve to do
Shall yet remain unknown. Thou in the mean
Shalt from our royal presence banish'd be,
Until our princely pleasure further shall
To thee be show'd. Depart therefore our sight,
Accursed child!

[*Exit* PORREX.]
What cruel destiny,

1168   *bewray'd:* revealed, exposed   1184   *in ure:* into practice
1178   *Even:* just, impartial   1191   *unknown:* unrevealed
1183   *protract:* delay   *in the mean:* in the meantime

What froward fate, hath sorted us this chance,
That even in those where we should comfort find,
Where our delight now in our aged days
Should rest and be, even there our only grief
And deepest sorrows to abridge our life,   1200
Most pining cares and deadly thoughts do grow?
AROSTUS: Your grace should now in these grave years of yours
Have found ere this the price of mortal joys,
How short they be, how fading here in earth,
How full of change, how brittle our estate,
Of nothing sure, save only of the death,
To whom both man and all the world doth owe
Their end at last. Neither should Nature's power
In other sort against your heart prevail
Than as the naked hand whose stroke assays   1210
The armed breast where force doth light in vain.
GORBODUC: Many can yield right sage and grave advice
Of patient sprite to others wrapp'd in woe,
And can in speech both rule and conquer kind,
Who if by proof they might feel Nature's force,
Would show themselves men as they are in deed,
Which now will needs be gods. [*Looking offstage.*]
                                    But what doth mean
The sorry cheer of her that here doth come?
        [*Enter* MARCELLA.]
MARCELLA: Oh, where is ruth? Or where is pity now?
Whither is gentle heart and mercy fled?   1220
Are they exil'd out of our stony breasts,
Never to make return? Is all the world

1196	*froward:* adverse	1211	*light:* comfort
	sorted: assigned	1213	*sprite:* spirit
1205	*brittle:* fragile, perishable	1215	*proof:* experience
1209	*sort:* manner	1218	*sorry cheer:* sorrowful expression
1210	*assays:* assails	1219	*ruth:* compassion

Drowned in blood, and sunk in cruelty?
If not in women mercy may be found –
If not, alas, within the mother's breast
To her own child, to her own flesh and blood –
If ruth be banish'd thence, if pity there
May have no place, if there no gentle heart
Do live and dwell, where should we seek it then?

1230   GORBODUC: Madam, alas! what means your woeful tale?

MARCELLA: O silly woman I, why to this hour
Have kind and fortune thus deferr'd my breath,
That I should live to see this doleful day?
Will ever wight believe that such hard heart
Could rest within the cruel mother's breast,
With her own hand to slay her only son?
But out, alas! these eyes beheld the same;
They saw the dreary sight, and are becomen
Most ruthful records of the bloody fact.

1240   Porrex, alas, is by his mother slain,
And with her hand, a woeful thing to tell,
While slumb'ring on his carefull bed he rests,
His heart, stabb'd in with knife, is reft of life!

GORBODUC: O Eubulus, oh draw this sword of ours,
And pierce this heart with speed! O hateful light!
O loathsome life! O sweet and welcome death!
Dear Eubulus, work this we thee beseech!

EUBULUS: Patient your grace, perhaps he liveth yet,
With wound received, but not of certain death.

1250   GORBODUC: Oh, let us then repair unto the place,
And see if Porrex live, or thus be slain.

      [*Exeunt* GORBODUC *and* EUBULUS.]

1231   *silly:* pitiful (see note)   1239   *records:* witnesses
1232   *deferr'd:* prolonged   *fact:* crime
1238   *dreary:* bloody, horrible   1242   *carefull:* full of care

MARCELLA: Alas, he liveth not; it is too true,
    That with these eyes of him, a peerless prince,
    Son to a king, and in the flower of youth,
    Even with a twink a senseless stock I saw.
AROSTUS: O damned deed!
MARCELLA: But hear his ruthful end.
    The noble Prince, pierc'd with the sudden wound,
    Out of his wretched slumber, hastily start,
    Whose strength now failing, straight he overthrew,
    When in the fall his eyes, even new unclos'd,   1260
    Beheld the Queen, and cried to her for help.
    We then, alas, the ladies which that time
    Did there attend, seeing that heinous deed,
    And hearing him oft call the wretched name
    Of mother, and to cry to her for aid,
    Whose direful hand gave him the mortal wound,
    Pitying, alas – for nought else could we do –
    His ruthful end, ran to the woeful bed,
    Dispoiled straight his breast, and all we might,
    Wiped in vain with napkins next at hand,   1270
    The sudden stream of blood that flushed fast
    Out of the gaping wound. Oh, what a look,
    Oh, what a ruthful, steadfast eye methought
    He fix'd upon my face, which to my death
    Will never part from me, when with a braid
    A deep-fet sigh he gave, and therewithal
    Clasping his hands, to Heaven he cast his sight;
    And straight pale Death pressing within his face,
    The flying ghost his mortal corpse forsook.

1255   *with a twink:* in a twinkling
      senseless stock: lifeless trunk (see note)
1258   *hastily start:* swiftly started
1259   *overthrew:* fell down
1266   *direful:* dreadful (see note)
1269   *Dispoiled straight:* immediately uncovered, stripped
1275   *braid:* start, sudden jerk
1276   *fet:* fetched, drawn

1280 AROSTUS: Never did age bring forth so vile a fact.

MARCELLA: O hard and cruel hap, that thus assign'd
   Unto so worthy a wight so wretched end!
   But most hard, cruel heart, that could consent
   To lend the hateful destinies that hand
   By which, alas, so heinous crime was wrought!
   O queen of adamant! O marble breast!
   If not the favour of his comely face,
   If not his princely cheer and countenance,
   His valiant, active arms, his manly breast,
1290   If not his fair and seemly personage,
   His noble limbs in such proportion cast
   As would have rapt a silly woman's thought –
   If this mought not have mov'd thy bloody heart
   And that most cruel hand the wretched weapon
   Even to let fall, and kiss'd him in the face,
   With tears for ruth to reave such one by death,
   Should Nature yet consent to slay her son?
   O mother, thou to murder thus thy child!
   Even Jove with justice must with lightning flames
1300   From Heaven send down some strange revenge on thee!
   Ah, noble Prince, how oft have I beheld
   Thee mounted on thy fierce and trampling steed,
   Shining in armour bright before the tilt
   And with thy mistress' sleeve tied on thy helm,
   And charge thy staff to please thy lady's eye
   That bow'd the headpiece of thy friendly foe?
   How oft in arms on horse to bend the mace?

1280	*fact:* deed, crime	1304	*sleeve:* token (see note)
1292	*rapt:* enraptured	1305	*charge:* level, aim
	silly: frail, simple (see note)		*staff:* spear, lance
1297	*Nature:* natural feelings, affection	1306	*bow'd:* brought low
1303	*tilt:* combat on horseback	1307	*bend:* level, direct, aim

How oft in arms on foot to break the sword,
Which never now these eyes may see again?
AROSTUS: Madam, alas, in vain these plaints are shed. 1310
Rather with me depart, and help to suage
The thoughtfull griefs that in the aged King
Must needs by nature grow, by death of this
His only son, whom he did hold so dear.
MARCELLA: What wight is that which saw that I did see,
And could refrain to wail with plaint and tears?
Not I, alas; that heart is not in me.
But let us go, for I am griev'd anew,
To call to mind the wretched father's woe.
                              [*Exeunt.*]
CHORUS: When greedy lust in royal seat to reign 1320
Hath reft all care of gods and eke of men,
And cruel heart, wrath, treason, and disdain
Within ambitious breast are lodged, then
Behold how mischief wide herself displays,
And with the brother's hand the brother slays.

When blood thus shed doth stain the heaven's face,
Crying to Jove for vengeance of the deed,
The mighty god even moveth from his place,
With wrath to wreak. Then sends he forth with speed
The dreadful Furies, daughters of the night, 1330
With serpents girt, carrying the whip of ire,
With hair of stinging snakes, and shining bright
With flames and blood, and with a brand of fire:
These for revenge of wretched murder done
Do make the mother kill her only son.

1311   *suage:* assuage, alleviate   1324   *mischief:* evil
1320   *lust:* obsessive desire   1331   *ire:* anger
1321   *reft:* eradicated

Blood asketh blood, and death must death requite;
Jove by his just and everlasting doom
Justly hath ever so requited it.
The times before record, and times to come,
1340 Shall find it true, and so doth present proof
Present before our eyes for our behoof.

O happy wight that suffers not the snare
Of murderous mind to tangle him in blood!
And happy he that can in time beware
By other's harms and turn it to his good:
But woe to him that, fearing not to offend,
Doth serve his lust, and will not see the end.

[*The* CHORUS *exits.*]

THE ORDER AND SIGNIFICATION OF THE DUMB-SHOW
BEFORE THE FIFTH ACT

First the drums and flutes began to sound, during which there
came forth upon the stage a company of harquebusiers and of
armed men, all in order of battle. These, after their pieces
discharged and that the armed men had three times marched
about the stage, departed, and then the drums and flutes did
cease. Hereby was signified tumults, rebellions, arms and civil
wars to follow, as fell in the realm of Great Britain, which by
the space of fifty years and more continued in civil war
between the nobility after the death of King Gorboduc, and of
his issues, for want of certain limitation, in the succession of

1337 *doom:* judgement   *pieces:* firearms
1340 *proof:* evidence   *certain limitation:* firm definition
1341 *behoof:* benefit   *reduced:* restored
1344 *beware:* take warning
Dumb-show
       harquebusiers: men armed with
       guns (see note)

the crown, till the time of Dunwallo Molmutius, who reduced
the land to monarchy.

ACT V SCENE I

[*An open plain*]
[*Enter* CLOTYN, MANDUD, GWENARD, FERGUS, *and*
EUBULUS.]

CLOTYN: Did ever age bring forth such tyrants' hearts?
  The brother hath bereft the brother's life,
  The mother she hath dy'd her cruel hands   1350
  In blood of her own son, and now at last
  The people, lo, forgetting truth and love,
  Contemning quite both law and loyal heart,
  Even they have slain their sovereign lord and Queen.
MANDUD: Shall this their traitorous crime unpunish'd rest?
  Even yet they cease not, carried on with rage,
  In their rebellious routs, to threaten still
  A new bloodshed unto the prince's kin,
  To slay them all, and to uproot the race
  Both of the King and Queen, so are they mov'd   1360
  With Porrex' death wherein they falsely charge
  The guiltless King without desert at all,
  And traitorously have murder'd him therefore,
  And eke the Queen.
GWENARD: Shall subjects dare with force
  To work revenge upon their prince's fact?
  Admit the worst that may — as sure in this
  The deed was foul, the Queen to slay her son —
  Shall yet the subject seek to take the sword,

1353   *contemning:* despising   1362   *desert:* deserving it
1354   *Even they:* those very people   1365   *fact:* crime
1357   *routs:* mobs, 'gangs'

Arise against his lord, and slay his King?
1370   O wretched state, where those rebellious hearts
Are not rent out even from their living breasts,
And with the body thrown unto the fowls
As carrion food, for terror of the rest!
FERGUS: There can no punishment be thought too great
For this so grievous crime; let speed therefore
Be used therein, for it behoveth so.
EUBULUS: Ye all, my lords, I see, consent in one,
And I as one consent with ye in all;
I hold it more than need with sharpest law
1380   To punish this tumultuous bloody rage.
For nothing more may shake the common state
Than sufferance of uproars without redress;
Whereby how some kingdoms of mighty power
After great conquests made, and flourishing
In fame and wealth, have been to ruin brought:
I pray to Jove that we may rather wail
Such hap in them than witness in ourselves.
Eke fully with the Duke my mind agrees
That no cause serves, whereby the subject may
1390   Call to account the doings of his prince;
Much less in blood by sword to work revenge
No more than may the hand cut off the head:
In act nor speech, no, not in secret thought
The subject may rebel against his lord,
Or judge of him that sits in Caesar's seat,
With grudging mind to damn those he mislikes.
Though kings forget to govern as they ought,
Yet subjects must obey as they are bound.
But now, my lords, before ye farther wade

| 1372 | *fowls:* birds | 1386 | *wail:* bewail |
| 1373 | *carrion:* dead flesh meat | 1387 | *hap:* misfortune |

Or spend your speech what sharp revenge shall fall   1400
By justice' plague on these rebellious wights,
Methinks ye rather should first search the way
By which in time the rage of this uproar
Might be repress'd, and these great tumults ceas'd.
Even yet the life of Britain land doth hang
In traitors' balance of unequal weight:
Think not, my lords, the death of Gorboduc,
Nor yet Videna's blood, will cease their rage.
Even our own lives, our wives and children dear,
Our country, dearest of all, in danger stands,   1410
Now to be spoil'd, now, now made desolate,
And by ourselves a conquest to ensue.
For give once sway unto the people's lusts
To rush forth on, and stay them not in time,
And as the stream that rolleth down the hill,
So will they headlong run with raging thoughts
From blood to blood, from mischief unto moe,
To ruin of the realm, themselves and all;
So giddy are the common people's minds,
So glad of change, more wavering than the sea.   1420
Ye see, my lords, what strength these rebels have,
What hugy number is assembled still;
For though the traitorous fact for which they rose
Be wrought and done, yet lodge they still in field,
So that how far their furies yet will stretch
Great cause we have to dread. That we may seek
By present battle to repress their power,
Speed must we use to levy force therefore;
For either they forthwith will mischief work,

1411   *spoil'd:* plundered, destroyed   1427   *present:* immediate
1417   *moe:* more   1429   *mischief:* damage, evil
1423   *fact:* crime, deed

1430   Or their rebellious roars forthwith will cease:
These violent things may have no lasting long.
Let us therefore use this for present help:
Persuade by gentle speech, and offer grace
With gift of pardon, save unto the chief;
And that upon condition that forthwith
They yield the captains of their enterprise
To bear such guerdon of their traitorous fact
As may be both due vengeance to themselves
And wholesome terror to posterity.

1440   This shall, I think, scatter the greatest part
That now are holden with desire of home,
Wearied in field with cold of winter's nights,
And some, no doubt, stricken with dread of law.
When this is once proclaimed, it shall make
The captains to mistrust the multitude,
Whose safety bids them to betray their heads,
And so much more because the rascal routs
In things of great and perilous attempts
Are never trusty to the noble race.

1450   And while we treat and stand on terms of grace,
We shall both stay their fury's rage the while,
And eke gain time, whose only help sufficeth
Withouten war to vanquish rebels' power.
In the meanwhile, make you in readiness
Such band of horsemen as ye may prepare;
Horsemen, you know, are not the commons' strength,
But are the force and store of noble men,

1437	*guerdon:* due recompense, 'medicine'	1449	*trusty:* loyal, trustworthy
1441	*holden with:* restrained by	1450	*treat:* negotiate
1446	*heads:* leaders	1452	*only help:* help alone
1447	*rascal routs:* good-for-nothing rabble	1457	*store:* resource

Whereby the unchosen and unarmed sort
Of skilless rebels, whom none other power
But number makes to be of dreadful force,   1460
With sudden brunt may quickly be oppress'd.
And if this gentle mean of proffer'd grace
With stubborn hearts cannot so far avail
As to assuage their desperate courages,
Then do I wish such slaughter to be made
As present age and eke posterity
May be adread with horror of revenge
That justly then shall on these rebels fall.
This is, my lords, the sum of mine advice.
CLOTYN: Neither this case admits debate at large,   1470
And though it did, this speech that hath been said
Hath well abridg'd the tale I would have told.
Fully with Eubulus do I consent
In all that he hath said, and if the same
To you, my lords, may seem for best advice,
I wish that it should straight be put in ure.
MANDUD: My lords, then let us presently depart
And follow this that liketh us so well.
            [*Exeunt all but* FERGUS.]
FERGUS: If ever time to gain a kingdom here
Were offer'd man, now it is offer'd me: 1480
The realm is reft both of their King and Queen;
The offspring of the Prince is slain and dead;
No issue now remains, the heir unknown;
The people are in arms and mutinies;

1458	*unchosen:* unfavoured, undistinguished, 'common'	1473	*consent:* agree
1461	*brunt:* assault, onslaught	1476	*in ure:* into practice
1464	*courages:* spirits	1477	*presently:* immediately
1467	*adread:* greatly frightened	1478	*liketh us:* pleases us
		1483	*unknown:* uncertain, dubious

The nobles they are busi'd how to cease
The great rebellious tumults and uproars;
And Britain land, now desert, left alone
Amid these broils uncertain where to rest,
Offers herself unto that noble heart
1490   That will or dare pursue to bear her crown.
Shall I that am the Duke of Albany,
Descended from that line of noble blood
Which hath so long flourish'd in worthy fame
Of valiant hearts, such as in noble breasts
Of right should rest above the baser sort,
Refuse to venture life to win a crown?
Whom shall I find enemies that will withstand
My fact herein, if I attempt by arms
To seek the same now in these times of broil?
1500   These dukes' power can hardly well appease
The people that already are in arms,
But if perhaps my force be once in field,
Is not my strength in power above the best
Of all these lords now left in Britain land?
And though they should match me with power of men,
Yet doubtful is the chance of battles joined:
If victors of the field we may depart,
Ours is the sceptre then of great Britain;
If slain amid the plain this body lie,
1510   Mine enemies yet shall not deny me this,
But that I died giving the noble charge
To hazard life for conquest of a crown.

1485   *cease:* bring to a halt   1506   *doubtful:* uncertain
1487   *desert:* desolate   *battles:* forces
1488   *broils:* tumults   *joined:* encountered in conflict
1493   *fame:* renown, reputation   1511   *giving the noble charge:* assuming
1498   *fact:* deed, action   the glorious task
1500   *appease:* pacify

Forthwith therefore will I in post depart
To Albany, and raise in armour there
All power I can. And here my secret friends
By secret practice shall solicit still
To seek to win to me the people's hearts.

[*Exit.*]

ACT V SCENE 2

[*Enter* EUBULUS.]

EUBULUS: O Jove, how are these people's hearts abus'd!
What blind fury thus headlong carries them!
That though so many books, so many rolls   1520
Of ancient time, record what grievous plagues
Light on these rebels aye, and though so oft
Their ears have heard their aged fathers tell
What just reward these traitors still receive,
Yea, though themselves have seen deep death and blood,
By strangling cord and slaughter of the sword
To such assign'd, yet can they not beware,
Yet cannot stay their lewd rebellious hands,
But suffering, lo, foul treason to distain
Their wretched minds, forget their loyal heart,   1530
Reject all truth and rise against their prince.
A ruthful case, that those whom duty's bond,
Whom grafted law by nature, truth and faith
Bound to preserve their country and their King,
Born to defend their commonwealth and prince,

1513	*in post:* in haste (see note)	1525	*deep:* solemn
1520	*rolls:* historical documents (see note)	1527	*beware:* take warning
		1528	*lewd:* vile, wicked
1522	*aye:* always	1529	*distain:* stain, defile
1524	*still:* always	1533	*grafted:* implanted

Even they should give consent thus to subvert
Thee, Britain land, and from thy womb should spring,
O native soil, those that will needs destroy
And ruin thee and eke themselves in fine.
For lo, when once the dukes had offer'd grace
Of pardon sweet, the multitude, misled
By traitorous fraud of their ungracious heads,
One sort, that saw the dangerous success
Of stubborn standing in rebellious war,
And knew the difference of prince's power
From headless number of tumultuous routs,
Whom common country's care and private fear
Taught to repent the error of their rage,
Laid hands upon the captains of their band,
And brought them bound unto the mighty dukes.
Another sort, not trusting yet so well
The truth of pardon, or mistrusting more
Their own offence than that they could conceive
Such hope of pardon for so foul misdeed,
Or for that they their captains could not yield
(Who, fearing to be yielded, fled before),
Stale home by silence of the secret night.
The third unhappy and enraged sort
Of desperate hearts, who, stain'd in princes' blood,
From traitorous furor could not be withdrawn
By love, by law, by grace, ne yet by fear,
By proffer'd life, ne yet by threaten'd death,

1540

1550

1560

1536　*subvert:* overthrow
1539　*in fine:* at last
1541　*misled:* who had (till then) been
　　　misled
1542　*fraud . . . etc.:* deception of their
　　　wicked leaders (see note)
1543　*success:* outcome
1544　*standing:* confrontation

1546　*routs:* hordes
1547　*common country's care:* a shared
　　　concern for their native land
1552　*truth:* genuineness
1557　*Stale:* stole
1558　*unhappy:* unfortunate, miserable
1560　*furor:* anger, madness
　　　withdrawn: detached, dissuaded

With minds hopeless of life, dreadless of death,
Careless of country, and aweless of God,
Stood bent to fight, as Furies did them move,
With violent death to close their traitorous life.
These all by power of horsemen were oppress'd
And with revenging sword slain in the field,
Or with the strangling cord hang'd on the trees
Where yet their carrion carcasses do preach   1570
The fruits that rebels reap of their uproars
And of the murder of their sacred prince.
[*Looking offstage*] But lo, where do approach the noble dukes
By whom these tumults have been thus appeas'd.
    [*Enter* CLOTYN, MANDUD, GWENARD *and* AROSTUS.]
CLOTYN: I think the world will now at length beware
  And fear to put on arms against their prince.
MANDUD: If not, those traitorous hearts that dare rebel
  Let them behold the wide and hugy fields
  With blood and bodies spread of rebels slain,
  The lofty trees cloth'd with the corpses dead   1580
  That strangled with the cord do hang thereon.
AROSTUS: A just reward, such as all times before
  Have ever lotted to those wretched folks.
GWENARD: But what means he that cometh here so fast?
    [*Enter* NUNTIUS.]
NUNTIUS: My lords, as duty and my truth doth move
  And of my country work a care in me,
  That, if the spending of my breath avail'd
  To do the service that my heart desires,
  I would not shun to embrace a present death:
  So have I now in that wherein I thought   1590

1565	*bent:* braced	1583	*lotted:* allotted
	as: as if	1586	*care:* concern
	Furies: avenging gods	1589	*present:* instant
1567	*oppress'd:* crushed		

My travail might perform some good effect,
Ventur'd my life to bring these tidings here.
Fergus, the mighty Duke of Albany,
Is now in arms and lodgeth in the field
With twenty thousand men. Hither he bends
His speedy march, and minds to invade the crown.
Daily he gathereth strength, and spreads abroad
That to this realm no certain heir remains;
That Britain land is left without a guide;
1600 That he the sceptre seeks for nothing else
But to preserve the people and the land,
Which now remain as ship without a stern.
Lo, this is that which I have here to say.

CLOTYN: Is this his faith? And shall he falsely thus
Abuse the vantage of unhappy times?
O wretched land, if his outrageous pride,
His cruel and untemper'd wilfulness,
His deep dissembling shows of false pretence,
Should once attain the crown of Britain land!
1610 Let us, my lords, with timely force resist
The new attempt of this our common foe,
As we would quench the flames of common fire.

MANDUD: Though we remain without a certain prince
To wield the realm or guide the wand'ring rule,
Yet now the common mother of us all,
Our native land, our country, that contains
Our wives, children, kindred, ourselves and all
That ever is or may be dear to man,
Cries unto us to help ourselves and her.

1592 *Ventur'd:* risked (see note)
1596 *invade:* seize, usurp
1602 *stern:* rudder (see note)
1605 *vantage:* opportunity
1607 *untemper'd:* immoderate
1613 *certain:* indubitable, acknowledged
1614 *wield:* rule
rule: realm? sway? (see note)

Let us advance our powers to repress   1620
This growing foe of all our liberties.
GWENARD: Yea, let us so, my lords, with hasty speed:
And ye, O gods, send us the welcome death
To shed our blood in field, and leave us not
· In loathsome life to linger out our days,
To see the hugy heaps of these unhaps
That now roll down upon the wretched land
Where empty place of princely governance,
No certain stay now left of doubtless heir,
Thus leave this guideless realm an open prey   1630
To endless storms and waste of civil war.
AROSTUS: That ye, my lords, do so agree in one
To save your country from the violent reign
And wrongfully usurped tyranny
Of him that threatens conquest of you all,
To save your realm, and in this realm yourselves,
From foreign thraldom of so proud a prince,
Much do I praise; and I beseech the gods
With happy honour to requite it you.
But, O my lords, sith now the heaven's wrath   1640
Hath reft this land the issue of their prince;
Sith of the body of our late sovereign lord
Remains no moe, since the young kings be slain;
And of the title of descended crown
Uncertainly the diverse minds do think
Even of the learned sort, and more uncertainly
Will partial fancy and affection deem,
But most uncertainly will climbing pride

1620	*repress:* withstand	1632	*in one:* together
1626	*unhaps:* misfortunes	1639	*requite:* reward
1629	*certain stay:* reliable prop	1640	*sith:* since
	doubtless: undoubted	1647	*partial:* biased

And hope of reign withdraw to sundry parts
1650   The doubtful right and hopeful lust to reign.
When once this noble service is achiev'd
For Britain land, the mother of ye all;
When once ye have with armed force repress'd
The proud attempts of this Albanian prince
That threatens thraldom to your native land;
When ye shall vanquishers return from field
And find the princely state an open prey
To greedy lust and to usurping power;
Then, then, my lords, if ever kindly care
1660   Of ancient honour of your ancestors,
Of present wealth and nobless of your stocks,
Yea, of the lives and safety yet to come
Of your dear wives, your children, and yourselves,
Might move your noble hearts with gentle ruth;
Then, then, have pity on the torn estate.
Then help to salve the well-near hopeless sore,
Which ye shall do, if ye yourselves withhold
Then slaying knife from your own mother's throat.
Her shall you save, and you, and yours in her,
1670   If ye shall all with one assent forbear
Once to lay hand or take unto yourselves
The crown, by colour of pretended right,
Or by what other means soever it be,
Till first by common counsel of you all
In parliament the regal diadem
Be set in certain place of governance,
In which your parliament, and in your choice,

1649	*withdraw:* disperse, divert	1665	*estate:* state, kingdom
1661	*nobless:* nobility	1666	*salve:* heal
	stocks: kindred		*well-near:* almost, virtually
1664	*ruth:* compassion	1672	*colour:* pretext, semblance

Prefer the right, my lords, without respect
Of strength or friends, or whatsoever cause
That may set forward any other's part: 1680
For right will last, and wrong cannot endure.
Right mean I his or hers, upon whose name
The people rest by mean of native line,
Or by the virtue of some former law
Already made their title to advance.
Such one, my lords, let be your chosen king;
Such one so born within your native land;
Such one prefer, and in no wise admit
The heavy yoke of foreign governance:
Let foreign titles yield to public wealth.   1690
And with that heart wherewith ye now prepare
Thus to withstand the proud invading foe,
With that same heart, my lords, keep out also
Unnatural thraldom of [a] stranger's reign,
Ne suffer you against the rules of kind
Your motherland to serve a foreign prince.

EUBULUS: Lo, here the end of Brutus' royal line,
And, lo, the entry to the woeful wrack
And utter ruin of this noble realm;
The royal King and eke his sons are slain;   1700
No ruler rests within the regal seat;
The heir, to whom the sceptre longs, unknown;
That to each force of foreign prince's power,
Whom vantage of our wretched state may move
By sudden arms to gain so rich a realm
And to the proud and greedy mind at home,

1683	*rest:* rely, trust	1702	*longs:* belongs
	by mean of: as a result of	1703	*That:* So that
1690	*wealth:* welfare, good	1704	*vantage:* opportunity
1694	*stranger's:* alien's		*of:* provided by
1698	*wrack:* wreckage		*move:* impel, prompt

Whom blinded lust to reign leads to aspire,
Lo, Britain realm is left an open prey,
A present spoil by conquest to ensue.
1710   Who seeth not now how many rising minds
Do feed their thoughts with hope to reach a realm?
And who will not by force attempt to win
So great a gain, that hope persuades to have?
A simple colour shall for title serve:
Who wins the royal crown will want no right,
Nor such as shall display by long descent
A lineal race to prove him lawful king.
In the meanwhile these civil arms shall rage
And thus a thousand mischiefs shall unfold,
1720   And far and near spread thee, O Britain land:
All right and law shall cease, and he that had
Nothing today, tomorrow shall enjoy
Great heaps of gold, and he that flow'd in wealth,
Lo, he shall be bereft of life and all,
And happiest he that then possesseth least.
The wives shall suffer rape, the maids deflower'd,
And children fatherless shall weep and wail;
With fire and sword thy native folk shall perish,
One kinsman shall bereave another's life;
1730   The father shall unwitting slay the son,
The son shall slay the sire and know it not,
Women and maids the cruel soldier's sword
Shall pierce to death, and silly children, lo,
That playing in the streets and fields are found
By violent hand shall close their latter day.
Whom shall the fierce and bloody soldier
Reserve to life? Whom shall he spare from death?

1714   *colour:* pretext   1729   *bereave:* rob
1720   *spread:* overrun, cover   1733   *silly:* defenceless
1726   *deflower'd:* ravished   1737   *Reserve:* preserve for

Even thou, O wretched mother, half alive,
Thou shalt behold thy dear and only child
Slain with the sword while he yet sucks thy breast!   1740
Lo, guiltless blood shall thus each where be shed:
Thus shall the wasted soil yield forth no fruit,
But dearth and famine shall possess the land.
The towns shall be consum'd and burnt with fire,
The peopled cities shall wax desolate,
And thou, O Britain, whilom in renown,
Whilom in wealth and fame, shalt thus be torn,
Dismember'd thus, and thus be rent in twain,
Thus wasted and defac'd, spoil'd and destroy'd!
These be the fruits your civil wars will bring;   1750
Hereto it comes when kings will not consent
To grave advice, but follow wilful will;
This is the end, when in young princes' hearts
Flattery prevails and sage rede hath no place;
These are the plagues, when murder is the mean
To make new heirs unto the royal crown.
Thus wreak the gods, when that the mother's wrath
Nought but the blood of her own child may suage;
These mischiefs spring when rebels will arise,
To work revenge and judge their prince's fact;   1760
This, this ensues, when noble men do fail
In loyal truth and subjects will be kings.
And this doth grow when, lo, unto the prince,
Whom death or sudden hap of life bereaves,
No certain heir remains, such certain heir,

1741	*each where:* in every place	1757	*wreak:* avenge
1746	*whilom:* formerly	1758	*suage:* assuage, appease
1749	*spoil'd:* stripped	1759	*mischiefs:* evils, troubles
1751	*Hereto:* to this	1760	*fact:* crime, deed
	consent: agree	1764	*hap:* occurrence
1754	*rede:* counsel		

As not all only is the rightful heir
But to the realm is so made known to be,
And truth thereby vested in subjects' hearts,
To owe faith there where right is known to rest.
1770 Alas, in parliament what hope can be,
When is of parliament no hope at all?
Which, though it be assembled by consent,
Yet is not likely with consent to end,
While each one for himself, or for his friend,
Against his foe, shall travail what he may;
While now the state, left open to the man
That shall with greatest force invade the same,
Shall fill ambitious minds with gaping hope:
When will they once with yielding hearts agree?
1780 Or in the while, how shall the realm be us'd?
No, no! Then parliament should have been holden,
And certain heirs appointed to the crown
To stay the title of establish'd right
And in the people plant obedience
While yet the prince did live, whose name and power
By lawful summons and authority
Might make a parliament to be of force
And might have set the state in quiet stay.
But now, O happy man, whom speedy death
1790 Deprives of life, ne is enforc'd to see
These hugy mischiefs and these miseries,
These civil wars, these murders and these wrongs.
Of justice yet must Jove in fine restore
This noble crown unto the lawful heir,

1766 *all only:* merely (see note)   1780 *while:* meantime
1775 *travail:* labour to effect   *us'd:* treated, maintained
1778 *gaping:* eager   1783 *stay:* stabilize, uphold
                                               1793 *in fine:* finally

For right will always live and rise at length,
But wrong can never take deep root to last.

[*Exeunt.*]

THE SPANISH TRAGEDY

THOMAS KYD

THE

SPANISH TRAGE-

die, Containing the lamentable
end of *Don Horatio,* and *Bel-imperia*:
with the pittifull death of
olde *Hieronimo.*

Newly correcred and amended of such grosse faults as
passed in the first impression.

AT LONDON

Printed by *Edward Allde,* for
Edward White.

Facsimile of the title-page of the first known edition of 1592.
Reproduced by permission of the British Museum.

The earliest surviving text of *The Spanish Tragedy* is undated, but bears the name of the printer, Edward Allde, and that of the publisher, Edward White; on the title-page it also announces that the version of the play as set forth has been 'Newly corrected and amended of such grosse faults as passed in the first impression'. This looks to be a reference to a probably corrupted edition published by one Abell Jeffes before he became involved in a dispute with the officers of the Stationers' Company in late July 1592. Not long afterwards, however, White brought out his version, based on a far superior manuscript possibly supplied by the playhouse company (in that it contains a number of apparent instructions to the players); unfortunately White lacked any authority from the licensing officials to issue the play, and Jeffes protected his lawful interests by paying sixpence to secure his position through an entry in the Stationers' Register, which reads:

vj^{to} die Octobris

Abell   Entred for his copie under thandes of mr Hart-
            welland mr Stirrop, a booke
Jeffes   w^{che} is called the Spanishe tragedie of Don Hora-
            tio and Bellimpera &c.

It is at least feasible that White's edition had appeared in print by this date; certainly it was out by 18 December, because on this day, as a result of Jeffes' complaint, White was found guilty by the Stationers 'in havinge printed the spanish tragedie belonging to Abell Jeffes' and fined ten shillings for doing so. It may have given him some wry satisfaction, however, that Jeffes had also flouted the rules by publishing a pirated version of *Arden of Feversham*, another Elizabethan crime play, of which the right to print belonged to White, and was therefore himself fined an identical sum as punishment. All the remaining unsold copies of the two offending texts were 'forfayted' and confiscated by the Company, although it seems that White and Jeffes were able to buy back their stock at a later date. Of White's product a single known copy, now preserved in the British Library (shelfmark C 34. d. 7), has survived its vicissitudes; all traces of the version Jeffes printed have vanished.

Since Jeffes had the licence to print the play, but White had produced the superior text, a stalemate might have ensued, but a compromise was effected so that when Jeffes published his edition of 1594, which is a virtual reprint of White's 1592 version, it was announced as

Printed by Abell Jeffes, and are / to be sold by Edward White.

Jeffes sold his rights in the play to another printer, William White (probably unrelated to his namesake Edward), on 13 August 1599, and this White produced his edition before the year was out, advertising it as

Printed by William White, / dwelling in Cow-lane.

No publisher or bookseller is mentioned, but perhaps Edward White was recompensed in some way for the use of 'his' text; when William White relinquished his rights in *The Spanish Tragedy* to Thomas Pavier on 14 August 1600, Edward

White authorized the transaction as Warden of the Stationers'
Company, but seems to have had no personal stake in the
matter.

William White, however, continued to be an interested party;
when Pavier published his expanded edition of the play in
1602, White was his printer, as his pelican trademark on the
title-page makes clear. The full provenance is given as:

Imprinted at London by W.W. for / T. Pavier, and are to
be sold at the signe of the Catte and Parrats / neare the
Exchange / 1602.

and its 'selling feature' may be deemed to have resided in the
fact that the text was warranted to be

Newly corrected, amended, and enlarged with / new
additions of the Painters part, and / others, as it hath of
late been / divers times acted.

This change involved the addition of five new passages
totalling some 340 lines of dialogue to the text of the 1592
Quarto edition; these are set out in the present edition after the
main text. In other respects the 1602 version kept fairly closely
to the readings of its predecessors. Other editions were called
for in at least the following years: 1603, 1610, 1615 (the first to
have an illustrative woodcut on the title-page), 1618, 1623, and
1633. William White was involved in several of them: as
printer for Thomas Pavier in 1603; then as partial printer of the
1610 version (which Pavier seems to have wrested from him
before completion, as their agreement entitled him to do, and
had undertaken by another firm); finally, as printer of the
'illustrated' edition of 1615. His son, John, printed the Quarto
of 1618 for Thomas Langley, but in 1623, although Langley
remained the bookseller, the printer is given as Augustine
Matthewes, who also brought out the 1633 Quarto for Francis

Grove. Although the authority to print was technically vested in Pavier, all the later editions of *The Spanish Tragedy* ignore his rights in the affair, and Matthewes, who leased his printing-house from John White, may well have laid claim to the printing rights in the play through his connection with John White or his father. Perhaps Thomas Pavier waived his claims and left the piece to sink or swim. However, the issue of ten separate extant editions produced between 1592 and 1633, in addition to Jeffes' vanished volume of 1592, is testimony to the fact that *The Spanish Tragedy* stayed triumphantly afloat through the first fifty or so years of its life.

The date of the play's first performance is hard to pin down, conjectures ranging from the early 1580s to the early 1590s. Lord Strange's Men performed a work referred to as *Jeronimo* at the Rose Theatre (partially excavated in 1989) on Bankside in February/March 1592, identified as an already established piece, thirteen performances being given by the following January. The play crops up again in January 1597 when Philip Henslowe, impresario and manager of the Lord Admiral's Men, then occupying the Rose, recorded its presentation as 'new', which suggests that the play may have received revision before the company took it into their repertory. On the other hand, it may simply indicate that the piece was newly introduced into the current repertoire.

Whether the additions preserved in the 1602 printing constituted the 'new' element in 1597 cannot now be ascertained, but it is known that Henslowe paid Edward Alleyn, his son-in-law and leading actor, on 25 September 1601 forty shillings 'to lend unto Bengemen Johnson upon his writinge of his adicions in geronymo . . .', and again on 22 June 1602 'bengemy Johnsone' was 'lent' ten shillings 'in earneste of a Boocke called Richard crookbacke & for new adicyons for Jeronymo'. However, it seems doubtful if the additions preserved in the 1602 edition were those supplied by Jonson – the style is unlike his known work, though Kydean pastiche cannot be ruled out – and it is more plausible that the surviving additions are those of 1597 which enabled Henslowe to present the Lord Admiral's Men in performances some elements of which were 'new' to their spectators at the Rose. Perhaps, too, the additions of 1597 were originally more extensive than those surviving in the 1602 printing, and the five passages which we have are all that Pavier could secure for his new edition. But their existence certainly adds an important dimension to our knowledge and enjoyment of Kyd's original piece.

In his excellent edition of the play for the Revels series in 1959, Philip Edwards conjectured very convincingly that copy for the 1592 edition may well have been supplied in two forms: one a fairly reliable author's manuscript (Edwards is sceptical of its bearing traces of adaptation for playhouse use) which ran to line 2176 of the present edition, the other a far less reliable copy, corrupted and garbled in a number of places, used for the final portion of the text. It may well be that the printer had to rely in some areas on the now-lost edition of Abell Jeffes or some other version lacking authorial supervision. Yet the 1592 text must remain the ultimate authority for resolving any textual issues which arise in the case of *The Spanish Tragedy*.

The present text derives from the unique 1592 copy of the text in the British Library, also available in facsimile in the Malone Society's volume of 1948; I have also consulted the Society's edition of the 1602 version, from which the additions which follow the main text are taken.

The chief modern editions of the play are:

F. S. Boas, ed., *The Works of Thomas Kyd*, Oxford, 1901; reissued with supplement, 1955.

W. W. Greg, ed., *The Spanish Tragedy with Additions* [1602], Malone Society Reprints, Oxford, 1925.

W. W. Greg, and D. Nichol Smith, eds., *The Spanish Tragedy (1592)*, Malone Society Reprints, Oxford, 1948 (1949).

Philip EDWARDS, ed., *The Spanish Tragedy*, The Revels Plays, 1959.

B. L. JOSEPH, ed., *The Spanish Tragedy*, The New Mermaids, 1964.

Andrew S. CAIRNCROSS, ed., *The First Part of Hieronimo and The Spanish Tragedy*, Regents Renaissance Drama Series, Lincoln, Nebraska and London, 1967.

Thomas W. ROSS, ed., *The Spanish Tragedy*, Fountainwell Drama Texts, Edinburgh, 1968.

J. R. MULRYNE, ed., *The Spanish Tragedy*, The New Mermaids, 1970.

T. W. CRAIK, ed., *Minor Elizabethan Drama: Tragedy*, Everyman University Library, 1974.

The present edition owes something to most of these versions; the cast-list has been developed from that printed by Greg and Nichol Smith in 1948.

LIST OF CHARACTERS

The GHOST OF ANDREA
REVENGE
The KING of Spain
The DUKE OF CASTILE, Cyprian, his brother
LORENZO, son of the Duke
BEL-IMPERIA, Lorenzo's sister
HIERONIMO, the Knight Marshal of Spain
ISABELLA, his wife
HORATIO, son to Hieronimo and Isabella
The VICEROY OF PORTUGAL
PEDRO, his brother
BALTHAZAR, son of the Viceroy
ALEXANDRO ⎫
VILLUPPO ⎬ Portuguese noblemen
The Portuguese AMBASSADOR
PEDRINGANO, Bel-imperia's servant
SERBERINE, Balthazar's servant
CHRISTOPHILL, Lorenzo's servant and Bel-imperia's gaoler
PAGE to Lorenzo
A Spanish GENERAL
A DRUMMER, three KNIGHTS, and three KINGS in the first
  dumb-show

Knight Marshal: a law officer of the   VILLUPPO: linked to the Italian term
crown   for 'entanglement', 'enfold' and 'grasp'

Two Portuguese NOBLEMEN
Three WATCHMEN
A MESSENGER
The DEPUTY or Judge
The HANGMAN
Isabella's MAID
Two PORTINGALES
A SERVANT to Hieronimo
Three CITIZENS
BAZULTO, an old man
Two TORCH-BEARERS and HYMEN in the second dumb-show
SOLDIERS, SERVANTS, GUARDS, ATTENDANTS, OFFICERS,
   HALBERDIERS

[In Hieronimo's play SOLIMAN, the Turkish Sultan, is played
by BALTHAZAR; ERASTO, a Knight of Rhodes, by LORENZO;
PERSEDA, an Italian Lady, by BEL-IMPERIA; and the BASHAW
by HIERONIMO.]

Three roles are added in the additions contained in the text of
1602:
PEDRO
        ⎫
        ⎬ Servants to Hieronimo
JACQUES ⎭
BAZARDO, a painter

The play is set in Spain and Portugal.

PORTINGALES: Portuguese   BASHAW: Pasha (see note)

THE SPANISH TRAGEDY

ACT I SCENE I

Enter the GHOST OF ANDREA, *and with him* REVENGE.

GHOST: When this eternal substance of my soul
　　Did live imprison'd in my wanton flesh,
　　Each in their function serving other's need,
　　I was a courtier in the Spanish court.
　　My name was Don Andrea, my descent,
　　Though not ignoble, yet inferior far
　　To gracious fortunes of my tender youth:
　　For there in prime and pride of all my years,
　　By duteous service and deserving love,
　　In secret I possess'd a worthy dame,
　　Which hight sweet Bel-imperia by name.
　　But in the harvest of my summer joys,
　　Death's winter nipp'd the blossoms of my bliss,
　　Forcing divorce betwixt my love and me.
　　For in the late conflict with Portingale,
　　My valour drew me into danger's mouth,

2　*wanton:* wayward, amorously in-
　　clined (see note)
8　*prime:* 'the prime of life'
　　pride: 'the pink', 'the top of my
　　form'
10　*possess'd:* enjoyed sexually (see
　　note)

11　*hight:* was called, named
13　*nipp'd:* destroyed with frost,
　　'nipped in the bud' (see note)
14　*divorce:* separation
15　*Portingale:* Portugal

Till life to death made passage through my wounds.
When I was slain, my soul descended straight
To pass the flowing stream of Acheron:
20   But churlish Charon, only boatman there,
Said that, my rites of burial not perform'd,
I might not sit amongst his passengers.
Ere Sol had slept three nights in Thetis' lap,
And slak'd his smoking chariot in her flood,
By Don Horatio, our Knight Marshal's son,
My funerals and obsequies were done.
Then was the ferryman of Hell content
To pass me over to the slimy strand
That leads to fell Avernus' ugly waves:
30   There pleasing Cerberus with honey'd speech,
I pass'd the perils of the foremost porch.
Not far from hence amidst ten thousand souls
Sate Minos, Eacus, and Rhadamant,
To whom no sooner gan I make approach
To crave a passport for my wand'ring ghost,
But Minos, in graven leaves of lottery,
Drew forth the manner of my life and death.
'This knight,' quoth he, 'both liv'd and died in love
And for his love tried fortune of the wars,
40   And by war's fortune lost both love and life.'
'Why then,' said Eacus, 'convey him hence
To walk with lovers in our fields of love,

19	*Acheron:* an underworld river	30	*Cerberus:* Hell's guard-dog
20	*Charon:* the infernal ferryman	31	*foremost porch:* principal entrance
23	*Sol:* the sun	33	*Minos* etc.: see note
	Thetis': the ocean's	35	*passport:* letter of safe conduct
24	*slak'd:* quenched, extinguished	36	*graven leaves:* engraved writings
28	*strand:* shore		(see note)
29	*fell:* deadly (see note)		*lottery:* chance, fortune
	Avernus': the lake, entrance to Hell		

And spend the course of everlasting time
Under green myrtle trees and cypress shades.'
'No, no,' said Rhadamant, 'it were not well
With loving souls to place a martialist;
He died in war, and must to martial fields
Where wounded Hector lives in lasting pain,
And Achilles' Myrmidons do scour the plain.'
Then Minos, mildest censor of the three,   50
Made this device to end the difference:
'Send him,' quoth he, 'to our infernal King
To doom him as best seems his Majesty.'
To this effect my passport straight was drawn.
In keeping on my way to Pluto's court,
Through dreadfull shades of ever-glooming night,
I saw more sights than thousand tongues can tell,
Or pens can write, or mortal hearts can think.
Three ways there were: that on the right-hand side
Was ready way unto the foresaid fields,   60
Where lovers live, and bloody martialists,
But either sort contain'd within his bounds.
The left-hand path declining fearfully
Was ready downfall to the deepest Hell,
Where bloody Furies shakes their whips of steel,
And poor Ixion turns an endless wheel,
Where usurers are chok'd with melting gold,
And wantons are embrac'd with ugly snakes,

46	*martialist:* soldier, warrior	62	*either:* both
49	*scour:* roam vigorously over, skirmish		*his:* its own
50	*mildest censor:* most lenient judge	63	*declining:* downward sloping
51	*device:* plan	64	*ready downfall:* precipice leading directly
52	*infernal:* hellish, underworldly	65	*Furies:* avengers (see note)
53	*doom:* pronounce judgement on	66	*Ixion:* a figure punished by the gods (see note)
55	*Pluto's:* the King of the underworld's	68	*wantons:* lechers
56	*dreadfull:* full of dread		

And murderers groan with never-killing wounds,
70   And perjur'd wights scalded in boiling lead,
And all foul sins with torments overwhelm'd.
'Twixt these two ways, I trod the middle path,
Which brought me to the fair Elysian green,
In midst whereof there stands a stately tower,
The walls of brass, the gates of adamant.
Here finding Pluto with his Proserpine,
I showed my passport humbled on my knee,
Whereat fair Proserpine began to smile,
And begg'd that only she might give my doom.
80   Pluto was pleas'd and seal'd it with a kiss.
Forthwith, Revenge, she rounded thee in th'ear,
And bade thee lead me through the gates of horn,
Where dreams have passage in the silent night.
No sooner had she spoke but we were here,
I wot not how, in twinkling of an eye.
REVENGE: Then know, Andrea, that thou art arriv'd
Where thou shalt see the author of thy death,
Don Balthazar, the Prince of Portingale,
Depriv'd of life by Bel-imperia.
90   Here sit we down to see the mystery
And serve for Chorus in this tragedy.

ACT I SCENE 2
[*A field of battle*]

70	*wights:* folk, people	82	*gates of horn:* twin doors of Hell
75	*adamant:* hard rock	85	*wot:* know
76	*Proserpine:* Pluto's wife	87	*author:* causer, instigator
79	*only she:* she alone	90	*mystery:* unknown outcome, events with hidden meaning (see note)
	doom: sentence		
81	*rounded:* whispered		

Enter Spanish KING, *the* GENERAL, *the* DUKE OF
   CASTILE, HIERONIMO.
KING: Now say, Lord General, how fares our camp?
GENERAL: All well, my sovereign liege, except some few
   That are deceased by fortune of the war.
KING: But what portends thy cheerful countenance,
   And posting to our presence thus in haste?
   Speak, man, hath Fortune given us victory?
GENERAL: Victory, my liege, and that with little loss.
KING: Our Portingales will pay us tribute then?
GENERAL: Tribute and wonted homage, therewithal.   100
KING: Then bless'd be Heaven, and guider of the Heavens,
   From whose fair influence such justice flows.
CASTILE: *O multum dilecte Deo, tibi militat aether,*
   Et conjuratae curvato poplite gentes
   Succumbunt: recti soror est victoria juris.
KING: Thanks to my loving brother of Castile.
   But, General, unfold in brief discourse
   Your form of battle and your war's success,
   That adding all the pleasure of thy news
   Unto the height of former happiness,   110
   With deeper wage and greater dignity
   We may reward thy blisful chivalry.
GENERAL: Where Spain and Portingale do jointly knit
   Their frontiers, leaning on each other's bound,
   There met our armies in their proud array,

92   *camp:* army, 'host' (see note)
96   *posting:* hurrying
99   *our Portingales:* 'our friends the
      Portuguese'
      tribute: money as tribute
100 *wonted:* customary (for a defeated
      foe)
103–5   *O multum* etc.: see note

107 *unfold:* reveal, explain
108 *war's:* battle's
      success: outcome, result
111 *deeper wage:* larger reward
112 *blisful:* joyous, 'glorious'
      chivalry: prowess in war
114 *bound:* frontier, boundary

Both furnish'd well, both full of hope and fear:
Both menacing alike with daring shows,
Both vaunting sundry colours of device,
Both cheerly sounding trumpets, drums and fifes,
120 Both raising dreadful clamours to the sky,
That valleys, hills, and rivers made rebound
And Heaven itself was frighted with the sound.
Our battles both were pitch'd in squadron form,
Each corner strongly fenc'd with wings of shot,
But ere we join'd and came to push of pike,
I brought a squadron of our readiest shot
From out our rearward to begin the fight;
They brought another wing to encounter us.
Meanwhile our ordnance play'd on either side,
130 And captains strove to have their valours tried.
Don Pedro, their chief horsemen's colonel,
Did with his cornet bravely make attempt
To break the order of our battle ranks.
But Don Rogero, worthy man of war,
March'd forth against him with our musketeers,
And stopp'd the malice of his fell approach.
While they maintain hot skirmish to and fro,
Both battles join and fall to handy blows,
Their violent shot resembling th'ocean's rage,
140 When, roaring loud and with a swelling tide,

116 *furnish'd:* equipped
117 *shows:* displays
118 *vaunting:* proudly exhibiting
colours of device: military ensigns bearing special designs
123 *battles:* bodies of troops
in squadron form: in a square (see note)
124 *fenc'd:* protected, fortified
wings of shot: musketeers on the flanks
125 *push of pike:* a hand-to-hand engagement
129 *ordnance:* artillery
130 *tried:* put to the test
132 *cornet:* company of cavalry
136 *malice:* harmfulness, injurious nature
fell: deadly
138 *handy:* hand-to-hand
139 *shot:* firing

It beats upon the rampiers of huge rocks,
And gapes to swallow neighbour-bounding lands.
Now while Bellona rageth here and there,
Thick storms of bullets rain like winter's hail,
And shiver'd lances dark the troubled air.
Pede pes et cuspide cuspis,
Arma sonant armis, vir petiturque viro.
On every side drop captains to the ground
And soldiers, some ill maim'd, some slain outright:
Here falls a body scinder'd from his head,   150
There legs and arms lie bleeding on the grass,
Mingled with weapons and unbowelled steeds
That scattering overspread the purple plain.
In all this turmoil, three long hours and more
The victory to neither part inclin'd,
Till Don Andrea with his brave launciers
In their main battle made so great a breach
That half dismay'd, the multitude retir'd:
But Balthazar, the Portingales' young Prince,
Brought rescue and encourag'd them to stay.   160
Here-hence the fight was eagerly renew'd,
And in that conflict was Andrea slain,
Brave man-at-arms, but weak to Balthazar,
Yet while the Prince, insulting over him,
Breath'd out proud vaunts, sounding to our reproach,
Friendship and hardy valour join'd in one

141	*rampiers:* ramparts	155	*inclin'd:* tended to favour
142	*neighbour-bounding:* adjacent, adjoining	156	*launciers:* lancers
		161	*Here-hence:* as a result
143	*Bellona:* the Roman goddess of war (see note)	163	*man-at-arms:* an armoured horse-soldier
146	*Pede pes* etc.: see note		*weak to:* feeble compared with
149	*ill maim'd:* badly injured	164	*insulting:* exulting arrogantly
150	*scinder'd:* severed	165	*sounding to:* implying, tending towards
153	*purple:* i.e. bloody		

       Prick'd forth Horatio, our Knight Marshal's son,
       To challenge forth that Prince in single fight:
       Not long between these twain the fight endur'd
170   But straight the Prince was beaten from his horse
       And forc'd to yield him prisoner to his foe.
       When he was taken, all the rest they fled,
       And our carbines pursu'd them to the death,
       Till, Phoebus waning to the western deep,
       Our trumpeters were charg'd to sound retreat.
  KING: Thanks, good Lord General, for these good news;
       And for some argument of more to come,
       Take this and wear it for thy sovereign's sake.
          Give him his chain.
       But tell me now, hast thou confirm'd a peace?
180 GENERAL: No peace, my liege, but peace conditional,
       That if with homage tribute be well paid,
       The fury of your forces will be stay'd,
       And to this peace their Viceroy hath subscrib'd
          Give the K[ING] *a paper.*
       And made a solemn vow that during life
       His tribute shall be truly paid to Spain.
  KING: These words, these deeds, become thy person well.
       But now, Knight Marshal, frolic with thy King,
       For 'tis thy son that wins this battle's prize.
  HIERONIMO: Long may he live to serve my sovereign liege,
190   And soon decay unless he serve my liege.
       A tucket afar off.

167	*Prick'd forth:* inspired	182	*stay'd:* halted, abated
173	*carbines:* carabins, armed and mounted soldiers (see note)	183	*subscrib'd:* given his signature
		187	*frolic:* make merry, 'live it up'
174	*Phoebus:* the sun	190	*decay:* decline in health and strength
	deep: the ocean		
175	*charg'd:* enjoined, ordered		s.d. *tucket:* trumpet flourish (see note)
177	*argument:* token, manifestation		
180	*but:* only		

KING: Nor thou nor he shall die without reward –
   What means this warning of this trumpet's sound?
GENERAL: This tells me that your grace's men of war,
   Such as war's fortune hath reserv'd from death,
   Come marching on towards your royal seat
   To show themselves before your Majesty,
   For so I gave in charge at my depart.
   Whereby by demonstration shall appear
   That all (except three hundred or few more)
   Are safe returned and by their foes enrich'd.   200

   The army enters, BALTHAZAR *between* LORENZO *and*
   HORATIO *captive.*

KING: A gladsome sight! I long to see them here.
   They enter and pass by.
   Was that the warlike Prince of Portingale
   That by our nephew was in triumph led?
GENERAL: It was, my liege, the Prince of Portingale.
KING: But what was he that on the other side
   Held him by th'arm as partner of the prize?
HIERONIMO: That was my son, my gracious sovereign,
   Of whom though from his tender infancy
   My loving thoughts did never hope but well,
   He never pleas'd his father's eyes till now,   210
   Nor fill'd my heart with overcloying joys.
KING: Go, let them march once more about these walls,
   That staying them we may confer and talk
   With our brave prisoner and his double guard.
   Hieronimo, it greatly pleaseth us
   That in our victory thou have a share,
   By virtue of thy worthy son's exploit.
   Enter [the Spanish army] again.

194   *reserv'd:* kept from, preserved   211   *overcloying:* excessively satiating
197   *depart:* departure   213   *staying:* halting

Bring hither the young Prince of Portingale;
The rest march on, but ere they be dismiss'd,
220   We will bestow on every soldier
Two ducats, and on every leader ten,
That they may know our largesse welcomes them.

> *Exeunt all [the army] but* BALTHAZAR, LORENZO,
> HORATIO.

Welcome, Don Balthazar, welcome, nephew,
And thou, Horatio, thou art welcome too:
Young Prince, although thy father's hard misdeeds
In keeping back the tribute that he owes
Deserve but evil measure at our hands,
Yet shalt thou know that Spain is honourable.

BALTHAZAR: The trespass that my father made in peace
230   Is now control'd by fortune of the wars;
And cards once dealt, it boots not ask why so.
His men are slain, a weakening to his realm,
His colours seiz'd, a blot unto his name,
His son distress'd, a corsive to his heart:
These punishments may clear his late offence.

KING: Aye, Balthazar, if he observe this truce,
Our peace will grow the stronger for these wars;
Meanwhile live thou, though not in liberty,
Yet free from bearing any servile yoke:
240   For in our hearing thy deserts were great,
And in our sight thyself art gracious.

BALTHAZAR: And I shall study to deserve this grace.

---

222   *largesse:* bounty, liberality
227   *measure:* treatment, recompense
230   *control'd:* curbed, restrained
231   *it boots not:* it is no good to
234   *distress'd:* crushed in battle
       corsive: corrosive or eating sub-
       stance

235   *clear:* expunge, purge
       late: recent
242   *study:* apply myself, seek to
       achieve

KING: But tell me, for their holding makes me doubt,
To which of these twain art thou prisoner?
LORENZO: To me, my liege.
HORATIO: To me, my sovereign.
LORENZO: This hand first took his courser by the reins.
HORATIO: But first my lance did put him from his horse.
LORENZO: I seiz'd his weapon and enjoy'd it first.
HORATIO: But first I forc'd him lay his weapons down.
KING: Let go his arm upon our privilege.   250

   [LORENZO *and* HORATIO] *let him go.*

Say, worthy Prince, to whether did'st thou yield?
BALTHAZAR: To him in courtesy, to this perforce:
He spake me fair, this other gave me strokes;
He promis'd life, this other threaten'd death;
He won my love, this other conquer'd me;
And truth to say I yield myself to both.
HIERONIMO: But that I know your grace for just and wise,
And might seem partial in this difference,
Enforc'd by nature and by law of arms,
My tongue should plead for young Horatio's right.   260
He hunted well that was a lion's death,
Not he that in a garment wore his skin:
So hares may pull dead lions by the beard.
KING: Content thee, Marshal, thou shalt have no wrong,
And for thy sake thy son shall want no right.
Will both abide the censure of my doom?
LORENZO: I crave no better than your grace awards.
HORATIO: Nor I, although I sit beside my right.

243	*their holding:* the fact they both hold you	
246	*courser:* war-horse	
248	*enjoy'd:* possessed	
250	*privilege:* royal prerogative	
251	*whether:* which of the two	
253	*strokes:* blows	
261	*was:* caused	
266	*censure:* judgement	
	of my doom: arising from my opinion	
268	*sit beside:* set to one side, discount	

KING: Then by my judgement thus your strife shall end:
270   You both deserve and both shall have reward.
      Nephew, thou took'st his weapon and his horse,
      His weapons and his horse are thy reward.
      Horatio, thou didst force him first to yield,
      His ransom therefore is thy valour's fee:
      Appoint the sum as you shall both agree.
      But, nephew, thou shalt have the Prince in guard,
      For thine estate best fitteth such a guest:
      Horatio's house were small for all his train,
      Yet in regard thy substance passeth his,
280   And that just guerdon may befall desert,
      To him we yield the armour of the Prince.
      How likes Don Balthazar of this device?
BALTHAZAR: Right well my liege, if this proviso were,
      That Don Horatio bear us company,
      Whom I admire and love for chivalry.
KING: Horatio, leave him not that loves thee so.
      Now let us hence to see our soldiers paid,
      And feast our prisoner as our friendly guest.
                                        Exeunt.

ACT I SCENE 3

      [*The Portuguese court*]
      Enter VICEROY, ALEXANDRO, VILLUPPO [*and* GUARDS].
VICEROY: Is our ambassador despatch'd for Spain?
290   ALEXANDRO: Two days, my liege, are past since his depart.
VICEROY: And tribute payment gone along with him?

---

277   *estate:* rank, status   281   *him:* i.e. Horatio
279   *in regard:* seeing that   282   *device:* plan, scheme
      substance: means, estate, riches 290   *depart:* departure
280   *that:* in order that
      guerdon: reward

ALEXANDRO: Aye, my good lord.
VICEROY: Then rest we here awhile in our unrest
  And feed our sorrows with some inward sighs,
  For deepest cares break never into tears.
  But wherefore sit I in a regal throne?
    Falls to the ground.
  This better fits a wretch's endless moan.
  Yet this is higher than my fortunes reach,
  And therefore better than my state deserves.
  Aye, aye, this earth, image of melancholy,   300
  Seeks him who fates adjudge to misery:
  Here let me lie, now am I at the lowest.
  Qui jacet in terra non habet unde cadat;
  In me consumpsit vires fortuna nocendo,
  Nil superest ut jam possit obesse magis.
  Yes, Fortune may bereave me of my crown:
  Here take it now; [*Takes crown off.*]
                    let Fortune do her worst,
  She will not rob me of this sable weed.
  Oh no, she envies none but pleasant things,
  Such is the folly of despiteful chance: 310
  Fortune is blind and sees not my deserts,
  So is she deaf and hears not my laments:
  And could she hear, yet is she wilful mad,
  And therefore will not pity my distress.
  Suppose that she could pity me, what then?
  What help can be expected at her hands,

---

293 *unrest:* turmoil, anxiety
299 *state:* condition
300 *image:* reflection, symbol
     melancholy: state of grief (see note)
301 *adjudge:* sentence, condemn
303 *Qui jacet* etc.: see note

308 *sable weed:* black clothing
309 *none:* nobody
     but: anything except
310 *despiteful:* malignant, malicious
311 *my deserts:* what I truly deserve
313 *wilful mad:* obstinately unreasonable

Whose foot is standing on a rolling stone,
And mind more mutable than fickle winds?
Why wail I then where's hope of no redress?
320   Oh yes, complaining makes my grief seem less.
My late ambition hath distain'd my faith,
My breach of faith occasion'd bloody wars,
Those bloody wars have spent my treasure,
And with my treasure my people's blood,
And with their blood, my joy and best belov'd,
My best belov'd, my sweet and only son.
Oh wherefore went I not to war myself?
The cause was mine, I might have died for both:
My years were mellow, his but young and green,
330   My death were natural, but his was forc'd.

ALEXANDRO: No doubt, my liege, but still the Prince
   survives.

VICEROY: Survives? Aye, where?

ALEXANDRO: In Spain, a prisoner by mischance of war.

VICEROY: Then they have slain him for his father's fault.

ALEXANDRO: That were a breach to common law of arms.

VICEROY: They reck no laws that meditate revenge.

ALEXANDRO: His ransom's worth will stay from foul
   revenge.

VICEROY: No, if he liv'd the news would soon be here.

ALEXANDRO: Nay, evil news fly faster still than good.

340   VICEROY: Tell me no more of news, for he is dead.

VILLUPPO: My sovereign, pardon the author of ill news,
   And I'll bewray the fortune of thy son.

VICEROY: Speak on; I'll guerdon thee whate'er it be:

318	*mutable:* changeable, fickle	337	*stay:* hold (them) back
321	*distain'd:* sullied, defiled	341	*author:* promoter, 'voucher for'
330	*forc'd:* imposed on him	342	*bewray:* expose, reveal
334	*fault:* offence, culpability	343	*guerdon:* reward
336	*reck:* heed, regard		

Mine ear is ready to receive ill news,
My heart grown hard 'gainst mischief's battery;
Stand up, I say, and tell thy tale at large.

VILLUPPO: Then hear that truth which these mine eyes have
    seen.
When both the armies were in battle join'd,
Don Balthazar, amidst the thickest troops,
To win renown, did wondrous feats of arms;   350
Amongst the rest I saw him hand to hand
In single fight with their Lord General:
Till Alexandro, that here counterfeits
Under the colour of a duteous friend,
Discharg'd his pistol at the Prince's back,
As though he would have slain their General.
But therewithal Don Balthazar fell down,
And when he fell, then we began to fly,
But had he liv'd the day had sure been ours.

ALEXANDRO: O wicked forgery! O traitorous miscreant!   360

VICEROY: Hold thou thy peace! But now, Villuppo, say:
Where then became the carcass of my son?

VILLUPPO: I saw them drag it to the Spanish tents.

VICEROY: Aye, aye, my nightly dreams have told me this.
[to ALEXANDRO] Thou false, unkind, unthankful,
    traitorous beast,
Wherein had Balthazar offended thee
That thou shouldst thus betray him to our foes?
Was't Spanish gold that bleared so thine eyes
That thou couldst see no part of our deserts?

346   *at large:* freely, fully, openly
354   *colour:* pretext, pretence
360   *forgery:* falsehood
        miscreant: villain, rogue
362   *Where then became:* what became
        of

365   *unkind:* cruel, unnatural (see
        note)
368   *bleared:* deceived by blurring, dis-
        torted the vision
369   *deserts:* merits, deserving

370   Perchance because thou art Terceira's lord,
    Thou hadst some hope to wear this diadem,
    If first my son and then myself were slain:
    But thy ambitious thought shall break thy neck.
    Aye, this was it that made thee spill his blood,
      Take the crown and put it on again.
    But I'll now wear it till thy blood be spilt.
ALEXANDRO: Vouchsafe, dread sovereign, to hear me speak!
VICEROY: Away with him! His sight is second Hell:
    Keep him till we determine of his death.
      [GUARDS *lead* ALEXANDRO *off.*]
    If Balthazar be dead, he shall not live.
380   Villuppo, follow us for thy reward.
                Exit VICEROY.
VILLUPPO: Thus have I with an envious forged tale
    Deceiv'd the King, betray'd mine enemy,
    And hope for guerdon of my villainy.
                    Exit.

ACT I   SCENE 4

[*The Spanish court*]
Enter HORATIO *and* BEL-IMPERIA
BEL-IMPERIA: Señor Horatio, this is the place and hour
    Wherein I must entreat thee to relate
    The circumstance of Don Andrea's death:
    Who, living, was my garland's sweetest flower,
    And in his death hath buried my delights.
HORATIO: For love of him and service to yourself,
390   I nill refuse this heavy doleful charge:
    Yet tears and sighs I fear will hinder me.

---

378 *Keep:* hold captive, guard   381 *envious:* spiteful, odious
    determine of: decide on the   390 *nill:* will not
    method of

When both our armies were enjoin'd in fight,
Your worthy chevalier amidst the thick'st,
For glorious cause still aiming at the fairest,
Was at the last by young Don Balthazar
Encounter'd hand to hand: their fight was long,
Their hearts were great, their clamours menacing,
Their strength alike, their strokes both dangerous.
But wrathful Nemesis, that wicked power,
Envying at Andrea's praise and worth,   400
Cut short his life to end his praise and worth.
She, she herself, disguised in armour's mask
(As Pallas was before proud Pergamus),
Brought in a fresh supply of halberdiers,
Which paunch'd his horse and ding'd him to the ground.
Then young Don Balthazar with ruthless rage,
Taking advantage of his foe's distress,
Did finish what his halberdiers begun,
And left not till Andrea's life was done.
Then, though too late, incens'd with just remorse,   410
I with my band set forth against the Prince,
And brought him prisoner from his halberdiers.

BEL-IMPERIA: Would thou hadst slain him that so slew my
    love!
But then was Don Andrea's carcass lost?

HORATIO: No, that was it for which I chiefly strove,
Nor stepp'd I back till I recover'd him:
I took him up and wound him in mine arms,
And wielding him unto my private tent,

392 *enjoin'd:* joined together, engaged
393 *chevalier:* knight, cavalier
     thick'st: thickest
394 *the fairest:* i.e. Bel-imperia
400 *Envying at:* filled with evil to-
     wards
402 *mask:* 'cloak', 'cover'
403 *Pergamus:* Troy
405 *paunch'd:* slit up the belly
     ding'd: knocked, smashed
418 *wielding:* carrying

There laid him down and dew'd him with my tears,
420   And sigh'd and sorrow'd as became a friend.
But neither friendly sorrow, sighs nor tears
Could win pale death from his usurped right.
Yet this I did, and less I could not do:
I saw him honour'd with due funeral;
This scarf I pluck'd from off his lifeless arm
And wear it in remembrance of my friend.
BEL-IMPERIA: I know the scarf — would he had kept it still,
For had he liv'd he would have kept it still,
And worn it for his Bel-imperia's sake:
430   For 'twas my favour at his last depart.
But now wear thou it both for him and me,
For after him thou hast deserv'd it best.
But, for thy kindness in his life and death,
Be sure while Bel-imperia's life endures,
She will be Don Horatio's thankful friend.
HORATIO: And, Madam, Don Horatio will not slack
Humbly to serve fair Bel-imperia.
But now, if your good liking stand thereto,
I'll crave your pardon to go seek the Prince,
440   For so the Duke your father gave me charge.
BEL-IMPERIA: Aye, go, Horatio, leave me here alone,
For solitude best fits my cheerless mood.
                              Exit HORATIO.
Yet what avails to wail Andrea's death,
From whence Horatio proves my second love?
Had he not lov'd Andrea as he did,
He could not sit in Bel-imperia's thoughts.
But how can love find harbour in my breast,
Till I revenge the death of my belov'd?

---

419   *dew'd:* damped, moistened   430   *favour:* love-token
                                                depart: departure

Yes, second love shall further my revenge.
I'll love Horatio, my Andrea's friend,   450
The more to spite the Prince that wrought his end,
And where Don Balthazar that slew my love
Himself now pleads for favour at my hands,
He shall in rigour of my just disdain
Reap long repentance for his murderous deed:
For what was't else but murderous cowardice,
So many to oppress one valiant knight,
Without respect of honour in the fight? –
And here he comes that murder'd my delight.

    Enter LORENZO *and* BALTHAZAR.

LORENZO: Sister, what means this melancholy walk?   460
BEL-IMPERIA: That for a while I wish no company.
LORENZO: But here the Prince is come to visit you.
BEL-IMPERIA: That argues that he lives in liberty.
BALTHAZAR: No, Madam, but in pleasing servitude.
BEL-IMPERIA: Your prison then belike is your conceit.
BALTHAZAR: Aye, by conceit my freedom is enthrall'd.
BEL-IMPERIA: Then with conceit enlarge yourself again.
BALTHAZAR: What if conceit have laid my heart to gage?
BEL-IMPERIA: Pay that you borrow'd and recover it.
BALTHAZAR: I die if it return from whence it lies.   470
BEL-IMPERIA: A heartless man and live? A miracle.
BALTHAZAR: Aye, lady, love can work such miracles.
LORENZO: Tush, tush, my lord, let go these ambages,
    And in plain terms acquaint her with your love.

---

454 *rigour:* strict enforcement
     disdain: indignation
456 *was't else:* was it otherwise
457 *oppress:* overwhelm, crush in battle

465 *your conceit:* all in your imagination
466 *enthrall'd:* imprisoned, enslaved
468 *to gage:* as a pledge
473 *ambages:* ambiguous remarks

BEL-IMPERIA: What boots complaint, when there's no
    remedy?
BALTHAZAR: Yes, to your gracious self must I complain,
    In whose fair answer lies my remedy,
    On whose perfection all my thoughts attend,
    [In] whose aspect mine eyes find beauty's bower,
480   In whose translucent breast my heart is lodg'd.
BEL-IMPERIA: Alas, my lord, these are but words of course,
    And but devis'[d] to drive me from this place.
    She, in going in, lets fall her glove, which HORATIO, *coming
    out, takes up.*
HORATIO: Madam, your glove.
BEL-IMPERIA: Thanks, good Horatio; take it for thy pains.
BALTHAZAR: Señor Horatio stoop'd in happy time.
HORATIO: I reap'd more grace than I deserv'd or hop'd.
LORENZO [*to* BALTHAZAR]: My lord, be not dismay'd for
    what is past;
    You know that women oft are humorous:
    These clouds will overblow with little wind;
490   Let me alone; I'll scatter them myself.
    Meanwhile let us devise to spend the time
    In some delightful sports and revelling.
HORATIO: The King, my lords, is coming hither straight
    To feast the Portingale Ambassador:
    Things were in readiness before I came.
BALTHAZAR: Then here it fits us to attend the King,
    To welcome hither our Ambassador,
    And learn my father and my country's health.
    Enter the banquet, trumpets, the KING *and* AMBASSADOR
    [*and the* DUKE OF CASTILE].

475	*boots:* profits	488	*humorous:* moody, temperamental
	complaint: amorous pleading	491	*devise:* plan
479	*aspect:* looks, appearance	496	*fits us:* behoves us
481	*words of course:* stock remarks, 'sweet nothings'		

KING: See, Lord Ambassador, how Spain entreats
 Their prisoner Balthazar, thy Viceroy's son: 500
 We pleasure more in kindness than in wars.
AMBASSADOR: Sad is our King, and Portingale laments,
 Supposing that Don Balthazar is slain.
BALTHAZAR [*to himself*]: So I am slain by beauty's tyranny.
 [*Aloud*] You see, my lord, how Balthazar is slain:
 I frolic with the Duke of Castile's son,
 Wrapp'd every hour in pleasures of the court
 And grac'd with favours of his Majesty.
KING: Put off your greetings till our feast be done;
 Now come and sit with us and taste our cheer.   510
 [*They*] *sit to the banquet.*
 Sit down, young Prince, you are our second guest:
 Brother, sit down, and nephew, take your place;
 Señor Horatio, wait thou upon our cup,
 For well thou hast deserved to be honour'd.
 Now, lordings, fall to; Spain is Portugal,
 And Portugal is Spain, we both are friends,
 Tribute is paid, and we enjoy our right.
 But where is old Hieronimo our Marshal?
 He promis'd us in honour of our guest
 To grace our banquet with some pompous jest.   520
 Enter HIERONIMO *with a drum* [*i.e. a* DRUMMER], THREE
 KNIGHTS, *each* [*with*] *his scutcheon, then he fetches* THREE
 KINGS; *they* [*the* KNIGHTS] *take their crowns and them
 captive.*
 Hieronimo, this masque contents mine eye,

---

499   *Spain:* members of the Spanish
      court
      entreats: behaves towards
501   *pleasure:* take pleasure
506   *frolic:* sport, make merry

511   *second guest:* i.e. in importance
515   *fall too:* fall to, start eating
520   *pompous jest:* stately performance
      s.d. *scutcheon:* a shield with a coat
      of arms on

Although I sound not well the mystery.

HIERONIMO: The first arm'd knight that hung his scutcheon
up —

He takes the scutcheon and gives it to the KING.

Was English Robert, Earl of Gloucester,
Who, when King Stephen bore sway in Albion,
Arriv'd with five and twenty thousand men
In Portingale, and by success of war,
Enforc'd the King, then but a Saracen,
To bear the yoke of the English monarchy.

530   KING: My Lord of Portingale, by this you see
That which may comfort both your king and you,
And make your late discomfort seem the less.
But say, Hieronimo, what was the next?

HIERONIMO: The second knight that hung his scutcheon
up —

He doth as he did before.

Was Edmund, Earl of Kent in Albion,
When English Richard wore the diadem.
He came likewise and razed Lisbon walls,
And took the King of Portingale in fight:
For which, and other suchlike service done,
540   He after was created Duke of York.

KING: This is another special argument
That Portingale may deign to bear our yoke,
When it by little England hath been yok'd.
But now, Hieronimo, what was the last?

HIERONIMO: The third and last, not least in our account —

Doing as before.

Was as the rest a valiant Englishman,

522   *sound:* fathom, understand
        mystery: hidden significance
525   *Albion:* England

537   *razed:* obliterated, destroyed
541   *special argument:* appropriate dem-
        onstration, illustration

Brave John of Gaunt, the Duke of Lancaster,
As by his scutcheon plainly may appear.
He with a puissant army came to Spain,
And took our King of Castile prisoner.   550
AMBASSADOR: This is an argument for our Viceroy,
That Spain may not insult for her success,
Since English warriors likewise conquer'd Spain,
And made them bow their knees to Albion.
KING: Hieronimo, I drink to thee for this device,
Which hath pleas'd both the Ambassador and me:
Pledge me, Hieronimo, if thou love [thy] King.
    Takes the cup of HORATIO [*and they drink*].
My lord, I fear we sit but over-long,
Unless our dainties were more delicate,
But welcome are you to the best we have.   560
Now let us in, that you may be dispatch'd;
I think our council is already set.
                    Exeunt omnes.
GHOST: Come we for this from depth of underground,
To see him feast that gave me my death's wound?
These pleasant sights are sorrow to my soul –
Nothing but league, and love, and banqueting?
REVENGE: Be still, Andrea; ere we go from hence,
I'll turn their friendship into fell despite,
Their love to mortal hate, their day to night,
Their hope into despair, their peace to war,   570

---

549 *puissant:* powerful, strong
552 *insult for:* brag about, behave arrogantly over
555 *device:* ingenious entertainment
557 s.d. *cup of:* cup from
559 *Unless:* unless it happened to be the case that
     dainties: dishes, fare
561 *dispatch'd:* sent on your way
566 *league:* alliances, friendship
568 *fell despite:* cruel aversion
569 *mortal:* deathly

Their joys to pain, their bliss to misery.

ACT II SCENE I

[Lorenzo's palace]
Enter LORENZO *and* BALTHAZAR.

LORENZO: My lord, though Bel-imperia seem thus coy,
Let reason hold you in your wonted joy:
In time the savage bull sustains the yoke,
In time all haggard hawks will stoop to lure,
In time small wedges cleave the hardest oak,
In time the flint is pierc'd with softest shower,
And she in time will fall from her disdain,
And rue the sufferance of your friendly pain.

580 BALTHAZAR: No, she is wilder and more hard withal
Than beast, or bird, or tree, or stony wall.
But wherefore blot I Bel-imperia's name?
It is my fault, not she, that merits blame.
My feature is not to content her sight,
My words are rude and work her no delight.
The lines I send her are but harsh and ill,
Such as do drop from Pan and Marsyas' quill.
My presents are not of sufficient cost,
And being worthless all my labour's lost.
590 Yet might she love me for my valiancy,
Aye, but that's slander'd by captivity;

---

574 *sustains:* submits to
575 *haggard:* untamed, in a wild state
  stoop: swoop, plunge
  lure: training-aid (see note)
576 *wedges:* metal blocks for slitting timber
578 *fall from:* abandon
579 *rue:* have pity on
  sufferance: long suffering, patient endurance
580 *wilder:* more passionate, erratic
  withal: besides
584 *feature:* bodily shape, bearing
  to: such as to
585 *rude:* rough, unpolished
587 *Pan and Marsyas':* see note
  quill: a pipe from a hollow stem
590 *valiancy:* courage, valour
591 *slander'd:* discredited, lowered in esteem

Yet might she love me to content her sire,
Aye, but her reason masters his desire;
Yet might she love me as her brother's friend,
Aye, but her hopes aim at some other end;
Yet might she love me to uprear her state,
Aye, but perhaps she hopes some nobler mate;
Yet might she love me as her beauty's thrall,
Aye, but I fear she cannot love at all.

LORENZO: My lord, for my sake leave these ecstasies,   600
And doubt not but we'll find some remedy,
Some cause there is that lets you not be lov'd:
First that must needs be known and then remov'd.
What if my sister love some other knight?

BALTHAZAR: My summer's day will turn to winter's night.

LORENZO: I have already found a stratagem
To sound the bottom of this doubtful theme.
My lord, for once you shall be rul'd by me,
Hinder me not whate'er you hear or see.
By force or fair means will I cast about   610
To find the truth of all this question out.
Ho, Pedringano!

PEDRINGANO [off]: Signor?

LORENZO: Vien qui presto.

       Enter PEDRINGANO.

PEDRINGANO: Hath your lordship any service to command me?

LORENZO: Aye, Pedringano, service of import.
And not to spend the time in trifling words,
Thus stands the case: it is not long, thou know'st,

---

596 *uprear her state:* elevate her social   612 *Vien qui presto:* come here
     status   quickly (see note)
600 *ecstasies:* rapturous outbursts (see   614 *import:* significance
     note)
607 *sound the bottom:* plumb the
     depths

Since I did shield thee from my father's wrath
For thy conveyance in Andrea's love,
For which thou wert adjudg'd to punishment:
620 I stood betwixt thee and thy punishment,
And since, thou know'st how I have favour'd thee.
Now to these favours will I add reward,
Not with fair words, but store of golden coin,
And lands and living join'd with dignities,
If thou but satisfy my just demand:
Tell truth and have me for thy lasting friend.
PEDRINGANO: Whate'er it be your lordship shall demand,
My bounden duty bids me tell the truth,
If case it lie in me to tell the truth.
630 LORENZO: Then, Pedringano, this is my demand:
Whom loves my sister Bel-imperia
(For she reposeth all her trust in thee)?
Speak, man, and gain both friendship and reward –
I mean, whom loves she in Andrea's place?
PEDRINGANO: Alas, my lord, since Don Andrea's death,
I have no credit with her as before,
And therefore know not if she love or no.
LORENZO: Nay, if thou dally then I am thy foe,
    [Draw[s] his sword.]
And fear shall force what friendship cannot win:
640 Thy death shall bury what thy life conceals.
Thou diest for more esteeming her than me.
PEDRINGANO: Oh stay, my lord!
LORENZO: Yet speak the truth and I will guerdon thee,
And shield thee from whatever can ensue,
And will conceal whate'er proceeds from thee,

618	*conveyance:* cunning dealing	638	*dally:* trifle
623	*store:* abundance	642	*stay:* hold off
629	*If case* etc.: if it proves I can	643	*guerdon:* recompense

But if thou dally once again, thou diest.
PEDRINGANO: If Madam Bel-imperia be in love –
LORENZO: What, villain, ifs and ands?
    Offer[s] to kill him.
PEDRINGANO: O stay, my lord, she loves Horatio!
    BALTHAZAR *starts back.*
LORENZO: What, Don Horatio, our Knight Marshal's son?   650
PEDRINGANO: Even him, my lord.
LORENZO: Now say but how know'st thou he is her love,
    And thou shalt find me kind and liberal:
    Stand up, I say, and fearless tell the truth.
PEDRINGANO: She sent him letters which myself perus'd,
    Full fraught with lines and arguments of love,
    Preferring him before Prince Balthazar.
LORENZO: Swear on this cross that what thou say'st is true,
    And that thou wilt conceal what thou hast told.
PEDRINGANO: I swear to both by him that made us all.   660
    [Kisses LORENZO's *sword.]*
LORENZO: In hope thine oath is true, here's thy reward.
    [Gives him money.]
    But if I prove thee perjur'd and unjust,
    This very sword whereon thou took'st thine oath
    Shall be the worker of thy tragedy.
PEDRINGANO: What I have said is true, and shall for me
    Be still conceal'd from Bel-imperia.
    Besides your honour's liberality
    Deserves my duteous service, even till death.
LORENZO: Let this be all that thou shalt do for me:
    Be watchful when and where these lovers meet,   670
    And give me notice in some secret sort.

---

648 s.d. *Offer[s] to:* threaten(s) to
656 *fraught:* laden, weighed down
658 *cross:* i.e. the sword-hilt
662 *unjust:* faithless

665 *for me:* for my part
671 *in some secret sort:* by some con-
    cealed method

PEDRINGANO: I will, my lord.

LORENZO: Then shalt thou find that I am liberal;
    Thou know'st that I can more advance thy state
    Than she; be therefore wise and fail me not.
    Go and attend her as thy custom is,
    Lest absence make her think thou dost amiss.

                Exit PEDRINGANO.

    Why, so; *Tam armis quam ingenio:*
    Where words prevail not, violence prevails,
680   But gold doth more than either of them both.
    How likes Prince Balthazar this stratagem?

BALTHAZAR: Both well, and ill; it makes me glad and sad:
    Glad, that I know the hinderer of my love;
    Sad, that I fear she hates me whom I love;
    Glad, that I know on whom to be reveng'd;
    Sad, that she'll fly me if I take revenge,
    Yet must I take revenge or die myself,
    For love resisted grows impatient.
    I think Horatio be my destin'd plague,
690   First in his hand he brandished a sword,
    And with that sword he fiercely waged war,
    And in that war he gave me dangerous wounds,
    And by those wounds he forced me to yield,
    And by my yielding I became his slave.
    Now in his mouth he carries pleasing words,
    Which pleasing words do harbour sweet conceits,
    Which sweet conceits are lim'd with sly deceits,
    Which sly deceits smooth Bel-imperia's ears,
    And through her ears dive down into her heart,

---

674 *state:* status and condition
678 *Tam armis* etc.: 'as much by force as by cunning'.
696 *sweet conceits:* pleasing concepts, notions
697 *lim'd:* smeared, made sticky (see note)
698 *smooth:* flatter

And in her heart set him where I should stand.   700
Thus hath he ta'en my body by his force,
And now by sleight would captivate my soul:
But in his fall I'll tempt the destinies,
And either lose my life, or win my love.
LORENZO: Let's go, my lord; your staying stays revenge:
    Do you but follow me and gain your love;
    Her favour must be won by his remove.
                                        Exeunt.

ACT II   SCENE 2

Enter HORATIO *and* BEL-IMPERIA.

HORATIO: Now, Madam, since by favour of your love
    Our hidden smoke is turn'd to open flame,
    And that with looks and words we feed our thoughts,   710
    Two chief contents, where more cannot be had,
    Thus in the midst of love's fair blandishments,
    Why show you sign of inward languishments?
        PEDRINGANO *showeth all to the* PRINCE [BALTHAZAR]
        and LORENZO, *placing them in secret* [*above the stage?*].
BEL-IMPERIA: My heart, sweet friend, is like a ship at sea;
    She wisheth port, where, riding all at ease,
    She may repair what stormy times have worn,
    And leaning on the shore may sing with joy
    That pleasure follows pain, and bliss annoy.
    Possession of thy love is th'only port
    Wherein my heart, with fears and hopes long toss'd,   720
    Each hour doth wish and long to make resort,

701   *ta'en:* taken   711   *chief contents:* major means of hap-
702   *sleight:* trickery, craft   piness
703   *in his fall:* in bringing him down   712   *blandishments:* allurements
710   *thoughts:* imaginings, 'wishful   714   *friend:* lover
      thinking'

There to repair the joys that it hath lost;
And sitting safe, to sing in Cupid's choir
That sweetest bliss is crown of love's desire.

BALTHAZAR [*above*]: O sleep, mine eyes, see not my love
   profan'd;
Be deaf, my ears, hear not my discontent;
Die, heart; another joys what thou deserv'st.

LORENZO [*above*]: Watch still, mine eyes, to see this love
   disjoin'd;
Hear still, mine ears, to hear them both lament;

730   Live, heart, to joy at fond Horatio's fall.

BEL-IMPERIA: Why stands Horatio speechless all this while?

HORATIO: The less I speak, the more I meditate.

BEL-IMPERIA: But whereon dost thou chiefly meditate?

HORATIO: On dangers past, and pleasures to ensue.

BALTHAZAR [*above*]: On pleasures past, and dangers to ensue.

BEL-IMPERIA: What dangers, and what pleasures dost thou
   mean?

HORATIO: Dangers of war, and pleasures of our love.

LORENZO [*above*]: Dangers of death, but pleasures none at all.

BEL-IMPERIA: Let dangers go, thy war shall be with me,

740   But such a war as breaks no bond of peace.
Speak thou fair words, I'll cross them with fair words,
Send thou sweet looks, I'll meet them with sweet looks;
Write loving lines, I'll answer loving lines;
Give me a kiss, I'll countercheck thy kiss;
Be this our warring peace, or peaceful war.

HORATIO: But, gracious Madam, then appoint the field
Where trial of this war shall first be made.

722	*repair:* replace, restore	730	*fond:* amorously foolish
723	*sing:* see note	741	*cross:* encounter, match
725	s.d. *above:* see note	744	*countercheck:* halt by interposing
727	*joys:* enjoys	747	*trial:* determination, 'testing'
728	*disjoin'd:* 'undone'		

BALTHAZAR [*above*]: Ambitious villain, how his boldness
    grows!
BEL-IMPERIA: Then be thy father's pleasant bower the field
    Where first we vow'd a mutual amity: 750
    The court were dangerous, that place is safe.
    Our hour shall be when Vesper gins to rise,
    That summons home distressful travailers.
    There none shall hear us but the harmless birds;
    Haply the gentle nightingale
    Shall carol us asleep ere we be ware,
    And singing with the prickle at her breast,
    Tell our delight and mirthful dalliance.
    Till then each hour will seem a year or more.
HORATIO: But, honey sweet and honourable love,   760
    Return we now into your father's sight;
    Dangerous suspicion waits on our delight.
LORENZO [*above*]: Aye, danger, mix'd with jealous despite
    Shall send thy soul into eternal night.
                        Exeunt.

ACT II SCENE 3

[*The Spanish court*]
Enter KING of Spain, Portingale AMBASSADOR, *the* DUKE
OF CASTILE *etc.*
KING: Brother of Castile, to the Prince's love
    What says your daughter Bel-imperia?

749 *bower:* leafy recess, arbour (see
     note)
750 *amity:* friendship, love
752 *Vesper:* the planet Venus, the
     'evening star'
     gins: begins
753 *distressful:* troubled, anxious
     travailers: labourers, those who
     travail (see note)

755 *Haply:* perhaps, maybe
757 *prickle:* thorn (see note)
758 *dalliance:* amorous play
763 *jealous:* vigilant, watchful (see
     note)
     despite: hatred

CASTILE: Although she coy it as becomes her kind,
　　　　And yet dissemble that she loves the Prince,
　　　　I doubt not, I, but she will stoop in time.
770　　And were she froward, which she will not be,
　　　　Yet herein shall she follow my advice,
　　　　Which is to love him or forgo my love.
KING: Then, Lord Ambassador of Portingale,
　　　　Advise thy King to make this marriage up,
　　　　For strengthening of our late confirmed league;
　　　　I know no better means to make us friends.
　　　　Her dowry shall be large and liberal:
　　　　Besides that, she is daughter and half heir
　　　　Unto our brother here, Don Cyprian,
780　　And shall enjoy the moiety of his land,
　　　　I'll grace her marriage with an uncle's gift —
　　　　And this it is: in case the match go forward,
　　　　The tribute which you pay shall be releas'd,
　　　　And if by Balthazar she have a son,
　　　　He shall enjoy the kingdom after us.
AMBASSADOR: I'll make the motion to my sovereign liege,
　　　　And work it if my counsel may prevail.
KING: Do so, my lord, and if he give consent,
　　　　I hope his presence here will honour us
790　　In celebration of the nuptial day,
　　　　And let himself determine of the time.
AMBASSADOR: Wilt please your grace command me aught
　　　　　　beside?
KING: Commend me to the King, and so farewell.

767　*coy it:* pretends to be indifferent
　　　her kind: her sex or nature
769　*stoop:* acquiesce, 'come to heel'
　　　(see note)
770　*froward:* awkward, perverse
774　*make . . . up:* arrange, settle

780　*the moiety of:* half share in
782　*in case:* provided that
786　*make the motion:* put the proposi-
　　　tion
787　*work it:* bring it off, have it
　　　agreed

But where's Prince Balthazar to take his leave?
AMBASSADOR: That is performed already, my good lord.
KING: Amongst the rest of what you have in charge,
   The Prince's ransom must not be forgot:
   That's none of mine, but his that took him prisoner,
   And well his forwardness deserves reward.
   It was Horatio, our Knight Marshal's son.   800
AMBASSADOR: Between us there's a price already pitch'd,
   And shall be sent with all convenient speed.
KING: Then once again farewell, my lord.
AMBASSADOR: Farewell, my lord of Castile and the rest.
                                                    Exit.

KING: Now, brother, you must take some little pains
   To win fair Bel-imperia from her will.
   Young virgins must be ruled by their friends;
   The Prince is amiable and loves her well;
   If she neglect him and forgo his love,
   She both will wrong her own estate and ours.   810
   Therefore, whiles I do entertain the Prince
   With greatest pleasure that our court affords,
   Endeavour you to win your daughter's thought.
   If she give back, all this will come to naught.
                                                    Exeunt.

ACT II   SCENE 4

[*The grounds of Hieronimo's house*]
Enter HORATIO, BEL-IMPERIA, *and* PEDRINGANO.
HORATIO: Now that the night begins with sable wings
   To over-cloud the brightness of the sun,

---

799   *forwardness:* zeal, initiative   814   *give back:* withdraws, pulls out,
801   *pitch'd:* fixed, determined   rejects him (see note)
806   *will:* wilful attitude   815   *sable:* black
813   *thought:* mind, 'fancy'

And that in darkness pleasures may be done,
Come, Bel-imperia, let us to the bower,
And there in safety pass a pleasant hour.

820 BEL-IMPERIA: I follow thee, my love, and will not back,
Although my fainting heart controls my soul.

HORATIO: Why, make you doubt of Pedringano's faith?

BEL-IMPERIA: No, he is as trusty as my second self:
Go, Pedringano, watch without the gate
And let us know if any make approach.

PEDRINGANO [aside]: Instead of watching, I'll deserve more
gold
By fetching Don Lorenzo to this match.

Exit PEDRINGANO.

HORATIO: What means my love?

BEL-IMPERIA: I know not what myself;
And yet my heart foretells me some mischance.

830 HORATIO: Sweet, say not so; fair fortune is our friend,
And heavens have shut up day to pleasure us.
The stars, thou seest, hold back their twinkling shine,
And Luna hides herself to pleasure us.

BEL-IMPERIA: Thou hast prevail'd; I'll conquer my
misdoubt,
And in thy love and counsel drown my fear:
I fear no more; love now is all my thoughts:
Why sit we not? for pleasure asketh ease.

HORATIO: The more thou sitt'st within these leafy bowers,
The more will Flora deck it with her flowers.

840 BEL-IMPERIA: Aye, but if Flora spy Horatio here,
Her jealous eye will think I sit too near.

---

821 *controls:* curbs, restrains
824 *without:* outside
827 *match:* encounter
828 *What means* etc.: i.e. what does
     your behaviour signify?

833 *Luna:* the moon
834 *misdoubt:* misgiving, distrust
837 *asketh:* requires, demands
839 *Flora:* Roman goddess of
     flowers

HORATIO: Hark, Madam, how the birds record by night,
  For joy that Bel-imperia sits in sight.
BEL-IMPERIA: No, Cupid counterfeits the nightingale,
  To frame sweet music to Horatio's tale.
HORATIO: If Cupid sing, then Venus is not far;
  Aye, thou art Venus or some fairer star.
BEL-IMPERIA: If I be Venus thou must needs be Mars;
  And where Mars reigneth there must needs be war[s].
HORATIO: Then thus begin our wars: put forth thy hand,   850
  That it may combat with my ruder hand.
BEL-IMPERIA: Set forth thy foot to try the push of mine.
HORATIO: But first my looks shall combat against thine.
BEL-IMPERIA: Then ward thyself; I dart this kiss at thee.
  [*They kiss.*]
HORATIO: Thus I retort the dart thou threw'st at me.
  [*They kiss.*]
BEL-IMPERIA: Nay, then, to gain the glory of the field,
  My twining arms shall yoke and make thee yield.
  [*They embrace.*]
HORATIO: Nay, then, my arms are large and strong withal:
  Thus elms by vines are compass'd till they fall.
BEL-IMPERIA: Oh, let me go, for in my troubled eyes   860
  Now may'st thou read that life in passion dies.
HORATIO: Oh, stay awhile and I will die with thee;
  So shalt thou yield, and yet have conquered me.
  [*A sound off.*]
BEL-IMPERIA: Who's there? Pedringano? We are betray'd!
  Enter LORENZO, BALTHAZAR, SERBERINE,
  PEDRINGANO, *disguised.*

842	*record:* warble, sing	855	*retort:* repay, return
845	*frame:* contrive, compose	858	*large:* broad, ample
851	*ruder:* coarser, clumsier		*withal:* besides, as well
854	*ward:* shield, guard	861	*dies:* see note

LORENZO [*to* BALTHAZAR]: My lord, away with her, take her
    aside!
[*To* HORATIO] O sir, forbear, your valour is already tried.
    Quickly dispatch, my masters.
        They hang him [HORATIO] *in the arbour.*
HORATIO: What, will you murder me?
LORENZO: Aye, thus, and thus; these are the fruits of love.
        They stab him.
870 BEL-IMPERIA: Oh, save his life and let me die for him!
    Oh, save him, brother, save him, Balthazar!
    I loved Horatio but he loved not me.
BALTHAZAR: But Balthazar loves Bel-imperia.
LORENZO: Although his life were still ambitious proud,
    Yet is he at the highest now he is dead.
BEL-IMPERIA: Murder! murder! Help, Hieronimo, help!
LORENZO: Come, stop her mouth; away with her!
                                    Exeunt.
        Enter HIERONIMO *in his shirt, etc.*
HIERONIMO: What outcries pluck me from my naked bed
    And chill my throbbing heart with trembling fear,
880 Which never danger yet could daunt before?
    Who calls Hieronimo? Speak, here I am:
    I did not slumber, therefore, 'twas no dream;
    No, no, it was some woman cried for help,
    And here within this garden did she cry;
    And in this garden must I rescue her.
    But stay, what murd'rous spectacle is this?
    A man hang'd up and all the murderers gone,
    And in my bower to lay the guilt on me:
    This place was made for pleasure, not for death.
        He cuts him down.

866   *tried:* proved (see note)   877   *stop:* gag, block
874   *ambitious proud:* arrogant in aspir-
      ing to honours

Those garments that he wears I oft have seen –   890
Alas, it is Horatio, my sweet son!
Oh, no, but he that whilom was my son.
Oh, was it thou that call'dst me from my bed?
Oh, speak if any spark of life remain!
I am thy father; who hath slain my son?
What savage monster, not of human kind,
Hath here been glutted with thy harmless blood
And left thy bloody corpse dishonour'd here,
For me amidst this dark and deathful shades
To drown thee with an ocean of my tears?   900
O heavens, why made you night to cover sin? –
By day this deed of darkness had not been.
O earth, why didst thou not in time devour
The vild profaner of this sacred bower?
O poor Horatio, what hadst thou misdone
To lose thy life ere life was new begun?
O wicked butcher, whatsoe'er thou wert,
How could thou strangle virtue and desert?
Aye me most wretched, that have lost my joy
In losing my Horatio, my sweet boy.   910
    Enter ISABELLA.
ISABELLA: My husband's absence makes my heart to throb:
    Hieronimo!
HIERONIMO: Here, Isabella, help me to lament,
    For sighs are stopp'd, and all my tears are spent.
ISABELLA: What world of grief! – My son Horatio?
    Oh, where's the author of this endless woe?
HIERONIMO: To know the author were some ease of grief,

892	*whilom:* once, formerly	906	*was new begun:* entered a new
899	*this:* these (see note)		phase
903	*in time:* at the right moment	913	*stopp'd:* obstructed, dammed up
904	*vild:* vile	915	*author:* causer
905	*misdone:* done wrong		

For in revenge my heart would find relief.

ISABELLA: Then is he gone? and is my son gone too?
Oh, gush out tears, fountains and floods of tears;
920 Blow sighs and raise an everlasting storm;
For outrage fits our cursed wretchedness.

HIERONIMO: Sweet lovely rose, ill-pluck'd before thy time;
Fair worthy son, not conquer'd but betray'd.
I'll kiss thee now, for words with tears are stay'd.
[*Kisses* HORATIO.]

ISABELLA: And I'll close up the glasses of his sight,
For once these eyes were only my delight.

HIERONIMO: See'st thou this handkercher besmear'd with
blood?
It shall not from me till I take revenge;
See'st thou those wounds that yet are bleeding fresh?
930 I'll not entomb them till I have reveng'd;
Then will I joy amidst my discontent,
Till then my sorrow never shall be spent.

ISABELLA: The Heavens are just, murder cannot be hid;
Time is the author both of truth and right,
And time will bring this treachery to light.

HIERONIMO: Meanwhile, good Isabella, cease thy plaints,
Or at the least dissemble them awhile,
So shall we sooner find the practice out,
And learn by whom all this was brought about.
940 Come, Isabel, now let us take him up,
   They take him up.
And bear him in from out this cursed place;
I'll say his dirge, singing fits not this case.

921	*outrage:* extravagant behaviour	930	*entomb:* inter, bury
924	*stay'd:* held back (see note)	934	*author:* agent, originator
925	*glasses of his sight:* eyes	936	*plaints:* lamentations
927	*handkercher:* kerchief or small	938	*practice:* conspiracy
	handkerchief (see note)	942	*dirge:* funeral hymn (see note)

O aliquis mihi quas pulchrum ver educat herbas
   HIERONIMO *sets his breast unto his sword.*
Misceat, et nostro detur medicina dolori;
Aut, si qui faciunt animis oblivia succos
Praebeat; ipse metam magnum quaecunque per orbem
Gramina Sol pulchras effert in luminis oras;
Ipse bibam quicquid meditatur saga veneni,
Quicquid et herbarum vi caeca nenia nectit:
Omnia perpetiar, lethum quoque, dum semel omnis   950
Noster in extincto moriatur pectora sensus.
Ergo tuos oculos nunquam mea vita, videbo,
Et tua perpetuus sepelivit lumina somnus?
Emoriar tecum: sic, sic juvat ire sub umbras.
At tamen absistam properato cedere letho,
Ne mortem vindicta tuam tum nulla sequatur.
   Here he throws it [*the sword*] *away from him and* [*with*
   ISABELLA] *bears the body away.*
GHOST: Brought'st thou me hither to increase my pain?
   I look'd that Balthazar should have been slain:
   But 'tis my friend Horatio that is slain,
   And they abuse fair Bel-imperia,   960
   On whom I doted more than all the world
   Because she lov'd me more than all the world.
REVENGE: Thou talk'st of harvest when the corn is green;
   The end is crown of every work well done:
   The sickle comes not till the corn be ripe.
   Be still, and ere I lead thee from this place,
   I'll show thee Balthazar in heavy case.

943–56 *O aliquis* etc.: see note   961 *doted:* loved to excess
958 *look'd:* expected, anticipated   967 *in heavy case:* 'in a sorry state'

ACT III SCENE I

[*The court of Portugal. A stake prepared*]
Enter VICEROY *of Portingale,* NOBLES, VILLUPPO.

VICEROY: Infortunate condition of kings,
  Seated amidst so many helpless doubts!
970 First we are plac'd upon extremest height,
  And oft supplanted with exceeding heat,
  But ever subject to the wheel of chance;
  And at our highest never joy we so,
  As we both doubt and dread our overthrow.
  So striveth not the waves with sundry winds,
  As Fortune toileth in the affairs of kings,
  That would be fear'd, yet fear to be belov'd,
  Sith fear or love to kings is flattery.
  For instance, lordings, look upon your King,
980 By hate deprived of his dearest son,
  The only hope of our successive line.
FIRST NOBLEMAN: I had not thought that Alexandro's heart
  Had been envenom'd with such extreme hate:
  But now I see that words have several works,
  And there's no credit in the countenance.
VILLUPPO: No, for, my lord, had you beheld the train
  That feigned love had colour'd in his looks,
  When he in camp consorted Balthazar,
  Far more inconstant had you thought the sun
990 That hourly coasts the centre of the earth

---

968 *Infortunate:* luckless, ill-fortuned
969 *seated:* positioned
  helpless: without remedy
  doubts: apprehensions, dangers
971 *heat:* strife, fury
978 *sith:* since
979 *For instance:* As an example
  lordings: my lords
981 *successive line:* line of succession

984 *have several works:* can convey a
  number of lines of conduct (see
  note)
985 *credit:* credence, reliability
986 *train:* guile, deceit
987 *colour'd:* counterfeited
988 *consorted:* attended, associated
  with

Than Alexandro's purpose to the Prince.
VICEROY: No more, Villuppo; thou hast said enough,
  And with thy words thou slay'st our wounded thoughts.
  Nor shall I longer dally with the world,
  Procrastinating Alexandro's death:
  Go some of you and fetch the traitor forth,
  That as he is condemned he may die.
       Enter ALEXANDRO *with a* NOBLEMAN *and halberts.*
SECOND NOBLEMAN: In such extremes will nought but
       patience serve.
ALEXANDRO: But in extremes what patience shall I use?
  Nor discontents it me to leave the world,   1000
  With whom there nothing can prevail but wrong.
SECOND NOBLEMAN: Yet hope the best.
ALEXANDRO: 'Tis Heaven is my hope.
  As for the earth it is too much infect
  To yield me hope of any of her mould.
VICEROY: Why linger ye? Bring forth that daring fiend,
  And let him die for his accursed deed.
ALEXANDRO: Not that I fear the extremity of death
  – For nobles cannot stoop to servile fear –
  Do I, O King, thus discontented live.
  But this, O this, torments my labouring soul,   1010
  That thus I die suspected of a sin
  Whereof, as Heavens have known my secret thoughts,
  So am I free from this suggestion.
VICEROY: No more, I say! To the tortures! When?
  Bind him, and burn his body in those flames,
       They bind him to the stake.

991 *purpose to:* intention towards
995 *Procrastinating:* delaying
997 s.d. *halberts:* halberdiers (see note)
998 *extremes:* extreme circumstances
1003 *infect:* corrupted, diseased
1004 *mould:* shaping, making (i.e. of earth) (see note)
1013 *suggestion:* false accusation

That shall prefigure those unquenched fires
Of Phlegethon prepared for his soul.

ALEXANDRO: My guiltless death will be aveng'd on thee,
On thee, Villuppo, that hath malic'd thus,
1020   Or for thy meed hast falsely me accus'd.

VILLUPPO: Nay Alexandro, if thou menace me,
I'll lend a hand to send thee to the lake
Where those thy words shall perish with thy works,
Injurious traitor, monstrous homicide!

Enter AMBASSADOR.

AMBASSADOR: Stay! Hold a while,
And here, with pardon of his Majesty,
Lay hands upon Villuppo!

VICEROY: Ambassador,
What news hath urg'd this sudden entrance?

AMBASSADOR: Know, sovereign lord, that Balthazar doth
live!

1030 VICEROY: What say'st thou? Liveth Balthazar our son?

AMBASSADOR: Your Highness' son, Lord Balthazar, doth
live;
And, well entreated in the court of Spain,
Humbly commends him to your Majesty.
These eyes beheld, and these my followers'
With these the letters of the King's commends

Gives him letters.

Are happy witnesses of his Highness' health.

The [VICEROY] *looks on the letters, and proceeds.*

VICEROY [*reading*]: 'Thy son doth live, your tribute is receiv'd,
Thy peace is made, and we are satisfied:
The rest resolve upon as things propos'd

1019 *malic'd:* entertained malice
1020 *meed:* gain, reward
1022 *lake:* Avernus, a lake in Hell
1024 *homicide:* killer, murderer

1032 *entreated:* treated
1035 *commends:* greetings, compliments
1039 *resolve upon:* decide on

For both our honours and thy benefit.'   1040
AMBASSADOR: These are his Highness' farther articles.
    He gives him more letters.
VICEROY [*to* VILLUPPO]: Accursed wretch, to intimate these
    ills
  Against the life and reputation
  Of noble Alexandro. [*To* ALEXANDRO] Come, my lord,
  Let him unbind thee that is bound to death,
  To make a quital for thy discontent.
    They unbind him.
ALEXANDRO: Dread lord, in kindness you could do no less,
  Upon report of such a damned fact;
  But thus we see our innocence hath sav'd
  The hopeless life which thou, Villuppo, sought   1050
  By thy suggestions to have massacred.
VICEROY: Say, false Villuppo, wherefore didst thou thus
  Falsely betray Lord Alexandro's life?
  Him whom thou knowest that no unkindness else,
  But even the slaughter of our dearest son,
  Could once have mov'd us to have misconceiv'd.
ALEXANDRO: Say, treacherous Villuppo, tell the King,
  Wherein hath Alexandro us'd thee ill?
VILLUPPO: Rent with remembrance of so foul a deed,
  My guilty soul submits me to thy doom: 1060
  For not for Alexandro's injuries,
  But for reward, and hope to be preferr'd,
  Thus have I shamelessly hazarded his life.

1041	*articles:* terms, points	1048	*fact:* crime
1042	*intimate:* proclaim publicly	1051	*suggestions:* false accusations
	ills: evils	1056	*misconceiv'd:* suspected
1046	*a quital:* reparation, amends	1060	*doom:* judgement
	discontent: vexation	1062	*preferr'd:* promoted, advanced
1047	*in kindness:* i.e. by virtue of your office (see note)		

VICEROY: Which, villain, shall be ransom'd with thy death,
 And not so mean a torment as we here
 Devis'd for him, who thou said'st slew our son;
 But with the bitterest torments and extremes
 That may be yet invented for thine end.
   ALEXANDRO *seems to entreat.*
 Entreat me not; go, take the traitor hence.
    Exit VILLUPPO [*guarded*]
1070 And Alexandro, let us honour thee
 With public notice of thy loyalty.
 To end those things articulated here
 By our great lord, the mighty King of Spain,
 We with our council will deliberate:
 Come, Alexandro, keep us company.

ACT III   SCENE 2

[*Near Lorenzo's palace*]
Enter HIERONIMO.

HIERONIMO: O eyes, no eyes, but fountains fraught with
  tears;
 O life, no life, but lively form of death;
 O world, no world, but mass of public wrongs,
 Confus'd and fill'd with murder and misdeeds.
1080 O sacred Heavens, if this unhallow'd deed,
 If this inhuman and barbarous attempt,
 If this incomparable murder thus
 Of [son of] mine, but now no more my son,
 Shall unreveal'd and unrevenged pass,

1065	*mean:* moderate, lenient	1077	*lively:* lifelike
1067	*extremes:* stringent punishments	1078	*mass:* dense aggregation
1072	*articulated:* listed as items	1079	*Confus'd:* disordered, unruly
1076	*fraught:* filled	1082	*incomparable:* without precedent

How should we term your dealings to be just,
If you unjustly deal with those that in your justice trust?
The night, sad secretary to my moans,
With direful visions wake my vexed soul,
And with the wounds of my distressful son
Solicit me for notice of his death.   1090
The ugly fiends do sally forth of Hell,
And frame my steps to unfrequented paths,
And fear my heart with fierce inflamed thoughts.
The cloudy day my discontents records,
Early begins to register my dreams,
And drive me forth to seek the murderer.
Eyes, life, world, Heavens, Hell, night and day,
See, search, show, send, some man, some mean, that may —
    A letter falleth [*onto the stage*].
What's here? a letter? tush, it is not so —
A letter written to Hieronimo!   1100
    Red ink.
'For want of ink receive this bloody writ:
Me hath my hapless brother hid from thee;
Revenge thyself on Balthazar and him,
For these were they that murdered thy son.
Hieronimo, revenge Horatio's death,
And better fare than Bel-imperia doth.'
What means this unexpected miracle?
My son slain by Lorenzo and the Prince?
What cause had they Horatio to malign?

1087 *secretary:* confidant
1088 *direful:* terrible, dreadful
1089 *distressful:* badly distressed
1090 *Solicit:* importunes, entreats
      notice: knowledge
1092 *frame:* direct
1093 *fear:* frighten
1095 *register:* set down
1098 *mean:* means
1101 *writ:* document, writing
1102 *hapless:* ill-luck-bearing, ill-omened (see note)
1109 *malign:* regard with envy or hate

1110   Or what might move thee, Bel-imperia,
        To accuse thy brother, had he been the mean?
        Hieronimo, beware; thou art betray'd,
        And to entrap thy life this train is laid.
        Advise thee therefore; be not credulous:
        This is devised to endanger thee,
        That thou by this Lorenzo shouldst accuse,
        And he, for thy dishonour done, should draw
        Thy life in question, and thy name in hate.
        Dear was the life of my beloved son,
1120   And of his death behoves me be reveng'd:
        Then hazard not thine own, Hieronimo,
        But live t'effect thy resolution.
        I therefore will by circumstances try
        What I can gather to confirm this writ,
        And hark'ning near the Duke of Castile's house,
        Close if I can with Bel-imperia,
        To listen more, but nothing to bewray.

        Enter PEDRINGANO.

        Now, Pedringano?
PEDRINGANO: Now, Hieronimo?
HIERONIMO: Where's thy lady?
PEDRINGANO: I know not; here's my lord.

        Enter LORENZO.

LORENZO: How now! Who's this? Hieronimo?
1130 HIERONIMO: My lord.
PEDRINGANO: He asketh for my Lady Bel-imperia.

1111	*mean:* agent, instrument	1123 *by circumstances:* see note
1113	*train:* trap, plot	*try:* ascertain, determine
1114	*Advise thee:* consider, reflect	1126 *close:* contract, come to an agree-
1117	*done:* i.e. done him	ment
	draw: put, bring	1127 *bewray:* let out, disclose
1121	*thine own:* i.e. life	
1122	*resolution:* what you have re-solved upon	

LORENZO: What to do, Hieronimo? The Duke my father hath
  Upon some disgrace awhile remov'd her hence,
  But if it be aught I may inform her of,
  Tell me, Hieronimo, and I'll let her know it.
HIERONIMO: Nay, nay, my lord, I thank you, it shall not need;
  I had a suit unto her, but too late,
  And her disgrace makes me unfortunate.
LORENZO: Why so, Hieronimo? Use me.
HIERONIMO: Oh no, my lord, I dare not; it must not be.   1140
  I humbly thank your lordship.
LORENZO: Why then, farewell.
HIERONIMO: My grief no heart, my thoughts no tongue, can tell.
          Exit.
LORENZO: Come hither, Pedringano, see'st thou this?
PEDRINGANO: My lord, I see it, and suspect it too.
LORENZO: This is that damned villain Serberine,
  That hath, I fear, reveal'd Horatio's death.
PEDRINGANO: My lord, he could not, 'twas so lately done,
  And since he hath not left my company.
LORENZO: Admit he have not, his condition's such
  As fear or flattering words may make him false;   1150
  I know his humour, and therewith repent
  That e'er I used him in this enterprise.
  But Pedringano, to prevent the worst,
  And cause I know thee secret as my soul,
  Here for thy further satisfaction take thou this
      Gives him more gold.

1139	*Use me:* employ me (in your suit)	1149	*condition:* nature, personality
1146	*reveal'd:* i.e. the details of	1151	*humour:* tendency, temperament
1147	*lately:* recently	1152	*used:* employed, made use of
		1154	*cause:* because

And harken to me. Thus it is devis'd:
This night thou must, and prithee so resolve,
Meet Serberine at St Luigi's Park —
Thou know'st 'tis here hard behind the house —
1160   There take thy stand, and see thou strike him sure,
For die he must, if we do mean to live.

PEDRINGANO: But how shall Serberine be there, my lord?

LORENZO: Let me alone; I'll send to him to meet
The Prince and me, where thou must do this deed.

PEDRINGANO: It shall be done, my lord, it shall be done,
And I'll go arm myself to meet him there.

LORENZO: When things shall alter, as I hope they will,
Then shalt thou mount for this; thou know'st my mind.

                                    Exit PEDRINGANO.

    Che le Jeron!
        Enter PAGE.

PAGE: My lord?

LORENZO: Go, sirrah, to Serberine,
1170   And bid him forthwith meet the Prince and me
At St Luigi's Park, behind the house,
This evening, boy.

PAGE: I go, my lord.

LORENZO: But, sirrah, let the hour be eight o'clock.
Bid him not fail.

PAGE: I fly, my lord.
                                    Exit.

LORENZO: Now to confirm the complot thou has cast
Of all these practices, I'll spread the watch,
Upon precise commandment from the King,

1163   *Let me alone:* leave it to me
1168   *mount:* climb socially (see note)
1169   *Che le Jeron:* see note
1175   *confirm:* strengthen, support
        complot: conspiracy
        cast: arranged, affected

1176   *practices:* intrigues, deceptions
        spread the watch: distribute the
        watchmen

Strongly to guard the place where Pedringano
This night shall murder hapless Serberine.
Thus must we work that will avoid distrust;   1180
Thus must we practise to prevent mishap;
And thus one ill another must expulse.
This sly inquiry of Hieronimo
For Bel-imperia breeds suspicion,
And this suspicion bodes a further ill.
As for myself, I know my secret fault,
And so do they, but I have dealt for them.
They that for coin their souls endangered
To save my life, for coin shall venture theirs:
And better 'tis that base companions die   1190
Than by their life to hazard our good haps.
Nor shall they live for me, to fear their faith:
I'll trust myself, myself shall be my friend,
For die they shall; slaves are ordain'd to no other end.

Exit.

ACT III SCENE 3

[*St Luigi's park*]
Enter PEDRINGANO *with a pistol.*
PEDRINGANO: Now, Pedringano, bid thy pistol hold,
And hold on, Fortune! once more favour me;
Give but success to mine attempting spirit,
And let me shift for taking of mine aim.
Here is the gold, this is the gold propos'd;

1181 *practise:* scheme, contrive
1182 *expulse:* expel
1190 *companions:* 'nobodies', 'low
      types'
1191 *good haps:* chances of success,
      good luck
1192 *faith:* trustworthiness

1194 *slaves:* men beneath contempt,
      'scum'
1195 *hold:* work accurately, correctly
1196 *hold on:* remain constant
1198 *let me shift:* leave it to me
1199 *propos'd:* looked forward to, an-
      ticipated

1200   It is no dream that I adventure for,
       But Pedringano is possess'd thereof.
       And he that would not strain his conscience
       For him that thus his liberal purse hath stretch'd,
       Unworthy such a favour may he fail,
       And wishing, want when such as I prevail.
       As for the fear of apprehension,
       I know, if need should be, my noble lord
       Will stand between me and ensuing harms.
       Besides, this place is free from all suspect:
1210   Here therefore will I stay and take my stand.
           Enter the WATCH.
   1 WATCH: I wonder much to what intent it is
       That we are thus expressly charged to watch?
   2 WATCH: 'Tis by commandment in the King's own name.
   3 WATCH: But we were never wont to watch and ward
       So near the Duke his brother's house before.
   2 WATCH: Content yourself, stand close, there's somewhat
       in't.
                           [*The* WATCH *retire.*]
           Enter SERBERINE.
SERBERINE: Here, Serberine, attend and stay thy pace,
       For here did Don Lorenzo's page appoint
       That thou by his command should'st meet with him.
1220   How fit a place, if one were so dispos'd,
       Methinks this corner is, to close with one.
PEDRINGANO: Here comes the bird that I must seize upon.

1200   *adventure:* take risks
1201   *But Pedringano* etc.: i.e. 'I actu-
       ally have the reward already'
1204   *fail:* become bankrupt
1209   *suspect:* anything to create suspi-
       cion
1212   *expressly:* explicitly, positively

1214   *watch and ward:* guard, patrol
       (see note)
1216   *close:* hidden
1217   *stay thy pace:* stop your walk
1221   *close with:* grapple, 'come to
       grips'

Now, Pedringano, or never, play the man!

SERBERINE: I wonder that his lordship stays so long,
 Or wherefore should he send for me so late?

PEDRINGANO: For this, Serberine, and thou shalt ha't.

   Shoots the dag.

 So, there he lies; my promise is perform'd.

   The WATCH [*appear*].

1 WATCH: Hark, gentlemen, this is a pistol shot!

2 WATCH: And here's one slain; stay the murderer!

PEDRINGANO: Now, by the sorrows of the souls in Hell,   1230

   He strives with the WATCH.

 Who first lays hand on me, I'll be his priest! [*The* WATCH
   subdue him.]

3 WATCH: Sirrah, confess, and therein play the priest:
 Why hast thou thus unkindly kill'd the man?

PEDRINGANO: Why, because he walk'd abroad so late.

3 WATCH: Come, sir, you had been better kept your bed
 Than have committed this misdeed so late.

2 WATCH: Come, to the Marshal's with the murderer.

1 WATCH: On to Hieronimo's; help me here
 To bring the murder'd body with us too.

PEDRINGANO: Hieronimo! Carry me before whom you will;   1240
 Whate'er he be I'll answer him and you,
 And do your worst, for I defy you all.

                              Exeunt.

1226 *ha't:* have it
      s.d. *dag:* a heavy pistol

1229 *stay:* detain, arrest

1231 *I'll be his priest!:* I'll kill him
      (see note)

1233 *unkindly:* in an inhuman manner
      (see note)

1234 *abroad:* in the open air, 'outside'

ACT III SCENE 4

[*Lorenzo's palace*]
Enter LORENZO *and* BALTHAZAR.

BALTHAZAR: How now, my lord, what makes you rise so
    soon?

LORENZO: Fear of preventing our mishaps too late.

BALTHAZAR: What mischief is it that we not mistrust?

LORENZO: Our greatest ills we least mistrust, my lord,
    And inexpected harms do hurt us most.

BALTHAZAR: Why, tell me, Don Lorenzo, tell me, man,
    If aught concerns our honour and your own?

1250 LORENZO: Nor you nor me, my lord, but both in one.
    For I suspect, and the presumption's great,
    That by those base confederates in our fault,
    Touching the death of Don Horatio,
    We are betray'd to old Hieronimo.

BALTHAZAR: Betray'd, Lorenzo? tush, it cannot be.

LORENZO: A guilty conscience, urged with the thought
    Of former evils, easily cannot err:
    I am persuaded, and dissuade me not,
    That all's revealed to Hieronimo.

1260   And therefore know that I have cast it thus –
      [*Enter* PAGE.]
    But here's the page; how now, what news with thee?

PAGE: My lord, Serberine is slain.

BALTHAZAR: Who? Serberine, my man?

PAGE: Your Highness' man, my lord.

1244 *preventing:* forestalling
1245 *not mistrust:* 'haven't already anticipated'
1246 *mistrust:* suspect the existence of
1247 *inexpected:* unexpected, unlooked for
1251 *presumption:* assumption
1252 *base:* lowly, mean
    confederates: accomplices
    fault: crime
1256 *urged:* provoked, stimulated
1260 *cast:* planned, devised

LORENZO: Speak, page, who murder'd him?

PAGE: He that is apprehended for the fact.

LORENZO: Who?

PAGE: Pedringano.

BALTHAZAR: Is Serberine slain, that loved his lord so well?
  Injurious villain, murderer of his friend!

LORENZO: Hath Pedringano murder'd Serberine?   1270
  My lord, let me entreat you to take the pains
  To exasperate and hasten his revenge
  With your complaints unto my lord the King.
  This their dissension breeds a greater doubt.

BALTHAZAR: Assure thee, Don Lorenzo, he shall die,
  Or else his Highness hardly shall deny.
  Meanwhile, I'll haste the Marshal Sessions,
  For die he shall for this his damned deed.

Exit BALTHAZAR.

LORENZO: Why so, this fits our former policy,
  And this experience bids the wise to deal.   1280
  I lay the plot, he prosecutes the point;
  I set the trap, he breaks the worthless twigs,
  And sees not that wherewith the bird was lim'd.
  Thus hopeful men that mean to hold their own
  Must look like fowlers to their dearest friends.
  He runs to kill whom I have holp to catch,
  And no man knows it was my reaching fatch.
  'Tis hard to trust unto a multitude,

1266 *fact:* crime	1279 *policy:* crafty stratagem (see note)
1269 *Injurious:* wickedly hurtful	
1272 *exasperate:* intensify, increase the severity of	1281 *prosecutes:* seeks to bring about
	point: resolution, culmination
1273 *complaints:* expressions of grievance	1283 *lim'd:* trapped, caught (see note)
1274 *doubt:* anxiety	1286 *holp:* helped
1276 *hardly:* harshly, unreasonably (see note)	1287 *reaching:* far-seeing, shrewd
	fatch: trick, contrivance

Or anyone, in mine opinion,
1290   When men themselves their secrets will reveal.
    Enter a MESSENGER *with a letter.*
LORENZO: Boy!
PAGE: My lord?
LORENZO: [*Indicating* MESSENGER] What's he?
MESSENGER: I have a letter to your lordship.
LORENZO: From whence?
MESSENGER: From Pedringano that's imprison'd.
LORENZO: So, he is in prison then?
MESSENGER: Aye, my good lord.
LORENZO: What would he with us? [*Reads*] He writes us here
To stand good lord and help him in distress.
Tell him I have his letters, know his mind,
And what we may let him assure him of.
1300   Fellow, begone: my boy shall follow thee.
                Exit MESSENGER.
This works like wax; yet once more try thy wits:
Boy, go convey this purse to Pedringano;
Thou know'st the prison, closely give it him:
And be advis'd that none be there about.
Bid him be merry still, but secret;
And though the Marshal Sessions be today,
Bid him not doubt of his delivery.
Tell him his pardon is already sign'd,
And thereon bid him boldly be resolv'd.
1310   For were he ready to be turned off
(As 'tis my will the uttermost be tried)

1297   *stand good lord:* support him as a
       protector
1301   *works like wax:* goes the way I
       intend (see note)
1303   *closely:* secretly
1304   *be advis'd:* be careful, make sure
1305   *secret:* circumspect, uncommuni-
       cative

1309   *resolv'd:* convinced, satisfied
1310   *turned off:* hanged (see note)
1311   *uttermost:* the most extreme pen-
       alty
       tried: selected

Thou with his pardon shalt attend him still;
Show him this box, tell him his pardon's in't,
But open't not, and if thou lov'st thy life:
But let him wisely keep his hopes unknown,
He shall not want while Don Lorenzo lives:
Away!

PAGE: I go, my lord; I run.

LORENZO: But, sirrah, see that this be cleanly done.

                     Exit PAGE.

Now stands our fortune on a tickle point,
And now or never ends Lorenzo's doubts.   1320
One only thing is uneffected yet,
And that's to see the executioner –
But to what end? I list not trust the air
With utterance of our pretence therein,
For fear the privy whisp'ring of the wind
Convey our words amongst unfriendly ears,
That lie too open to advantages.
E quel che voglio io, nessun lo sa;
Intendo io; quel mi basterà.

                    Exit.

ACT III SCENE 5

Enter PAGE *with the box.*

PAGE: My master hath forbidden me to look in   1330
    this box, and by my troth 'tis likely, if he had
    not warned me, I should not have had so much idle
    time: for we men's-kind in our minority are like

1314	*and if:* if	1327	*advantages:* taking advantage
1318	*cleanly:* efficiently (see note)	1328	*E quel* etc.: and what I desire,
1319	*tickle:* precarious, insecure		nobody knows; I understand,
1320	*doubts:* fears		that's enough for me
1323	*I list not:* I don't choose to	1333	*men's-kind:* male creatures
1324	*pretence:* false purpose		*minority:* while under age

women in their uncertainty: that they are most
forbidden, they will soonest attempt. So I now.
    [*Looks in box.*]
By my bare honesty, here's nothing but
the bare empty box. Were it not sin against
secrecy, I would say it were a piece of
gentlemanlike knavery. I must go to Pedringano,
1340   and tell him his pardon is in this box; nay, I
would have sworn it, had I not seen the contrary.
I cannot choose but smile to think how the villain
will flout the gallows, scorn the audience, and
descant on the hangman, and all presuming of his
pardon from hence. Will't not be an odd jest for
me to stand and grace every jest he makes, pointing
my finger at this box: as who would say, 'Mock on,
here's thy warrant'? Is't not a scurvy jest, that a man
should jest himself to death? Alas, poor
1350   Pedringano, I am in a sort sorry for thee, but if I
should be hanged with thee, I cannot weep.
                                        Exit.

ACT III SCENE 6

    [*The Marshal's Sessions. A gallows prepared*]
    Enter HIERONIMO *and the* DEPUTY.
HIERONIMO: Thus must we toil in other men's extremes,
    That know not how to remedy our own;
    And do them justice, when injustly we,

1334 *uncertainty:* fickle nature	1348 *scurvy:* shabby, 'dirty'
1336 *bare:* meagre, simple	1350 *in a sort:* in a way
1343 *flout:* mock	1351 s.d. DEPUTY: Knight Marshal's
1344 *descant on:* 'go on about', 'give a	assistant
commentary on'	1352 *extremes:* crises, dire circum-
1346 *grace:* embellish	stances

For all our wrongs, can compass no redress.
But shall I never live to see the day
That I may come, by justice of the Heavens,
To know the cause that may my cares allay?
This toils my body, this consumeth age,
That only I to all men just must be,   1360
And neither gods nor men be just to me.
DEPUTY: Worthy Hieronimo, your office asks
    A care to punish such as do transgress.
HIERONIMO: So is't my duty to regard his death,
    Who when he liv'd deserv'd my dearest blood;
    But come, for that we came for let's begin,
    For here lies that which bids me to be gone.

    Enter OFFICERS, [PAGE, *the* HANGMAN] *and*
        PEDRINGANO, *with a letter in his hand, bound* [*and guarded*].

DEPUTY: Bring forth the prisoner, for the court is set.
PEDRINGANO: Gramercy, boy, but it was time to come,
    For I had written to my lord anew   1370
    A nearer matter that concerneth him,
    For fear his lordship had forgotten me;
    But sith he hath rememb'red me so well —
    Come, come, come on, when shall we to this gear?
HIERONIMO: Stand forth, thou monster, murderer of men,
    And here, for satisfaction of the world,
    Confess thy folly and repent thy fault,
    For there's thy place of execution.

1355	*compass:* bring about, effect	1369	*Gramercy:* thank goodness!
1358	*the cause:* the facts of the matter	1371	*nearer:* more vital
1359	*toils:* wearies, fatigues	1373	*sith:* since
	consumeth age: wastes, devours my life	1374	*to this gear:* get down to this business
1362	*asks:* requires, demands	1376	*for satisfaction:* in order to satisfy, atone to
1364	*regard:* concern myself with, have an eye to	1377	*fault:* crime
1365	*deserv'd:* was worthy of		

PEDRINGANO: This is short work! Well, to your Marshalship
1380 First I confess, nor fear I death therefore,
I am the man, 'twas I slew Serberine.
But, sir, then you think this shall be the place
Where we shall satisfy you for this gear?

DEPUTY: Aye, Pedringano.

PEDRINGANO: Now I think not so.

HIERONIMO: Peace, impudent, for thou shalt find it so.
For blood with blood shall while I sit as judge
Be satisfied, and the law discharg'd.
And though myself cannot receive the like,
Yet will I see that others have their right.
1390 Dispatch, the fault's approved and confess'd,
And by our law he is condemn'd to die.

HANGMAN: Come on, sir, are you ready?

PEDRINGANO: To do what, my fine officious knave?

HANGMAN: To go to this gear.

PEDRINGANO: O sir, you are too forward; thou would'st
fain furnish me with a halter, to disfurnish me
of my habit. So I should go out of this gear,
my raiment, into that gear, the rope. But hangman,
now I spy your knavery; I'll not change without boot,
1400 that's flat.

HANGMAN: Come, sir.

PEDRINGANO: So then I must up?

HANGMAN: No remedy.

PEDRINGANO: Yes, but there shall be for my coming down.

1379 *This is short work!*: i.e. 'you
don't hang about!'
1383 *satisfy you*: make expiation to
you
gear: business, 'little matter'
1387 *discharg'd*: executed
1390 *Dispatch*: hurry up
approved: proved

1394 *this gear*: i.e. the hanging
1395 *forward*: presumptuous, eager
1396 *disfurnish*: divest, strip
1397 *habit*: clothing (see note)
1398 *gear*: 'affair'
1399 *knavery*: crafty trick
without boot: without remedy,
compensation

HANGMAN: Indeed, here's a remedy for that.

PEDRINGANO: How? Be turned off?

HANGMAN: Aye, truly; come, are you ready? I pray, sir, dispatch; the day goes away.

PEDRINGANO: What, do you hang by the hour? If you do, I may chance to break your old custom.   1410

HANGMAN: Faith, you have reason, for I am like to break your young neck.

PEDRINGANO: Dost thou mock me, hangman? Pray God I be not preserved to break your knave's pate for this.

HANGMAN: Alas, sir, you are a foot too low to reach it, and I hope you will never grow so high while I am in the office.

PEDRINGANO: Sirrah, dost see yonder boy with the box in his hand?   1420

HANGMAN: What, he that points to it with his finger?

PEDRINGANO: Aye, that companion.

HANGMAN: I know him not, but what of him?

PEDRINGANO: Do'st thou think to live till his old doublet will make thee a new truss?

HANGMAN: Aye, and many a fair year after, to truss up many an honester man than either thou or he.

PEDRINGANO: What hath he in his box as thou think'st?

HANGMAN: Faith, I cannot tell, nor I care not greatly. Methinks you should rather hearken to your soul's health.   1430

PEDRINGANO: Why, sirrah hangman? I take it that that is good for the body is likewise good for the soul; and it may be, in that box is balm for both.

1406	*turned off:* hanged	1425	*truss:* a tight jacket
1409	*by the hour:* at fixed times	1426	*truss up:* hang, 'string up'
1414	*pate:* head	1430	*hearken to:* attend to
1422	*that companion:* 'my mate'	1434	*balm:* a soothing restorative

HANGMAN: Well, thou art even the merriest piece of man's
    flesh that e'er groaned at my office door.

PEDRINGANO: Is your roguery become an 'office' with a
    knave's name?

HANGMAN: Aye, and that shall all they witness that see you
1440   seal it with a thief's name.

PEDRINGANO: I prithee, request this good company to pray
    with me.

HANGMAN: Aye, marry sir, this is a good motion; my masters,
    you see here's a good fellow.

PEDRINGANO: Nay, nay, now I remember me, let them alone
    till some other time, for now I have no great need.

HIERONIMO: I have not seen a wretch so impudent:
    O monstrous times where murder's set so light,
    And where the soul that should be shrin'd in Heaven
1450   Solely delights in interdicted things,
    Still wand'ring in the thorny passages –
    That intercepts itself of happiness!
    Murder, O bloody monster, God forbid
    A fault so foul should scape unpunished!
    Dispatch and see this execution done –
    This makes me to remember thee, my son.

                    Exit HIERONIMO.

PEDRINGANO: Nay, soft, no haste.

DEPUTY: Why, wherefore stay you? Have you hope of life?

PEDRINGANO: Why, aye.

1460 HANGMAN: As how?

PEDRINGANO: Why, rascal, by my pardon from the King.

HANGMAN: Stand you on that? Then you shall off with this!

1436	*office door:* i.e. prior to being hanged	1452	*intercepts itself of:* cuts itself off from (see note)
1443	*motion:* impulse, proposal	1455	*Dispatch:* make haste
1448	*set so light:* treated to casually	1457	*soft:* wait, hang on
1450	*interdicted:* forbidden	1462	*Stand you:* are you relying? (see note)
1451	*Still:* eternally, always		

He turns him off.
DEPUTY: So, executioner, convey him hence,
   But let his body be unburied:
   Let not the earth be choked or infect
   With that which Heaven contemns and men neglect.

                                            Exeunt.

ACT III   SCENE 7

   [*Hieronimo's house*]
   Enter HIERONIMO.
HIERONIMO: Where shall I run to breathe abroad my woes,
   My woes whose weight hath wearied the earth?
   Or mine exclaims that have surcharg'd the air   1470
   With ceaseless plaints, for my deceased son?
   The blust'ring winds, conspiring with my words,
   At my lament have mov'd the leafless trees,
   Disrob'd the meadows of their flow'red green,
   Made mountains marsh with spring-tides of my tears,
   And broken through the brazen gates of Hell.
   Yet still tormented is my tortur'd soul,
   With broken sighs and restless passions
   That winged mount, and hovering in the air,
   Beat at the windows of the brightest Heavens,   1480
   Soliciting for justice and revenge:
   But they are plac'd in those imperial heights,

1463   s.d. *turns him off:* hangs him
1466   *infect:* infected, corrupted
1467   *contemns:* scorns, disdains
       neglect: disregard, leave unat-
       tended
1468   *breathe abroad:* express freely
1470   *exclaims:* exclamations, outcries
       surcharg'd: weighed down, over-
       loaded

1471   *plaints:* lamentations
1478   *passions:* sufferings, strong feel-
       ings
1481   *Soliciting:* entreating, importun-
       ing
1482   *imperial:* empyreal, of highest
       heaven

Where, countermur'd with walls of diamond,
I find the place impregnable, and they
Resist my woes, and give my words no way.

    Enter HANGMAN *with a letter.*

HANGMAN: O lord, sir, God bless you, sir, the man
sir, Petergade, sir, he that was so full of merry
conceits –

HIERONIMO: Well, what of him?

1490 HANGMAN: O lord, sir, he went the wrong way; the
fellow had a fair commission to the contrary.
Sir, here is his passport; I pray you, sir, we
have done him wrong.

HIERONIMO: I warrant thee, give it me.

HANGMAN: You will stand between the gallows and me?

HIERONIMO: Aye, aye.

HANGMAN: I thank your lord worship.

    Exit HANGMAN.

HIERONIMO: And yet, though somewhat nearer me concerns,
I will, to ease the grief that I sustain,

1500 Take truce with sorrow while I read on this:
'My lord, I writ as mine extremes requir'd
That you would labour my delivery;
If you neglect, my life is desperate,
And in my death I shall reveal the truth.
You know, my lord, I slew him for your sake,
And as confederate with the Prince and you,
Won by rewards and hopeful promises,

1483 *countermur'd:* enclosed within double walls
1485 *no way:* no form of entrance
1487 *Petergade:* i.e. Pedringano (see note)
1488 *conceits:* quips, 'gags'
1491 *fair commission:* proper warrant
1492 *passport:* authorization

1498 *nearer:* more serious, more personal
1501 *extremes:* dire circumstances
1502 *labour:* work hard for, engineer
1503 *desperate:* hopeless, in danger
1506 *as confederate:* as an associate, an accomplice

I holp to murder Don Horatio too.'
Holp he to murder mine Horatio?
And actors in th'accursed tragedy   1510
Wast thou Lorenzo – Balthazar and thou,
Of whom my son, my son deserv'd so well?
What have I heard, what have mine eyes beheld?
O sacred Heavens, may it come to pass
That such a monstrous and detested deed,
So closely smother'd, and so long conceal'd,
Shall thus by this be vented or reveal'd!
Now see I what I durst not then suspect,
That Bel-imperia's letter was not feign'd
Nor feigned she, though falsely they have wrong'd   1520
Both her, myself, Horatio, and themselves.
Now may I make compare, 'twixt hers and this,
Of every accident; I ne'er could find
Till now, and now I feelingly perceive,
They did what Heaven unpunish'd would not leave.
O false Lorenzo, are these thy flattering looks?
Is this the honour that thou didst my son?
And Balthazar, bane to thy soul and me,
Was this the ransom he reserv'd thee for?
Woe to the cause of these constrained wars,   1530
Woe to thy baseness and captivity!
Woe to thy birth, thy body and thy soul,
Thy cursed father, and thy conquer'd self

1509   *holp:* helped
1515   *detested:* hateful, disgusting
1516   *closely smother'd:* secretly covered
       up
1517   *vented:* disclosed, divulged (see
       note)
1522   *this:* i.e. Pedringano's letter
1523   *accident:* happening, incidental
       detail
       find: discern, find out

1524   *feelingly:* with a sense of pain,
       acutely
1526   *flattering:* complimentary, be-
       guiling
1528   *bane:* agent of ruin, poisoner
1529   *reserv'd:* preserved, spared
1530   *constrained:* enforced, needless
1531   *baseness:* contemptible character

And bann'd with bitter execrations be
The day and place where he did pity thee!
But wherefore waste I mine unfruitful words,
When naught but blood will satisfy my woes?
I will go plain me to my lord the King,
And cry aloud for justice through the court,
1540   Wearing the flints with these my withered feet,
And either purchase justice by entreats,
Or tire them all with my revenging threats.

                                        Exit.

ACT III SCENE 8

[*The same*]
Enter ISABELLA *and her* MAID.

ISABELLA: So that you say this herb will purge the eye
And this the head?
Ah, but none of them will purge the heart:
No, there's no medicine left for my disease,
Nor any physic to recure the dead:
     She runs lunatic.
Horatio! Oh, where's Horatio?

MAID: Good Madam, affright not thus yourself
1550   With outrage for your son Horatio;
He sleeps in quiet in the Elysian Fields.

ISABELLA: Why, did I not give you gowns and goodly
          things,
Bought you a whistle and a whipstalk too,
To be revenged on their villainies?

1534	*bann'd:* cursed	1541 *entreats:* entreaty, supplication
1538	*plain me:* express my complaint, grief	1543 *purge:* cleanse, purify
1540	*Wearing:* wearing out	1547 *recure:* restore to life, recover
	flints: i.e. the flagstones	1553 *whipstalk:* a whip with a handle

MAID: Madam, these humours do torment my soul.
ISABELLA: My soul? Poor soul, thou talk'st of things
    Thou knowst not what – my soul hath silver wings
    That mounts me up unto the highest Heavens;
    To Heaven? Aye, there sits my Horatio,
    Back'd with a troop of fiery cherubins,   1560
    Dancing about his newly-healed wounds,
    Singing sweet hymns and chanting heavenly notes,
    Rare harmony to greet his innocence,
    That died, aye, died, a mirror in our days.
    But say, where shall I find the men, the murderers,
    That slew Horatio? Whither shall I run
    To find them out, that murdered my son?
                              Exeunt.

ACT III   SCENE 9

[*Lorenzo's palace*]
BEL-IMPERIA *at a window.*
BEL-IMPERIA: What means this outrage that is offer'd me?
    Why am I thus sequester'd from the court?
    No notice? Shall I not know the cause   1570
    Of this my secret and suspicious ills?
    Accursed brother, unkind murderer,
    Why bend'st thou thus thy mind to martyr me?
    Hieronimo, why writ I of thy wrongs,
    Or why art thou so slack in thy revenge?
    Andrea, O Andrea, that thou saw'st

1555	*humours:* freaks of behaviour, strange 'turns'	1570	*No notice?:* not kept informed?
1560	*Back'd with:* supported by a background of	1571	*this:* these
			suspicious: suspicion-arousing
1563	*greet:* salute, honour	1572	*unkind:* unnatural, inhuman
1564	*mirror:* model, example	1573	*bend'st:* applies
1569	*sequester'd:* isolated, secluded	1576	*that thou:* if only you

Me for thy friend Horatio handled thus,
And him for me thus causeless murdered!
Well, force perforce, I must constrain myself
1580 To patience, and apply me to the time,
Till Heaven, as I have hop'd, shall set me free.

          Enter CHRISTOPHILL.

CHRISTOPHILL: Come, Madam Bel-imperia, this may not
    be.

                              Exeunt.

ACT III SCENE 10

    [*The same*]
    Enter LORENZO, BALTHAZAR, *and the* PAGE

LORENZO: Boy, talk no further; thus far things go well.
    Thou art assured that thou saw'st him dead?
PAGE: Or else, my lord, I live not.
LORENZO: That's enough.
    As for his resolution in his end,
    Leave that to him with whom he sojourns now.
    Here, take my ring, and give it Christophill,
    And bid him let my sister be enlarg'd
1590 And bring her hither straight.

                      Exit PAGE.

    This that I did was for a policy
    To smooth and keep the murder secret,
    Which as a nine days' wonder being o'er-blown,

1577 *for:* because of
1579 *force perforce:* through sheer ne-
        cessity
      constrain: compel, exert
1580 *apply me to the time:* accept the
        situation
1584 *saw'st him:* i.e. Pedringano

1586 *resolution:* confidence, determina-
        tion
1589 *enlarg'd:* set free
1591 *policy:* stratagem, crafty purpose
1592 *smooth:* gloss over
1593 *being o'er blown:* having blown
        over

My gentle sister will I now enlarge.
BALTHAZAR: And time, Lorenzo, for my lord the Duke,
  You heard, enquired for her yesternight.
LORENZO: Why, and, my lord, I hope you heard me say
  Sufficient reason why she kept away?
  But that's all one. My lord, you love her?
BALTHAZAR: Aye.
LORENZO: Then in your love beware, deal cunningly,   1600
  Salve all suspicions; only soothe me up,
  And if she hap to stand on terms with us,
  As for her sweetheart and concealment so,
  Jest with her gently; under feigned jest
  Are things conceal'd that else would breed unrest.
  But here she comes.
    Enter BEL-IMPERIA.
                Now, sister.
BEL-IMPERIA: Sister? no!
  Thou art no brother, but an enemy.
  Else wouldst thou not have us'd thy sister so:
  First, to affright me with thy weapons drawn
  And with extremes abuse my company;   1610
  And then to hurry me like whirlwind's rage,
  Amidst a crew of thy confederates;
  And clap me up where none might come at me
  Nor I at any, to reveal my wrongs.
  What madding fury did possess thy wits?
  Or wherein is't that I offended thee?

1595 *And time:* i.e. it's high time you did
1599 *all one:* 'neither here nor there'
1601 *Salve:* allay
    soothe me up: back me up
1602 *hap:* happens, chances
    stand on terms: insists on her rights, makes conditions
1610 *extremes:* the harshest severity (see note)
1612 *confederates:* accomplices
1613 *clap me up:* bundle me into custody
1615 *madding:* frenzied

LORENZO: Advise you better, Bel-imperia,
  For I have done you no disparagement:
  Unless by more discretion than deserv'd,
1620   I sought to save your honour and mine own.
BEL-IMPERIA: Mine honour? Why, Lorenzo, wherein is't
  That I neglect my reputation so,
  As you, or any, need to rescue it?
LORENZO: His Highness and my father were resolv'd
  To come confer with old Hieronimo
  Concerning certain matters of estate
  That by the Viceroy was determined.
BEL-IMPERIA: And wherein was mine honour touch'd in
    that?
BALTHAZAR: Have patience, Bel-imperia; hear the rest.
1630 LORENZO: Me next in sight as messenger they sent,
  To give him notice that they were so nigh:
  Now when I came, consorted with the Prince,
  And unexpected in an arbour there
  Found Bel-imperia with Horatio –
BEL-IMPERIA: How then?
LORENZO: Well then, remembering that old disgrace
  Which you for Don Andrea had endur'd
  And now were likely longer to sustain
  By being found so meanly accompanied,
1640   Thought rather, for I knew no readier mean,
  To thrust Horatio forth my father's way.
BALTHAZAR: And carry you obscurely somewhere else,

1618 *disparagement:* indignity	1632 *consorted:* accompanied
1619 *discretion:* exercise of judgement, prudence	1636 *old disgrace:* i.e. loving an inferior clandestinely (see note)
1626 *estate:* state (see note)	1639 *meanly:* i.e. Horatio was equally inferior socially to Andrea
1627 *determined:* settled, decided upon? (see note)	
1630 *Me next in sight:* me being handy, clapping eyes on me nearby	1640 *readier mean:* handier method
	1641 *forth:* out of, but see note

Lest that his Highness should have found you there.
BEL-IMPERIA: Even so, my lord? And you are witness
That this is true which he entreateth of!
You, gentle brother, forg'd this for my sake,
And you, my lord, were made his instrument:
A work of worth, worthy the noting too!
But what's the cause that you conceal'd me since?
LORENZO: Your melancholy, sister, since the news   1650
Of your first favourite Don Andrea's death,
My father's old wrath hath exasperate.
BALTHAZAR: And better was't for you, being in disgrace,
To absent yourself and give his fury place.
BEL-IMPERIA: But why had I no notice of his ire?
LORENZO: That were to add more fuel to your fire,
Who burnt like Aetna for Andrea's loss.
BEL-IMPERIA: Hath not my father then enquir'd for me?
LORENZO: Sister, he hath, and thus excus'd I thee.
        He whispereth in her ear.
But Bel-imperia, see the gentle Prince;   1660
Look on thy love, behold young Balthazar,
Whose passions by thy presence are increas'd,
And in whose melancholy thou mayest see
Thy hate, his love; thy flight, his following thee.
BEL-IMPERIA: Brother, you are become an orator –
I know not, I, by what experience –
Too politic for me, past all compare
Since last I saw you; but content yourself:
The Prince is meditating higher things.

1645	*entreateth of:* pleads with me to believe	1652	*exasperate:* exacerbated
1646	*gentle:* kind, well-bred (ironic)	1654	*give his fury place:* see note
	forg'd: devised, carried out, feigned	1657	*Aetna:* Mount Etna (see note)
		1667	*politic:* shrewd, artful (see note)
1650	*melancholy:* depression (see note)		*compare:* comparison

1670 BALTHAZAR: 'Tis of thy beauty then that conquers kings;
  Of those thy tresses, Ariadne's twines,
  Wherewith my liberty thou hast surpris'd;
  Of that thine ivory front, my sorrow's map,
  Wherein I see no haven to rest my hope.

BEL-IMPERIA: To love, and fear, and both at once, my lord,
  In my conceit are things of more import
  Than women's wits are to be busied with.

BALTHAZAR: 'Tis I that love.

BEL-IMPERIA: Whom?

BALTHAZAR: Bel-imperia.

BEL-IMPERIA: But I that fear.

BALTHAZAR: Whom?

BEL-IMPERIA: Bel-imperia.

LORENZO: Fear yourself?

BEL-IMPERIA: Aye, brother.

LORENZO: How?

1680 BEL-IMPERIA: As those
  That what they love are loth and fear to lose.

BALTHAZAR: Then, fair, let Balthazar your keeper be.

BEL-IMPERIA: No, Balthazar doth fear as well as we.
  Et tremulo metui pavidum jungere timorem
  Est vanum stolidae proditionis opus.
         Exit.

LORENZO: Nay, and you argue things so cunningly,
  We'll go continue this discourse at court.

BALTHAZAR: Led by the loadstar of her heavenly looks,
  Wends poor oppressed Balthazar

1671	*Ariadne's:* Minos's daughter (but see note)	1676	*import:* significance, weight
	twines: threads	1684	*Et tremulo* etc.: see note
1672	*surpris'd:* taken prisoner	1686	*and:* if
1673	*front:* brow, forehead		*cunningly:* cleverly, knowingly
	map: guidebook (see note)	1688	*loadstar:* 'guiding light' (see note)

As o'er the mountains walks the wanderer,   1690
Incertain to effect his pilgrimage.

ACT III SCENE 11

Enter TWO PORTINGALES, *and* HIERONIMO *meets them.*

1 PORTINGALE: By your leave, sir.

HIERONIMO: Good leave have you; nay, I pray you go,
For I'll leave you, if you can leave me so.

2 PORTINGALE: Pray you which is the next way to my lord
the Duke's?

HIERONIMO: The next way from me.

1 PORTINGALE: To his house, we mean.

HIERONIMO: Oh, hard by; 'tis yon house that you see.

2 PORTINGALE: You could not tell us if his son were there?

HIERONIMO: Who, my lord Lorenzo?

1 PORTINGALE: Aye, sir.

He [HIERONIMO] *goeth in at one door and comes out at
another.*

HIERONIMO: Oh, forbear,
For other talk for us far fitter were.   1700
But if you be importunate to know
The way to him, and where to find him out,
Then list to me, and I'll resolve your doubt:
There is a path upon your left-hand side
That leadeth from a guilty conscience
Unto a forest of distrust and fear,
A darksome place and dangerous to pass;
There shall you meet with melancholy thoughts,
Whose baleful humours if you but uphold,

1691 *Incertain* etc.: unsure of carrying out
1695 *next:* nearest, handiest
1707 *darksome:* dark and gloomy

1709 *baleful humours:* pernicious tendencies
uphold: sustain, entertain

1710 It will conduct you to despair and death:
Whose rocky cliffs, when you have once beheld,
Within a hugy dale of lasting night,
That kindl'd with the world's iniquities
Doth cast up filthy and detested fumes;
Not far from thence where murderers have built
A habitation for their cursed souls,
There in a brazen caldron fix'd by Jove
In his fell wrath upon a sulphur flame,
Yourselves shall find Lorenzo bathing him
1720 In boiling lead and blood of innocents.

1 PORTINGALE: Ha, ha, ha!

HIERONIMO: Ha, ha, ha! Why, ha, ha, ha!
Farewell, good, ha, ha, ha!
                                                    Exit.

2 PORTINGALE: Doubtless this man is passing lunatic,
Or imperfection of his age doth make him dote.
Come, let's away to seek my lord the Duke.
                                                    Exeunt.

ACT III SCENE 12

Enter HIERONIMO: *with a poniard in one hand, and a rope in
the other.*

HIERONIMO: Now, sir, perhaps I come and see the King;
The King sees me, and fain would hear my suit –
Why, is not this a strange and seld seen thing,
That standers-by with toys should strike me mute?
1730 Go to, I see their shifts, and say no more:

1712	*hugy dale:* vast valley	1725	s.d. *poniard:* dagger (see note)
1714	*detested:* detestable, revolting	1728	*seld:* seldom
1718	*fell:* cruel	1729	*toys:* trifles, trivial points
1723	*passing:* exceedingly, utterly	1730	*Go to:* 'come now!'
1724	*imperfection* etc.: senility		*shifts:* 'clever tricks'
	dote: act madly		

Hieronimo, 'tis time for thee to trudge.
Down by the dale that flows with purple gore
Standeth a fiery tower; there sits a judge
Upon a seat of steel and molten brass,
And 'twixt his teeth he holds a fire-brand
That leads unto the lake where Hell doth stand.
Away, Hieronimo, to him be gone!
He'll do thee justice for Horatio's death.
    [*Indicating poniard*]
Turn down this path; thou shalt be with him straight –
    [*Indicating rope*]
Or this, and then thou needst not take thy breath.   1740
This way, or that way? Soft and fair, not so:
For if I hang or kill myself, let's know
Who will revenge Horatio's murder then?
No, no, fie no! pardon me, I'll none of that:
    He flings away the dagger and halter.
This way I'll take, and this way comes the King;
    He takes them up again.
And here I'll have a fling at him, that's flat.
And, Balthazar, I'll be with thee to bring,
And thee, Lorenzo! Here's the King! Nay, stay,
And here, aye, here; there goes the hare away.
    Enter KING, AMBASSADOR, *the* DUKE OF CASTILE, *and*
    LORENZO.
KING: Now show, Ambassador, what our Viceroy saith;   1750
    Hath he receiv'd the articles we sent?

1731	*trudge:* get going, move on	1742	*kill:* stab
1732	*purple:* crimson	1746	*have a fling at:* tackle, 'have a go at'
1736	*leads:* indicates the route		
1739	*straight:* immediately	1747	*I'll be with thee* etc.: I'll get my own back on you
1740	*take thy breath:* bother to keep breathing		
1741	*Soft and fair:* take it easy now! Hang on!	1749	*there goes the hare away:* 'the King's eluding me' (see note)

HIERONIMO: Justice, O justice to Hieronimo!

LORENZO: Back! see'st thou not the King is busy?

HIERONIMO: Oh, is he so?

KING: Who is he that interrupts our business?

HIERONIMO: Not I; Hieronimo, beware! Go by, go by.

AMBASSADOR: Renowned King, he hath receiv'd and read
    Thy kingly proffers, and thy promis'd league,
    And, as a man extremely overjoy'd
    To hear his son so princely entertain'd,
1760   Whose death he had so solemnly bewail'd,
    This for thy further satisfaction
    And kingly love, he kindly lets thee know:
    First, for the marriage of his princely son
    With Bel-imperia, thy beloved niece,
    The news are more delightful to his soul
    Than myrrh or incense to the offended Heavens.
    In person therefore will he come himself
    To see the marriage rites solemniz'd,
    And, in the presence of the court of Spain,
1770   To knot a sure inexplicable band
    Of kingly love and everlasting league
    Betwixt the crowns of Spain and Portingale:
    There will he give his crown to Balthazar,
    And make a queen of Bel-imperia.

KING: Brother, how like you this our Viceroy's love?

CASTILE: No doubt, my lord, it is an argument
    Of honourable care to keep his friend,
    And wondrous zeal to Balthazar his son;
    Nor am I least indebted to his grace,

1755 *Go by:* let it go, keep out of
      trouble
1757 *proffers:* proposals
1770 *inexplicable:* permanently tied
      (see note)

1776 *argument:* indication, demonstra-
      tion

That bends his liking to my daughter thus.   1780
AMBASSADOR: Now last, dread lord, here hath his Highness
  sent —
  Although he send not that his son return —
  His ransom due to Don Horatio.
    [*Gives* KING *the money.*]
HIERONIMO: Horatio! Who calls Horatio?
KING: And well remember'd; thank his Majesty.
  Here, see it given to Horatio.
HIERONIMO: Justice! O justice, justice, gentle King!
KING: Who is that? Hieronimo?
HIERONIMO: Justice, O justice! O my son, my son,
  My son whom naught can ransom or redeem!   1790
LORENZO: Hieronimo, you are not well advis'd.
HIERONIMO: Away, Lorenzo, hinder me no more,
  For thou hast made me bankrupt of my bliss!
  Give me my son, you shall not ransom him:
  Away! I'll rip the bowels of the earth,
      He diggeth *with his* dagger.
  And ferry over to th'Elysian plains,
  And bring my son to show his deadly wounds.
  Stand from about me.
  I'll make a pickaxe of my poniard,
  And here surrender up my marshalship: 1800
  For I'll go marshal up the fiends in Hell,
  To be avenged on you all for this.
KING: What means this outrage?
  Will none of you restrain his fury?
HIERONIMO: Nay, soft and fair, you shall not need to strive;

1780	*bends:* inclines, directs	1803	*outrage:* violent outburst
1782	*that:* in order to ensure that	1804	*fury:* fierce emotion
1791	*well advis'd:* being sensible		
1796	*th'Elysian plains:* the Elysian Fields (see note)		

Needs must he go that the devils drive.
Exit.

KING: What accident hath happ'd Hieronimo?
I have not seen him to demean him so.

LORENZO: My gracious lord, he is with extreme pride
1810 Conceiv'd of young Horatio his son,
And covetous of having to himself
The ransom of the young Prince Balthazar,
Distract and in a manner lunatic.

KING: Believe me, nephew, we are sorry for't:
This is the love that fathers bear their sons.
But, gentle brother, go give to him this gold,
The Prince's ransom; let him have his due,
For what he hath Horatio shall not want.
Haply Hieronimo hath need thereof.

1820 LORENZO: But if he be thus helplessly distract,
'Tis requisite his office be resign'd
And given to one of more discretion.

KING: We shall increase his melancholy so;
'Tis best that we see further in it first:
Till when, ourself will [not] exempt the place.
And, brother, now bring in the Ambassador,
That he may be a witness of the match
'Twixt Balthazar and Bel-imperia;
And that we may prefix a certain time
1830 Wherein the marriage shall be solemniz'd
That we may have thy lord the Viceroy here.

AMBASSADOR: Therein your Highness highly shall content

1807 *accident:* event, incident
happ'd: happened to
1808 *demean him:* conduct himself, behave
1810 *Conceiv'd of:* imagined concerning
1813 *Distract:* deranged
1819 *Haply:* maybe
1823 *melancholy:* depression (see note)
1824 *see further* etc.: explore it more thoroughly
1825 *[not] exempt* etc.: will not debar him from office (see note)
1829 *prefix:* arrange in advance

His Majesty, that longs to hear from hence.
KING: On then, and hear you, Lord Ambassador.
                                    Exeunt.

ACT III   SCENE 13

[*Hieronimo's house*]
Enter HIERONIMO *with a book in his hand.*
HIERONIMO: *Vindicta mihi!*
Aye, Heaven will be reveng'd of every ill,
Nor will they suffer murder unrepaid.
Then stay, Hieronimo, attend their will,
For mortal men may not appoint their time.
'*Per scelus semper tutum est sceleribus iter*' –   1840
Strike, and strike home, where wrong is offer'd thee,
For evils unto ills conductors be,
And death's the worst of resolution.
For he that thinks with patience to contend
To quiet life, his life shall easily end.
'*Fata si miseros juvant, habes salutem:*
Fata si vitam negant, habes sepulchrum.'
If destiny thy miseries do ease,
Then hast thou health, and happy shalt thou be;
If destiny deny thee life, Hieronimo,   1850
Yet shalt thou be assured of a tomb:
If neither, yet let this thy comfort be:
Heaven covereth him that hath no burial –

1835 *Vindicta mihi:* vengeance be-   1843 *And death's* etc.: at the worst
      longs to me (see note)   resolute behaviour can only
1838 *stay:* hold on   lead to death
      attend: await   1844 *contend:* battle his way
      their will: the pleasure of the 1846 '*Fata si*' etc.: see note
      heavens
1840 '*Per scelus*' etc.: 'in crime the way
      to safety is always through
      more crimes' (see note)

And to conclude, I will revenge his death!
But how? not as the vulgar wits of men,
With open, but inevitable ills,
As by a secret, yet a certain mean,
Which under kindship will be cloaked best.
Wise men will take their opportunity,
1860   Closely and safely fitting things to time;
But in extremes advantage hath no time,
And therefore all times fit not for revenge.
Thus therefore will I rest me in unrest,
Dissembling quiet in unquietness,
Not seeming that I know their villainies,
That my simplicity may make them think
That ignorantly I will let all slip:
For ignorance, I wot (and well they know),
'*Remedium malorum iners est.*'
1870   Nor aught avails it me to menace them,
Who, as a wintry storm upon a plain,
Will bear me down with their nobility.
No, no, Hieronimo, thou must enjoin
Thine eyes to observation, and thy tongue
To milder speeches than thy spirit affords,
Thy heart to patience, and thy hands to rest,
Thy cap to courtesy, and thy knee to bow,

1855   *vulgar wits:* commonplace intelligences
1856   *inevitable:* inescapable
ills: harmful acts (see note)
1857   *mean:* method, course of action
1858   *kindship:* kindness, good will
cloaked: concealed
1860   *Closely:* secretly, subtly
1861   *But in extremes:* only in crises
advantage: a favourable opportunity
1862   *fit not:* are unsuitable
1863   *rest me* etc.: remain content with
uneasiness of mind
1866   *simplicity:* apparent naivety
1869   '*Remedium*' etc.: '[ignorance] is a
poor cure for evils' (see note)
1872   *nobility:* noble status
1873   *enjoin:* strictly command, impose
on

Till to revenge thou know, when, where, and how.
  A noise within.
How now! What noise? What coil is that you keep?
  Enter a SERVANT.

SERVANT: Here are a sort of poor petitioners   1880
  That are importunate, and it shall please you, sir,
  That you should plead their cases to the King.

HIERONIMO: That I should plead their several actions?
  Why, let them enter, and let me see them.
    Enter three CITIZENS *and an* OLD MAN [SENEX].

1 CITIZEN [*to the others*]: So I tell you this: for learning and
    for law,
  There [is] not any advocate in Spain
  That can prevail, or will take half the pain,
  That he will in pursuit of equity.

HIERONIMO: Come near, you men, that thus importune me.
  [*To himself*] Now must I bear a face of gravity,   1890
  For thus I us'd, before my marshalship,
  To plead in causes as corregidor.
  [*Aloud*] Come on, sirs, what's the matter?

2 CITIZEN: Sir, an action.

HIERONIMO: Of battery?

1 CITIZEN: Mine of debt.

HIERONIMO: Give place.

2 CITIZEN: No, sir; mine is an action of the case.

3 CITIZEN: Mine an *Ejectione firmae* by a lease.

HIERONIMO: Content you, sirs; are you determin'd
  That I should plead your several actions?

1 CITIZEN: Aye, sir, and here's my declaration.

1879 *coil:* rumpus	1888 *equity:* justice, fair play
1880 *a sort of:* several, 'a bit of a	1892 *corregidor:* advocate (see note)
crowd'	1894 *Give place:* take your turn
1881 *and:* if	1896 *Ejectione firmae:* a writ to evict a
1883 *plead:* i.e. in court	tenant
actions: lawsuits	

2 CITIZEN: And here is my band.

1900 3 CITIZEN: And here is my lease.

　　　They give him papers.

HIERONIMO [*seeing the* OLD MAN]: But wherefore stands yon
　　silly man so mute,

　　With mournful eyes and hands to heaven uprear'd?

　　Come hither, father, let me know thy cause.

SENEX: O worthy sir, my cause but slightly known

　　May move the hearts of warlike Myrmidons,

　　And melt the Corsic rocks with ruthful tears.

HIERONIMO: Say, father, tell me, what's thy suit?

SENEX: No, sir, could my woes

　　Give way unto my most distressful words,

1910 　　Then should I not in paper, as you see,

　　With ink bewray what blood began in me.

HIERONIMO: What's here? 'The humble supplication

　　Of Don Bazulto for his murdered son.'

SENEX: Aye, sir.

HIERONIMO: No, sir, it was my murder'd son –

　　O my son! My son, O my son Horatio!

　　But mine, or thine, Bazulto, be content.

　　Here, take my handkercher and wipe thine eyes,

　　Whiles wretched I in thy mishaps may see

　　The lively portrait of my dying self.

　　　He draweth out a bloody napkin.

1920 Oh no, not this; Horatio, this was thine,

　　And when I dy'd it in thy dearest blood,

1899	*declaration:* statement of claim	1909	*Give way:* allow free scope
1900	*band:* bond	1911	*bewray:* disfigure, soil
1901	*silly:* simple, helpless (see notes)		*blood:* bloodshed
1904	*but:* only	1917	*handkercher:* handkerchief
1905	*Myrmidons:* see note	1918	*mishaps:* wretched fortune
1906	*Corsic:* Corsican (see note)	1919	*lively:* living
	ruthful: pitiful		

This was a token 'twixt thy soul and me,
That of thy death revenged I should be.
But here, take this [*gives* OLD MAN *money*], and this. What,
   my purse? —
Aye, this and that, and all of them are thine,
For all as one are our extremities.
1 CITIZEN: Oh, see the kindness of Hieronimo!
2 CITIZEN: This gentleness shows him a gentleman.
HIERONIMO: See, see, oh see thy shame, Hieronimo,
   See here a loving father to his son!   1930
   Behold the sorrows and the sad laments
   That he delivereth for his son's decease.
   If love's effects so strive in lesser things,
   If love enforce such moods in meaner wits,
   If love express such power in poor estates —
   Hieronimo, whenas a raging sea,
   Tossed with the wind and tide, o'erturne[th] then
   The upper billows, course of waves to keep,
   Whilst lesser waters labour in the deep,
   Then sham'st thou not, Hieronimo, to neglect   1940
   The sweet revenge of thy Horatio?
   Though on this earth justice will not be found,
   I'll down to Hell and in this passion
   Knock at the dismal gates of Pluto's court,
   Getting by force, as once Alcides did,
   A troop of Furies and tormenting hags,
   To torture Don Lorenzo and the rest.
   Yet lest the triple-headed porter should

1926	*extremities:* dire straits	1944	*Pluto's:* the king of Hell's
1934	*meaner:* less exalted	1945	*Alcides:* Hercules (see note)
1935	*estates:* social classes	1946	*Furies:* the avenging deities (see
1937	*o'erturne[th]:* revolves (see note)		note)
1938	*keep:* maintain (see note)	1948	*triple-headed porter:* Cerberus (see
1943	*passion:* distressed condition, upset state		note)

Deny my passage to the slimy strand,
1950   The Thracian poet thou shalt counterfeit:
Come on, old father, be my Orpheus,
And if thou canst no notes upon the harp,
Then sound the burden of thy sore heart's grief,
Till we do gain that Proserpine may grant
Revenge on them that murdered my son.
Then will I rent and tear them thus and thus,
Shivering their limbs in pieces with my teeth.
       Tear[s] the papers.
1 CITIZEN: O sir, my declaration!
                    Exit HIERONIMO *and they after.*
2 CITIZEN: Save my bond!
       Enter HIERONIMO [*with the* CITIZENS *in pursuit*].
Save my bond!
3 CITIZEN: Alas, my lease, it cost me ten pound,
1960   And you, my lord, have torn the same.
HIERONIMO: That cannot be; I gave it never a wound;
Show me one drop of blood fall from the same:
How is it possible I should slay it then?
Tush, no, run after, catch me if you can.
              Exeunt all but the OLD MAN.
       [*The* OLD MAN] *remains till* HIERONIMO *enters again, who,*
       staring him in the face, speaks.
HIERONIMO: And art thou come, Horatio, from the depth,
To ask for justice in this upper earth?
To tell thy father thou art unreveng'd?
To wring more tears from Isabella's eyes

1949	*strand:* shore, beach (see note)	1953	*burden:* musical refrain or theme
1950	*The Thracian poet:* Orpheus (see		(see note)
	note)	1954	*gain:* obtain agreement
	counterfeit: impersonate, imitate	1956	*rent:* rend, pull apart
1952	*canst no notes:* lack the skill to		
	play		

Whose lights are dimm'd with over-long laments?
Go back, my son; complain to Eacus,   1970
For here's no justice; gentle boy, be gone,
For justice is exiled from the earth.
Hieronimo will bear thee company;
Thy mother cries on righteous Rhadamant
For just revenge against the murderers.

SENEX: Alas, my lord, whence springs this troubled speech?

HIERONIMO: But let me look on my Horatio:
Sweet boy, how art thou chang'd in death's black shade!
Had Proserpine no pity on thy youth,
But suffer'd thy fair crimson-coloured spring   1980
With wither'd winter to be blasted thus?
Horatio, thou art older than thy father:
Ah, ruthless [fate], that favour thus transforms!

[SENEX]: Ah, my good lord, I am not your young son.

HIERONIMO: What, not my son? Thou then a Fury art,
Sent from the empty kingdom of black night,
To summon me to make appearance
Before grim Minos and just Rhadamant,
To plague Hieronimo that is remiss,
And seeks not vengeance for Horatio's death.   1990

[SENEX]: I am a grieved man, and not a ghost,
That came for justice for my murder'd son.

HIERONIMO: Aye, now I know thee; now thou nam'st [thy]
son,
Thou art the lively image of my grief;
Within thy face, my sorrows I may see:

1969	*lights:* gleams, rays	1981	*blasted:* blighted by frost
1970	*Eacus:* Aeacus, an underworld judge (see note)	1983	*favour thus transforms:* that so changes the appearance
1974	*cries on:* appeals to	1988	*Minos:* a third judge
	Rhadamant: Rhadamanthus, another underworld judge (see note to line 33 above)	1994	*lively:* living

Thy eyes are gumm'd with tears, thy cheeks are wan,
Thy forehead troubled, and thy mutt'ring lips
Murmur sad words abruptly broken off;
By force of windy sighs thy spirit breathes;
2000   And all this sorrow riseth for thy son:
And self-same sorrow feel I for my son.
Come in, old man, thou shalt to Isabel;
Lean on my arm; I thee, thou me shalt stay,
And thou, and I, and she will sing a song,
Three parts in one, but all of discords fram'd –
Talk not of cords, but let us now be gone,
For with a cord Horatio was slain.
                              Exeunt.

ACT III SCENE 14

[*The Spanish court*]
Enter KING *of Spain, the* DUKE OF CASTILE, VICEROY,
and LORENZO, BALTHAZAR, DON PEDRO, *and* BEL-
IMPERIA [*and* SERVANTS].

KING: Go, brother; it is the Duke of Castile's cause.
    Salute the Viceroy in our name.
CASTILE: I go. [*Crosses stage.*]
2010 VICEROY: Go forth, Don Pedro, for thy nephew's sake,
    And greet the Duke of Castile.
PEDRO: It shall be so.
    [*Crosses to greet* CASTILE.]
KING: And now to meet these Portuguese;
    For as we now are, so sometimes were these,
    Kings and commanders of the western Indies.

1996 *gumm'd:* sticky, stuck tight   2008 *cause:* business, affair
2003 *stay:* support   2014 *western Indies:* Portuguese
2005 *fram'd:* composed, made up   Brazil? (see note)

Welcome, brave Viceroy, to the court of Spain,
And welcome all his honourable train.
'Tis not unknown to us for why you come,
Or have so kingly cross'd the seas:
Sufficeth it in this we note the troth
And more than common love you lend to us.   2020
So is it that mine honourable niece
(For it beseems us now that it be known)
Already is betroth'd to Balthazar,
And by appointment and our condescent,
Tomorrow are they to be married.
To this intent we entertain thyself,
Thy followers, their pleasure, and our peace:
Speak, men of Portingale, shall it be so?
If aye, say so: if not, say flatly no.

VICEROY: Renowned King, I come not as thou think'st,   2030
With doubtful followers, unresolved men,
But such as have upon thine articles
Confirm'd thy motion and contented me.
Know, sovereign, I come to solemnize
The marriage of thy beloved niece,
Fair Bel-imperia, with my Balthazar,
With thee, my son, whom sith I live to see,
Here take my crown, I give it her and thee;
And let me live a solitary life,
In ceaseless prayers,   2040
To think how strangely Heaven hath thee preserv'd!
      [*He weeps.*]

2016	*train:* suite, retinue
2019	*troth:* trust, faith
2020	*lend:* grant, impart
2022	*beseems us:* appears befitting to us
2024	*condescent:* consent, agreement

2026	*entertain:* maintain, cherish
2027	*their:* i.e. the engaged couple's
2033	*motion:* proposal
2037	*sith:* since
2041	*strangely:* wonderfully

KING [*to* CASTILE]: See, brother, see, how Nature strives in
    him!
  Come, worthy Viceroy, and accompany
  Thy friend, with thine extremities:
  A place more private fits this princely mood.
VICEROY: Or here or where your Highness thinks it good.
               Exeunt all but CASTILE *and* LORENZO.
CASTILE: Nay stay, Lorenzo, let me talk with you:
  Seest thou this entertainment of these kings?
LORENZO: I do, my lord, and joy to see the same.
CASTILE: And knowest thou why this meeting is?
LORENZO: For her, my lord, whom Balthazar doth love,
  And to confirm their promis'd marriage.
CASTILE: She is thy sister?
LORENZO: Who, Bel-imperia?
  Aye, my gracious lord, and this is the day
  That I have long'd so happily to see.
CASTILE: Thou wouldst be loth that any fault of thine
  Should intercept her in her happiness?
LORENZO: Heavens will not let Lorenzo err so much.
CASTILE: Why then, Lorenzo, listen to my words:
  It is suspected, and reported too,
  That thou, Lorenzo, wrong'st Hieronimo,
  And in his suits towards his Majesty
  Still keep'st him back, and seeks to cross his suit.
LORENZO: That I, my lord – ?
CASTILE: I tell thee, son, myself have heard it said,
  When, to my sorrow, I have been asham'd
  To answer for thee, though thou art my son.
  Lorenzo, know'st thou not the common love

2050

2060

2042 *strives:* contends, struggles
2044 *extremities:* deep emotions
2046 *Or:* either
2048 *entertainment:* social exchanges

2057 *intercept:* obstruct
2063 *cross:* thwart, oppose
2068 *common:* general

And kindness that Hieronimo hath won
By his deserts within the court of Spain?   2070
Or see'st thou not the King my brother's care,
In his behalf, and to procure his health?
Lorenzo, should'st thou thwart his passions,
And he exclaim against thee to the King,
What honour wer't in this assembly,
Or what a scandal wer't among the kings,
To hear Hieronimo exclaim on thee?
Tell me, and look thou tell me truly too,
Whence grows the ground of this report in court?
LORENZO: My lord, it lies not in Lorenzo's power   2080
To stop the vulgar, liberal of their tongues:
A small advantage makes a water-breach,
And no man lives that long contenteth all.
CASTILE: Myself have seen thee busy to keep back
Him and his supplications from the King.
LORENZO: Yourself, my lord, hath seen his passions
That ill beseem'd the presence of a king,
And for I pitied him in his distress,
I held him thence with kind and courteous words,
As free from malice to Hieronimo   2090
As to my soul, my lord.
CASTILE: Hieronimo, my son, mistakes thee then?
LORENZO: My gracious father, believe me so he doth:
But what's a silly man, distract in mind,
To think upon the murder of his son?

2069	*kindness:* affection	2081	*vulgar:* common folk
2070	*deserts:* merits, worthiness		*liberal* etc.: who gossip freely
2072	*procure:* care for	2082	*advantage:* opportunity for criticism
2073	*passions:* strong feelings		
2074	*exclaim against:* protest, denounce		*water-breach:* an irruption of water, a spate of abuse
2075	*wer't:* would it be	2088	*for:* since, because
2079	*ground:* basis	2094	*silly:* weak, simple, 'poor'

Alas, how easy is it for him to err!
But for his satisfaction and the world's,
'Twere good, my lord, that Hieronimo and I
Were reconciled, if he misconster me.
2100 CASTILE: Lorenzo, thou has said; it shall be so.
Go, one of you, and call Hieronimo.
                    [*Exit a* SERVANT.]
        Enter BALTHAZAR *and* BEL-IMPERIA.
BALTHAZAR: Come, Bel-imperia, Balthazar's content,
    My sorrow's ease and sovereign of my bliss;
    Sith Heaven hath ordain'd thee to be mine,
    Disperse those clouds and melancholy looks,
    And clear them up with those thy sun-bright eyes
    Wherein my hope and Heaven's fair beauty lies.
BEL-IMPERIA: My looks, my lord, are fitting for my love,
    Which new begun, can show [no] brighter yet.
BALTHAZAR: New-kindl'd flames should burn as morning
2110   sun.
BEL-IMPERIA: But not too fast, lest heat and all be done.
    I see my lord my father.
BALTHAZAR: Truce, my love;
    I will go salute him.
CASTILE: Welcome, Balthazar,
    Welcome brave prince, the pledge of Castile's peace:
    And welcome Bel-imperia! How now, girl?
    Why com'st thou sadly to salute us thus?
    Content thyself, for I am satisfi'd;
    It is not now as when Andrea liv'd:
    We have forgotten and forgiven that,
2120   And thou art graced with a happier love.

2099 *misconster:* misconstrue, 'gets me   2112 *Truce:* i.e. 'let's stop sparring'
        wrong'   2113 *salute:* greet
2102 *content:* contentment   2116 *sadly:* thoughtfully, pensively
2104 *Sith:* since   2120 *happier:* fitter, more suitable

But, Balthazar, here comes Hieronimo.
I'll have a word with him.
    Enter HIERONIMO *and a* SERVANT.

HIERONIMO: And where's the Duke?

SERVANT: Yonder.

HIERONIMO [*aside*]: Even so:
  What new device have they devised, trow?
  Pocas palabras, mild as the lamb,
  Is't I will be reveng'd? No, I am not the man.

CASTILE: Welcome, Hieronimo.

LORENZO: Welcome, Hieronimo.

BALTHAZAR: Welcome, Hieronimo.

HIERONIMO: My lords, I thank you for Horatio.   2130

CASTILE: Hieronimo, the reason that I sent
  To speak with you, is this.

HIERONIMO: What, so short?
  Then I'll be gone, I thank you for't. [*Going.*]

CASTILE: Nay, stay, Hieronimo; go call him, son.

LORENZO: Hieronimo, my father craves a word with you.

HIERONIMO: With me, sir? Why, my lord, I thought you had
    done.
    [*Returning.*]

LORENZO: [*aside*] No, would he had.

CASTILE: Hieronimo, I hear
  You find yourself aggrieved at my son,
  Because you have not access unto the King,
  And say 'tis he that intercepts your suits.   2140

HIERONIMO: Why, is not this a miserable thing, my lord?

CASTILE: Hieronimo, I hope you have no cause,
  And would be loth that one of your deserts

2124 *device:* plot, stratagem
      trow?: do you reckon
2125 *Pocas palabras:* few words (Span-
      ish) (see note)

2140 *intercepts:* obstructs, hinders
2143 *deserts:* deserving, merits

Should once have reason to suspect my son,
Considering how I think of you myself.

HIERONIMO: Your son Lorenzo? whom, my noble lord?
The hope of Spain, mine honourable friend?
Grant me the combat of them, if they dare;
   Draws out his sword.
I'll meet him face to face, to tell me so.

2150   These be the scandalous reports of such
As love not me, and hate my lord too much.
Should I suspect Lorenzo would prevent
Or cross my suit, that lov'd my son so well?
My lord, I am asham'd it should be said.

LORENZO: Hieronimo, I never gave you cause.

HIERONIMO: My good lord, I know you did not.

CASTILE: There then pause,
And for the satisfaction of the world,
Hieronimo, frequent my homely house,
The Duke of Castile Cyprian's ancient seat,
2160   And when thou wilt, use me, my son, and it.
But here before Prince Balthazar and me,
Embrace each other, and be perfect friends.

HIERONIMO: Aye, marry, my lord, and shall:
Friends, quoth he? See, I'll be friends with you all,
[*to* LORENZO] Specially with you, my lovely lord,
For divers causes it is fit for us
That we be friends; the world is suspicious,
And men may think what we imagine not.

BALTHAZAR: Why, this is friendly done, Hieronimo.

2170 LORENZO: And [thus] I hope old grudges are forgot.

2148 *the combat of:* the chance to duel with
2152 *prevent:* frustrate
2153 *cross:* frustrate, oppose
2157 *for the satisfaction:* in order to remove the doubts
2158 *homely:* kindly (see note)
2160 *use:* ask support of, make use of

HIERONIMO: What else? It were a shame it should not be so.

CASTILE: Come on, Hieronimo, at my request;
　Let us entreat your company today.

　　　　　　　　　　　　Exeunt.

HIERONIMO: Your Lordship's to command – [*aside*] Pha! keep
　your way.
　Chi mi fa più carezze che non suole,
　Tradito mi ha, o tradir mi vuole.

　　　　　　　　　　　　Exit.

　GHOST *and* REVENGE

GHOST: Awake, Erichtho! Cerberus, awake!
　Solicit Pluto, gentle Proserpine;
　To combat, Acheron and Erebus!
　For ne'er by Styx and Phlegethon in Hell . . .　　　　2180
　Nor ferried Charon to the fiery lakes
　Such fearful sights as poor Andrea sees:
　Revenge, awake!

REVENGE:　　　　Awake? for why?

GHOST: Awake, Revenge, for thou art ill advis'd
　To sleep away what thou art warn'd to watch!

REVENGE: Content thyself, and do not trouble me.

GHOST: Awake, Revenge, if love, as love hath had,
　Have yet the power of prevalance in Hell;
　Hieronimo with Lorenzo is join'd in league,
　And intercepts our passage to revenge:　　　　　　　2190
　Awake, Revenge, or we are woe-begone!

2174　*Pha!:* faugh! (an expression of
　disgust)
2175–6　*Chi mi fa* etc.: the man who
　gives me more embraces than
　is customary has either be-
　trayed me, or wishes to (see
　note)
2177–81　*Erichtho* etc.: See notes
2184　*ill advis'd:* injudicious

2185　*sleep away:* sleep through
　warn'd: cautioned, ordered
　watch: guard, tend
2188　*prevalance:* mastery, predomi-
　nance
2190　*intercepts:* hinders, blocks
2191　*woe-begone:* oppressed with mis-
　fortune

REVENGE: Thus worldlings ground what they have dream'd
    upon.
    Content thyself, Andrea; though I sleep,
    Yet is my mood soliciting their souls:
    Sufficeth thee that poor Hieronimo
    Cannot forget his son Horatio,
    Nor dies Revenge although he sleep awhile,
    For in unquiet, quietness is feign'd,
    And slumb'ring is a common worldly wile.
2200   Behold, Andrea, for an instance how
    Revenge hath slept, and then imagine thou
    What 'tis to be subject to destiny.
        Enter a dumb-show [of two TORCHBEARERS, *and* HYMEN.
        They mime, and then exeunt].
GHOST: Awake, Revenge! Reveal this mystery.
REVENGE: The two first the nuptial torches bore,
    As brightly burning as the midday's sun;
    But after them doth Hymen hie as fast,
    Clothed in sable, and a saffron robe,
    And blows them out, and quencheth them with blood,
    As discontent that things continue so.
2210 GHOST: Sufficeth me; thy meaning's understood,
    And thanks to thee and those infernal powers
    That will not tolerate a lover's woe;
    Rest thee, for I will sit to see the rest.

2192 *worldlings:* mundane beings
     ground: found, base their behav-
     iour on (see note)
2194 *mood:* fierce spirit
     soliciting: ensnaring, enticing
2198 *unquiet:* times of turmoil
2199 *wile:* crafty device
2200 *instance:* instant, moment
2203 *Reveal:* explain, disclose
     mystery: hidden meaning

2206 *Hymen:* god of marriage
     hie: speed, chase
2207 *sable:* black
     saffron: orange yellow, 'crocus
     yellow'
2209 *As discontent:* as being dissatis-
     fied
2212 *tolerate:* allow to persist

REVENGE: Then argue not, for thou hast thy request.

Exeunt[?].

ACT IV SCENE I

[*Hieronimo's house*]
Enter BEL-IMPERIA *and* HIERONIMO

BEL-IMPERIA: Is this the love thou bear'st Horatio?
Is this the kindness that thou counterfeit'st?
Are these the fruits of thine incessant tears?
Hieronimo, are these thy passions,
Thy protestations, and thy deep laments,
That thou wert wont to weary men withal?   2220
O unkind father! O deceitful world!
With what excuses canst thou show thyself?
With what . . .
From this dishonour and the hate of men,
Thus to neglect the loss and life of him
Whom both my letters, and thine own belief,
Assures thee to be causeless slaughtered?
Hieronimo, for shame, Hieronimo!
Be not a history to after-times
Of such ingratitude unto thy son.   2230
Unhappy mothers of such children then,
But monstrous fathers, to forget so soon
The death of those whom they with care and cost
Have tender'd so, thus careless should be lost!

2218 *passions:* painful sufferings, expressions of emotion
2220 *That:* with which
2221 *unkind:* unnatural
2222 *With what* etc.: how can you justify yourself in public?
2223 *With what . . .:* a defective line (see note)

2227 *causeless:* without good cause
2229 *history:* exemplary case-history
2231 *then:* in such cases
2234 *tender'd:* cherished, nurtured
careless: lacking care

Myself, a stranger in respect of thee,
So lov'd his life, as still I wish their deaths,
Nor shall his death be unreveng'd by me,
Although I bear it out for fashion's sake.
For here I swear in sight of Heaven and earth,

2240 Should'st thou neglect the love thou should'st retain
And give it over and devise no more,
Myself should send their hateful souls to Hell,
That wrought his downfall with extremest death.

HIERONIMO: But may it be that Bel-imperia
Vows such revenge as she hath deign'd to say?
Why, then I see that Heaven applies our drift,
And all the saints do sit soliciting
For vengeance on those cursed murderers.
Madam, 'tis true, and now I find it so:

2250 I found a letter, written in your name,
And in that letter, how Horatio died.
Pardon, oh pardon, Bel-imperia,
My fear and care in not believing it,
Nor think I thoughtless think upon a mean
To let his death be unreveng'd at full,
And here I vow, so you but give consent
And will conceal my resolution,
I will ere long determine of their deaths
That causeless thus have murdered my son.

2260 BEL-IMPERIA: Hieronimo, I will consent, conceal,

2235	*in respect of:* by comparison with	2245	*deign'd:* thought fit
		2247	*soliciting:* pleading, entreating
2238	*bear it out:* pretend, 'carry it off'	2253	*care:* caution
	fashion's: mere form's	2254	*thoughtless:* without reflecting carefully
2241	*give it over:* abandon		*mean:* method
	devise: plot, scheme	2255	*at full:* totally, utterly
2243	*extremest:* cruellest	2258	*determine of:* definitely fix

And aught that may effect for thine avail,
Join with thee to revenge Horatio's death.

HIERONIMO: On then: whatsoever I devise,
Let me entreat you grace my practices,
For why the plot's already in mine head –
Here they are.
Enter BALTHAZAR *and* LORENZO.

BALTHAZAR: How now, Hieronimo? What, courting
Bel-imperia?

HIERONIMO: Aye, my lord,
Such courting as, I promise you,
She hath my heart but you, my lord, have hers.

LORENZO: But now, Hieronimo, or never,   2270
We are to entreat your help.

HIERONIMO: My help?
Why, my good lords, assure yourselves of me,
For you have given me cause –
[*aside*] Aye, by my faith, have you.

BALTHAZAR: It pleas'd you
At the entertainment of the Ambassador
To grace the King so much as with a show;
Now were your study so well furnished,
As, for the passing of the first night's sport,
To entertain my father with the like,
Or any such-like pleasing motion,   2280
Assure yourself it would content them well.

HIERONIMO: Is this all?

2261 *effect:* be effectual
avail: benefit, help
2264 *grace:* countenance, back up
practices: actions, schemes
2265 *For why:* because
2276 *grace:* honour
as with: in that you staged
show: display, presentation

2277 *study:* private room, library
so well furnished: sufficiently well
stocked
2279 *the like:* a similar show or spectacle
2280 *motion:* show? (but see note)

BALTHAZAR: Aye, this is all.

HIERONIMO: Why, then I'll fit you, say no more.
When I was young I gave my mind
And plied myself to fruitless poetry:
Which, though it profit the professor naught,
Yet is it passing pleasing to the world.

LORENZO: And how for that?

HIERONIMO: Marry, my good lord, thus
(And yet methinks you are too quick with us):
2290   When in Toledo there I studied,
It was my chance to write a tragedy –
See here, my lords –

    He shows them a book.

Which long forgot, I found this other day.
Now would your lordships favour me so much
As but to grace me with your acting it –
I mean each one of you to play a part –
Assure you it will prove most passing strange,
And wondrous plausible to that assembly.

BALTHAZAR: What, would you have us play a tragedy?

2300   HIERONIMO [*irritably*]: Why, Nero thought it no
disparagement,
And kings and emperors have ta'en delight
To make experience of their wits in plays!

LORENZO: Nay, be not angry, good Hieronimo;
The Prince but asked a question.

2283	*fit you:* satisfy your need, 'fix you up' (see note)	2297	*strange:* notable, remarkable
2286	*professor:* practitioner, creator	2298	*plausible:* praiseworthy, pleasing
2287	*passing:* exceedingly	2300	*disparagement:* indignity
2288	*Marry:* why, to be sure	2301	*ta'en:* taken
2289	*quick:* sharp, importunate, 'quick off the mark'	2302	*experience:* trial
			wits: skill, talent
2291	*chance:* fortune, 'it happened that'	2305	*and you be:* if you are

BALTHAZAR: In faith, Hieronimo, and you be in earnest,
   I'll make one.
LORENZO: And I another.
HIERONIMO: Now, my good lord, could you entreat
   Your sister Bel-imperia to make one –
   For what's a play without a woman in it?
BEL-IMPERIA: Little entreaty shall serve me, Hieronimo,   2310
   For I must needs be employ'd in your play.
HIERONIMO: Why, this is well. I tell you, lordings,
   It was determin'd to have been acted
   By gentlemen and scholars too,
   Such as could tell what to speak.
BALTHAZAR: And now it shall be play'd by princes and
      courtiers,
   Such as can tell how to speak,
   If, as it is our country manner,
   You will but let us know the argument.
HIERONIMO: That shall I roundly. The Chronicles of Spain   2320
   Record this written of a knight of Rhodes:
   He was betroth'd and wedded at the length
   To one Perseda, an Italian dame,
   Whose beauty ravish'd all that her beheld,
   Especially the soul of Soliman,
   Who at the marriage was the chiefest guest.
   By sundry means sought Soliman to win
   Perseda's love, and could not gain the same:
   Then gan he break his passions to a friend,

2306	*make one:* join the cast	2319	*but:* only
2310	*serve:* suffice		*argument:* subject-matter, plot
2313	*determin'd:* resolved, agreed	2320	*roundly:* readily
2315	*could tell:* knew what they had to say (see note)	2322	*at the length:* in the fullness of time
2317	*tell how to speak:* know the rules of elocution (see note)	2329	*gan he:* he began
2318	*country manner:* national custom (see note)		*break:* reveal, confess

2330 One of his bashaws whom he held full dear;
Her had this bashaw long solicited,
And saw she was not otherwise to be won
But by her husband's death, this knight of Rhodes,
Whom presently by treachery he slew.
She, stirr'd with an exceeding hate therefore,
As cause of this slew Soliman,
And to escape the bashaw's tyranny,
Did stab herself. And this the tragedy.

LORENZO: Oh, excellent!

BEL-IMPERIA: But say, Hieronimo,
2340 What then became of him that was the bashaw?

HIERONIMO: Marry, thus: mov'd with remorse of his misdeeds,
Ran to a mountain-top and hung himself.

BALTHAZAR: But which of us is to perform that part?

HIERONIMO: Oh, that will I, my lords, make no doubt of it;
I'll play the murderer, I warrant you,
For I already have conceited that.

BALTHAZAR: And what shall I?

HIERONIMO: Great Soliman, the Turkish Emperor.

LORENZO: And I?

HIERONIMO: Erastus, the knight of Rhodes.

BEL-IMPERIA: And I?

2350 HIERONIMO: Perseda, chaste and resolute.
And here, my lords, are several abstracts drawn,
For each of you to note your parts,
And act it as occasion's offer'd you.

[*to* BALTHAZAR] You must provide a Turkish cap,

2330 *bashaws:* Pashas, officers
2331 *solicited:* pestered for sexual favours
2334 *presently:* immediately
2346 *conceited:* 'worked that out', formed a conception of
2351 *abstracts:* synopses, plot-outlines
  drawn: drawn up, drafted
2353 *occasion's:* opportunity's

A black mustachio and a fauchion.
   Gives a paper to BALTHAZAR.
You with a cross like to a knight of Rhodes.
   Gives another to LORENZO.
And, Madam, you must attire yourself
   He giveth BEL-IMPERIA *another.*
Like Phoebe, Flora, or the huntress,
Which to your discretion shall seem best.
And as for me, my lords, I'll look to one;   2360
And, with the ransom that the Viceroy sent,
So furnish and perform this tragedy,
As all the world shall say Hieronimo
Was liberal in gracing of it so.
BALTHAZAR: Hieronimo, methinks a comedy were better.
HIERONIMO: A comedy?
Fie, comedies are fit for common wits,
But to present a kingly troop withal,
Give me a stately-written tragedy,
Tragoedia cothurnata, fitting kings,   2370
Containing matter, and not common things.
My lords, all this must be perform'd,
As fitting for the first night's revelling:
The Italian tragedians were so sharp of wit
That in one hour's meditation
They would perform anything in action.
LORENZO: And well it may, for I have seen the like

2355	*mustachio:* moustache	2368	*to present* etc.: to set before a
	fauchion: a broad carved sword		royal party
	(see note)	2370	*Tragoedia cothurnata:* high
2358	*the huntress:* Diana		tragedy (see note)
2359	*Which:* whichever	2371	*matter:* content of significance
2360	*look to one:* prepare a suitable cos-	2374	*tragedians:* tragic actors (see
	tume		note)
2362	*furnish:* set up, provide for	2375	*meditation:* study, preparation-
2364	*gracing:* adorning, 'mounting'		time

In Paris, 'mongst the French tragedians.

HIERONIMO: In Paris, Mass and well remembered!
2380   There's one thing more that rests for us to do.

BALTHAZAR: What's that, Hieronimo? Forget not anything.

HIERONIMO: Each one of us must act his part
    In unknown languages,
    That it may breed the more variety.
    [*to* BALTHAZAR] As you, my lord, in Latin, I in Greek,
    [*to* LORENZO] You in Italian, and for because I know
    That Bel-imperia hath practised the French,
    In courtly French shall all her phrases be.

BEL-IMPERIA: You mean to try my cunning then,
    Hieronimo?

2390   BALTHAZAR: But this will be a mere confusion,
    And hardly shall we all be understood.

HIERONIMO: It must be so, for the conclusion
    Shall prove the invention, and all was good:
    And I myself in an oration,
    And, with a strange and wond'rous show besides
    That I will have there behind a curtain,
    Assure yourself shall make the matter known:
    And all shall be concluded in one scene,
    For there's no pleasure ta'en in tediousness.

BALTHAZAR [*aside to* LORENZO]: How like you this?

2400   LORENZO [*aside*]:   Why thus, my lord:
    We must resolve to soothe his humours up.

BALTHAZAR: On then, Hieronimo, farewell till soon.

2379   *Mass:* by the Mass!
2380   *rests:* remains
2383   *unknown:* non-native (i.e. not
        Spanish)
2387   *practised:* studied
2389   *cunning:* skill
2391   *hardly:* with difficulty
2393   *invention:* contrivance, design

2395   *strange:* rare
        show: spectacle, tableau (see
        note)
2399   *ta'en:* taken
2401   *soothe his humours up:* humour
        him, indulge his fancies

HIERONIMO: You'll ply this gear?
LORENZO: I warrant you.
                    Exeunt all but HIERONIMO.
HIERONIMO: Why so;
    Now shall I see the fall of Babylon
    Wrought by the Heavens in this confusion.
    And if the world like not this tragedy,
    Hard is the hap of old Hieronimo.
                              Exit.

ACT IV   SCENE 2

[*The grounds of Hieronimo's house*]
Enter ISABELLA *with a weapon.*
ISABELLA: Tell me no more! O monstrous homicides!
    Since neither piety nor pity moves
    The King to justice or compassion,   2410
    I will revenge myself upon this place,
    Where thus they murder'd my beloved son.
        She cuts down the arbour.
    Down with these branches and these loathsome boughs
    Of this unfortunate and fatal pine!
    Down with them, Isabella, rent them up,
    And burn the roots from whence the rest is sprung!
    I will not leave a root, a stalk, a tree,
    A bough, a branch, a blossom, nor a leaf,
    No, not an herb within this garden plot:
    Accursed complot of my misery,   2420
    Fruitless for ever may this garden be!
    Barren the earth, and blissless whosoever

2403   *ply this gear:* put your backs into
       this business
2407   *hap:* luck, fortune
2408   *homicides:* killers

2414   *unfortunate:* disastrous, unlucky
2415   *rent:* rend, tear
2420   *complot of:* conspirer in? (see
       note)

Imagines not to keep it unmanur'd;
An eastern wind commix'd with noisome airs
Shall blast the plants and the young saplings;
The earth with serpents shall be pestered,
And passengers, for fear to be infect,
Shall stand aloof, and looking at it, tell
'There murder'd died the son of Isabel.'

2430 Aye, here he died, and here I him embrace;
See where his ghost solicits with his wounds
Revenge on her that should revenge his death.
Hieronimo, make haste to see thy son,
For sorrow and despair hath cited me
To hear Horatio plead with Rhadamant;
Make haste, Hieronimo, to hold excus'd
Thy negligence in pursuit of their deaths,
Whose hateful wrath bereav'd him of his breath.
Ah nay, thou dost delay their deaths,

2440 Forgives the murderers of thy noble son,
And none but I bestir me [–] to no end;
And as I curse this tree from further fruit,
So shall my womb be cursed for his sake
And with this weapon will I wound the breast,
The hapless breast that gave Horatio suck.

> *She stabs herself.*
> [*Exit.*]

2423	*Imagines:* plans	2427	*passengers:* passers-by
	unmanur'd: unfertilized, unculti-		*infect:* infected
	vated	2431	*solicits:* urges
2424	*commix'd:* mingled	2434	*cited:* summoned to court
	noisome: noxious, offensive	2436	*hold:* have adjudged to be
	airs: vapours, winds	2440	*Forgives:* i.e. Hieronimo
2426	*pestered:* plagued, encumbered	2445	*hapless:* unfortunate, unlucky

ACT IV   SCENE 3

[*The Spanish court*]
Enter HIERONIMO; *he knocks up the curtain.*
Enter the DUKE OF CASTILE.

CASTILE: How now, Hieronimo! Where's your fellows,
That you take all this pain?
HIERONIMO: O sir, it is for the author's credit
To look that all things may go well:
But, good my lord, let me entreat your grace   2450
To give the King the copy of the play:
[*Gives him a book.*]
This is the argument of what we show.
CASTILE: I will, Hieronimo.
HIERONIMO: One thing more, my good lord.
CASTILE: What's that?
HIERONIMO: Let me entreat your grace
That, when the train are pass'd into the gallery,
You would vouchsafe to throw me down the key.
CASTILE: I will, Hieronimo.
          Exit CASTILE.
HIERONIMO [*calling off*]: What, are you ready, Balthazar?
Bring a chair and a cushion for the King.
     Enter BALTHAZAR *with a chair* [*and a title-board*].
Well done, Balthazar; hang up the title.   2460
'Our scene is Rhodes.' What, is your beard on?
BALTHAZAR: Half on, the other is in my hand.

2445 s.d. *knocks up:* fixes, fastens up? 2455 *train:* retinue
      (see note)   *gallery:* see note
2446 *fellows:* fellow-players   2456 *vouchsafe:* deign, graciously con-
2447 *That you take* etc.: i.e. that every-   sent
      thing devolves on you   *me:* for me (see note)
2449 *To look that:* to make sure that   2460 *title:* placard with the location
2452 *argument:* synopsis, scenario   on (see note)

HIERONIMO: Dispatch, for shame! Are you so long?

Exit BALTHAZAR.

Bethink thyself, Hieronimo;
Recall thy wits; recount thy former wrongs
Thou hast receiv'd by murder of thy son;
And lastly, not least, how Isabel,
Once his mother and thy dearest wife,
All woe-begone for him hath slain herself.
2470 Behoves thee then, Hieronimo, to be reveng'd:
The plot is laid of dire revenge:
On then, Hieronimo, pursue revenge,
For nothing wants but acting of revenge.

Exit HIERONIMO.

ACT IV SCENE 4

Enter Spanish KING, VICEROY, *the* DUKE OF CASTILE, *and their train.*

KING [*consulting his copy*]: Now, Viceroy, shall we see the tragedy
Of Soliman the Turkish Emperor:
Perform'd of pleasure by your son the Prince,
My nephew, Don Lorenzo, and my niece.
VICEROY: Who, Bel-imperia?
KING: Aye, and Hieronimo our Marshal,
2480 At whose request they deign to do't themselves –
These be our pastimes in the court of Spain.
Here, brother, you shall be the book-keeper;
This is the argument of that they show.

2463	*Dispatch:* hurry up!	2473	*wants:* is lacking
2465	*recount:* consider, reckon up, go over		*but:* except
		2476	*of pleasure:* to amuse themselves
2469	*woe-begone:* grief-stricken	2480	*deign:* think fit
2470	*Behoves thee:* it befits you	2482	*book-keeper:* prompter (see note)

He giveth him [CASTILE] *a book.*
  Gentlemen, this play of Hieronimo in sundry languages was
    thought good to be set down in English more largely,
      for the easier understanding to every
        public reader.
  Enter [*to perform*] BALTHAZAR, BEL-IMPERIA, *and*
  HIERONIMO.
BALTHAZAR: *Bashaw, that Rhodes is ours, yield heavens the*
  honour,
  And holy Mahomet our sacred Prophet;
  And be thou grac'd with every excellence
  That Soliman can give, or thou desire.
  But thy desert in conquering Rhodes is less
  Than in reserving this fair Christian nymph,
  Perseda, blissful lamp of excellence: 2490
  Whose eyes compel, like powerful adamant,
  The warlike heart of Soliman to wait.
KING: See, Viceroy, that is Balthazar your son
  That represents the Emperor Soliman;
  [*aside*] How well he acts his amorous passion!
VICEROY [*aside*]: Aye, Bel-imperia hath taught him that.
CASTILE [*aside*]: That's because his mind runs all on Bel-
  imperia.
HIERONIMO: *Whatever joy earth yields betide your Majesty!*
BALTHAZAR: *Earth yields no joy without Perseda's love.*
HIERONIMO: *Let then Perseda on your grace attend.*   2500
BALTHAZAR: *She shall not wait on me, but I on her;*
  Drawn by the influence of her lights, I yield.
  But let my friend the Rhodian knight come forth,

2483	s.d. *more largely:* more fully, more freely (see note)	2491	*adamant:* magnetic stone (see note)
2486	*grac'd:* honoured	2492	*wait:* look forward hopefully
2488	*desert:* merit	2498	*betide:* befall
2489	*reserving:* rescuing, saving	2502	*lights:* 'bright glances'

> *Erasto, dearer than my life to me,*
> *That he may see Perseda my beloved.*
>> *Enter* [LORENZO *as*] ERASTO.

KING: Here comes Lorenzo; [*to* CASTILE] look upon the
   plot,
   And tell me, brother, what part plays he?

BEL-IMPERIA: *Ah, my Erasto, welcome to Perseda!*

LORENZO: *Thrice happy is Erasto, that thou livest;*
2510   *Rhodes' loss is nothing to Erasto's joy:*
   Sith his Perseda lives, his life survives.

BALTHAZAR: *Ah, bashaw, here is love between Erasto*
   And fair Perseda, sovereign of my soul.

HIERONIMO: *Remove Erasto, mighty Soliman,*
   And then Perseda will be quickly won.

BALTHAZAR: *Erasto is my friend, and while he lives,*
   Perseda never will remove her love.

HIERONIMO: *Let not Erasto live, to grieve great Soliman.*

BALTHAZAR: *Dear is Erasto in our princely eye.*

2520 HIERONIMO: *But if he be your rival, let him die.*

BALTHAZAR: *Why, let him die, so love commandeth me.*
   Yet grieve I that Erasto should so die.

HIERONIMO: *Erasto, Soliman saluteth thee,*
   And lets thee wit by me his highness' will,
   Which is, thou should'st be thus employed.
>> *Stabs him.*

BEL-IMPERIA: *Ay me,*
   Erasto! See Soliman, Erasto's slain!

BALTHAZAR: *Yet liveth Soliman to comfort thee.*
   Fair queen of beauty, let not favour die,
2530   *But with a gracious eye behold his grief,*
   That with Perseda's beauty is increas'd,

2506 *plot:* scenario (with cast-list)	2524 *wit:* know
2510 *to:* compared with	2529 *favour:* Perseda's love
2511 *Sith:* since	

If by Perseda grief be not releas'd.

BEL-IMPERIA: *Tyrant, desist soliciting vain suits;*
  Relentless are mine ears to thy laments,
  As thy butcher is pitiless and base,
  Which seiz'd on my Erasto, harmless knight.
  Yet by thy power thou thinkest to command,
  And to thy power Perseda doth obey:
  But were she able, thus she would revenge
  Thy treacheries on thee, ignoble Prince —   2540
    Stab[s] him.
  And on herself she would be thus reveng'd.
    Stab[s] herself.

KING: Well said, old Marshal, this was bravely done.

HIERONIMO: But Bel-imperia plays Perseda well.

VICEROY: Were this in earnest, Bel-imperia,
  You would be better to my son than so.

KING: But now what follows for Hieronimo?

HIERONIMO: Marry, this follows for Hieronimo:
  Here break we off our sundry languages,
  And thus conclude I in our vulgar tongue.
  Haply you think — but bootless are your thoughts —   2550
  That this is fabulously counterfeit,
  And that we do as all tragedians do:
  To die today, for fashioning our scene,
  The death of Ajax, or some Roman peer,
  And in a minute starting up again,
  Revive to please tomorrow's audience.

2533 *soliciting:* urging	2550 *Haply:* perhaps
2535 *thy butcher:* i.e. the bashaw	*bootless:* useless
2538 *obey:* submit	2551 *fabulously counterfeit:* a fictional
2542 *Well said:* well executed, well	imitation only
done (see note)	2553 *fashioning our scene:* shaping our
bravely: worthily	drama
2549 *vulgar tongue:* the common	
speech of Spain	

No, princes; know I am Hieronimo,
The hopeless father of a hapless son,
Whose tongue is tun'd to tell his latest tale,
2560   Not to excuse gross errors in the play.
I see your looks urge instance of these words;
Behold the reason urging me to this —
     Shows his dead son [behind the curtain].
See here my show, look on this spectacle.
Here lay my hope, and here my hope hath end;
Here lay my heart, and here my heart was slain;
Here lay my treasure, here my treasure lost;
Here lay my bliss, and here my bliss bereft;
But hope, heart, treasure, joy, and bliss,
All fled, fail'd, died, yea, all decay'd with this.
2570   From forth these wounds came breath that gave me life;
They murder'd me that made these fatal marks.
The cause was love, whence grew this mortal hate:
The hate, Lorenzo and young Balthazar;
The love, my son to Bel-imperia.
But night, the coverer of accursed crimes,
With pitchy silence hush'd these traitors' harms,
And lent them leave, for they had sorted leisure,
To take advantage in my garden plot
Upon my son, my dear Horatio.
2580   There merciless they butcher'd up my boy,
In black dark night, to pale dim cruel death;
He shrieks; I heard, and yet methinks I hear
His dismal outcry echo in the air.
With soonest speed I hasted to the noise,

2558   *hopeless:* void of hope
2559   *latest:* final
2561   *instance:* proof
2563   *show:* tableau, display
2570   *breath that gave* etc.: the breath
        which gave life to me (see note)

2576   *pitchy:* pitch-black, 'deepest'
        harms: evil acts
2577   *sorted:* contrived, arranged
2584   *soonest:* quickest

Where, hanging on a tree, I found my son,
Through-girt with wounds, and slaughter'd as you see.
And griev'd I, think you, at this spectacle?
Speak, Portuguese, whose loss resembles mine!
If thou canst weep upon thy Balthazar,
'Tis like I wail'd for my Horatio.   2590
And you, my lord, whose reconciled son
March'd in a net, and thought himself unseen,
And rated me for brainsick lunacy,
With 'God amend that mad Hieronimo' —
How can you brook our play's catastrophe?
And here behold this bloody handkercher
Which at Horatio's death I weeping dipp'd
Within the river of his bleeding wounds;
It as propitious, see, I have reserv'd,
And never hath it left my bloody heart,   2600
Soliciting remembrance of my vow
With these, O these accursed murderers,
Which now perform'd, my heart is satisfied.
And to this end the bashaw I became,
That might revenge me on Lorenzo's life,
Who therefore was appointed to the part,
And was to represent the knight of Rhodes,
That I might kill him more conveniently.
So, Viceroy, was this Balthazar thy son
That Soliman, which Bel-imperia   2610
In person of Perseda murdered,

2586 *Through-girt:* struck through   2599 *propitious:* as a good sign (that
2591 *reconciled:* i.e. with Hieronimo   revenge will occur)
2592 *March'd in a net* etc.: made his   *reserv'd:* preserved, kept
        deceit obvious (see note)   2601 *Soliciting:* demanding
2593 *rated:* reproached, reproved   2606 *appointed to:* assigned to
2595 *brook:* endure, stand
        catastrophe: dénouement, 'terrible
        finale'

Solely appointed to that tragic part
That she might slay him that offended her.
Poor Bel-imperia miss'd her part in this,
For though the story saith she should have died,
Yet I of kindness, and of care to her,
Did otherwise determine of her end;
But love of him whom they did hate too much
Did urge her resolution to be such.

2620 And, princes, now behold Hieronimo,
Author and actor in this tragedy,
Bearing his latest fortune in his fist;
And will as resolute conclude his part
As any of the actors gone before:
And, gentles, thus I end my play;
Urge no more words: I have no more to say.

He runs to hang himself.

KING: Oh, hearken, Viceroy! Hold, Hieronimo!
Brother, my nephew and thy son are slain!
VICEROY: We are betray'd! My Balthazar is slain!
2630 Break ope the doors; run, save Hieronimo!

[*They* [ATTENDANTS] *break in and hold* HIERONIMO.]

Hieronimo, do but inform the King of these events;
Upon mine honour thou shalt have no harm.
HIERONIMO: Viceroy, I will not trust thee with my life,
Which I this day have offer'd to my son.
Accurs'd wretch,
Why stay'st thou him that was resolved to die?
KING: Speak, traitor; damned, bloody murderer, speak;
For now I have thee I will make thee speak:
Why hast thou done this undeserving deed?

2614 *miss'd her part:* went beyond her role
2622 *latest:* final
       fortune: destiny (see note)
2625 *gentles:* gentlefolk
2627 *Hold:* stop, hold your hand (see note)
2636 *stay'st:* do you restrain
2639 *undeserving:* unjustified

VICEROY: Why hast thou murdered my Balthazar?   2640
CASTILE: Why hast thou butcher'd both my children thus?
HIERONIMO: Oh, good words!
   As dear to me was my Horatio
   As yours, or yours, or yours, my lord, to you.
   My guiltless son was by Lorenzo slain,
   And by Lorenzo and that Balthazar
   Am I at last revenged thoroughly,
   Upon whose souls may heavens be yet aveng'd
   With greater far than these afflictions.
CASTILE: But who were thy confederates in this?   2650
VICEROY: That was thy daughter Bel-imperia:
   For by her hand my Balthazar was slain;
   I saw her stab him.
KING: Why speakest thou not?
HIERONIMO: What lesser liberty can kings afford
   Than harmless silence? Then afford it me:
   Sufficeth I may not, nor I will not tell thee.
KING: Fetch forth the tortures:
   Traitor as thou art, I'll make thee tell.
HIERONIMO: Indeed, thou mayest torment me as his wretched
      son
   Hath done in murd'ring my Horatio.   2660
   But never shalt thou force me to reveal
   The thing which I have vow'd inviolate:
   And therefore, in despite of all thy threats,
   Pleas'd with their deaths, and eas'd with their revenge,
   First take my tongue, and afterwards my heart.
    [He bites out his tongue.]
KING: O monstrous resolution of a wretch!
   See, Viceroy, he hath bitten forth his tongue
   Rather than to reveal what we requir'd.

2646   *by:* through the deaths of   2659   *his wretched son:* i.e. Castile's
2658   *Traitor:* betrayer   2662   *inviolate:* impervious to inquiry

CASTILE: Yet can he write.

2670 KING: And if in this he satisfy us not,
We will devise th'extremest kind of death
That ever was invented for a wretch.

*Then he [HIERONIMO] makes signs for a knife to mend his
pen.*

CASTILE: Oh, he would have a knife to mend his pen.

VICEROY: Here, and advise thee that thou write the troth.

He [HIERONIMO] with a knife stabs the DUKE and himself.

[KING]: Look to my brother! Save Hieronimo!
What age hath ever heard such monstrous deeds?
My brother and the whole succeeding hope
That Spain expected after my decease!
Go bear his body hence, that we may mourn
2680 The loss of our beloved brother's death,
That he may be entomb'd whate'er befall.
I am the next, the nearest, last of all.

VICEROY: And thou, Don Pedro, do the like for us;
Take up our hapless son untimely slain:
Set me with him, and he with woeful me,
Upon the mainmast of a ship unmann'd
And let the wind and tide haul me along
To Scylla's barking and untamed [reef],
Or to the loathsome pool of Acheron,
2690 To weep my want for my sweet Balthazar:
Spain hath no refuge for a Portingale.

*The trumpets sound a dead march, the KING of Spain
mourning after his brother's body, and the [VICEROY] of
Portingale bearing the body of his son.*

2672 s.d. *mend his pen:* improve by
sharpening (see note)
2674 *advise thee:* ponder well, take
care
troth: truth

2678 *expected:* awaited, anticipated
2688 *barking:* see note
2689 *Acheron:* one of the rivers of
Hell (see note)
2690 *my want for:* my loss of

Enter GHOST *and* REVENGE.

GHOST: Aye, now my hopes have end in their effects,
    When blood and sorrow finish my desires:
    Horatio murder'd in his father's bower,
    Vild Serberine by Pedringano slain,
    False Pedringano hang'd by quaint device,
    Fair Isabella by herself misdone,
    Prince Balthazar by Bel-imperia stabb'd,
    The Duke of Castile and his wicked son
    Both done to death by old Hieronimo.   2700
    My Bel-imperia fall'n as Dido fell,
    And good Hieronimo slain by himself:
    Aye, these were spectacles to please my soul.
    Now will I beg at lovely Proserpine,
    That, by the virtue of her princely doom,
    I may consort my friends in pleasing sort,
    And on my foes work just and sharp revenge.
    I'll lead my friend Horatio through those fields
    Where never-dying wars are still inur'd;
    I'll lead fair Isabella to that train   2710
    Where pity weeps but never feeleth pain;
    I'll lead my Bel-imperia to those joys
    That vestal virgins and fair queens possess;
    I'll lead Hieronimo where Orpheus plays,
    Adding sweet pleasure to eternal days.
    But say, Revenge, for thou must help or none,
    Against the rest how shall my hate be shown?
REVENGE: This hand shall hale them down to deepest Hell,

2695	*Vild:* vile	
2696	*quaint:* ingenious, cunning	
	device: trick, scheme	
2697	*Fair:* sweet	
	misdone: destroyed	
2704	*beg at:* entreat	

2705	*princely doom:* royal sentence	
2706	*consort:* escort, accompany	
2709	*inur'd:* practised, conducted	
2710	*train:* company	
2713	*vestal:* chaste (see note)	
2718	*hale:* drag	

Where none but Furies, bugs and tortures dwell.
2720 GHOST: Then, sweet Revenge, do this at my request:
Let me be judge and doom them to unrest:
Let loose poor Titius from the vulture's gripe,
And let Don Cyprian supply his room;
Place Don Lorenzo on Ixion's wheel,
And let the lover's endless pains surcease:
Juno forgets old wrath and grants him ease.
Hang Balthazar about Chimera's neck,
And let him there bewail his bloody love,
Repining at our joys that are above;
2730 Let Serberine go roll the fatal stone,
And take from Sisyphus his endless moan;
False Pedringano, for his treachery,
Let him be dragg'd through boiling Acheron,
And there live dying still in endless flames,
Blaspheming gods and all their holy names.
REVENGE: Then haste we down to meet thy friends and foes,
To place thy friends in ease, the rest in woes:
For here, though death hath end their misery,
I'll there begin their endless tragedy.

Exeunt.

FINIS

2719 *bugs:* hobgoblins, 'bogies'
2721 *doom:* sentence
       unrest: discomfort
2723 *supply his room:* fill his place
2725 *the lover's:* i.e. Ixion's
       surcease: cease, come to an end
2727 *Chimera's:* a monster's (see note)
2729 *Repining at:* begrudging, resenting
2734 *still:* permanently
2735 *Blaspheming:* uttering impieties against
2738 *end:* ended, completed

ADDITIONS TO THE 1602 TEXT OF
THE SPANISH TRAGEDY

ADDITION A (between lines 921 and 922)

[ISABELLA: For outrage fits our cursed wretchedness.]
    Aye me, Hieronimo; sweet husband, speak.
HIERONIMO: He supp'd with us tonight, frolic and merry,
    And said he would go visit Balthazar
    At the Duke's palace: there the Prince doth lodge.
    He had no custom to stay out so late;
    He may be in his chamber; some go see.
    Roderigo, ho!
        Enter PEDRO *and* JAQUES.
ISABELLA: Aye me, he raves. Sweet Hieronimo!
HIERONIMO: True, all Spain takes note of it.
    Besides he is so generally belov'd,
    His Majesty the other day did grace him
    With waiting on his cup: these be favours
    Which do assure [he] cannot be short-liv'd.
ISABELLA: Sweet Hieronimo!
HIERONIMO: I wonder how this fellow got his clothes?
    Sirrah, sirrah, I'll know the truth of all:
    Jaques, run to the Duke of Castile's presently,

---

2 *frolic:* 'full of fun'
5 *had no custom:* was not in the habit
10 *generally:* by all
12 *waiting on his cup:* serving him wine
13 *assure:* make certain
17 *presently:* straightaway

And bid my son Horatio to come home.
I and his mother have had strange dreams tonight.
Do you hear me, sir?

JAQUES: Aye, sir.

20 HIERONIMO: Well, sir, begone.
                                    [*Exit* JAQUES.]
Pedro, come hither: knowest thou who this is?
    [*indicating* HORATIO'*s corpse.*]

PEDRO: Too well, sir.

HIERONIMO: Too well? Who? Who is it? Peace, Isabella:
Nay, blush not, man.

PEDRO: It is my lord Horatio.

HIERONIMO: Ha, ha! By Saint James, but this doth make me
    laugh
That there are more deluded than myself.

PEDRO: Deluded?

HIERONIMO: Aye, I would have sworn myself within this
    hour
That this had been my son Horatio;
30 His garments are so like –
Ha! are they not great persuasions?

ISABELLA: Oh, would to God it were not so!

HIERONIMO: Were not, Isabella? Dost thou dream it is?
Can thy soft bosom entertain a thought
That such a black deed of mischief should be done
On one so poor and spotless as our son?
Away! I am asham'd.

ISABELLA: Dear Hieronimo,
Cast a more serious eye upon thy grief;
Weak apprehension gives but weak belief.

---

31 *persuasions:* convincing pieces of   39 *apprehension:*   comprehension,
    evidence   grasp on the situation

36 *poor:* unfortunate, humble (but see
    note)

HIERONIMO: It was a man, sure, that was hang'd up here;   40
  A youth, as I remember; I cut him down:
  If it should prove my son now after all!
  Say you, say you, light! Lend me a taper;
  Let me look again. O God!
  Confusion, mischief, torment, death and hell,
  Drop all your stings at once in my cold bosom,
  That now is stiff with horror; kill me quickly:
  Be gracious to me, thou infective night,
  And drop this deed of murder down on me;
  Gird in my waste of grief with thy large darkness,   50
  And let me not survive to see the light
  May put me in the mind I had a son.
ISABELLA: O, sweet Horatio! O, my dearest son!
HIERONIMO: How strangely had I lost my way to grief:
  [Sweet lovely rose, ill-pluck'd before thy time;]

ADDITION B (to be substituted for line 1140
and part of line 1141)

[LORENZO: Why so, Hieronimo? Use me.]
HIERONIMO: Who, you, my lord?
  I reserve your favour for a greater honour;
   This is a very toy, my lord, a toy.
LORENZO: All's one, Hieronimo; acquaint me with it.
HIERONIMO: I'faith, my lord, 'tis an idle thing:
  I must confess, I ha' been too slack,
  Too tardy, too remiss unto your honour.
LORENZO: How now, Hieronimo?
HIERONIMO: In troth, my lord, it is a thing of nothing:

48 *infective:* infection-bearing   3 *a very toy:* a mere trifle (see note)
50 *Gird in:* confine   9 *In troth:* in truth
     waste: devastated void

10   The murder of a son or so;
       A thing of nothing, my lord.
[LORENZO: Why then, farewell.]

ADDITION C (between line 1692 and line 1693)

[1 PORTINGALE: By your leave, sir.]
HIERONIMO: 'Tis neither as you think, nor as you think,
       Nor as you think: you're wide all.
       These slippers are not mine, they were my son Horatio's –
       My son, and what's a son? A thing begot
       Within a pair of minutes, thereabout;
       A lump bred up in darkness, and doth serve
       To ballace these light creatures we call women;
       And at nine months' end, creeps forth to light.
       What is there yet in a son
10   To make a father dote, rave or run mad?
       Being born, it pouts, cries, and breeds teeth.
       What is there yet in a son? He must be fed,
       Be taught to go, and speak – Aye, or yet?
       Why might not a man love a calf as well,
       Or melt in passion o'er a frisking kid,
       As for a son? Methinks a young bacon
       Or a fine little smooth horse-colt
       Should move a man as much as doth a son:
       For one of these in very little time
20   Will grow to some good use, whereas a son
       The more he grows in stature and in years,
       The more unsquar'd, unbevell'd he appears,

---

 2   *wide:* wide of the mark   16   *bacon:* pig
 7   *ballace:* ballast, weigh down 22   *unsquar'd:* out of true (cf. 'needs
11   *breeds teeth:* cuts teeth   the corners knocked off')
13   *to go:* to walk   *unbevell'd:* raw, unpolished
     Aye, or yet?: Yes, and what else?

Reckons his parents among the rank of fools,
Strikes care upon their heads with his mad riots,
Makes them look old before they meet with age:
This is a son:
And what a loss were this, considered truly?
Oh, but my Horatio
Grew out of reach of these insatiate humours;
He lov'd his loving parents,   30
He was my comfort, and his mother's joy;
The very arm that did hold up our house:
Our hopes were stored up in him;
None but a damned murderer could hate him.
He had not seen the back of nineteen year,
When his strong arm unhors'd the proud Prince Balthazar,
And his great mind, too full of honour,
Took him [unto] mercy,
That valiant but ignoble Portingale.
Well, Heaven is Heaven still,   40
And there is Nemesis and Furies,
And things call'd whips,
And they sometimes do meet with murderers;
They do not always scape – that's some comfort.
Aye, aye, aye, and then time steals on;
And steals, and steals, till violence leaps forth
Like thunder wrapp'd in a ball of fire,
And so doth bring confusion to them all.
[Good leave have you; nay, I pray you go,]

---

24 *mad riots:* crazy revelry, 'daft   38 *Took him [unto] mercy:* decided to
    pranks'   have mercy on
29 *insatiate:* unsatisfied, discontented   48 *confusion:* ruin, overthrow, destruc-
    humours: fancies, whims   tion
35 *the back of nineteen year:* i.e. was
    not yet twenty

ADDITION D (between line 1834 and line 1835, i.e. between the end of Act III Scene 12 and the start of Act III Scene 13)

Enter JAQUES *and* PEDRO.

JAQUES: I wonder, Pedro, why our master thus
    At midnight sends us with our torches' light,
    When man and bird and beast are all at rest,
    Save those that watch for rape and bloody murder?

PEDRO: O Jaques, know thou that our master's mind
    Is much distraught since his Horatio died,
    And now his aged years should sleep in rest,
    His heart in quiet – like a desperate man,
    Grows lunatic and childish for his son.
10   Sometimes as he doth at his table sit,
    He speaks as if Horatio stood by him,
    Then starting in a rage, falls on the earth,
    Cries out, 'Horatio, where is my Horatio?'
    So that with extreme grief and cutting sorrow,
    There is not left in him one inch of man:
    See, where he comes.

        Enter HIERONIMO.

HIERONIMO: I pry through every crevice of each wall,
    Look on each tree, and search through every brake,
    Beat at the bushes, stamp our grandam earth,
20   Dive in the water, and stare up to Heaven,
    Yet cannot I behold my son Horatio.
    How now? Who's there? Spirits, spirits?

PEDRO: We are your servants that attend you, sir.

HIERONIMO: What make you with your torches in the dark?

---

18 *brake:* bushy thicket
19 *grandam:* grandmother
22 *Spirits:* demons

24 *What make you:* what are you doing

PEDRO: You bid us light them, and attend you here.

HIERONIMO: No, no, you are deceiv'd, not I; you are
    deceiv'd:
  Was I so mad to bid you light your torches now?
  Light me your torches at the mid of noon,
  Whenas the sun-god rides in all his glory:
  Light me your torches then.

PEDRO: Then we burn daylight.   30

HIERONIMO: Let it be burnt; night is a murderous slut
  That would not have her treasons to be seen,
  And yonder pale-faced [Hecate] there, the moon,
  Doth give consent to that is done in darkness;
  And all those stars that gaze upon her face
  Are aggots on her sleeve, pins on her train,
  And those that should be powerful and divine
  Do sleep in darkness when they most should shine.

PEDRO: Provoke them not, fair sir, with tempting words;
  The Heavens are gracious, and your miseries   40
  And sorrow makes you speak you know not what.

HIERONIMO: Villain, thou liest, and thou doest nought
  But tell me I am mad; thou liest, I am not mad.
  I know thee to be Pedro, and he Jaques:
  I'll prove it to thee, and were I mad, how could I?
  Where was she that same night when my Horatio
  Was murder'd? She should have shone: search thou the
    book.
  Had the moon shone, in my boy's face there was a kind of
    grace,
  That I now (nay, I do know), had the murderer seen him,

---

30 *burn daylight:* waste our time (see   39 *tempting:* provocative
    note)   47 *the book:* the almanac (see note)
36 *aggots:* aiglets, shiny lace-tags (see
    note)
    pins: spangled decorations

50 His weapon would have fallen and cut the earth,
    Had he been fram'd of naught but blood and death.
    Alack, when mischief doth it knows not what,
    What shall we say to mischief?
        Enter ISABELLA.
ISABELLA: Dear Hieronimo, come in a-doors:
    Oh, seek not means so to increase thy sorrow.
HIERONIMO: Indeed, Isabella, we do nothing here;
    I do not cry; ask Pedro and ask Jaques.
    Not I, indeed; we are very merry, very merry.
ISABELLA: How be merry here, be merry here?
60 Is not this the place, and this the very tree,
    Where my Horatio hied, where he was murder'd?
HIERONIMO: Was — do not say what: let her weep it out.
    This was the tree — I set it of a kernel,
    And when our hot Spain could not let it grow,
    But that the infant and the humane sap
    Began to wither, duly twice a morning
    Would I be sprinkling it with fountain water;
    At last it grew, and grew, and bore and bore,
    Till at the length it grew a gallows,
70 And did bear our son.
    It bore thy fruit and mine: O wicked, wicked plant!
        One knocks within at the door.
    See who knock there.
        [PEDRO *goes to the gate*.]
PEDRO: It is a painter, sir.
HIERONIMO: Bid him come in, and paint some comfort,
    For surely there's none lives but painted comfort.
    Let him come in: one knows not what may chance.
    God's will! that I should set this tree — but even so

51 *fram'd:* constructed, created
52 *mischief:* evil, wickedness
61 *hied:* went, betook himself
65 *humane:* kindly
66 *wither:* dry up
74 *painted:* feigned, dissembled, super-
    ficial

Masters ungrateful servants rear from nought,
And then they hate them that did bring them up.
Enter the PAINTER.

PAINTER: God bless you, sir.

HIERONIMO: Wherefore? Why, thou scornful villain?   80
How, where, or by what means should I be blest?

ISABELLA: What would'st thou have, good fellow?

PAINTER: Justice, Madam.

HIERONIMO: Oh, ambitious beggar, wouldest thou have that
That lives not in the world?
Why, all the undelv'd mines cannot buy
An ounce of justice: 'tis a jewel so inestimable.
I tell thee,
God hath engross'd all justice in his hands,
And there is none but what comes from him.

PAINTER: Oh, then I see   90
That God must right me for my murdered son.

HIERONIMO: How? Was thy son murder'd?

PAINTER: Aye, sir; no man did hold a son so dear.

HIERONIMO: What not as thine? That's a lie
As massy as the earth: I had a son,
Whose least unvalu'd hair did weigh
A thousand of thy sons – and he was murder'd.

PAINTER: Alas, sir; I had no more but he.

HIERONIMO: Nor I, nor I; but this same one of mine
Was worth a legion: but all is one.   100
Pedro, Jaques, go in a-doors; Isabella, go;
And this good fellow here and I
Will range this hideous orchard up and down,
Like to two lions reaved of their young.

---

88 *engross'd:* concentrated, monopo-
    lized
95 *massy:* solid, weighty
100 *all is one:* it doesn't matter
103 *range:* stroll about
104 *reaved:* deprived, bereft

Go in a-doors, I say.

Exeunt [PEDRO, JAQUES, ISABELLA].

The PAINTER *and he sits down.*

Come, let's talk wisely now. Was thy son
murder'd?

PAINTER: Aye, sir.

HIERONIMO: So was mine. How dost take it? Art thou not
sometimes mad? Is there no tricks that comes before thine
eyes?

PAINTER: O lord, yes, sir.

HIERONIMO: Art a painter? Canst paint me a tear, or a
wound, a groan, or a sigh? Canst paint me such a tree as
this?

PAINTER: Sir, I am sure you have heard of my painting; my
name's Bazardo.

HIERONIMO: Bazardo – afore God, an excellent fellow.
Look you, sir, do you see, I'd have you paint
me [in] my gallery in your oil colours matted,
and draw me five years younger than I am. Do ye
see, sir? Let five years go, let them go like the
Marshal of Spain. My wife Isabella standing by me,
with a speaking look to my son Horatio, which
should intend to this or some such-like purpose:
'God bless thee, my sweet son': and my hand
leaning upon his head, thus, sir; do you see? May it
be done?

PAINTER: Very well, sir.

HIERONIMO: Nay, I pray mark me, sir. Then, sir, would I
have you paint me this tree, this very tree. Canst paint a
doleful cry?

PAINTER: Seemingly, sir.

---

120   *gallery:* a covered walk (see note)   124   *speaking:* eloquent, meaningful
      matted: with a 'matt finish' (?)   125   *intend to:* signify
      (see note)   133   *Seemingly:* giving that impression

HIERONIMO: Nay, it should cry: but all is one. Well, sir,
paint me a youth run through and through with villains'
swords, hanging upon this tree. Canst thou draw a
murderer?

PAINTER: I'll warrant you, sir, I have the pattern of
the most notorious villains that ever liv'd
in all Spain. 140

HIERONIMO: Oh, let them be worse, worse: stretch thine art,
and let their beards be of Judas his own colour, and let
their eye-brows jutty over: in any case, observe that. Then,
sir, after some violent noise, bring me forth in my shirt,
and my gown under mine arm, with my torch in my hand,
and my sword rear'd up thus: and with these words:
What noise is this? Who calls Hieronimo?
May it be done?

PAINTER: Yea, sir.

[HIERONIMO]: Well, sir, then bring me forth, bring 150
me through alley and alley, still with a
distracted countenance going along, and let my
hair heave up my night-cap. Let the clouds
scowl, make the moon dark, the stars extinct,
the winds blowing, the bells tolling, the owl
shrieking, the toads croaking, the minutes jarring,
and the clock striking twelve. And then at last,
sir, starting, behold a man hanging: and tottering,
and tottering, as you know the wind will weave a
man, and I with a trice to cut him down. And 160
looking upon him by the advantage of my torch,
find it to be my son Horatio. There you may

138 *pattern:* 'blueprint', model
142–3 *Judas . . . colour:* red (see note)
143 *jutty:* jut out, project
154 *extinct:* extinguished, 'out'
156 *jarring:* ticking by
158 *tottering:* swaying
159–60 *weave a man:* make a man
swing, swerve about
160 *with a trice:* immediately
161 *advantage:* help, assistance

[show] a passion, there you may show a passion.
Draw me like old Priam of Troy, crying,
'The house is a-fire, the house is a-fire as the
torch over my head!' Make me curse, make me rave,
make me cry, make me mad, make me well again,
make me curse Hell, invocate Heaven, and in the
end, leave me in a trance, and so forth.

170 PAINTER: And is this the end?

HIERONIMO: Oh, no, there is no end: the end is death and
madness! As I am never better than when I am mad,
then methinks, I am a brave fellow, then I do
wonders: but reason abuseth me, and there's the
torment, there's the Hell. At the last, sir,
bring me to one of the murderers; were he as strong
as Hector, thus would I tear and drag him up and
down.

> *He beats the* PAINTER *in, then comes out again with a book in his hand.*

[HIERONIMO: *Vindicta mihi!*]

ADDITION E (to be substituted for lines 2642 to 2664)

[CASTILE: Why hast thou butcher'd both my children thus?]

HIERONIMO: But are you sure they are dead?

CASTILE: Aye, slave, too sure.

HIERONIMO [*to* VICEROY]: What, and yours too?

VICEROY: Aye, all are dead, not one of them survive.

HIERONIMO: Nay, then I care not; come, and we shall be
        friends;
    Let us lay our heads together:
    See, here's a goodly noose will hold them all.

173   *brave:* 'smart', splendid   174   *abuseth:* deceives, deludes

VICEROY: O damned devil, how secure he is!

HIERONIMO: Secure? Why dost thou wonder at it?
  I tell thee, Viceroy, this day I have seen revenge,
  And in that sight am grown a prouder monarch   10
  Than ever sat under the crown of Spain;
  Had I as many lives as there be stars,
  As many heavens to go to as those lives,
  I'd give them all, aye, and my soul to boot,
  But I would see thee ride in this red pool.

CASTILE: Speak! Who were thy confederates in this?

VICEROY: That was thy daughter Bel-imperia
  For by her hand my Balthazar was slain:
  I saw her stab him.

HIERONIMO: Oh, good words:
  As dear to me was my Horatio   20
  As yours, or yours, or yours, my lord, to you.
  My guiltless son was by Lorenzo slain,
  And by Lorenzo and that Balthazar
  Am I at last revenged thoroughly,
  Upon whose souls may heavens be yet reveng'd
  With greater far than these afflictions.
  Methinks since I grew inward with revenge,
  I cannot look with scorn enough on death.

KING: What, dost thou mock us, slave? Bring tortures forth.

HIERONIMO: Do, do, do, and meantime I'll torture you.   30
  [to VICEROY] You had a son (as I take it) and your son
  Should ha' been married [to CASTILE] to your daughter –
  Ha, was't not so? You had a son too;
  He was my liege's nephew. He was proud

7	*secure:* assured, confident, 'cocky'	27	*grew inward:* became intimate
14	*to boot:* as well, also	29	*tortures:* means of torture
15	*red pool:* i.e. of blood	33	*a son:* i.e. Lorenzo
24	*thoroughly:* utterly, completely		

And politic: had he liv'd, he might 'a come
To wear the crown of Spain, I think 'twas so:
'Twas I that kill'd him; look you, this same hand,
'Twas it that stabb'd his heart. Do you see this hand?
For one Horatio, if you ever knew him, a youth;
40   One that they hang'd up in his father's garden;
       [*to* VICEROY] One that did force your valiant son to yield,
       [*to* CASTILE] While your more valiant son did take him
          prisoner.

VICEROY: Be deaf, my senses, I can hear no more.
KING: Fall, Heaven, and cover us with thy sad ruins!
CASTILE: Roll all the world within thy pitchy cloud.
HIERONIMO: Now do I applaud what I have acted.
    Nunc iners cadat manus.
    Now to express the rupture of my part,
    [First take my tongue, and afterwards my heart.]

35   *politic:* shrewd, scheming, cun-   48   *rupture of my part:* breaking-off in
     ning   my role in the action
     'a: have
47   *Nunc iners* etc.: now let my hand
     fall idle

NOTES

The following abbreviations are used in the notes:

Newton   *Seneca His Tenne Tragedies, Translated into English*, edited
          by Thomas Newton (1581). The Tudor Translations
          Second Series XI, XII, ed. Charles Whibley, 2 vols.,
          1927.

OED   *A New English Dictionary on a Historical Basis* (the 'Oxford
          English Dictionary').

Tilley   M. P. Tilley, *A Dictionary of Proverbs in England*, Ann
          Arbor, Michigan, 1950.

References to the works of Shakespeare are taken from *William Shakespeare: The Complete Works*, ed. Peter Alexander, London and Glasgow,
1951.

GORBODUC

THE P[RINTER]. TO THE READER
This statement occurs only in the 1570 edition.

the Inner Temple: One of the four Inns of Court, the Inner Temple, like the
   Middle Temple, Gray's Inn and Lincoln's Inn, originated in the reign
   of Edward I (1272–1307); its buildings share with the Middle Temple
   the area south of Fleet Street known as 'the Temple' which has been
   associated with the legal profession since the fourteenth century. For
   'the grand Christmas' see the Introduction.

now Lord Buckhurst: Sackville was knighted in the presence of Queen
   Elizabeth I by the Duke of Norfolk on 8 June 1567, and the same day
   ennobled as Baron Buckhurst.

before her Majesty: Queen Elizabeth witnessed a command performance of *Gorboduc* at her palace of Whitehall on 18 January 1561–2.

one W.G.: William Griffith, publisher of the first edition of the play in 1565. It is of interest to note that the churchyard of St Dunstan's-in-the-West where Griffith carried on his trade was only a short distance from the Inner Temple.

the last great plague: Epidemics of bubonic plague were frequent in Europe during the late medieval and early modern periods; London was often visited, culminating in the Great Plague of 1664–5. It was common for prominent citizens to seek the safety of the provinces during such outbreaks.

out of England: Sackville was often employed on diplomatic missions, and appears to have been in Rome and Paris at intervals between 1563 and 1566.

new apparelled etc.: It may have been Thomas Norton who corrected the slightly faulty text published in 1565, thus justifying in some measure Day's confident claim.

the house from whence she is descended: i.e. the Inner Temple.

Lucrece's part: Lucretia was the celebrated Roman matron of tradition, wife to Lucius Tarquinius Collatinus, who, after being raped by Sextus Tarquinius, son of the King of Rome, stabbed herself to death, exhorting her relatives to avenge her. The rape and other crimes and acts of oppression led to the expulsion of the Tarquins from Rome. Lucrece's fate was a popular subject for literary and pictorial treatment (see cover illustration); Shakespeare's famous narrative poem appeared in 1594.

this one poor black gown: This suggests that the binding of Day's edition was black, as befitted the solemn tragic genre to which *Gorboduc* was seen to belong.

THE NAMES OF THE SPEAKERS
Great Britain: a good deal of interest attaches to this early use of a term which achieved general currency only after James I's accession in 1603, when he was proclaimed 'King of Great Britain, France, and Ireland' by virtue of uniting the English and Scottish kingdoms. *OED*, however, records the usage in a life of Joseph of Arimathea printed around 1500. In the present context the term seems intended to indicate the united state of Gorboduc's kingdom before its partition had taken place.

Duke of Cornwall: The term is of course an anachronism from the strictly historical standpoint, dukes only being introduced into Britain under Edward III, who in 1337 created Edward Prince of Wales ('the Black Prince') Duke of Cornwall. However, the title was employed as one appropriate to foreign nobility, including William the Conqueror, who was known in Britain as the Duke of Normandy. It is possible that the term is employed in *Gorboduc* to convey its earlier sense of 'leader, chief or ruler' (cf. Latin *'dux'*). Thus Wycliffe writes of 'Jesus Christ duke of our batel', Lydgate refers to 'Duke Moses', Wat Tyler is named by John Capgrave (1460) as 'duke' of the Peasants' Revolt, while Fabyan's *Chronicle* (see Appendix) uses the term frequently.

Cornwall: Although Norton and Sackville are not adhering to historical fact in any way, it is worth noting that Cornwall was the last Celtic area of southern Britain to be conquered by the Saxons; not before the reign of Athelstan (*c.* 925–40) were the Cornish confined beyond the Tamar.

CLOTYN: The 1565 reading, preferred to 1570's 'CLOYTON'. Cloten is mentioned in Geoffrey of Monmouth's *Historia* as King of Cornwall and father to Dunwallo Molmutius.

Albany: According to Geoffrey's *Historia* the sons of Brutus, the legendary founder of Britain, divided the kingdom on his death into three parts: to the lot of the youngest, Albanactus, fell 'the region which is nowadays called Scotland', which he named Albany after himself. But Holinshed was to claim that in fact Albany stretched 'from the river Humber to the point of Caithness', a far larger domain (see note to line 414).

Loegris: Loegria was the region of Britain allocated to Brutus's elder son Locrinus or Locrine, and which seems to have corresponded to present-day England, although it may not have been regarded as including the region north of the Humber (see previous note).

[Camberland]: Line 232 of the 1570 text indicates that this, rather than 'Cumberland' as printed in 'The names of the speakers' in the early quartos, is the correct reading. Cambria or Kambria was the share of Brutus's kingdom given to his second son, Kamber, who imposed his name on it; this synonym for Wales (actually a Latinized form of 'Cymry') survived for centuries.

younger son Porrex: 1570 reads 'yongest'; although Elizabethan and modern usage are often slack on the point, 1565 gives the grammatically correct form adopted here.

parasite: The term was a recent importation from Greek or Latin, and meant literally someone who fed at the table of another; the figure was embodied in a stock character of Roman comedy whose role was never precisely assimilated into English Renaissance drama, though its influence is detectable in *Roister Doister* and elsewhere.

DUMB-SHOW

violins: The early use of the word 'violin' (as well as of the instrument itself) is of interest, *OED*'s earliest citation stemming from Spenser's *Shepheardes Calender* of 1579, where the Muses in the April eclogue are described as bearing 'violines'. The instrument was of recent development when *Gorboduc* was first presented, three-string versions featuring in paintings of the 1530s, and the four-string version being perfected by Andrea Amati of Cremona (*c.* 1520–1611), from whom the French King, François II, ordered thirty-eight stringed instruments in 1560. The reference to 'violenze' in the first dumb-show seems odd, since they were regarded primarily as best suited to accompany dancing, yet analogous phrases in descriptions of the other dumb-shows suggest that violins *are* meant, and that the term does not mean 'music of violence' (Italian *violenza*), however tempting this interpretation may be.

wild men: These figures, often known as 'woodwoses', were a regular feature of royal entries, pageants, masques and disguisings, banquet entertainments and the popular iconography of the late Middle Ages and early Renaissance. Usually depicted or portrayed as clad in leaves or skins of beasts, these denizens of the woodland were often equated with satyrs or savages, and embodied the spirit of unsophisticated primitivism, in both its negative and positive aspects. Here their presence seems intended to universalize the adage that 'Unity is strength', rather than to suggest that these are some of Gorboduc's barbaric subjects, or the rebels of Act V.

faggot: Aesop tells in one of his fables of a labourer who convinced his contentious children that their frequent quarrels made them vulnerable to enmity, by inviting them to attempt to break a bundle of canes in half. However, the anecdote and the moral it illustrated were Renaissance commonplaces, and there is no necessity to seek a precise source for the play's first dumb-show.

Duke: The editions of 1565 and 1570 both print 'Duke Gorboduc' here, possibly by false analogy with the various 'Dukes' of the cast, perhaps employing the term in its original sense of 'leader, chief or ruler' (see

note to 'The names of the speakers' under 'Duke of Cornwall' above).
It is certainly notable that Fabyan's *Chronicle* employs the term, since
Sackville and Norton may have drawn on this account.

1-6. *The silent night* etc.: One may compare similar descriptions in classical
literature: the first Chorus of Seneca's *Hercules Furens* is relevant, but
the opening of his *Oedipus*, which takes the form of a duologue between
Oedipus and his mother, is of greater significance. Lines 1-5 in
Alexander Nevyle's version of 1560 run:

The Night is gon: and dreadfull day begins at length t'appeere:
And Phoebus all bedim'de with Clowdes, himself aloft doth reere.
And glyding forth with deadly hue, a dolefull blase in Skies
Doth beare: Great terror and dismay to the beholders Eyes.
                                        (Newton, I. 192)

4. *The slow Aurore*: The Romans personified dawn as the 'rosy-fingered'
goddess Aurora arising daily from Tithonus's bed to cross the heavens
in a chariot.

11. *all course of kind:* The term 'kind' and variants upon it occur with great
frequency in *Gorboduc*. Etymologically connected with 'kin' and often
used in the same sense, as a noun 'kind' comes to signify a type or
species, but its other principal meaning is 'descent' or 'birth', and thus
it can refer to those related to a common stock, and hence indicate a
birthright or a heritage. Simultaneously it denotes *characteristics* deriving
from one's birth, and thus equates with 'one's natural disposition or
innate mode of behaviour'; from this it can be extended to convey traits
generally accepted as lying within the accustomed practices to be found
in nature. Here the two main meanings appear to be combined: Videna
suggests that Gorboduc is acting unnaturally both as a human being
and as a father in showing equal favour to Porrex; by flouting the
notion of primogeniture, he is denying not only his responsibilities as a
parent but also the natural order of the universe. (Cf. line 18, where the
word 'kindliness' also carries its modern meaning of 'gentleness, benign
disposition'.)

18. *In kind a father* etc.: cf. *Hamlet* I. 2. 65: 'A little more than kin, and less
than kind'.

25. *spoil me of thy sight:* The early quartos read 'thee of my sight', but 'me
of thy sight' seems a more natural complaint for a mother to voice, as
well as balancing out 'But thee of thy birthright' of line 26. This is a
very plausible error for a scribe or printer to make. Either way the

phrase might suggest that the scene represents a clandestine meeting between mother and son at dawn, which, skilfully staged, could point up Gorboduc's authoritarian disposition, and also add to the tension engendered by the play's opening.

35. *the gods:* Like Shakespeare in *King Lear*, *Gorboduc*'s authors are normally careful to avoid the intrusion of Christian imagery into the play's texture. The image of Videna making a burnt offering as a sacrifice to pagan deities conforms to the play's classical inspiration and the attempt to evoke a primitive past, and the phrase 'heaven's throne' is supported from classical mythology by the concept of Jupiter or Zeus seated in majesty. On the frequent use of the term 'the gods' and the invocation of heathen deities in both *Gorboduc* and *Lear*, see Barbara H. C. de Mendonca's article in the Guide to Further Reading.

54. *There resteth all:* i.e. 'Everything depends on that factor.'

59–67. *When lords, and trusted rulers* etc.: A typical *sententia* on Senecan lines, although lacking a precise parallel in his work.

65. *Jove's:* Jupiter or Jove, the supreme deity of the Roman pantheon, was equated with the Greek Zeus. The allusion is again appropriate to the spirit of a primitive British past.

69. *The end?* etc.: An almost jaunty piece of word-play to bring the scene to a close.

Act I Scene 2: With the succession of an episode or scene of private and personal intimacy by one of public import or display, compare the opening scenes of Shakespeare's *Henry V*, or Act I Scene 1 of *King Lear* or *The Winter's Tale*.

72. *to this age:* Chronicle tradition maintained that Gorboduc reigned for 'about the term of 62 years' (Holinshed).

117. *commonweals:* In sixteenth-century usage 'common weal' (two words) possessed two main significances: (a) the public good, the common well-being; (b) the body politic, the state, the commonwealth. In the case of *Gorboduc* an editor has to decide which of the two permissible senses is primarily intended where the term occurs, and only elide the two words where the second meaning applies. Often this is impossible to determine from the context, but in this instance (as in lines 311, 324 etc.), the intention seems unequivocal. However, in line 205 etc. it has been thought best to allow the words to bear as their primary meaning sense (a), even if (b) is entirely proper.

122. *spend their hopeful days:* The 1570 text omits 'their', but the scansion, if not the sense, demands that it should appear as it does in the 1565 version.

123. *with their mother here:* Either the writer has forgotten the embargo on Ferrex's access to his mother, mentioned in line 25, or Gorboduc is concealing his alienation from his elder son from the assembly.

126–9. *mine to greater ease* etc.: cf. *King Lear*, I. 1. 37–40:

> 'tis our fast intent
> To shake all cares and business from our age,
> Conferring them on younger strengths, while we
> Unburden'd crawl toward death . . .
> (One may also compare *Gorboduc*, lines 417–19.)

131. *the younger:* 1565 reads 'the other', which is a possible reading, although the contrast with 'elder son' is thereby lost.

143. *Show forth* etc.: The line lacks one iambic foot to make it scan regularly; various insertions such as 'to me' or 'I pray' have been canvassed. Craik suggests 'Show forth such further means', comparing line 210.

159–62. *unload your aged mind* etc.: cf. the quotation from *King Lear* noted at lines 126–9 above.

172–3. *crooked age* etc.: Generic portraits of Age were rife in medieval and Tudor allegorical poetry, and followed conventional principles. Sackville himself provides an instance in lines 295–336 of his *Induction to A Mirror for Magistrates* (1563 edition) (ed. Lily B. Campbell, Cambridge, 1938, pp. 308–10). Lines 330–31 run:

> Crookbacked he was, toothshaken, and blear eyed,
> Went on three feet, and sometime crept on four . . .

182. *hazard:* 'Hasard' was the Old French term for a species of dice-game, and probably originally derived from an Arabic place-name. It soon came to indicate 'chance', 'risk' or 'peril'. Here it suggests that the experiment in joint monarchy will be most vulnerable at the time of its initial introduction.

184. *insolence:* Unlikely here to carry its usual meaning of 'arrogance' or 'cheek', but rather its less frequent one of 'inexperience' or 'unfamiliarity'.

187. *green-bending:* One of the infrequent touches of figurative language in the play, the adjective suggests 'pliable because youthful', 'green' being

often employed to convey inexperience and immaturity. Cf. *Hamlet*, I. 3. 101: 'You speak like a green girl'; *Antony and Cleopatra*, I. 5. 73–4: 'My salad days, / When I was green in judgement'.

189. *Custom, O King* etc.: Proverbial wisdom; see Tilley C 933: 'Custom makes all things easy.'

196. *random*: The interchangeable forms random/randon derive from the Old French *randir* (to run fast or to gallop) and describe impetuosity or lack of control, and anything done carelessly or aimlessly, 'at random'. The sense here suggests a lack of steady purposefulness in government, with Ferrex and Porrex each following his own instinctive desires.

200. *with aged father's awe:* 'accompanied by fear of their elderly parent's authority'.

229. *I think not good for you* etc.: cf. line 139 above, and lines 326–7 below.

230. *civil*: Ultimately deriving from the Latin *civilis*, 'of or pertaining to a citizen', the term here indicates a battle involving members of a single community (cf. 'the Civil War').

231–2. *Morgan* etc.: Geoffrey of Monmouth's *Historia* (ii.15) tells how King Leir's grandsons, Marganus or Morgan, son of Maglaurus Duke of Albany and Goneril, and Cunedagius, son of Henwinus Duke of Cornwall and Regan, resented their aunt Cordelia's tenure of the throne of Britain following the deaths of her father and her husband, Aganippus King of the Franks. Rebelling against their aunt, Marganus and Cunedagius deposed Cordelia and capturing her, cast her into prison where she committed suicide in despair. The cousins thereupon divided the kingdom between them, Marganus ruling the land north of the Humber, Cunedagius's realm comprising the territory south of the river. But Marganus soon fell prey to troublemakers who encouraged him to invade Cunedagius's lands and to claim them for his own on the grounds of seniority. Cunedagius marched out to encounter his cousin and inflicted a heavy defeat on him and his forces; he then harried the fleeing Marganus 'from province to province', eventually slaying him at Margam near the coast of what is now West Glamorgan (see lines 961–2 below). Cunedagius then ruled the unified kingdom for thirty-three years.

234. *Three noble sons:* Brutus's three sons were, according to Geoffrey of Monmouth, Locrinus or Locrine, Kamber, and Albanactus (see notes

to 'The names of the speakers' above). Brutus or Brute, the legendary founder of Britain and its first king, was supposedly the son of Silvius, son of Ascanius, and thus great-grandson to Aeneas, the legendary founder of Rome. For the division of the kingdom at Brutus's death, see notes to 'The names of the speakers' above.

241–68. *And when the region* etc.: Philander's speech abounds in instances of dramatic irony; despite his arguments in favour of treating Ferrex and Porrex equally generously, the calamities predicted if Ferrex is given exclusive sway occur in any case.

254. *by course of kind:* cf. the parallel with line 11, and the note accompanying it.

263. *Gapes for his death:* The verb is frequently applied to those who eagerly await some much-coveted benefit, notably one attendant on a death; Thomas Hoccleve in 1412 writes of those who gape after 'some fat and rich benefice'; Corbaccio, one of the suppliants in Jonson's *Volpone* (*c.* 1605), is referred to as 'a gaping crow'. The Prologue to Act II of *Romeo and Juliet* expresses it thus:

Now old desire doth in his death-bed lie,
And young affection gapes to be his heir . . .

284. *cankers:* A cancer or any kind of corrosive ulcer; here the term is used figuratively, for corrupting thoughts festering secretly within.

289. *her order and her course:* The phrase was proverbial (cf. Tilley N 48: 'Nature will have her course'); compare the classic expression of this piece of philosophical/cosmological/sociological doctrine in *Troilus and Criseyde*, I. 3. 85–124. It is worth noting that the speaker of these lines, Ulysses, emphasizes dependence on 'The primogenity and due of birth' as one of the factors which prevent the principle of anarchy from dominating the universe.

290. *doth corrupt:* Singular verbs with plural subjects (and vice versa) are common in sixteenth-century English.

292. *My lord:* Both the 1565 and the 1570 texts of the play read 'My lordes' at this point, as if Philander were now addressing his fellows, but the speech is clearly still directed at Gorboduc, to whom alone it may be said that 'your sons may learn to rule of you'; I have therefore corrected what must be an error.

301. *Long may they learn:* The 1565 and 1570 texts both read 'But longe may they learne', a reading which gives the line a redundant syllable.

The reading 'But longer may they learne' creates an extra foot, which would be unusual though not impossible, and Craik argues for its retention on the grounds that the contrast requires it. However, my solution (like other editors') has been to treat 'But' as a scribal or printer's error, and suppress it, so restoring (not without regret) metrical regularity.

303. *immortal:* i.e. by deferring their succession until they reach years of wisdom, Ferrex and Porrex will achieve not deathlessness but everlasting fame because of their increased maturity.

310. *join you to themselves:* i.e. 'gather you to them in death'.

321. *which yourself have seemed best to like:* Given the need to create dramatic tension, it is unfortunate that Gorboduc has been permitted to express his own preference so firmly and prematurely; when he announces his decision at lines 406–12 there is a strong sense of anti-climax when it becomes clear that none of the arguments of Philander or Eubulus has had the slightest effect on his 'one self purpose'. One wonders what the dramatic justification for the debate is, unless to demonstrate Gorboduc's complacency and folly in asking for advice and then only taking into account views which echo his own (cf. lines 1751–2: 'when kings . . . follow wilful will'). A stage production would have to bring out the consternation that the King's decision would cause in some quarters.

339–51. *The mighty Brute* etc.: See notes to 'The names of the speakers' and to line 234. Geoffrey of Monmouth recounts how, when the kingdom was divided between Locrinus, Kamber and Albanactus, 'these three reigned in peace and harmony for a long time' until Humber King of the Huns invaded Albany, killed Albanactus in battle and forced his people to seek protection from Locrinus, who then defeated Humber who was drowned in the river which still bears his name. Thus the 'sundered unity' which Eubulus deplores was not a direct result of the tripartite division of Brutus's kingdom, his sons proving mutually supportive.

344. *British blood:* The 1565 text has 'brutish' here, an attractive alternative reading to 1570's 'Brittish', conveying as it does the sense of 'brutal, savage, passionate', as well as referring to the blood of Brutus's descendants.

346–51. *What princes slain* etc.: Several commentators have argued that to an audience in the 1560s these lines would convey a clear reminder of the dynastic turmoil and civil strife occasioned by the

Wars of the Roses (1455–85), which cast a long shadow over Tudor England.

357. *if power serve:* i.e. 'if the forces at his command are sufficiently strong to enable him to redress his grievances through his agency'.

373. *The younger:* The metrical stresses fall awkwardly in this line, although it is not defective syllabically; some degree of corruption may be possible.

399–400. *Too soon he clamb* etc.: Phaeton ('the shining one'), son of Helios or Phoebus Apollo the sun-god, extracted a promise from his father that he might drive the golden chariot of the sun across the sky for a day; he proved unable to control the four fiery horses which drew it, and so set the earth aflame, causing cities to be burnt, and rivers and seas to dry up. To save the universe Zeus struck Phaeton down with a thunderbolt; the dead youth became an epitome of impetuous recklessness and presumption (cf. lines 454–6, 666–8). Shakespeare's line in *Richard II*, III. 3. 178 – 'Down, down I come, like glist'ring Phaeton' – reminds us that the word is trisyllabic. (Cf. *3 Henry VI*, II. 6. 11–13:

O Phoebus, hadst thou never given consent
That Phaeton should check [control] thy fiery steeds,
Thy burning car never had scorch'd the earth!)

407–10. *But sith I see* etc.: One might compare the complacency of King Lear in Act I Scene 1 in reposing his trust in the good faith of Goneril and Regan.

414. *Humber:* The division between Ferrex's and Porrex's share of Gorboduc's kingdom resembles that between the shares allocated to Locrinus and Albanactus (according to Geoffrey of Monmouth) after the death of Brutus, although Ferrex appears to receive Cambria as well as Loegria (see notes to 'The names of the speakers' above). Porrex's share is presumably Albany which, according to Holinshed, reached from the north bank of the Humber to the point of Caithness. Geoffrey's *Historia* makes no precise allocations of territory (see Appendix).

449–50. *The sticks* etc.: Refers back to the dumb-show which introduced the act.

454–6. *the proud son:* Phaeton (see note to lines 399–400 above).

461. *A mirror* etc.: The term 'mirror' to suggest any kind of pattern or exemplar held up to scrutiny goes back to at least the late twelfth

century; Hoccleve writes of Henry V as a 'Mirror to Princes all' and Shakespeare refers to the same monarch as 'the mirror of all Christian kings' (*Henry V*, Chorus to Act II, line 6). In the anonymous play of *King Leir*, lines 755–6 read:

But he, the mirror of mild patience,
Puts up all wrongs, and never gives reply.

The term (*speculum* in Latin) derives its figurative significance from its literal capacity to reflect accurately the true state of affairs, and so provide an exemplary image. Although the word was not applied exclusively to admonitory cases, it did become a key term in the presentation of medieval and Renaissance 'tragedies' involving the rise and fall of great figures in secular authority, especially kings, princes and governors. Thus William Baldwin in *A Mirror for Magistrates* (1559), that major compilation of verse-accounts chronicling the fates of prominent members of the ruling classes, declares the work to be intended 'as a mirror for all men as well noble as others, to show the slippery deceits of the wavering lady [i.e. Fortune], and the due reward of all kind of vices . . . For here as in a looking glass, you shall see (if any vice be in you) how the like hath been punished in other heretofore, whereby admonished, I trust it will be a good occasion to move you to the sooner amendment.'

DUMB-SHOW
cup: i.e. a drink, a cupful.

> *a cup of gold filled with poison:* cf. Tilley P 458: 'poison is hidden in golden cups'.

> *destroyeth the prince:* The 1565 reading; 1570 has 'destroyed'.

> *parasites:* See note to 'The names of the speakers' above.

476–83. *The wreakful gods* etc.: A passage inspired by Senecan tragedy, relying heavily on infernal mythology and phraseology for its effect. One may compare Medea's speech in Act IV of Seneca's tragedy, or the soliloquy for Thyestes added by Jasper Heywood in his version of *Thyestes* published in 1560.

478. *The hellish prince:* Pluto or Hades, the King of the underworld to which departed spirits were conveyed, and where some of them suffered everlasting torments.

479. *Tantale's thirst:* Tantalus, King of Lydia, was condemned to the eternal torture of being placed within sight of food and drink he could never reach; his principal crime had been to dismember his son Pelops

and serve him as food to deceive the gods on Mount Sipylus. The verb 'to tantalize' derives from his name. Tantalus appears as a character in Act I of Seneca's *Thyestes*, urged on by one of the Furies to stir up strife between his nephews Atreus and Thyestes, who rule Mycenae by turns. His speeches contain memorable descriptions of Hell. Cf. note to s.d., line 1 of *The Spanish Tragedy*.

Ixion's wheel: Ixion, King of the Lapithae, attempted to seduce Hera or Juno, wife to Zeus or Jupiter; as a punishment he was bound hand and foot to a wheel which revolved ceaselessly through the air, or (in some versions of the legend) through the underworld.

480. *cruel gripe:* The Euboean giant Tityrus or Titias tried to violate Leto or Latona, mother to Apollo and Artemis; Zeus, who fathered them, punished the giant by confining him in Tartarus, where vultures or serpents devoured his liver which grew again either as fast as it was eaten or overnight. In *Thyestes* Seneca has Tantalus inquire:

Or shal my paynes be Tytius' panges th'encreasyng liver still,
Whose growing guttes the gnawing gripes and fylthy foules do fyll?
That styl by nyght repayres the panch [stomach] that was devourd by
    day,
And wondrous wombe unwasted lieth a new prepared pray [?]
        (transl. Jasper Heywood, Newton, I. 55)

508. *Love wrongs not* etc.: Another proverbial-sounding phrase, but not one found in the major collections.

510. *So large a reign:* If this means 'so generous an area to govern' it would connect with Dordan's earlier reference to Ferrex having been assigned the more prestigious half of the kingdom (lines 498–506), taking 'reign' to mean 'territory ruled by a king, a realm'. However, the phrase could mean 'so free a hand in ruling', 'so ample a say in government', both meanings of 'large' being permissible.

578. *fail:* Although the basic sense of 'let down' or 'disappoint' suits the context here, what *OED* claims as a nonce-usage in Spenser is of considerable importance. The line cited (*The Faerie Queene*, III. xi. 46: 'So lively and so like, that living sence it fayld') suggests that the verb there means 'to deceive or cheat'. In *Gorboduc* the adjacent verb 'betray' might justify the view that Spenser's usage is here anticipated, yet the duplication of the notions of betrayal and deceit might render the possibility less likely.

588–91. '*Wise men* . . .' etc.: These four lines are enclosed in inverted commas in the 1565 and 1570 editions in order to highlight their sententious nature; the same is true of lines 608–13, 744–7, 794, 922–6. I have retained the quotation marks in each case, although the passages selected appear to have been chosen on completely arbitrary principles, and other *sententiae* equally deserving of emphasis might have featured.

605–17. *Know ye that lust of kingdoms* etc.: i.e. 'desire for rule is not governed by regulations'. The phrase is a proverbial one; see Tilley K 90: 'For a kingdom any law may be broken.' With the entire passage, J. W. Cunliffe compares Seneca's *Agamemnon*, lines 264, 268–72, rendered by John Studley as follows:

One law doth rule in royal throne, and pompous princelye Towres,
Among the vulgar sorte, another in private simple bowers . . .
This is the chiefest priviledge that doth to Kinges belong.
What lawes forbiddeth other men, they doe, and doe no wronge.
        (Newton, II. 112–13)

Similar arguments to those advanced by Hermon were also a commonplace of doctrines being ascribed to Machiavelli and his disciples during the century. Cf. too *The Faerie Queene*, II. x. 35. 1–2 (see Appendix).

608–13. '*When kings . . .* ' etc.: The second passage to be set in quotation marks in the early editions to highlight its sententious quality (see note to lines 588–91 above).

616–17. *Yet none offence* etc.: The 1565 text places this pair of lines before lines 614–15, an obvious error corrected in 1570.

629. *present murder:* i.e. Ferrex would be put to death immediately his hand in the murder of Porrex was discovered.

666–8. *rash Phaeton:* A third reference to the Greek youth's folly (see note to lines 399–400 above).

673. *yet . . . green:* i.e. still recent and unentrenched.

682. *of armour . . . weapon:* The 1565 text reads 'of Armours, and of weapons there', use of the plural form 'armours' to indicate 'suits of mail' being quite common. The 1570 text amends 'Armours' to 'armour', replacing a specific concept with the idea of military equipment in general, but also converts 'weapons' to its singular form, which up to *c.* 1600 was commonly used like the plural to denote 'arms'. Since the 1570 edition is usually the more reliable, I have retained its readings here.

710. *hazard:* See note to line 182 above.

726. *That loves my brother* etc.: cf. Act I Scene 1, 22–5.

731. *Mischief for mischief* etc.: proverbial; see Tilley C 826: 'Crimes [Mischiefs] are made secure by greater crimes [mischiefs],' and cf. *The Spanish Tragedy*, line 1840. Marvin Herrick, 'Senecan Influence in *Gorboduc*' (see Guide to Further Reading), compares line 115 of Seneca's *Agamemnon*, which in Studley's translation runs: 'The safest path to mischiefe is by mischiefe open still' (Newton, II. 106). One might also cite *Macbeth*, III. 2. 55: 'Things bad begun make strong themselves by ill.'

734. *treat:* The 1565 reading is 'entreate', but 1570's 'and treate' maintains the accretive pressure of the conjunctions, and is therefore to be preferred. 'Treat' may still retain the sense of 'entreat', but entreaty seems alien to Porrex's state of mind at this point in the tragedy, and I prefer to see the term as meaning 'negotiate', rejection of which procedure seems to fit the speech's scornful mood.

744–7. *'O most unhappy state . . . '* etc.: The third sententious passage to be enclosed in inverted commas for greater stress.

752. *these poor remnants* etc.: It was popularly believed that the first settlers in Britain were survivors of the siege of Troy, led by Brutus, Aeneas's great-grandson. Geoffrey of Monmouth's *Historia* (i.17) states that Brutus's capital (which later developed into London) was named Troia Nova ('New Troy') or Trinovantum.

767. *laws [of] kind:* Both 1565 and 1570 print 'lawes kinde', and some editors have defended the reading by suggesting that 'lawes' spelt thus indicates a disyllable. But the spelling occurs elsewhere in the play (e.g. line 718) and represents an unequivocal monosyllable; moreover, the phrase is awkward in conveying the sense required. The Bodleian copy of the play (Malone 257) has the word 'of' inserted in the margin, and I prefer to follow Thomas Hawkins's lead of 1773 and retain the insertion he adopted. (Craik compares line 1171.)

770–71. *rede | Of best advice:* 'Rede' is often taken here to mean 'counsel, advice', yet this sense seems otiose in view of the phrase 'best advice' which succeeds. I prefer to adopt *OED*'s sense 5, which indicates 'the faculty of deliberation . . . judgement, prudence, reason'.

782–3. *poison in gold* etc.: The final rhyming couplet clearly refers back to the dumb-show to the Act (cf. lines 449–50 above), but the lines also echo Seneca's *Thyestes* yet again, lines 450–53 of which were translated by Jasper Heywood as:

And safer foode is fed upon, at narrow boorde alway,
While drunke in golde the poyson is by proofe well taught I say . . .
        (Newton, I. 70).

DUMB-SHOW

murder: The 1565 edition obviously has the correct reading here, 1570's 'murderer' probably being a careless alteration.

784. *O cruel fates!* etc.: The line requires an extra syllable to complete the iambic pentameter.

785. *Simois':* Simois and Scamander were the two chief rivers of ancient Troy, the Simois being identified today with the Dumrek Su. This and succeeding references to the Trojan war continue to emphasize the notion that the British are lineal descendants of the Trojans, 'the issues of destroyed Troy' (line 793).

787. *Phrygian:* The ancient kingdom of Phrygia occupied part of north-west and central Anatolia (Asia Minor), with its capital at Gordium where the famous Gordian knot hung; according to Homer its forces assisted those of Priam during the Trojan war.

789. *Priam's:* The aged Priam was King of Troy during the famous siege; his fifty offspring included Hector, Paris and Troilus. At the fall of Troy he was killed by Pyrrhus, son of Achilles.

790. *Ilion's fall:* Ilion was the name given to the colony founded around Troy by Greek settlers from Lesbos, *c.* 700 B.C., based on the ancient title of Ilium, the traditional site of Troy.

792. *our line:* The 1565 text reads 'lyves', 1570 'lynes', both of which make sense if 'lynes' is taken to mean 'lineage, stock, race', a meaning which accords with the sentiments expressed in lines 784–91, 'lynes' providing a better equivalent to 'issues' in line 793 than does 'lyves'. However, the unfamiliarity of the plural used to mean 'lineage' is puzzling, and one either has to take 'lyves' as the true reading, or explain 'lynes' as an error for the singular form. If one accepts that the printer worked from a corrected copy of the 1565 text, then it is possible that an 's' was caught up from the erroneous 'lyves' to produce 'lynes'. I have therefore amended the 1570 reading to produce what seems to be the best solution of the problem.

794. '*Oh no man happy . . .*' etc.: Another instance of a sententious statement being picked out through the use of inverted commas. The statement itself is a classical commonplace, and Tilley under M 333 cites Ecclesiasticus xi. 28, 'Judge none blessed before his death.' The most relevant citations in the present context are perhaps Solon (c. 640–c. 588 B.C.), quoted in Herodotus, *Histories*, I. 32, 'Call no man happy till he dies, he is at best fortunate'; Sophocles's *Oedipus Rex* ('. . . none can be called happy until that day when he carries / His happiness down to the grave in peace,' transl. E. F. Watling, Penguin Classics, 1947, p. 73); Seneca, *Oedipus*, Chorus prior to Act V Scene 2 ('Thinke no man blest before his ende,' Newton, I. 227).

797. *Hecuba:* Hecuba or Hecabe was the wife of King Priam and mother of some of his fifty children. She appears as the heroine of Euripides's *Hecuba* and of his *Trojan Women*, and of Seneca's *Troas*.

the woefullest wretch: Herrick, op. cit., thinks that the line may be indebted to Chaucer, *Troilus and Criseyde*, IV. 516–17 ('. . . that am the wofulleste wyght / That evere was . . .'), but it seems a weak parallel.

806. *kings of kings:* i.e. 'those that have sovereignty over kings'.

835. *the elder:* The words require to be elided ('th'elder') to preserve the metre.

842. *The gods:* cf. note on line 35. (Cf. 'The mighty Jove' in line 842, and 'Jove slay them both' in line 879.)

845. *Your son, sir, lives* etc.: cf. the cryptic response from Iago to Lodovico's inquiry after Cassio in *Othello*, IV. 1. 218: 'Lives, sir.'

849. *No end of woes:* The 1570 edition reads 'Not ende' which is clumsy, and 1565's 'No ende' has been preferred.

877. *kingdom's care:* The 1570 edition reads 'cares' which appears to be a careless alteration of 1565's 'care' (i.e. 'protection, concern for'); 'cares' meaning 'worries, anxieties' seems inappropriate in the context, and I adopt the original reading.

884. *The fire not quench'd* etc.: A proverbial phrase listed in Tilley under F 265 as 'Fire that's closest kept burns most of all,' citing the *Gorboduc* reference as its earliest example.

905. *And add it to the glory* etc.: The word 'latter' makes the line an alexandrine or iambic hexameter, and some editors suppress the word.

906. *And they your sons:* The 1570 edition text has 'our sonnes', a clear

error, which the Bodleian Library copy (Malone 257) corrects to 'your' in the margin.

907. *Beware, O King:* One might compare the English morality plays in which characters in their distress doubt the mercy of God, and thus become guilty of the sin of despair, from which they are only rescued by divine intervention. In the anonymous *Mankind*, and in Skelton's *Magnificence*, the eponymous heroes are tempted in this way.

921. *Sorrow doth dark* etc.: A typical aphorism for which there is little need to track down a specific source.

922–6. '*The heart unbroken . . .*' etc.: These lines are enclosed within inverted commas as having sententious merit. Cf. Tilley H 305: 'A good heart conquers ill fortune (overcomes all).'

937. s.d. [*Enter* NUNTIUS.]: The convention by which a herald or messenger arrived to impart to the Chorus or other characters news of a usually direful or disastrous nature was established in Greek tragedy and retained by Seneca.

938. *O King, the greatest grief* etc.: Another line with twelve syllables, like 905 above.

950. *Die with revenge:* i.e. 'die while executing revenge', a highly Senecan observation.

951. *The lust of kingdom* etc.: cf. lines 605–17 and note.

962. *Bereft Morgan* etc.: See note to lines 231–2.

967. *The wicked child:* The rhyme-scheme of the entire chorus calls for comment: all but the final stanza rhyme ABABCDCD, the last rhyming ABABCC, so that one might initially suspect that two lines have been lost from the final stanza. However, the sense is continuous, and the stanza must simply be assumed to be deliberately irregular. It is worth noting that all the choruses to Acts I and II follow a similar rhyme-pattern (ABABCC), except that the chorus to Act II has an extra-long final stanza which rhymes ABABCCDD! Uniformity clearly had no very high priority in the minds of the co-authors.

968. *very life:* The 1565 text reads 'wery life', a variation of only one letter from the 1570 reading. 1565's version is a very attractive variant, and some might wish to retain it in preference to the later alteration. Certainly the edition of 1590 reverts to 'weary' as its preferred reading.

DUMB-SHOW

hautboys: the *OED* gives as its earliest citation of the term 'Howboies' (which derives from the French '*hautbois*', literally 'high wood') Robert Laneham's *Letter* of 1575 describing the entertainment staged for Queen Elizabeth I at Kenilworth Castle that year, the so-called 'Princely Pleasures'.

under the stage: An interesting observation on the mode of staging employed, although it seems more appropriate to performance in a public playhouse than to methods usually associated with *Gorboduc*. If the Furies literally entered from 'under the stage', it would almost certainly have been one specially erected for the occasion, since a dais in a banquet-hall would scarcely have been high enough to permit people to be concealed beneath it. (See Introduction for further discussion.)

three Furies: The Furies or Erinyes in Greek myth were characterized as repulsive women with snakes for hair, who emerged from Hades to torment those guilty of particularly repugnant crimes such as infanticide. In Aeschylus's *Oresteia* they harry Orestes for the murder of his mother, Clytemnestra, but ultimately relent and are revered thereafter as the Eumenides or Kindly Ones. They play an important role in T. S. Eliot's re-working of the story of Orestes in modern dress, *The Family Reunion* of 1939. (Cf. lines 1330–33 below.)

Tantalus: See note to line 479.

Medea: The princess of Colchis, who assisted Jason and the Argonauts to steal the Golden Fleece and later married the hero, who later deserted her for Glauce. In revenge she murdered her two children by Jason.

Athamas, Ino: Athamas and his wife Ino, daughter of Cadmus, brought up the god Dionysus or Bacchus, son of Zeus, following the death of his mother Semele. In a fit of jealousy Juno drove the foster-parents mad, so that in their delusion they slew their own offspring, Learchus and Melicertes.

Cambises: Cambyses, King of Persia and son of Cyrus the Great, was reputedly a drunken tyrant with countless crimes to his name; he reigned from 529 to 522 B.C. He killed the Apis, the sacred Egyptian bull, and murdered his own brother; possibly he features in *Gorboduc* as having slain the son of his adviser Praxaspes as the result of a wager. His career was the subject of an early English tragedy by Thomas Preston, usually dated *c.* 1569.

Althea: The wife of Oeneus and mother of Meleager, one of the Argonauts, she was told that her son would die as soon as a log on the fire burnt to ashes. Althea retrieved the log and kept it in a chest unconsumed, but when Meleager killed her brothers in a quarrel, Althea took the brand from the chest and burnt it, so causing her son's death.

973–1053. *Why should I live* etc.: One might compare the lengthy female monologues which are such a feature of Seneca's tragedies: Juno and Megara have extensive soliloquies in Acts I and II of his *Hercules Furens*; Hecuba has a long opening speech in the *Troas*, as does Medea at the beginning of the tragedy which bears her name, as well as a long speech in the fourth act.

975. *most woeful wight:* cf. note on line 797 above; line 975 seems closer to the Chaucerian wording.

997. *Is my beloved son* etc.: Irby Cauthen suggests that the repetition of these lines may be the result of a compositor's error, derived from the two above, but it seems strange that the reviser of the text for the 1570 printing did not exclude them.

999. *Murder'd with cruel death?:* A fine example of pleonasm, or 'redundancy of expression' (*OED*), as in 'a false lie'.

1002–8. *Thou, Porrex* etc.: Speeches threatening vengeance abound in Seneca's tragedies: one might cite several of Atreus's speeches in Act II of *Thyestes*.

1010. *If such hard heart* etc.: A classical commonplace, but one might compare the accusation levelled at Aeneas by Dido in Virgil's *Aeneid*, Book IV: 'But of hard rocks Mount Caucase monstrous / Bred thee' (transl. the Earl of Surrey, lines 479–80). One might also cite Seneca's *Hercules Oetatus*, 143–6, Englished by John Studley as:

What Scythian crag, what stones engendered him?
What Rocky mountayne Rhodope thee bred . . .
Stipe [steep] Athos hill, the brutish Caspia land,
With teate unkinde, fed thee twixt rocke and stone . . .
(Newton, II. 198).

1032. *some young son:* Videna draws attention to Ferrex's lack of an heir, and this prefigures the strife which is to follow the death of Gorboduc.

1044–5. *Thou never suck'd* etc.: Another classical allusion, again familiar to many from Virgil's *Aeneid*, IV. 365–7, where Dido accuses Aeneas of a similar upbringing: '. . . teats of tiger gave thee suck' (transl. the Earl of Surrey, line 480) (cf. note to line 1010 above). Also of interest are lines 9–12 from a poem in 'Tottel's Miscellany' (1557) attributed to Sir Thomas Wyatt, beginning 'Pass forth my wonted cries'; they run:

For though hard rocks among
She seems to have been bred,
And of the tiger long
Been nourished and fed . . .

1048. *wild and desert woods bred thee:* cf. the similar charges cited in the note to line 1010 above.

1081. *thou art:* Elided – 'th'art'.

1090. *my doleful heart* etc.: It is impossible to glean from this speech whether Porrex is conceived of as being truly repentant or a specious liar at this point. The doubt is symptomatic of the authors' failure to reveal motivation through speech.

1097. *regrate:* The presence of 'sorrow' in the same line suggests that 'regreite' is here a form of 'regrate' meaning 'lamentation, complaint' rather than that of 'regret', which would only have a duplicating effect.

1101–2. *water troubled with the mud* etc.: The phrase is probably proverbial; see Tilley W 100: 'Muddy water is a bad looking glass,' which cites *Gorboduc* and James Howell's *Proverbs or Old Sayed-Sawes and Adages . . .* of 1659. It is possible that the proverbial function developed only after *Gorboduc* was written.

1114. *the gods:* See note on line 35 above, and cf. line 1321 below.

1123–4. *the mind | Stoops to no dread:* The traditional boast of the resolute hero who claims immunity from fears of death or future suffering.

1142. *he now remains:* Porrex at this point appears to be employing the historic present.

1171. *The law of kind:* See note to line 11 above.

1175–6. *Then saw I how* etc.: Many commentators have seen here a clear echo of Chaucer's *Knight's Tale* (*The Canterbury Tales,* I. 1995, 1999):

> Ther saugh I first . . .
> The smylere with the knyf under the cloke . . .

1202–8. *Your grace should now* etc.: The sentiments expressed are commonplace enough – Tilley under J 80 quotes from James Sanford, *The Garden of Pleasure* (1573): 'The mirth of this world dureth but a while' – but Herrick quotes a telling passage from Seneca's *Moral Epistles*: 'Everything is slippery, deceitful and more changeable than weather. Nothing is sure for anyone but death.'

1222–3. *Is all the world* etc.: Herrick parallels Seneca's *Hippolytus*, 551–2, translated thus by John Studley:

By meanes hereof eche Land is fild with clottred gore yshed,
With streames of bloud the Seas are dyed to hue of sanguine red . . .
(Newton, I. 156)

but the resemblance is perhaps too general to be significant.

1231. *O silly woman:* 'Silly' at this time has three principal meanings: (i) 'pitiful'; (ii) 'feeble'; (iii) 'ignorant', all of which interrelate to some extent. The context here would suggest that meaning (i) comes closest to what is implied.

1238. *becomen:* The archaic form of the past participle, a form later revived by Spenser to contribute to the antique flavour of *The Faerie Queene*.

1255. *a senseless stock:* 'Stock' was originally employed to indicate a tree-trunk, and then by transference the human torso; the phrase used here is a standard one, found, for example, in 'Tottel's Miscellany' (1557) in Nicholas Grimald's *Marcus Tullius Ciceroes death*.

1256–79. *But hear his ruthful end* etc.: One may compare similar announcements and descriptions in Seneca: cf. the Messenger's speech in Act IV of *Thyestes*; the account of the death of Hippolytus; that of the self-blinding of Oedipus in Act V of that tragedy.

1260. *new unclos'd:* Porrex had just woken up.

1262. *We then, alas, the ladies* etc.: Geoffrey of Monmouth stresses that Porrex's mother (called by him Judon) was assisted in her act of vengeance by her maidservants (see Appendix).

1266. *direful:* The earliest citation *OED* offers for this term as meaning 'dreadful' or 'full of dire effect' is from Philip Stubbes's *The Anatomy of Abuses* (1583), but it would seem that *Gorboduc* pre-dates it.

1292. *a silly woman's thought:* 'Silly' here would seem to convey a sense of 'weak' or 'vulnerable', even 'susceptible'; see note to line 1231 above.

1299–1300. *Even Jove* etc.: cf. note to line 65 above. (See also lines 1327, 1337 below.)

1301–9. *Ah, noble Prince* etc.: The description is of course entirely anachronistic for the period at which the play is set; the lines rely on the conventions of medieval chivalric romance to paint the figure of Porrex in colours appropriate to a knight taking part in a tournament.

1304. *sleeve:* The detachable sleeve of a medieval lady's costume was frequently employed as a recognized love-token to be worn in battle or the tourney by her knightly lover. Cf. Chaucer, *Troilus and Criseyde*, V. 1043: 'She made hym were [wear] a pencel [token] of hire sleve.' Spenser in *A View of the Present State of Ireland* (1596) also alludes to the custom: 'Knights in ancient times used to wear their mistress' or love's sleeve, upon their arms.'

1330–33 *The dreadful Furies* etc.: See note to the dumb-show to Act IV, p. 283.

1336. *Blood asketh blood:* cf. Tilley B 458, and *Macbeth*, III. 4. 121: '. . . blood will have blood'. Tilley and others cite Genesis ix. 6: 'Whoso sheddeth man's blood, by man shall his blood be shed,' but closer is *A Mirror for Magistrates* (ed. Lily B. Campbell, Cambridge, 1938, p. 99): 'Blood will have blood, either [at] first or last.'

1346. *to offend:* Elided ('t'offend').

DUMB-SHOW

harquebusiers: The harquebus or arquebus (variously spelt) was an early type of portable gun, often supported by a tripod or forked rest. It was popular in the sixteenth century, as being superior to the hand-gun, but was superseded later in the century by the musket.

the space of fifty years: Geoffrey of Monmouth does not specify the length of the period of civil war which commenced on the deaths of Ferrex and Porrex, nor does he mention Gorboduc's violent end. However, Fabyan's *Chronicle* (see Appendix) states that following Gorboduc's death the rival kings contended for the throne for fifty-one years.

Dunwallo Molmutius: As the son of Clotyn King of Cornwall Dunwallo (or Dunvallo) succeeded to the kingdom on his father's death, and then, according to Geoffrey of Monmouth, killed the Kings of Loegria, Cambria and Albany, subjecting the whole land to his personal rule, reigning successfully as king of all Britain for forty years.

reduced: Literally 'led back' (from the Latin *reducere*); hence 'restored'.

1368-9 *Shall yet the subject* etc.: It was a hallowed political axiom of the Tudor age that obedience to authority was required of the good citizen, and that anarchy and rebellion were not merely socially subversive, but crimes against nature and the laws of God. (Similar sentiments underlie lines 1388-98, and 1519-39.)

1370-73. *those rebellious hearts* etc.: The punishments for civil rebellion at this period were extreme in their ferocity: Robert Aske, a leader of the Pilgrimage of Grace in 1536, was hanged in chains at York Castle; Robert Ket, who led a rising in East Anglia in 1549, was hanged on 7 December at Norwich and his head put on public display.

1383. *some kingdoms of mighty power:* There is no reason to doubt that the quartos' 'some' is correct, although if we assume a mistake for 'soone' the lines gain extra force, and some editors amend accordingly. There is no need to seek reference here to any specific 'kingdoms', since the allusion is deliberately general; however, in the early 1560s the unstable political condition of France might well have occurred to observers of the European scene at this point in the drama.

1386. *I pray to Jove:* cf. note to line 65, etc.

1389-96. *That no cause serves* etc.: These eight lines appear in both the 1565 and the 1590 texts of the play, but are omitted from the 1570 version. They may have been dropped as merely reinforcing the sentiments of lines 1368-73, but mere iteration elsewhere in the 1570 text has not led to similar pruning, so the loss of lines 1389-96 may have been accidental. However, Craik advances the view that Norton as an ardent Calvinist may have disapproved of Sackville's political docility as expressed in these lines, and used the opportunity of revising the text for publication to suppress his colleague's opinions.

1395. *Caesar's seat:* The practice of referring to any one in civil or temporal authority as 'Caesar' can be traced in English through translations of Matthew xxii. 21 to references with more general application. Bishop Barlow in a sermon preached in 1601 speaks of 'The things due from subjects unto their Caesar' (*OED*), and one can compare Wyatt's sonnet 'Who so list to hunt', line 13 of which has the phrase 'for Caesar's I am', almost certainly referring to Henry VIII.

1396. *to damn:* The 1565 text has 'do damne', 1590 'doo damne', for what is clearly to be read as 'to damne'.

1412. *And by ourselves* etc.: 'We shall finish up having defeated ourselves in civil war.'

1419. *So giddy* etc.: Herrick finds parallels in Seneca, *Hercules Furens*, line 170 ('And commons more unconstant than the sea'), and in *Octavia*, lines 877–81, but only the first comparison between human inconstancy and the ocean seems significant. Sister Maureen Walsh in her critical edition (Ph.D. thesis, St Louis, 1964) draws attention to Sackville's own 'Complaint of Henry Duke of Buckingham' in *A Mirror for Magistrates* (Campbell edn, p. 332):

> O let no prince put trust in commonty [the common people],
> Nor hope in faith of giddy people's mind . . .
> Lo, where is truth or trust? or what could bind
> The vain people, but they will swerve and sway,
> As chance brings change, to drive and draw that way?
> (lines 421–2, 425–7)

1429. *mischief:* The term in sixteenth-century usage had far more sinister connotations than in modern parlance; its primary meaning 'misfortune' or 'distress' was often extended to include 'injury' or 'harm' (cf. 'do yourself a mischief'), and in some contexts 'wickedness' or 'evil'.

1431. *These violent things* etc.: Tilley (N 321 – 'Nothing violent can be permanent') cites *Gorboduc* for its earliest instance of the proverb's appearance.

1434–5. *gift of pardon* etc.: cf. note to lines 1370–73. In 1549 Protector Somerset issued a pardon to Ket's rebels on condition that they returned home and surrendered their arms. The offer was ignored, and the rising suppressed, Ket and the other leaders being captured.

1469. *my lords:* The 1565 text reads 'lordes' here, while 1570 has 'lord'. Although the latter reading makes perfect sense (the line could be addressed to Fergus or Clotyn as an individual), Eubulus has begun his speech at line 1377 by speaking to all the lords, and reiterates the plural mode of address at lines 1399, 1407 and 1421. Hence it seems logical to adopt the 1565 reading at line 1469.

1491–5. *Shall I that am* etc.: Fergus here foreshadows the appearance on the English stage of the ambitious usurper of regality, of whom Marlowe's Tamburlaine and Shakespeare's Richard III were to prove notable instances. (Line 1512, for example, might almost be a line from Marlowe's play.)

1500. *dukes':* Bisyllabic here to maintain the scansion.

1503. *above the best:* In Geoffrey's *Historia* the combined forces of the

Kings of Cambria and Albany defy Dunwallo's army of 30,000 men during much of the ultimate battle for mastery of Britain, and are defeated only by a ruse.

1513. *in post:* 'At full speed, express', deriving from the custom of having horsemen stationed at intervals along a route to convey messages and letters etc. on their way at speed. To 'ride in post' was to travel at the speed of a post-horseman.

1517. *To seek to win* etc.: Fergus's tactics here can be compared with those of Shakespeare's Richard of Gloucester in seeking public support in *Richard III*.

1518. *O Jove:* cf. note to line 65 etc.

1520. *rolls:* In early times formal or official records were often kept on a length of parchment, rolled up in a scroll for ease of handling, storage or carrying; the term 'roll' was thus employed to indicate any document in this form.

1532–9. *A ruthful case* etc.: A confused sentence, in that its syntax seems badly distorted; the sense is that it is pitiful that men whom 'duty's bond' and 'grafted law' oblige to preserve their country, and who are also born to defend the commonwealth and the prince, should prove disloyal, and that thus men of native stock should destroy their own inheritance.

1541–2. *the multitude, misled* etc.: This sentence appears incomplete, 'multitude' relating to no main clause, unless it is 'Laid hands upon' in line 1549, which obscures the distinction made between 'One sort' in line 1543 and 'Another' in line 1551. A line may well have dropped out at this point and one suspects textual corruption from line 1532 onwards.

1542. *By traitorous fraud* etc.: Other editors have assumed this to indicate that the unsophisticated intelligences of the rabble have been treacherously subverted, but the sentiment is hardly likely to be heard from Eubulus's lips, however elementary the characterization. The idea is surely that although the men's leaders, lost to grace or damned (the 'ungracious heads'), had 'led them up the garden path', the majority on hearing of the nobles' ultimatum came to their senses and either turned in their captains or deserted.

1551. *Another sort:* The 1570 edition has 'And other sort' here, which is a feasible reading, but 1565's 'An other sort' reads more naturally, and has been preferred.

1552–4. *mistrusting more* etc.: 'Being more convinced of their own guilt than assured that their vile crime merited any kind of forgiveness'.

1569. *trees*: Although the 1570 reading of 'tree' is entirely possible, the generic term 'tree' for 'gallows' being found as early as *c.* 1425 in *The Castle of Perseverance*, there is something strikingly graphic about 1565's more literal-minded 'trees' as a location for hanged bodies, and the reviser of the text may have rejected the plural form only through the proximity of 'field' in the singular in the previous line. I have allowed 'trees' to stand, the more especially because 'trees' occurs in line 1580 below. The 1590 text also has the plural form in line 1569.

1584. s.d. [*Enter* NUNTIUS]: See note to line 937, s.d., above.

1589. *to embrace:* Elided ('t'embrace').

1592. *Ventur'd my life:* Not a strictly necessary detail, but one which helps marginally to increase the tension created by the Messenger's entry.

1600–1602. *he the sceptre seeks* etc.: The characterization of Fergus as a machinating schemer is fitfully maintained by such small touches as this.

1602. *without a stern:* Cauthen reminds his readers that *OED* defines 'stern' as the complete steering-gear of a ship, i.e. rudder and helm, although the term is often applied to the rudder alone. Cf. Sir Thomas Wyatt's poem 'Who list his wealth and ease retain', line 24 of which reads 'Bear low, therefore, give God the stern.' The poem is of interest in the present context as having a refrain based on Seneca, *Hippolytus*, line 1140, 'The thunder rumbles round [Jupiter's] throne.'

1612. *common fire:* 'A fire which threatened all of us'.

1614. *rule*: The term appears here to equate with 'realm' or 'state' but *OED* does not offer such an interpretation, and it seems as if its significance is closer to 'management, sway, control', although a certain imprecision is inevitable.

1615–19. *the common mother of us all* etc.: Mandud reinforces here sentiments outlined by Eubulus in lines 1409–10; *Gorboduc* is perhaps the earliest play in English to develop an appeal to love of one's native land as a tactic for gaining audience support.

1617. *Our wives* etc.: Craik reads 'Our wives, our children, kindred, selves and all' to restore metrical regularity here.

1623. *O gods:* cf. note on line 35. (Cf., too, line 1638.)

1637. *foreign thraldom:* Commentators suggest that the play deviates from strict logic at this point to issue a warning of the dangers of European intervention in English affairs to its contemporary auditors (cf. lines 1689, 1690, 1696). The phrase may be used, however, not to suggest that Fergus is a 'foreigner' but that the servitude his accession would involve is alien to the people of Britain.

1643. *the young kings:* Ferrex and Porrex, the issue of Gorboduc's body, were each given a kingdom to rule.

1644-50. *And of the title* etc.: This complex statement appears to mean: 'And people (even those learned in such matters) are divided in their minds as to whom the true succession devolves on, while those who are prejudiced or influenced by personal feelings are even more fallible in their judgements; the most dubious situation of all will come about if the right to rule Britain is allowed to be disposed of to just anyone under pressure from those [like Fergus] whose ardent ambition it is to reign supreme regardless.'

1654. *the Albanian prince:* i.e. Fergus, Duke of Albany.

1668. *your own mother's:* i.e. Britain's.

1670-90. *If ye shall all* etc.: This passage clearly abounds in anachronisms, but it is equally clearly intended to have an impact on Elizabethan political and dynastic thinking (see Introduction). It may be that the authors had in mind the question of the succession not simply in general but in specific terms, and were seeking to further the claims of Lady Katherine Grey (see L. H. Courtney's article in *Notes and Queries*, Second Series, X (1860), 26-3) as opposed to the more dubious claims of either Mary Queen of Scots or King Philip of Spain ('a foreign prince'). Courtney bases his assumption in part on the reference to 'his or hers' in line 1682, and on Henry VIII's recognition of Lady Katherine's right to succeed, conveyed in line 1684's allusion to 'some former law'. There may be justification for the degree of specificity which Courtney and others attribute to the lines, but they may be intended to have broad application only, and 'his or hers' in line 1682 may merely acknowledge that a female heir had succeeded to the English throne in 1553 and another in 1558.

1678. *without respect:* This is the reading found in the 1565 version, which is both notionally and metrically correct; the 1570 text reads 'with', which is unaccountable and cannot be justified.

1679. *Of strength or friends:* The 1565 version reads 'of frends', which 1570 amends to the present reading; either version is permissible, but perhaps the later emendation should stand, as making perfect sense.

1681. *wrong cannot endure:* Possibly an early version of Tilley W 942: 'All wrong comes to wrack,' the earliest example of which (in Howell's *Proverbs and Old Sayed-Sawes . . .*) is dated 1659.

1695. *the rules of kind:* The central concept of 'kind' appears once again here, this time with its meaning of 'birthright', 'heritage' rather than 'natural behaviour', although line 1694 suggests that for the British to prefer a foreign ruler would also be 'unnatural' (see note to line 11).

1697. EUBULUS: Eubulus's lengthy speech of summarization has the effect of a choric rather than an individual utterance, perhaps because Act V has no place for the tragedy's own Chorus to sum up. This is in fact in keeping with Senecan practice, though not with that of the ancient Greek theatre. Only Seneca's *Hercules Oetatus* concludes with a final speech for the Chorus.

1708. *Britain realm:* The 1565 text reads 'Brittaine Land' here, but there seems to be no good reason for amending the 1570 version of the phrase.

1715–17. *Who wins* etc.: these lines must be intended ironically: 'Fabricated claims can easily be trumped up to support a usurper's right to the throne.'

1726–49. *The wives shall suffer* etc.: A powerful descriptive passage which seems to have clear affinities with comparable passages in Shakespeare, where the communal anguish occasioned by civil strife is invoked. Cf. *Richard II*, I. 3. 125–39; *1 Henry IV*, I. 1. 1–18; *Richard III*, V. 5. 23–41.

1730–31. *The father shall* etc.: One is forcibly struck by the foretaste of Act II Scene 5 of Shakespeare's *3 Henry VI*, where the king watches the entry of 'a Son that hath kill'd his Father . . . and a Father that hath kill'd his Son'. One might note especially the correspondence between line 1731 of *Gorboduc* and Shakespeare's 'Pardon me, God, I knew not what I did' (II. 5. 69).

1734. *That playing:* The 1570 text reads 'That play' at this point, but grammar and scansion require the present participle as indicated in the 1565 reading.

1751–62. *Hereto it comes* etc.: Craik astutely points out that Eubulus in these lines provides a succinct summary of the import of each act, in a sequence of four two-line synopses, with a quatrain to cover Act V.

1753. *young princes':* The text of 1570 has 'fonde' for 1565's 'yonge' here, used to mean 'foolish' and so enabling the remark to apply to Gorboduc as well as Ferrex and Porrex. Taken in this manner, however, it duplicates in essence lines 1751–2, and I think the retention of 1565's 'yonge' as having sole application to the conduct of Gorboduc's sons in Act II is justified.

1757. *the gods:* See note on line 35 above.

the mother's wrath: A clear reference to Videna.

1766–7. *As not all only* etc.: 'Who is not merely heir to the throne by right of inheritance, but is openly declared to be so, and accepted as such by the entire kingdom'.

1770–88. *in parliament* etc.: Another anachronism, with more political than dramatic justification.

1793. *Jove:* A final evocation of the pagan deity (see note on line 35 above), but the 1570 text inconsistently reads 'God' at this point, which in the Tudor context of foreign invaders, threats to the English crown, and the summoning of parliaments might be permitted to stand. However, the edition of 1565's 'Jove' is more in keeping with *Gorboduc*'s initially primitive setting, and I have retained it.

1795–6. *For right* etc.: An apparent conflation of the sentiments of two proverbs – Tilley T 579 ('Truth is mighty and will prevail') and W 942 ('All wrong comes to wrack' – cf. note to line 1681). It is appropriate that a play which abounds in both native and Senecan *sententiae* should culminate with such a pious adage.

THE SPANISH TRAGEDY

CAST LIST

BASHAW: The title given to Turkish officials of high rank, chiefly military commanders and governors of provinces, equivalent to the more recent term 'pasha'.

s.d. *the* GHOST OF ANDREA: Seneca's *Thyestes* opens with the entrance of the Ghost of Tantalus, accompanied by a Fury who insists he wreak vengeance on the house of Atreus, although Tantalus, unlike Andrea, is reluctant to punish others. The figure of Thyestes's ghost also initiates the action in Seneca's *Agamemnon*. Hattaway (*Elizabethan Popular Theatre*, p. 115) suggests that the Ghost and Revenge enter through a trap-door in the stage, as if rising from Hell.

1. *When this eternal substance* etc.: Such 'true confessions' became a common-place in Elizabethan drama, examples being found in *3 Henry VI*, III. 3. 153–95; *Titus Andronicus*, V. 1. 125–44; *The Jew of Malta*, II. 3. 179–203. Philip Edwards draws attention to the most celebrated parody of such speeches, in Beaumont's burlesque-comedy *The Knight of the Burning Pestle* (*c.* 1607), where Ralph begins his own funeral oration: 'When I was mortal, this my costive corpse, / Did lap up figs and raisins in the Strand; / Where sitting, I espied a lovely dame . . .' (V. 3. 277–9).

2. *wanton flesh: OED* cites a multiplicity of meanings for 'wanton', including 'unruly', 'rebellious', 'sportive', 'robust' and 'unrestrained' as well as 'lascivious', so that Andrea's phrase may only mean that his flesh, like that of humanity in general, is capriciously wayward in a general sense. However, given the use of 'possess'd' in line 10 and related allusions later, the inference is that Andrea and Bel-imperia were 'wanton' in sexual behaviour, *OED* citing this reference under the heading of 'lascivious, unchaste, lewd . . . given to amorous dalliance'. (Cf. line 68.)

6. *inferior far:* The first allusion to relative rank in a play which is strongly infused with an awareness of social gradations and class distinctions. Andrea's lineage, like that of Horatio later, is deemed unsuitable for a potential suitor to Bel-imperia; she incurs her father's wrath for engaging in a secret liaison (cf. lines 1636–7, 1650–53), Pedringano also suffering the threat of punishment for acting as their go-between (lines 616–20). Although the Duke of Castile later claims to have forgiven his daughter (lines 2116–20), there is a strong suspicion that Andrea's death was engineered. Hieronimo and Horatio are also portrayed as of inferior stock to the nobility they mingle with: the King deems Horatio's means insufficient for him to entertain Balthazar and his train (lines 276–8), Lorenzo considers his sister 'meanly accompanied' (line 1639) when consorting with Horatio, and unworthy strictures over the disputed ransom persuade the King that Hieronimo may be short of funds (lines 1809–19).

10. *In secret:* The central motifs of clandestine encounter and deceptive intrigue are established early in the action.

13. *Death's winter* etc.: cf. *Love's Labour's Lost*; V. 2. 789–90:

If frosts and fasts . . .
Nip not the gaudy blossoms of your love . . .

15. *the late conflict:* None of the military actions alluded to has any basis in fact.

18. *When I was slain* etc.: Descriptions of Hades abound in classical, medieval and Renaissance literature, one of the most seminal being found in Virgil's *Aeneid*, Book VI. Sackville's *Induction* to *A Mirror for Magistrates* contains another account based partly on Virgil's version. Kyd's description seems to have been drawn from no single source, but has obvious predecessors.

19. *Acheron:* One of the fabled rivers of the underworld, Acheron was said to be thronged with hovering shades seeking repose.

20. *Charon:* 'The ferryman of Hell', son of Erebus, was envisaged as a surly boatman transporting dead souls across the river Styx.

23. *Ere Sol* etc.: The sun god was traditionally portrayed as sleeping at night in the bed of Thetis, Nereid mother of Achilles and goddess of the ocean, leaving it at dawn to make his daily journey across the sky.

25. *Knight Marshal's:* The Knight Marshal was a legal officer of the English royal household, responsible for law and order among its members and within a twelve-mile radius ('the verge') of the palace. The irony of Hieronimo's plight later in the play is here anticipated: as the dispenser of justice he can get none himself.

26. *funerals and obsequies:* It is difficult to make any valid distinction between this pair of terms, thus rendering the combination of synonyms tautological.

29. *fell Avernus':* Lake Averno, near Pozzuoli (Puteoli) in the volcanic region near Naples, was traditionally deemed to form the entrance to the classical underworld. No bird was reckoned to be able to fly over it unscathed, so pungent was the stench arising from it.

30. *Cerberus:* The 'hellish hound' tamed by Orpheus and vanquished by Hercules, Cerberus was a monstrous dog chained up to guard the entrance to Hell, and depicted as having three barking heads.

33. *Minos* etc.: Hell was considered to be under the jurisdiction of three judges, Aeacus, Rhadamanthus and Minos, whose mortal incorruptibility obtained them the distinction of adjudicating in Hades; Minos was thought to have the final say in their deliberations.

36. *graven leaves* etc.: The sense seems a little obscure, but Minos appears to pick out from some vessel a form of engraved writing supplying an account of Andrea's 'lottery' in life, i.e. the fortune good or bad which he had enjoyed while living. There may be some confusion with the *Aeneid*, VI. 431–3, where Minos 'shakes the urn' and lots are drawn to

determine the final destination of the dead; Andrea's fate is not left to chance, however, but to judicial arbitration.

38–40. 'This knight . . .' etc.: The play's first example of the rhetorical figure known as anadiplosis, in which the lines are linked to one another by the echoing of certain words or phrases (see lines 321–6, 690–700).

48–9. Hector . . . Achilles' Myrmidons: Hector, Trojan hero and one of the sons of Priam, was according to Homer killed by Achilles during the Trojan war; the Myrmidons were aggressive warriors of ancient Thessaly led to Troy by Achilles.

52. our infernal king: Pluto was traditionally held to be the King of the underworld, though the name was originally a superstitious substitute for that of Hades.

63. the left-hand path: In Virgil's Aeneid, VI. 540–43 the Sibyl tells Aeneas that the road through the underworld splits in two, and that the left-hand track 'brings evil men to godless Tartarus, and with never a pause, exacts their punishment' (transl. W. F. Jackson Knight, Penguin Classics, 1956, p. 163). (Cf. line 1704.)

65. bloody Furies: The Furies or Erinyes were avenging deities who emerged from Tartarus to torment those guilty of the most revolting crimes (see note on the dumb-show to Act IV of Gorboduc, p.283). They were pictured as three women with wings, serpents for hair, and carrying whips of steel. A Fury accompanies Tantalus at the opening of Seneca's Thyestes.

shakes: The combination of singular verb with plural noun, and vice versa, is a common feature of Elizabethan English.

66. poor Ixion: See note to line 479 of Gorboduc; Ixion for attempting to ravage Juno was bound to an endlessly revolving wheel. At the close (lines 2724–6) Andrea is to plead that Lorenzo be forced to take Ixion's place.

73. Elysian green: The Elysian Fields were the traditional resting-place of the blessed ones in Greek mythology. It is probably this line that Nashe bore in mind when satirizing as ignorant those contemporary playwrights who 'thrust Elisium into hell' (see Introduction). Certainly Homer locates the Elysian Fields on the banks of Oceanus to the west of the earth, but Latin poets such as Virgil identify them with an area of the underworld separate from the depths of Hades where the damned dwelt.

76. Proserpine: Proserpine or Persephone was believed to have been carried

off to the underworld by Pluto (or Hades) as his bride, and restored to her mother Demeter or Ceres for six months of each year.

82. *the gates of horn:* In Greek mythology (and *Aeneid*, VI. 893–6) dreams were considered to issue forth from the underworld, false dreams emanating from an ivory gate, true ones through the gate of horn. Andrea's exit-route indicates that his dream (of revenge) will ultimately be accomplished.

90. *Here sit we down:* One of the most interesting indications of staging in the play. Did Revenge and Andrea take their seats on the stage, perhaps on opposite sides of the platform, and remain there during the action, or did they mount to one of the galleries to the rear or the side of the auditorium? (See Introduction and notes on the stage-directions at lines 2176 and 2214.) It might be unusual for the action to begin elsewhere than on the main platform.

the mystery: Again Kyd stresses the dimension of secrecy and conspiracy; Andrea and Revenge (like the audience) will watch the unfolding of events whose true significance is hidden from the characters enacting them (see Introduction).

91. *serve for Chorus:* The convention had evidently established itself by this time that tragedy required a choric commentary, but Kyd appears to have been one of the first English playwrights to frame his action with figures having a vested interest in the outcome, rather than ones who could look on in a relatively detached way as in *Gorboduc.*

92. *camp:* Used in the broadest sense to indicate the whole of an army engaged in a military campaign.

103. *O multum dilecte* etc.: 'The heavens fight on your side, O man most pleasing in God's eyes, and the people in alliance drop to their bended knees: victory is the sister of true justice.' Adapted, according to Boas, from Claudian's *De Tertio Consulatu Honorii*, 96–8, written *c.* A.D. 400.

113. *Where Spain and Portingale:* The General's account may appear unreasonably protracted since we already know how the battle went, but as Mulryne points out, it provides an objective version of events from which the rest of the action is to derive, while also offering Kyd an opportunity to set the scene with a martial narrative in approved rhetorical style, which his audience doubtless enjoyed. Of this speech Wolfgang Clemen (*English Tragedy before Shakespeare*, 1961, p. 104) says: 'Kyd could not have drawn out to such a length the Spanish General's account of the battle . . . had his audience not expected showy and elaborately rhetorical report-speeches of this kind . . .'

116–20. *Both furnish'd well* etc.: An example of the figure of anaphora, whereby a word or a phrase is repeated in several successive lines of verse or several clauses in prose, to create a special effect of emphasis.

123. *battles:* Battle-formations, dispositions of troops.

in squadron form: *OED* designates 1562 for its earliest usage of the term 'squadron', which derives from the Italian 'squadra' meaning 'a square'.

131. *colonel:* The text reads 'corlonell' here, and the forms 'coronel' and 'colonel' seem to have been used virtually interchangeably until the mid seventeenth century; Kyd or his printer appears to have found a compromise form. The form 'colonel' was certainly coming into more frequent use (from Italian) by about 1580–90.

143. *Bellona:* The Romans regarded Bellona as the wife or sister of Mars, their god of war, and as sharing his attributes.

144. *storms of bullets rain:* Collier suggested 'rain' as the appropriate emendation to 1592's 'ran', which shifts the tense from the present to the past for no good reason; the verb 'rain' also has a more graphic effect, and I have adopted the reading.

146–7. *Pede pes* etc.: 'Foot versus foot, lance against lance, weapons resound on weapons, man is attacked by man.' Boas finds a source in Statius's *Thebais* VIII. 399, but sees analogous structures in Virgil and Curtius.

173. *our carbines:* The words 'carbine', to indicate a hand-gun shorter than a musket and longer than a pistol, and 'carabin' (a musketeer on horseback) were never distinguished in English; according to Randle Cotgrave (1611) a carabin was 'an arquebusier [see note to dumb-show to Act V of *Gorboduc*, p. 287] armed with a morrian [helmet] and breast-plate, and serving on horseback'.

174. *Till, Phoebus waning:* The text of 1592 has 'waving' for 'waning' here, and *OED* cites this reference alone in support of a presumed meaning, 'to decline'. However, confusion between 'n' and 'u' in Elizabethan texts is frequent, and it seems more likely that 'waning' was intended.

178. s.d. *Give him his chain:* The form of this stage-direction and others (cf. s.d.s to lines 183, 251, 374, 510, etc.) might indicate that the text was set up from one used in the playhouse, although scholarly opinion generally favours the view that the source used was possibly Kyd's own manuscript. Edwards is sceptical, but possibly some instructions to the playhouse company became incorporated in the printed text.

186. *These words* etc.: cf. Duncan's words to the bleeding Sergeant in *Macbeth*, I. 2. 44–5:

So well thy words become thee as thy wounds;
They smack of honour both.

190. s.d. *A tucket afar off: OED* links 'tucket' with 'tuck' meaning a trumpet-blast, a blow or a tap, and with the Old French 'tuchet' (a blow or a stroke). The tucket appears to have been the signal to order cavalry troops to march, and thus unlike the 'sennet' had a genuine military function.

192. *this warning:* All early quartos read thus, though most recent editors prefer 'the'.

199. (*except three hundred or few more*): Mulryne compares *Much Ado About Nothing*, I. 1. 5–6:

LEONATO: How many gentlemen have you lost in this action?
MESSENGER: But few of any sort, and none of name

commenting that it adds to the general air of bland complacency at the Spanish court at this juncture in the play.

200. s.d. *The army enters:* Even with the limited resources available to the Elizabethan stage companies, military display offered an opportunity for some grandiose theatrical effects. It also adds to the impression of martial valour and flamboyance necessary to the play's opening phase before the warriors' rivalries become the dominating feature of the drama.

221. *Two ducats:* The ducat was a European gold coin of varying value, the first being struck in Venice in 1284.

242. *And I shall study* etc.: cf. Edmund in *King Lear*, I. 1. 30: 'Sir, I shall study deserving.'

243. *But tell me* etc.: Clemen notes the creation here of a stock dramatic situation of the period, whereby a ruler arbitrates between two rival disputants, as in the opening scene of *Richard II*, Act IV Scene 1 of *The Merchant of Venice*, and Act IV Scene 2 of *Gorboduc*.

252–6. *To him in courtesy* etc.: Balthazar's antithetical speech here supplies an excellent key to the relative characters of Lorenzo and Horatio.

261–2. *He hunted well* etc.: Edwards traces the reference to Caxton's edition of Avian's Fourth Fable in which a donkey presumptuously dons the skin of a dead lion. It has been a matter of frequent note that the same image appears in Shakespeare's *King John*, II. 1. 141–2, 145:

BLANCH: O, well did he become that lion's robe
  That did disrobe that lion of that robe! . . .
BASTARD: But, ass, I'll take that burden from your back . . .

263. *So hares* etc.: cf. Tilley H 165, and *King John*, II.1. 137–8:

You are the hare of whom the proverb goes,
Whose valour plucks dead lions by the beard . . .

The proverb occurs in Erasmus's *Adagia*; ultimately deriving from Publius Syrus and Martial. Thomas Nashe quotes Kyd's line (with 'beards' for 'beard') in his *Strange News, of the intercepting certain letters* (1592), adding '*Memorandum*: 'I borrowed this sentence out of a Play' (*The Works of Thomas Nashe*, ed. R. B. McKerrow, Oxford, 1958, I. 271).

283–5. *if this proviso were* etc.: A further indication of Horatio's moral superiority to the ruthless Lorenzo, despite their social distinction.

293. *Then rest we here:* Mulryne highlights the contrast between the Spanish King's self-congratulation and the Viceroy's grief; in a play which abounds in fathers lamenting over sons actually or presumed dead, it sets the tone for later developments.

296. s.d. *Falls to the ground:* This stage-direction occurs between lines 299 and 300 in the 1592 text, but it clearly needs to be placed a few lines earlier, since lines 297–9 make little sense unless delivered from the floor.

300. *melancholy:* Elizabethan physiologists and their predecessors postulated the existence in the human body of four 'humours': blood, phlegm, black bile or melancholy, and choler. Personal temperament and stability were determined by the relative balance or imbalance existing between these elements; an excess of black bile produced the sullen 'melancholy' or depressive personality also cultivated as a fashionable affectation towards the end of the sixteenth century; however, in a true melancholic an over-excess could result in madness. Melancholy was equated with the natural element of earth, which along with air, fire and water constituted all created matter; hence the Viceroy's association of his state of dejection with the earth he lies upon.

303–5. *Qui jacet* etc.: 'The man who falls prostrate to the ground has no further to fall; upon me Fortune has exhausted her capacity to hurt;

302] NOTES TO THE SPANISH TRAGEDY

nothing remains that can cause me greater harm.' The lines appear to
be a conflation of a line from Alanus de Insulis (Alain de l'Isle), line
698 of Seneca's *Agamemnon*, and an invented hexameter by Kyd himself.

317. *Whose foot is standing* etc.: Fortune was often depicted in illustrative
matter of the period as a goddess standing insecurely on a rolling
sphere; she was also characterized as being deaf to human complaints,
and blind to adversity (cf. lines 311–12). The 1592 text inadvertently
omits the word 'is', which has been restored.

321–6. *My late ambition* etc.: Another graphic instance of anadiplosis (see
note to lines 38–40).

331–4. *No doubt, my liege* etc.: A reproduction of a common device of
classical drama known as *stichomythia*, where disputacious dialogue is
conducted in alternating single lines, antithesis and repetition being
employed for extra sharpness in the exchanges. Kyd probably adapted
the device from Seneca. Cf. lines 460–72, 731–8, etc.

334. *Then they have slain him:* i.e. 'they will have slain him by now'.

336. *They reck no laws that meditate revenge:* The first use of the term
'revenge' in the main action is of importance, reminding spectators
of the reckless nature of acts of vengeance and what Bacon in his
Essays viewed as 'a kind of wild justice' outside the law (see Introduction).

339. *evil news fly faster* etc.: A variant form of several proverbs with the
same theme; cf. Tilley N 145, 147, 148, of which N 147 is the closest to
Kyd's line: line 1538 of Milton's *Samson Agonistes* runs: 'For evil news
rides post, while good news baits [takes its time].' The use of the plural
verb with 'newes' was standard until the nineteenth century.

365. *unkind:* As on frequent occasions in *Gorboduc* (see notes to that
play, lines 11, 18, 1695, etc.), the terms 'kind/unkind' carry not only
connotations of kindness/cruelty, but also natural/unnatural behaviour. The Viceroy accuses Alexandro of inhumanity as well as callous-
ness.

370. *Terceira's lord:* Terceira was one of the islands of the Portuguese
Azores, of which Alexandro appears to be *Capitao Donatorio*, a hereditary
title awarded to the original discoverer or colonizer, and hence confer-
ring virtually dictatorial powers (Boas). The attribution of ruthless
ambition to Alexandro, although unjustified, reflects the rivalries at the
Spanish court.

371. *diadem:* The 1592 text reads 'Diadome' which, since *OED* does not list it as an alternative spelling of 'diodeme', I have silently corrected.

374. s.d. *Take the crown* etc.: cf. note on line 178, s.d. above.

381–3. *Thus have I* etc.: Villuppo confides his villainy to the audience in very much the same spirit as the Vice figures of the late medieval morality plays had done, and as later embodiments of evil (Richard III, Iago, Flamineo in *The White Devil*) were to do. (See Bernard Spivack, *Shakespeare and the Allegory of Evil*, New York, 1958.) Again, Villuppo's deceit anticipates that of Lorenzo.

392–426. *When both our armies* etc.: Horatio's account may seem an over-lengthy recapitulation of events already described in the General's speech (lines 113–75), but it highlights the relative roles of Andrea, Balthazar and Horatio himself, and puts a less honourable gloss on the conduct of Balthazar in dispatching Don Andrea (lines 402–9). It also renders the seemingly abrupt transfer of Bel-imperia's affection from Andrea to Horatio less precipitate and unmotivated. Mulryne points out that Horatio's narrative is also, unsurprisingly, a more emotional version of events than the General's.

403. *As Pallas was* etc.: Edwards points out that in Virgil's *Aeneid* (II. 612–16) it is Juno rather than Pallas Athene who is clad in steel armour (*ferro accincta*).

414. *Don Andrea's carcass:* cf. the Viceroy of Portugal's question in line 362.

425–32. *This scarf* etc.: Kyd, like Sackville and Norton (cf. notes to lines 1301–9, 1304, of *Gorboduc*, above), here utilizes the trappings of chivalric convention. Scarves (like sleeves and handkerchiefs) were often employed as love-tokens worn in battles and tournaments by knights in honour of their ladies. Mulryne shrewdly remarks that by accepting Bel-imperia's scarf which was Andrea's, Horatio becomes his dead friend's proxy; he is also exposed to the same risks. If the scarf then becomes the 'handkercher besmear'd with blood' of line 927, the connection Andrea–Bel-imperia–Horatio–Hieronimo is visually maintained almost throughout the play.

442. s.d. *Exit* HORATIO: 1592 has Horatio exit after line 440 of the present edition, while the 1602 text omits his departure altogether. Horatio's approach is so correct, however – 'I'll crave your pardon' – and Bel-imperia addresses him in lines 441–2, that I have ventured to place the stage-direction two lines later than in the 1592 version.

453. *Himself now pleads* etc.: This is the first intimation we receive of the main factor in precipitating Horatio's murder.

456–8. *For what was't else* etc.: Bel-imperia again spells out the breach of honour of which Balthazar was guilty, reinforcing the impression of weakness of character conveyed elsewhere, notably in the Prince's ready acquiescence in Lorenzo's murderous schemes.

460–72. *Sister, what means* etc.: A further passage of *stichomythia*, in which Kyd exploits to the full the increase in pace and tension offered. He conveys brilliantly the respective positions and attitudes of the protagonists, Balthazar's ardour being courteously but wittily damped by Bel-imperia's caustic retorts until Lorenzo sardonically intervenes with his observations in lines 473–4 that the Prince should come to the point without obliquity.

479. [*In*] *whose aspect:* The 1592 text reads 'On whose', no doubt caught up from line 478.

482. *but devis'*[*d*]: The 1592 and 1594 texts read 'but devise' at this point, but the 1599 and 1602 quartos have 'but devised'. Although the earlier readings could be taken to mean 'merely a device', 'no more than a device', I find the phrase reads awkwardly, and despite Edwards's view that the later reading has no authority, I have substituted the verb for the noun.

483. s.d. *She . . . lets fall her glove:* A hackneyed piece of stage business, but possibly intended as a deliberate signal to Horatio by Bel-imperia that she is unimpressed with Balthazar's blandishments, or an agreed sign that an assignation is in prospect, so anticipating Act II Scene 2. It certainly precipitates the covert rivalry between the two men which lies behind the guarded courtesies of lines 485–6, as well as acting as a 'red rag' to the slighted Lorenzo.

498. s.d. *Enter the banquet:* However unelaborate on the stage, the ceremonial involved here, followed by Hieronimo's masque, parallels and foreshadows the final banquet entertainment of Act IV Scene 4. Elizabethan stage production would undoubtedly have exploited the visual potential of the courtly background.

513. *Wait thou upon our cup:* It was a sign of royal favour for a subject to be permitted to attend to some personal need of the sovereign's, in this case to see that his cup was replenished with wine at intervals.

520. s.d. *Enter* HIERONIMO etc.: Hieronimo establishes himself at this

point as a deviser of stage entertainments, a necessary requirement if his role as director of the final performance is not to appear arbitrary. The masque at this point was no doubt a more elaborate affair than the mere description suggests; deriving from the iconography of the tilt-yard, it reminds one in some measure of the dumb-shows preceding each act of *Gorboduc*, and may like them have some relationship to court masquings. Similar banquet entertainments were a feature of medieval and Renaissance feasts (see William Tydeman, *The Theatre in the Middle Ages*, Cambridge, 1978, pp. 70–79).

524–9. *English Robert* etc.: A celebration of English martial prowess scarcely seems a likely subject for a Spanish court entertainment, but as Mulryne observes, at the time when *The Spanish Tragedy* was first staged, patriotic feeling ran high in London, and Kyd capitalized on it. The reference in lines 524–9 is very inaccurate: Robert of Gloucester (d. 1147) was the natural son of Henry I and half-brother to the Empress Matilda, for whose cause he fought against King Stephen in England from 1139 to 1141. His association with the liberation of Portugal from Muslim rule appears to be purely apocryphal, though part of popular tradition.

529. *the English:* Elided, i.e. 'th'English'.

537. *razed Lisbon walls:* Edmund Langley, Duke of York, was associated in 1381–2 with the Portuguese in their conflict with Spain, but the 'razing of Lisbon's walls' may have become confused with the attack on Lisbon in 1190 by English crusaders, during which the city was sacked and burnt before King Sancho could intervene (see Rose Macaulay, *They Went to Portugal*, 1946, pp. 30–31).

547. *Brave John of Gaunt:* Fourth son of Edward III, John claimed the crown of Castile through his second marriage (to the former Infanta) in 1371 and in 1386 led an army to the Peninsula to claim his title. Despite the support of King John of Portugal, to whom Gaunt married his daughter Philippa, the expedition was a military failure, and he abandoned his claims on Castile. In 1367 John did take part in the battle of Najera, along with his brother the Black Prince, in support of Peter I of Castile, but Kyd can scarcely be alluding to this, since England favoured the Castilian cause.

574–7. *In time the savage bull* etc.: These four anaphoric lines are quoted, not quite verbatim, from a love poem (No. XLVII) composed by Thomas Watson for his *Hecatompathia, or Passionate Century of Love* (1582); the first two lines of Balthazar's reply (580–81) quote the succeeding lines of the poem in slightly modified form. The original runs:

> In time the bull is brought to wear the yoke;
> In time all haggard hawks will stoop the lures;
> In time small wedge will cleave the sturdiest oak;
> In time the marble wears with weakest showers:
>> More fierce is my sweet love, more hard withal,
>> Than beast, or bird, than tree, or stony wall.

All the images are commonplaces of contemporary love poems, in many cases deriving from such Italian sonneteers as Petrarch and Serafino, while the use of the sonnet convention in drama may be compared with *Romeo and Juliet*, I. 5. 91–104. 'In time the savage bull sustains the yoke' appears in virtually identical form in *Much Ado About Nothing*, I. 1. 226, Don Pedro predicting that the sworn bachelor Benedick will one day fall in love. The phrase became proverbial (see Tilley T 303), although its use in English seems to have been anticipated by Ovid.

575. *haggard hawks* etc.: In training a hawk learns to 'stoop' or plunge from a height and 'home in on' the lure, a dummy bird of feathers and leather; a haggard hawk is one which is untamed as yet, or has reverted to the wild state. This phrase too was proverbial (see Tilley T 298).

587. *Pan and Marsyas' quill:* Marsyas, a satyr of Phrygia, challenged Apollo to a musical contest and, losing, was flayed to death for presuming to compete (see Ovid, *Metamorphoses* VI. 382–99). The god Pan was said to have formed a pipe from the reed into which Syrinx was transformed, but it is not clear why his notes should here be regarded as 'harsh and ill'.

590–99. *Yet might she love me* etc.: To modern readers Balthazar's speech with its lavish display of anaphora (patterned repetitions) must appear strained and artificial in its blatantly structured organization. To the Elizabethans such artifice was not automatically deplorable; Mulryne observes that an element of obviousness may be intentional, Balthazar being characterized as indecisive, weak and in love.

598. *beauty's thrall:* The 1592 text has 'beauteous thrall' and the 1602 version 'beautious thrall' at this point; following the 1615 text Boas proposed to read 'beauties', which occurs in the version of lines 580–81, 592–3, 596–9, which is freely quoted by Tucca in Ben Jonson's *The Poetaster* of 1601 (III. 4. 215–22).

600. *ecstasies: OED* offers no instance of 'ecstasy' to mean 'an outburst, an utterance of tumultuous feeling' prior to 1695, but Lorenzo clearly

objects less to the intensity of Balthazar's feelings than to their unbridled expression in terms of extravagant rhetoric.

612. *Vien qui presto:* Lorenzo's use of Italian suggests that we are to assume that Pedringano (with his '*Signor?*') is Italian, or that Lorenzo's Machiavellian nature makes Italian a natural language for him to use when initiating his villainous plan (cf. line 1169, and note below).

629. *it lie in me:* An ingenious pun to typify the servant's penchant for mendacity.

638. s.d. [*Draw[s] his sword*]: The 1592 text has no stage-direction here, but 1602 offers the vivid touch which I have incorporated.

648. *ifs and ands:* Mulryne notes that Nashe possibly alludes to this moment when in the preface to Greene's *Menaphon* (see Introduction) he speaks of those who 'bodge up a blank verse with ifs and ands'.

s.d. *Offer[s] to kill him:* 1592 has no stage-direction here (cf. line 638, s.d., note), but 1602 again supplies the direction I have inserted.

658. *Swear on this cross:* The cross-piece of a sword- or dagger-hilt was often used in lieu of a crucifix for the purpose of swearing oaths. Cf., for example, the oaths sworn on Hamlet's sword in Act I Scene 5, lines 147–61, and *Henry V*, II. 1. 98: 'Sword is an oath, and oaths must have their course.'

678. *Tam armis quam ingenio:* A source for this Latin tag has not been discovered, but Edwards compares '*tam Marti quam Mercurio*' ('as much through strength as cunning').

679–80. *Where words prevail not* etc.: One might compare, though the parallel is not an exact one, Tilley G 295: 'You may speak with your gold and make other tongues dumb (Where gold speaks every tongue is silent).'

688. *love resisted grows impatient:* Similar proverbs on the dangers of repression are found in Tilley under F 265 and S 929, but Edwards points out that a closer parallel occurs in Marlowe's *Hero and Leander*, II. 139: 'But love resisted once, grows passionate'; Marlowe may possibly have been imitating Kyd here, though his poem did not appear in print until 1598.

690–700. *First in his hand* etc.: Another notable example of anadiplosis (see note to lines 38–40 above), of which Clemen remarks that its lack of substance and profusion of antithetical amplifications suits Balthazar's irresolute and dependent role in the action (cf. note to lines 590–99). (It has been argued that the lines echo Watson's *Hecatompathia*, No. XLI; see note to lines 574–7 above.)

697. *lim'd:* It was common at this period to catch birds by daubing the branches and twigs of trees with bird-lime, a glutinous substance made from holly–bark, from which the bird could not struggle free.

713. s.d. [*above the stage?*]: From the stage-direction 'BALTHAZAR [above]' at line 725, it seems fairly certain that Pedringano at line 713 ushers Lorenzo and Balthazar into one of the upper galleries of the Elizabethan public playhouse so that they can look down on the stage-platform. Michael Hattaway (*Elizabethan Popular Theatre*) suggests that they may have confronted Revenge and Andrea's Ghost seated in the gallery opposite theirs.

723. *sing:* The proximity of 'choir' may suggest that the modern meaning of 'sing' is applicable, but the term can also signify 'celebrate' in a general sense.

725. BALTHAZAR [*above*]: This appears as a stage-direction in the 1592 text, probably to clarify the situation not spelt out in the stage-direction at line 713. I have transferred it to its present position by incorporating it as a speech-prefix, to assimilate it into the text more effectively.

731–40. *Why stands Horatio* etc.: Another notable passage of *stichomythia*, with the 'unheard' interjections of Balthazar and Lorenzo a vital factor in building up tension.

740. *such a war:* The 1592 text has 'warring', which seems clumsy and unmetrical, and most editors since Dodsley (1744) have preferred to read 'war'.

748. *Ambitious villain* etc.: Horatio's presumption in aspiring to Bel-imperia's love is shown to rankle with the Portuguese Prince and Lorenzo (cf. note to line 6).

749. *bower:* The construction of leafy arbours as places of rest and resort in gardens and parks was popular from the sixteenth century on-wards.

751. *The court were dangerous* etc.: A neat piece of dramatic irony.

753. *travailers:* Elizabethan usage made no distinction between the text's 'travellers' and modern 'travailers', and one can only guess at which is intended here, journeys and hard manual labour both being 'distressful' at the time. However, the appearance of the evening star could be a signal to discontinue work, while it would not necessarily denote the

end of a journey, which would depend on other factors. The term is therefore modernized to mean 'labourers'.

757. *with the prickle at her breast:* It was a proverbial saying that the nightingale sang with its breast pressed against a thorn [see Tilley N 183). In Shakespeare's *Rape of Lucrece*, the ravished heroine addresses the nightingale:

Come, Philomel, that sing'st of ravishment,
Make thy sad grove in my dishevell'd hair . . .
And whiles against a thorn thou bear'st thy part . . .
                                        (lines 1128–9, 1135).

763. *jealous despite:* The term 'jealous' seems to require a third syllable to make the line scan regularly; hence some editors amend to 'jealious' here. The word itself is of interest, carrying as it does its meaning of 'suspiciously watchful, zealously vigilant' rather than its more common modern significance of 'enviously, resentfully possessive'.

769. *stoop in time:* cf. note to line 575 above; Bel-imperia will eventually be 'trained' like a hawk to do her father's bidding.

813. *your daughter's thought:* All early editions read 'thoughts' at this point, but most modern editors prefer the singular form which first appears in the quarto of 1615.

814. *If she give back:* Edwards takes this as analogous to the phrase 'to give one the back' meaning 'to turn away from'. However, I think it can be equated with the medieval and Elizabethan term 'give back' for 'retreat, turn tail, run away'; if Bel-imperia adamantly refuses to marry Balthazar, the alliance is null and void.

815-19. *Now that the night* etc.: The sinister connotations of these lines remind us that to the Elizabethans night was a more fitting time for deeds of evil to be done; cf. *Macbeth*, III. 2. 52–3:

Good things of day begin to droop and drowse,
Whiles night's black agents to their preys do rouse . . .

821. *my fainting heart:* Similar forebodings are found in other tragedies of the period; note Juliet's reservations in *Romeo and Juliet*, II. 2. 17–20 (cf. line 829).

823. *as trusty as my second self:* The scene abounds in dramatic ironies such as these; cf. lines 830–33.

848. *thou must needs be Mars:* Venus had an adulterous love-affair with Mars, the god of war, which was discovered by her husband Vulcan when he surprised the lovers together. The partial parallel would not be lost on an Elizabethan audience.

859. *Thus elms by vines* etc.: 'The vine embraces the elm' was a common saying (cf. Tilley V 61); *The Comedy of Errors*, II. 2. 173, reads: 'Thou art an elm, my husband, I a vine.' Edwards shows how Kyd inverts the intended meaning (that both are strengthened by the alliance), so that here a 'fall' is presaged as the vine (Bel-imperia) pulls the elm (Horatio) down to enjoy sex, although her lover's ultimate fate may also be touched on (see note to line 861).

861. *in passion dies:* 'To die' was a common Elizabethan synonym for experiencing sexual orgasm; here the literal meaning also prefigures the tragic fate about to overwhelm the lovers.

863. [*A sound off.*]: I have introduced a stage-direction here to motivate Bel-imperia's line which follows.

864. *Who's there? Pedringano?:* Previous editors have argued that 'Pedringano!' is the correct reading, Elizabethan printers often employing the mark of interrogation where we should expect an exclamation mark, but I am unconvinced. Surely Bel-imperia, surprised and scared, calls out to the servant she believes is keeping watch to check that he is still there, and to read 'Pedringano!' (as if she recognized him in disguise) contradicts the stage-direction which follows suggesting that all the murderers are masked. That she identifies Balthazar and Lorenzo is clear (see note to line 871).

866. *your valour is already tried:* A brutal response to Horatio's frantic efforts to grapple with the men holding him: 'you've already proved what a brave guy you are' (cf. Lorenzo's 'sick' joke at lines 874–5). Balthazar's defeats in love and war still seem to rankle with Lorenzo.

867. *They hang him* etc.: There has been some debate on the staging of this central incident, and particularly on whether a scenic tree from which to hang the body was used, or some part of the arbour structure served. The celebrated title-page illustration of the 1615 quarto shows very clearly that Horatio hangs from the centre of a trellis-archway stuck with leaves leading into the arbour, but this may not be based on stage practice. (The illustration is altogether a contrived one, since it shows a masked Lorenzo restraining a screaming Bel-imperia at the same time as a virtually fully dressed Hieronimo is depicted discovering

Horatio's corpse.) Certainly at lines 2413–14 Isabella, in cutting down the arbour, speaks of 'this unfortunate and fatal pine' as bearing especial responsibility in Horatio's demise, and curses it at line 2442; Hieronimo refers to his foray into the garden at line 2585, which says 'Where, hanging on a tree, I found my son', a cue taken up and expanded on by the author of Addition D at lines 60–71. Perhaps, as Mulryne suggests, leafy arbour and tree were conceived of as being one, and that when Isabella destroyed the arbour at line 2412 she stripped the foliage from the arbour or toppled a property-tree.

871. *Oh save him, brother* etc.: Lorenzo and Balthazar are masked, yet it seems likely that Bel-imperia pleads with them to spare her lover, rather than calls to them for assistance. From her letter to Hieronimo (lines 1101–6) it is evident that she knows the truth, and this seems to render the device of the masks redundant. (See note to lines 1606–16.)

877. s.d. *Enter* HIERONIMO *in his shirt, etc.*: Contrary to the illustration referred to under the note to line 867 above, in which he has merely discarded his cloak and doublet, Hieronimo appears here in his night-shirt, without outer garments. The popular belief that our ancestors slept completely naked does not seem borne out by such evidence as exists (see note to line 878 below, and Alan C. Dessen, *Elizabethan Stage Conventions and Modern Interpreters*, Cambridge, 1984, pp. 40–49).

878. *What outcries pluck me* etc.: One of the most famous moments in the play (see title-page to the 1615 edition) is accompanied by an equally celebrated soliloquy, 'which is not only spoken but acted' (Clemen, p. 109). It has been argued that the later part of the speech was probably suppressed when Addition A was incorporated into the text some time before 1602.

my naked bed: The phrase was perhaps originally used in a literal sense, but it came to indicate no more than that in going to bed one removed most of one's ordinary daytime clothing. It may also convey a sense of defencelessness and vulnerability.

899. *this:* The interchange of plural for singular forms and vice versa was common at the period.

901. *to cover sin?:* cf. lines 815–19, 830–33, and the note to lines 815–19.

906. *life was new begun?:* Horatio's career had presumably begun to 'take off' as a result of his gallant conduct on the battlefield; the King has made him his cup-bearer, and bestowed favours on him. In his father's estimation he was 'on his way'.

910. s.d. *Enter* ISABELLA: It is unfortunate that Isabella could not have been introduced into the action while her son was still alive; she has to establish herself as a character at a point when the tension is high and our interest is diverted from her as a character.

921. *For outrage fits our cursed wretchedness:* It is after this line that Addition A is inserted into the 1602 text.

922. *Sweet lovely rose:* Kyd here extends the traditional Christian notion that the rose is a symbol of perfection to suggest that Horatio was a youthful paragon; one may compare Ophelia's description of Hamlet as 'Th'expectancy and rose of the fair state' (III. 1. 152), or Hotspur's reference to the dead Richard II as 'that sweet lovely rose' (*1 Henry IV*, I. 3. 175), a phrase which might just possibly derive direct from *The Spanish Tragedy*.

924. *stay'd:* The 1592 quarto reads 'stainde' which at first sight seems plausible, but the emendation 'staide' makes better sense in explaining Hieronimo's resort to a kiss, tears preventing him from expressing his feelings verbally.

925. *glasses of his sight:* cf. *Coriolanus*, III. 2. 116–17: 'schoolboys' tears take up / The glasses of my sight!'

927. *this handkercher:* As with *Othello* we have to suppress any lowly associations which the humble handkerchief may possess. At this period a handkerchief could be a very costly and prized object, elaborately wrought and owned only by the well-to-do. Mulryne thinks that Hieronimo is referring here to Bel-imperia's scarf, and that the visual connection suggested in the note to lines 425–32 is thereby maintained throughout the action, but Craik feels it may simply be his own handkerchief with which the father attempts to staunch Horatio's bleeding wounds that is in question. Edwards compares *3 Henry VI*, I. 4, where a 'napkin' is dipped in the blood of the dead Rutland.

933–5. *murder cannot be hid* etc.: A little collocation of proverbial sayings; 'murder will out' (Tilley M 1315) goes back at least to Caxton's 'murdre abydeth not hyd' (*c.* 1481); 'time tries the truth' (cf. Tilley T 338), and 'time brings the truth to light' (cf. Tilley T 324) are clearly interrelated.

940. s.d. *They take him up:* Horatio's body has presumably remained on the ground after Hieronimo has cut him down at line 889; its removal is a necessity for the uninterrupted flow of action common on the Elizabethan stage. The removal of the corpse by the grieving parents could

be quite effective, but it would require to be delayed until much later in the scene, when Hieronimo's dirge is ended, unless the latter was actually left out in production. If not, perhaps the parents simply support Horatio during the dirge, and then carry him off after line 956.

942. *his dirge:* The 'Dirge' was originally given to the Matins service of the Roman Catholic Office of the Dead, deriving its title from the opening antiphon, *Dirige Domine* (Vulgate Psalm V. 19). It later came to indicate a song sung at a burial or any commemoration of the dead, or simply any kind of funeral hymn, or a song of mourning or lament. Hieronimo speaks the words, being too overcome with grief to sing them.

943–56. *O aliquis* etc.: (The Latin of the 1592 text has been corrected and normalized.) The passage appears to be a mish-mash of invented lines and selective quotations from Latin poets including Tibullus, Virgil, Ovid and Lucretius, but on the stage it constitutes a splendidly sonorous farrago. The translation runs: 'Oh, let someone blend for me those herbs which beauteous spring brings forth, and let a medicine be given for our grief, or, if there are any juices which bring oblivion to men's minds, let him supply those. I shall personally gather whatever plants throughout the great world the sun brings out into the glorious regions of light; I myself will take whatever poisoned drink the sorceress concocts, and whatever herbal preparation her incantation combines together through its secret powers: I shall endure all, even death, until all feeling we possess dies in my lifeless breast once and for all. Thus, my entire life, shall I never again behold your eyes; has an everlasting sleep buried your light in the grave? I shall die with you: thus, thus it delights me to go down to the shades below. But, none the less, I shall hold back from subjecting myself to a speedy end, lest in that way no vengeance should follow your death.'

943. s.d. HIERONIMO *sets his breast unto his sword:* The implication must be that he threatens suicide at this juncture, although it seems an arbitrary point in the speech to do so. The stage-direction might be more appropriately inserted at line 954, when Hieronimo speaks of dying with his son ('*Emoriar tecum*').

957. GHOST: A reminder that Andrea's Ghost and Revenge have watched in silence throughout. The brief scene between the two serves to round off the Act neatly, as well as offering a moment of choric commentary on the harrowing events witnessed. The sense that events are still under Revenge's control consoles both Andrea and audience. No entrance or exit for the Ghost and Revenge seems envisaged (cf. notes to lines 2176, 2214, and 2691 below).

963–5. *Thou talk'st of harvest* etc.: These lines all have a proverbial ring, but they do not appear in the principal collections, although line 964 translates a popular Latin tag, *Finis coronat opus.*

967. s.d. [. . . *A stake prepared*]: Hattaway, op. cit. p. 122, thinks that perhaps one of the pillars supporting the 'heavens' over the stage platform could have been pressed into service here.

968–78. *Infortunate condition* etc.: The opening of the Viceroy's speech is indebted to Seneca's *Agamemnon*, lines 57–73, which in John Studley's translation begin:

O Fortune, that does fayle the great estate of kinges,
On slippery sliding seat thou placest lofty thinges
And setst on tottring sort, where perils do abound
Yet never kingdome calme, nor quiet could be found . . .

However, the resemblances are mainly general, one exception being the parallel with Kyd's line 977, which in Studley's version runs:

Fayne woulde they dreaded bee, and yet not setled so
When as they feared are, they feare, and lyve in woe.

Speeches on the sufferings of kings are a familiar aspect of Elizabethan drama: one might compare *Richard II*, III. 2. 155–70; *2 Henry IV*, III. 1. 4–31; *Henry V*, IV. 1. 226–80; Marlowe's *Edward II*, IV. 6. 12–15; V. 1. 8–27.

972. *the wheel of chance:* The image of the wheel of Fortune, symbol of her inconstancy, is an ancient one, deriving from the notion that good or bad luck was an entirely arbitrary matter, and one had no control over Fortune's favours. In prosperity one occupied a place at the top of her wheel, but the 'blind goddess' could equally well bring one crashing down. For some further discussion, see Introduction.

984. *words have several works:* i.e. 'words are not always related to deeds'.

985. *no credit in the countenance:* cf. *Macbeth*, I. 4. 11–12: 'There's no art / To find the mind's construction in the face.'

986–7. *behold the train* etc.: i.e. 'had you been able to observe his feigned love for Balthazar disguised so effectively in his outward appearance . . .'

990. *That hourly coasts the centre of the earth:* 'That circles the earth in a regular number of hours'. Kyd here maintains the old Ptolemaic

explanation of the cosmos, whereby the earth is conceived of as lying at the centre of the universe, around which the sun, the planets and fixed stars revolve in their respective spheres. By Kyd's day the theories of Copernicus were known, but not widely accepted.

997. s.d. *halberts:* The halbert or halberd seems to have come into use in the fifteenth century; it was a combination of spear and battle-axe mounted on a shaft five to seven feet in length. A soldier armed with such a weapon was known as a halberdier or a halbert(d).

1004. *any of her mould:* There is a play on words here, 'mould' often being used as a synonym for 'earth' or 'the soil'.

1017. *Phlegethon:* Phlegethon derived its name from the Greek *phlego*, to burn; it was conceived of as a river of liquid fire which flowed into the Acheron (see note to line 19 above). The 'lake' of line 1022 is presumably Avernus (see note to line 29 above).

1023. *those thy words* etc.: cf. line 984: 'But now I see that words have several works.'

1028. *entrance:* Trisyllabic to maintain the scansion.

1036. *witnesses:* The metrical pattern would usually require 'witness' here, but I have maintained the 1592 reading.

s.d. *The* [VICEROY] etc.: The 1592 text has 'King' at this point, but in the interests of consistency his usual title has been restored (cf. line 2691 and note).

1044–6. *Come, my lord* etc.: 1592 follows this remark with the words 'unbinde him', which seem metrically redundant as well as tautological in the light of line 1045. It has been conjectured that a stage-direction has become incorporated into the dialogue, and perhaps should have been cancelled in view of '*They unbind him*' two lines below. Alternatively, the compositor may have caught up the words from line 1046, s.d., too early. Craik argues attractively that they apply to the Viceroy who himself begins to unbind Alexandro at this point with the words 'Come, my lord' by way of apology, and that others join in later, but the Viceroy's previous words seem to indicate that it can only be Villuppo ('that is bound to death') who has to unbind Alexandro from the stake at this point. It is just possible but grammatically unlikely that it is Alexandro 'that is bound to death'. It may be that in the interests of speed Villuppo needed assistance, hence the wording of the stage-direction at 1046, although many editors argue that this simply means 'he is unbound'.

1047. *in kindness:* See note to *Gorboduc*, line 11; Alexandro is defending the Viceroy's conduct by saying that, in his capacity as ruler, he had to act in accordance with what was expected of one in his position. Edwards suspects rewriting here, since Alexandro responds to an apology the King has not made, which throws us back to the vexed question as to who is referred to in lines 1044–6.

1058. *Wherein hath Alexandro:* The 1592 text begins 'Or wherein', but many editors have been content to suppress the redundant word.

1076–98. *O eyes, no eyes* etc.: A 'set speech' frequently ridiculed and parodied in its own day, the first line of which translates line 4 of Petrarch's sonnet *In Vita* 161, which runs 'o occhi miei, occhi non già, ma fonti'. In Jonson's *Every Man in his Humour*, I. 4, it is selected for special praise by Bobadil and Matthew, two characters whose antiquated tastes in drama are made much fun of. However, Clemen, op. cit. pp. 271–5, says of it, 'The speech is a masterpiece of rhetorical art. Its structure and proportions are worked out with an almost mathematical exactness, and a variety of stylistic figures are harmoniously dovetailed in order to make a powerful emotional impact.' Clemen's whole discussion merits close attention.

1083. *[son of]:* I gratefully adopt Craik's suggested emendation here, which restores the metrical line and improves the sense.

1086. *If you unjustly* etc.: Kyd unconsciously or consciously has introduced a fourteen-syllable line here, reproducing the standard unit in which large portions of the Senecan translations in Newton's collection of 1581 were composed.

1088. *wake:* The single subject of a plural verb is 'night' in the preceding line, but this is not an unusual feature of English usage at this time. However, Edwards notes that 'solicit' in line 1090 is also plural, although perhaps here 'night' and 'wounds' may be considered to constitute a plural subject.

1097–8. *Eyes, life* etc.: A typical Kydian conclusion in which the leading images of the speech are gathered into a culminating catalogue of predominantly monosyllabic terms (cf. lines 2564–9 below).

1098. s.d. *A letter falleth* etc.: A slightly unusual stage device, but an effective one for creating maximum dramatic surprise. Presumably the letter is assumed to be thrown through the window or over a wall; one may compare *Julius Caesar*, I. 2. 314–19, I. 3. 144–5; *King Lear*, I. 2.

57–8. Doubtless on stage the letter was actually dropped by Bel-imperia herself from the playhouse gallery, if that was assumed to constitute her prison (see line 1567, s.d. and note).

1100. s.d. *Red ink:* The insertion 'Red incke' would seem to indicate the author's insistence that the letter written in blood should be seen by the audience to be so, but it might possibly be a note inserted by the book-keeper as a reminder to himself. It could be a further indication that some playhouse instructions had become incorporated into the manu-script (see note to line 178, s.d. above).

1102. *hapless:* The usual meaning attributed to 'hapless' is 'unlucky' or 'unfortunate', neither of which terms can really be applied to Lorenzo; I have therefore ventured to suggest that its significance here is 'ill-luck-bearing' or 'ill-omened'.

1123. *by circumstances:* The noun derives from the Latin term for 'stand-ing around'; it has thence been assumed that the phrase means 'pro-ceeding indirectly'. However, Edwards prefers to take the phrase together with 'confirm' as meaning 'by way of circumstantial evi-dence'.

1128. *Now, Hieronimo?:* The servant's pert and casual response to Hier-onimo's superior tone tells us much that is relevant to Pedringano's social pretensions and his contempt for the niceties of verbal convention (cf. line 1240 and note).

1139. *Why so, Hieronimo? Use me:* It is after this line that Addition B is inserted in the 1602 text.

1158. *Luigi's:* The 1592 text renders the evidently unfamiliar name as 'Liugis', and 1602 repeats the error. However, 'Luigi' is essentially an Italian name, and perhaps Kyd had some other word in mind.

1168. *shalt thou mount:* The secondary sense of 'mount' obviously refers to Lorenzo's intention to have Pedringano hanged for Serberine's murder, when he will 'mount' the scaffold.

1169. *Che le Jeron!:* Boas says that this phrase may be a corrupted version of the page's name (cf. line 1158 and note above), but others think part of it is a form of the Italian *'chi è là?'* (Who's there?), with *Jeron* as the page's name or some reference to Hieronimo's (cf. line 612 and note). Mulryne objects to the theory that the cry is occasioned by Lorenzo hearing a noise off-stage, by saying that it would be somewhat implaus-ible dramatically; one might therefore note that this type of call for attendance is found elsewhere, as in *Macbeth*, III. 1. 71. Some scholars have conjectured that the phrase should be *'Che leggerone!'*, *leggerone* being Italian for an inconstant, thoughtless, talkative person. Lorenzo might be saying of Pedringano, 'What a crazy boy!'

1182. *And thus one ill* etc.: cf. Tilley D 174: 'One deceit driveth out another' (Richard Taverner's transl. of Erasmus).

1190. *And better 'tis:* 'better its' is the 1592 reading which many editors seem to have been happy to accept; however, 'better 'tis' would seem to be far more idiomatic and the quarto of 1599 adopts it, as do subsequent quartos. I have therefore included it, treating 'its' as a printer's or a scribe's error.

1193. *I'll trust myself* etc.: cf. *Richard III*, V. 3. 183: 'Richard loves Richard; that is, I am I.'

1194. *For die they shall:* Cairncross argues that these words have been interpolated from elsewhere, since they make the metrical line over-long, yet they seem needful to make sense of the whole.

1214. *watch and ward:* The performance of the duties of a sentry or watchman was often a feudal obligation in the Middle Ages, and the phrase 'watch and ward' had specific application in this legal sense. However, the phrase later simply serves as a more intensive synonym for 'watch', often for literary effect.

1230. *the sorrows of the souls in Hell:* Pedringano here employs an image constantly repeated in the course of the drama.

1231. *I'll be his priest!:* A phrase alluding to the priest's function in administering the last rites to the dead; hence it means 'I'll gladly perform the final acts necessary to his death.' Cf. *2 Henry VI*, III. 1. 272: 'Say but the word, and I will be his priest.' Tilley cites these and other illustrations under P 587.

1233. *unkindly:* See note to *Gorboduc*, line 11; the sense here is that Pedringano has acted as no normal human being should.

1240. *Hieronimo!:* Presumably this exclamation (like the contemptuous response in line 1129) is an indication of Pedringano's insolent scorn for the ageing Knight Marshal.

1272. *To exasperate:* Elided as 'T'exasperate'.

1276. *hardly:* The term could imply here that the King will have great difficulty in denying Balthazar's demands for the death penalty, but it seems more plausible for Balthazar to be arguing a little petulantly that the King will demonstrate a very harsh nature by so doing.

1279. *policy:* A key-word in many Elizabethan writings, 'policy', like related terms, was by now developing a distinctly adverse connotation as it became associated with the calculating, self-interested, cunning strategies of political opportunism as advocated by Machiavelli and his followers. Lorenzo's speech is a perfect instance of 'policy' in practice. Howard S. Babb ('"Policy" in Marlowe's *The Jew of Malta*', *English Literary History* 24, 1957, pp. 85–94) explores the ambivalent employment of the term to highlight hypocrisy and ruthless pragmatism.

1283. *the bird was lim'd:* See note to line 697 above.

1301. *This works like wax:* Wax was synonymous with softness and pliability, and known for its ability to receive impressions readily, so that speakers and writers used the phrase to indicate that matters were progressing favourably. Cf. *Mother Bombie* by John Lyly, lines 991–2: 'the time was wherein wit would work like wax'; lines 1431–2: 'This cottons, and works like wax in a sow's ear!' Other examples are found under W 138 in Tilley.

1308. *Tell him his pardon* etc.: There appears to be little real justification for this ruse except to discourage Pedringano from confessing what he knows, but its main purpose is to compound Lorenzo's villainy, and contribute an element of 'black comedy' to the execution scene.

1310. *turned off:* An alternative variant of the phrase was 'to turn off the ladder', i.e. to make a hanged corpse spin round above the steps of the gallows.

1318. *cleanly:* B. L. Joseph argues for the meaning 'innocently, without suspicion' here, but in the context I incline to the more plausible definition given; Lorenzo wants 'no mistakes'.

1322. *see the executioner:* Edwards suggests that 'fee the executioner' (i.e. 'pay him off, bribe him') is probably correct, but allows 'see' to stand as making sense.

1330–51. *My master* etc.: A notable monologue using idiomatic prose throughout.

1339. *gentlemanlike:* i.e. 'just what a member of the upper classes would do'.

1361. *neither gods nor men:* Such a reference to pagan deities may not be intentional or meaningful here, Kyd being less concerned than the authors of *Gorboduc* to create a non-Christian environment for his tragedy. However, his presumably extensive reading in the works of

Seneca may have led him to make the allusion without fully considering its significance, though the blend of classic and Christian reference is characteristic.

1367. *here lies that:* Speculation continues as to what gesture Hieronimo makes at this point; he may touch his heart in association with the reference in line 1365 to his 'dearest blood'; others prefer the head. Boas perhaps makes the most imaginative conjecture when he thinks that Hieronimo may touch the handkerchief stained with Horatio's blood which is concealed in his doublet. Bel-imperia's letter may also be considered as another possible focus for the allusion.

1370. *I had written to my lord anew:* A reference forward to lines 1486–1508.

1386–7. *For blood with blood* etc.: Proverbial; see note to line 1336 of *Gorboduc*.

1396–7. *disfurnish me of my habit:* It was the custom at judicial executions for the clothes of the deceased to be given to the executioner. Pedringano's speeches are full of word-play at this point, stressing his absolute confidence in Lorenzo's good offices. The dramatic irony of the action is apparent, made more enjoyable by the verbal sparring between the two low comedians.

1426. *truss up:* The Hangman puns on the word 'truss' meaning (a) 'breeches' and (b) 'stringing up' (i.e. 'hanging').

1437. *Is your roguery become an 'office':* Pedringano, like several of Shakespeare's clowns, comments on the universal habit of dignifying what are seen as menial or sordid tasks with high-falutin' titles; his contempt for the Hangman's craft is shown in such terms as 'roguery' and 'a knave's name'.

1452. *intercepts itself of* etc.: The sense of Hieronimo's remark seems clear enough – 'the soul, by taking pleasure exclusively in forbidden matters and exploring dubious experiences, finally deprives itself of ultimate bliss' – but the syntactic structure of the sentence seems odd. Mulryne locates the difficulty at the word 'That' (line 1452), agreeing that an 'And' by way of substitution would clarify the sense. One possible solution is to treat 'That' (i.e. 'all that kind of conduct') as the subject of the final clause, and to insert a hiatus mark after 'thorny passages'.

1462. *Stand you on that?:* The grim nature of the Hangman's pun would be more clearly emphasized on stage, if by this point the halter were already round Pedringano's neck, and he were 'standing' on the trap-door of the scaffold. Mulryne suggests that the mechanical device for hanging Horatio in the arbour was pressed into service here, but it does not necessarily follow.

1468–85. *Where shall I run* etc.: Clemen's comment on this speech (p. 275) is worthy of quotation: 'in the first part of the speech Kyd plays his own variations on the two well-worn themes of "Where shall I go to voice my grief?" and "Nature grieves with me"; then he embarks on a finely expressive image of a helpless suffering that is thrown back on itself, a suffering whose impassioned pleas cannot force their way through to heaven ... Here for the first time in pre-Shakespearean drama, it would seem, we have sorrow conceived of in terms of a coherent picture of movement, for it is not merely a state of mind that is described, but activity; and, moreover, all the conventional formulas are abandoned ...'

1483. *countermur'd:* Edwards compares a line from John Studley's translation of Seneca's *Hippolytus*: 'Nor countermured Castle strong the walled Townes to keepe' (Newton, II. 155).

1487. *Petergade:* The change in the Hangman's normally bluff demeanour is emphasized by his pathetic effort to recall or pronounce Pedringano's name.

1490. *went the wrong way:* i.e. 'he shouldn't have been hanged at all'.

1492. *here is his passport:* It is perhaps worth stating that the Hangman is illiterate.

1500. *Take truce with sorrow:* 'Give myself a little respite from my sadness.'

1501. *I writ:* The 1592 text has 'write' here, but it is clear from the form 'required' that Pedringano refers to his first letter of appeal (see line 1292), and that the past tense is therefore correct.

1506. *as confederate:* The 1592 edition reads 'was confederate', but this indicates some confusion about the precise syntax of the lines; 'as' must be the correct reading, though B. L. Joseph retains 'was', arguing that line 1508 is a separate sentence. Yet Hieronimo responds to the last three lines of the speech as a unit, and Pedringano had no confederates in killing Serberine.

1517. *vented:* The 1592 text reads 'venged' here, possibly because 'vengeance' and 'revenge' are such key-words in the context; however, 'vented' makes a far more satisfactory contrast to 'smother'd' and complements 'reveal'd' more neatly. See note to line 1538 below.

1519–20. *not feign'd/Nor feigned she:* i.e. Bel-imperia's letter was no forgery, nor was she spreading falsehood in what she said in it.

1528. *bane to thy soul and me:* i.e. Balthazar has poisoned his own immortal soul and Hieronimo's mortal life. The pronouns are hard to disentangle in these lines.

1529. *he reserv'd thee for:* i.e. Horatio ('he did pity thee!' in line 1535).

1538. *to my lord the King:* As Mulryne observes, it is worth noting that Hieronimo's first reaction is to seek redress at the hands of the rightful authorities; he does not plan to pursue vengeance on his own terms until baulked of satisfaction. The point has bearing on the reading of the line 1517 above.

1542. s.d. *Enter* ISABELLA etc.: Some editors argue for beginning a new (Fourth) Act here on the grounds that Act III as printed is preternaturally long, and that dividing it into two shorter Acts would restore a five-act structure to the tragedy (see Introduction). But four-act plays are not unknown, even in the classical theatre.

1551. *Elysian Fields:* A further instance of the classical imagery (see note to line 73) which runs through the play, contrasting strongly with the traditional Christian terminology in which Isabella describes Paradise in lines 1556–64.

1552. *Why, did I not give* etc.: Isabella in her madness is here conceived of as addressing Horatio in person.

1556–64. *My soul?* etc.: Edwards (Appendix D) makes a convincing case for Kyd's indebtedness in these lines to Thomas Watson's *Eglogue uppon the Death of . . . Sir Francis Walsingham* (1590); Watson's *Hecatompathia* (1582) had already supplied some lines for the dialogue between Lorenzo and Balthazar (see lines 574–7 and notes above). The diction is far more Christian than classical at this point, and the debt may account for the change of tone.

1567. s.d. *at a window:* It may well be that the scene which follows was performed in the gallery above the stage, the 'window' being imagined by audience and players.

1571. *this:* See note on line 899.

1574. *why writ I:* i.e. 'why did I bother to write?'

1581. s.d. *Enter* CHRISTOPHILL: Presumably he too enters 'above' and leads Bel-imperia out of the gallery.

1582. *this may not be:* i.e. 'I can't allow you to behave like this.'

1583. *talk no further:* This remark might offer support to part of the interpretation of line 1169 offered in the note above, i.e. that the Page is a 'chatterbox'.

1593. *a nine days' wonder:* The proverb 'a wonder lasts but nine days' was proverbial at least by 1525 (the earliest citation under Tilley W 728), but Kyd seems to have been one of the first, if not the first, to phrase the proverb in its best-known form.

1606–16. *Sister? no!* etc.: At first sight it seems curious that Bel-imperia makes slight reference to the cardinal reason for her anger, namely the murder of her lover, but in the circumstances it is plausible that she might seek to allay her brother's suspicions that she had precise knowledge as to who the masked assailants were (cf. note to line 871).

1610. *with extremes* etc.: 'Use the cruellest violence towards the person I was with.'

1626–7. *matters of estate* etc.: Some editors, including Edwards, prefer to suggest that it was on some question of the Viceroy's relinquished possessions that Lorenzo pretends that the King and Castile wished to consult Hieronimo, but 'matters of state' could be all that is meant. Lorenzo is lying to his sister anyway!

1636. *old disgrace:* See lines 1–11, and notes.

1641. *forth my father's way:* On the surface this means no more than 'out of my father's sight', suggesting that Lorenzo believes that Bel-imperia can be deceived as to Horatio's ultimate fate. William Empson, however, in *'The Spanish Tragedy'* (see Guide to Further Reading), argues that Lorenzo implies that he is employing his father's methods, and that the Duke of Castile was a prime mover in securing the demise of Andrea.

1644–5. *Even so, my lord?:* Bel-imperia's evident scorn for Balthazar's moral calibre is beautifully conveyed.

1650. *Your melancholy:* See note to line 300.

1654. *give his fury place:* i.e. 'allow his anger to expend itself in your absence'; the concept is slightly oddly phrased.

1657. *Aetna:* Mount Etna in Sicily was well-known for its frequently active volcano; Virgil mentions its activity in the *Aeneid*, Book III, alluding to the belief that Enceladus, one of the giants who conspired against Zeus, is buried beneath Etna, having been killed by Zeus, and that the volcanic eruptions are his exhaled breath.

1659. s.d. *He whispereth in her ear:* A slightly enigmatic rubric, the assumption being that Lorenzo has attributed his sister's absence to some female condition or ailment.

1655–9. *Brother, you are become an orator* etc.: The cool ironic tone of Bel-imperia's responses in this and later speeches is notable.

1667. *politic:* See note to line 1279; Lorenzo's sister is pretending to admire her brother's astuteness, but clearly aims at his falsity and deceit.

1671–2. *Ariadne's twines* etc.: Ariadne was a princess of Crete, and daughter to King Minos who built the Labyrinth to house the Minotaur. She assisted Theseus to kill the monster by guiding him through the maze with a thread ('twines'). Some commentators think Kyd here confuses Ariadne with Arachne, a princess of Lydia who hanged herself when the goddess Athene jealously destroyed her woven tapestry: Athene then turned Arachne into a spider. The story is found in Ovid's *Metamorphoses*, VI. 1–145. The origins of the legends tell us little about which mythical princess Kyd had in mind, but the image of a lover captured in his mistress's hair is found in Sonnet X of France's first sonnet-sequence, *L'Olive* (1549–50) by Joachim Du Bellay. The confusion is echoed in *Troilus and Cressida*, V. 2. 150, where Troilus speaks of 'Ariachne's broken woof', suggesting that Shakespeare too had trouble distinguishing between the two characters.

1673. *my sorrow's map:* Since the forehead or 'front' was believed to exhibit the emotions, Balthazar is assumed to be 'reading' Bel-imperia's feelings for him, to guide his response.

1684. *Et tremulo* etc.: 'To unit quaking fear with trembling horror is a futile deed of stupid treachery.' The source, if there is one, is unknown, and no two editors have agreed on a precise translation. It is doubtless a piece of concocted Latin, but to read *jungere* for *junxere* does render the sense a little less obscure.

1686–7. *Nay, and you argue* etc.: Lorenzo's quick mind perceives that his sister has got the better of the Portuguese Prince, and probably calls this after her to relieve his feelings.

1688. *loadstar:* A loadstar or lodestar was one which showed voyagers the route, and hence in figurative usage signified anyone or anything on which one could fix one's hopes, attention or desires.

1689. *Wends poor oppressed Balthazar:* This line is a metrical foot short;

Craik proposes the substitution of 'love-oppressèd', and pronouncing 'poore' as a disyllable.

1692. *By your leave, sir:* It is after this line that Addition C is inserted in the 1602 text.

1693–4. *Good leave have you* etc.: It is hard to make much sense of these lines, in that Hieronimo is intended to be distracted and confused. He appears to assume that the First 'Portingale' wishes to leave him, when in reality he simply says 'Excuse me' prior to putting his question. Line 1694 appears to mean 'You're not the only one who can depart; I can depart from you in just the same way.'

1699. s.d. *He* [HIERONIMO] *goeth in* etc.: This seems to be another physical indication of the dreadful agony of indecision that Hieronimo is undergoing, although Craik wants to postpone its performance until Hieronimo's exit at line 1722, feeling the 'pointless' act 'unthinkable' in the mid-line position. But it would surely lose its 'point' if it occurred at the end of a scene. His dramatic departure would also confirm his belief that Lorenzo has come from Hell (lines 1719–20), and that he is acting out the terrifying expedition to find him.

1704. *a path upon your left-hand side:* See note on line 63 above.

1725. s.d. *Enter* HIERONIMO etc.: Boas points out that Elizabethans would immediately recognize Hieronimo as a potential suicide at his entry, carrying as he does the poniard and the halter of tradition (cf. *The Faerie Queene*, I. ix. 29). The same point is made by Alan C. Dessen, *Elizabethan Stage Convention and Modern Interpreters*, Cambridge, 1984, pp. 65–6.

poniard: A poniard was any kind of short stabbing weapon, but was usually considered to be synonymous with a dagger.

1726. *Now, sir:* It is a little difficult to comprehend why Hieronimo addresses anyone at this point, except in the anguish of insanity, but it is possible that he speaks directly to the spectators, and that the line should really read 'Now, sirs . . .' I have not made the emendation, but it seems to merit consideration.

1729. *standers-by with toys:* Hieronimo uncannily anticipates his own fate at the hands of Lorenzo.

1732. *Down by the dale* etc.: cf. the landscape invoked in lines 63–71 above.

1733. *a judge:* It is unclear from the context which of the three infernal judges (see note to line 33), if any, is here referred to.

1736. *the lake:* Presumably Lake Avernus (see note to line 29).

1739–44. *Turn down this path* etc.: Schick in his edition of 1898 observes that the sense of these lines is substantially that of lines 954–6 incorporated into the Latin dirge. (See notes to lines 943–55.)

1749. *there goes the hare away:* A proverbial phrase cited by Tilley under H 157. The usage appears to indicate that one's most cherished or ardently desired plans often prove elusive in achievement, or that one can easily lose the fruits of one's painstaking labours.

1770. *inexplicable band:* The 1592 text contains the bizarre reading 'inexcrable band', of which no good sense can be made; later quartos substitute 'inexplicable', which in Elizabethan use means either 'inexpressible' or 'indissoluble, unable to be untied'. Since this term makes good sense, I see no reason to emend to 'inextricable' as so many editors following Hawkins prefer to do. The accent falling on the second syllable should make it clear to modern audiences that 'unexplainable' is not the sense here.

1786. *see it given to Horatio:* The King appears to have been kept in ignorance of a ghastly murder taking place within his jurisdiction; even if it were credible that the crime could be 'hushed up', it might be considered odd that Horatio's sudden disappearance had occasioned no regal inquiries as to his whereabouts. As Edwards says, everyone else seems to know about it!

1790. *whom naught can ransom* etc.: i.e. those unlike Balthazar.

1795. *I'll rip the bowels* etc.: Boas compares *The Jew of Malta*, I. 1. 147, 'Ripping the bowels of the earth for them', but it remains uncertain which play pioneered the use of the phrase.

1796. *th'Elysian plains:* See notes to lines 73 and 1551.

1806. *Needs must he go* etc.: A familiar proverb, cited by Tilley as D 278.

1814. *we are sorry for't:* cf. *Othello*, I. 3. 73: 'We are very sorry for't'.

1823. *melancholy:* See note to line 300.

1825. *[not] exempt the place:* One of the most awkward cruces in the text. The 1592 edition reads 'our selfe will exempt', which not only poses problems of meaning, but renders the line one syllable short. Mulryne chooses to retain the 1592 reading, opting to gloss 'exempt' as 'hold in suspense' (i.e. Hieronimo's duties will be waived, but he will not be deprived of his position). Other editors, including Collier and Craik, propose to emend 'exempt' to 'execute' here, implying that the King will take over his Knight Marshal's duties for a time. T. W. Ross sees the meaning of 'exempt' as 'vacate, declare vacant', and certainly in the next scene Hieronimo is exercising his function as corregidor, a position he occupied before becoming Knight Marshal. However, others like Philip Edwards prefer to restore sense and scansion by simply assuming that the word 'not' has fallen out of the 1592 text at this point. I accept this theory, taking *OED*'s third sense of 'exempt', i.e. 'take away', 'debar (him from)' as giving the most likely interpretation of the whole phrase.

1834. s.d. *Exeunt:* It is after this departure that Addition D appears in the 1602 edition.

s.d. *Enter* HIERONIMO *with a book:* It is made clear during the speech which follows that Hieronimo is carrying a copy of Seneca, from which he quotes later.

1835. *Vindicta mihi!:* Almost certainly quoted from St Paul's Epistle to the Romans (xii. 19): 'Vengeance is mine; I will repay, saith the Lord,' despite the fact that Hieronimo is about to read from the works of Seneca. The blend of classical wisdom and Christian admonition is very marked at this point (cf. line 1838).

1840. '*Per scelus . . .*' etc.: The line is adapted from Seneca, *Agamemnon*, line 115, which in John Studley's version of 1581 is translated as 'The safest path to mischiefe is by mischiefe open still' (Newton, II. 106). The phrase seems rapidly to have become proverbial in England (see Tilley C 826). Cf. *Gorboduc*, line 731 and note above, where the link with *Macbeth*, III. 2. 55 is highlighted.

1846–7. '*Fata si . . .*' etc.: The sentiments which are taken from Seneca's *Troas* (lines 511–12) are roughly translated in the ensuing four lines; Jasper Heywood renders them thus:

If ought the fates may wretches help thou has thy savegard here,
If not: already then pore foole thou has thy sepulchere.
    (Newton, II. 31)

1852. *neither:* Presumably if destiny does not ease his miseries, nor grant him death, Hieronimo still has the consolation of Heaven's protective influence.

1853. *Heaven covereth him* etc.: Taken from Lucan's *Pharsalia*, VII. 818.

1856. *With open, but inevitable ills:* A puzzling line, but the general sense appears to be 'with blatant acts of destruction certain to be detected'; the contrast is with Hieronimo's concealed but guaranteed methods. The problem lies with the word 'inevitable', none of *OED*'s citations of which supplies the precise meaning which seems to be required. It is tempting to suggest that 'With' should read 'Will', which then could supply the sense that 'men of common intelligences are prone merely to bring trouble on themselves', but this remedy to a textual puzzle is a desperate one.

1861–2. *But in extremes* etc.: i.e. 'except that in critical situations no precise moment offers a favourable opportunity, and therefore one cannot take revenge, just when one thinks one will'.

1869. '*Remedium malorum . . .*' etc.: Adapted from Seneca's *Oedipus*, line 515, translated by Alexander Nevyle as '. . . a simple remedy of little force and strength / Is ignoraunce of our estate when daungers us betyde' (Newton, I. 208).

1877. *Thy cap to courtesy:* Hieronimo will doff his cap reverently to the nobility.

1878. s.d. *A noise within:* This stage-direction appears after line 1879 in the 1592 text, but in the light of Hieronimo's remark I have placed it one line earlier.

1892. *corregidor:* The text reads 'Corregedor' but the proper term is *corregidor*, a judge or more strictly a Spanish chief magistrate, here simply a lawyer or advocate.

1895. *an action of the case*: A legal suit which required a special writ setting out the cause of the dispute, since it did not fall within the normal remit of the Court of Common Pleas. Kyd's legal knowledge seems much in evidence in this scene.

1896. *Ejectione firmae:* A writ permitting a tenant to be ejected from a property before the expiry of a lease; 'by a lease' thus seems awkward in the context.

1901. *silly:* See note to line 1231 of *Gorboduc*; the context here suggests 'pitiful' or 'pitiable' as the dominant sense.

1905. *Myrmidons:* See note to lines 48–9 above. The passage derives from Virgil, *Aeneid*, II. 6–8: 'What Mirmidon . . . could keep back the tears in recounting such a story?'

1906. *Corsic rocks:* In *Octavia*, line 382, Englished by Thomas Newton, there is a reference to 'the craggy corsicke rockes' (Newton, II. 163). (Whether or not Seneca composed *Octavia*, it has always been taken as part of the Senecan canon.)

1936–41. *whenas a raging sea* etc.: Perhaps the hardest passage in the play to elucidate satisfactorily. Hieronimo seems to be rebuking himself for his own manic efforts to obtain justice, contrasting the more controlled grief of the Old Man. The marine imagery suggests that while Hieronimo in the midst of storms of anguish has been diverted from 'the course of waves' (which the 'upper billows' should uphold, thus maintaining the façade of normal behaviour), the Old Man, despite being of inferior social status ('lesser waters'), refuses to 'labour in the deep', but keeps up persistent pressure fuelled by love for redress of his wrongs. The 1592 text reads 'oreturnest' in line 1937, and has no comma after 'billowes', but both readings seem to require amendment.

1945. *Alcides:* The original name of Hercules or Heracles. As his twelfth labour he was required to go down into Hades and carry off Cerberus, the monster guard-dog (see note on line 30), to the upper world and back again.

1946. *Furies:* See note to line 65.

1948. *the triple-headed porter:* i.e. Cerberus (see note to line 30).

1949. *the slimy strand:* cf. line 28: 'To pass me over to the slimy strand'.

1950. *The Thracian poet:* i.e. Orpheus, who descended to the underworld to persuade the infernal gods to release his dead wife Eurydice and charmed all the creatures below by playing to them on the lyre.

1953. *sound the burden:* Kyd puns on the meanings 'musical refrain' and 'distressing load'.

1954–5. *that Proserpine may grant* etc.: Mulryne remarks that this has already been agreed (see lines 76–80).

1958 s.d. *Exit* HIERONIMO etc.: Craik argues that the exits here anticipate those at line 1964, but this is to minimize the wild grotesque behaviour of a distraught old man. The abrupt departures and arrivals should be seen as part of Hieronimo's crazed condition.

1959. *Save my bond:* Possibly an erroneous repetition of the previous cry.

1964. *Tush, no, run after* etc.: cf. *King Lear*, IV. 6. 204–5: 'Nay, an you get it, you shall get it by running . . .' (both elderly men are 'running mad' at this point).

1970. *Eacus:* See line 33 and note (cf. lines 1974 and 1988).

1983. *Ah, ruthless [fate]:* 1592 reads 'ruthlesse Father', but it seems clear that the compositor has caught this up from 'Father' in line 1982, and that 'fate' is the correct version.

1984. [SENEX]: 1592 here and at line 1991 abandons the speech-prefix 'SENEX' for 'BA' (for 'BAZULTO'); I have observed consistency at both points.

1985. *a Fury:* See note to line 65.

1993. [*thy*] *son:* The 1592 text reads 'my sonne', but the sense appears to dictate the emendation given.

2014. *western Indies:* Arthur Freeman suggests that by this allusion Portuguese Brazil is meant; certainly, Spain and Portugal having been united from 1580 to 1640, the former Portuguese colony became part of the Spanish Empire. However, Kyd may have had the East Indies in mind, and made a careless error.

2108. *cross'd the seas:* This seems an extraordinary way to travel from Portugal to Spain, though if the action is mainly set in Seville, the Viceroy's party could have travelled by sea from Lisbon to Cadiz, and thence by land.

2044. *Thy friend* etc.: A defective line, which J. M. Manly rectified by reading 'to strive with thine extremities'.

2107. *lies:* The verb is singular, but the subject plural, a common occurrence in Elizabethan English (cf. note to line 2151).

2109. *can show [no] brighter yet:* The 1592 edition omits the word 'no' at this point; it appears in the 1594 text. Apart from being one syllable short, the line in its 1592 version can yield sense ('my love is quite capable of increasing'), but given Bel-imperia's resolve and her fondness for enigmatic statements, she surely means 'My love is too recent in origin to burn very brightly as yet.'

2118–20. *It is not now* etc.: Castile is making a magnanimous gesture in the hope of reconciling Bel-imperia to the match with Balthazar; the dramatic irony is plain.

2125. *Pocas palabras*: A Spanish phrase recommending taciturnity, it seems to have become rapidly popular in Elizabethan dramatic literature.

2135. LORENZO: The 1592 edition fails to insert this prefix, but 1602 restores it.

2151. *As love not me:* 1592 reads 'loves', offering another example of a singular verb with a plural subject (cf. note to line 2107 above), but Edwards sees a printer's error, since 'hate' is regular.

2155. *I never gave you cause:* cf. *Othello*, V. 2. 302: 'Dear General, I never gave you cause.'

2157. *And for the satisfaction of the world:* cf. line 1376 above.

2158. *homely:* Castile may be engaging in conventional denigration of his ducal seat here (cf. 'my humble home'), but I believe he is extolling its hospitable atmosphere where Hieronimo will feel 'at home'.

2170. *And [thus] I hope:* Many editors follow Dodsley and amend to 'And thus' here, feeling that Lorenzo's 'and that' in the 1592 text lacks an introductory clause. B. L. Joseph relates the remark to Hieronimo's preceding 'it is fit for us / That we be friends', but the grammatical logic is awkward ('it is fit for us . . . that I hope, old grudges . . .'?'). Edwards punctuates 'And thus, I hope, old grudges are forgot'.

2175–6. *Chi mi fa* etc.: The Italian of the original has been corrected; slightly different versions of the proverb occur elsewhere.

2176. s.d. GHOST *and* REVENGE: The 1592 direction reads 'Enter Ghoast' etc., but one assumes that Andrea and Revenge remain present throughout the preceding action, and Edwards and Ross omit the 'enter' (but see note to line 2214 for a caveat about this assumption).

2177–81. *Erichtho* (1592 reads 'Erictha'): A Thessalian sorceress or possibly an error for Alecto, one of the Furies.

Cerberus: See note to line 30.
Pluto . . . Proserpine: See notes to lines 478 of *Gorboduc* and line 76 of *The Spanish Tragedy*.

Acheron ('Achinon' 1592): See note to line 19.

Erebus ('Ericus' 1592): The son of Chaos and thus the name given to the dark passage through which the dead passed into Hades.

Styx: The principal river of the underworld, which flowed round it seven times.

Phlegethon: See note to line 1017.

Charon: See note to line 20.

2180. *For ne'er by Styx* etc.: It is generally agreed that a line has dropped out following this one, making nonsense of line 2180 as it stands; the missing line perhaps ran something like 'Was wretch more woeful yet conveyed to death' or 'Was I distress'd with outrage sore as this' (Edwards). I have transposed 'in Hell' to line 2180, from the previous line.

2185. *To sleep away* etc.: An awkward line to punctuate since 1592 prints commas after 'sleepe', 'away' and 'what', which has enabled editors to change the sense of the line in an infinite number of minor ways. However, good sense and fewer interjections result if the commas are suppressed as here. Others prefer to read 'to sleep; awake!'

2192. *Thus worldlings ground* etc.: The line departs from normal word-order (anastrophe); the sense is that mundane creatures tend to found their beliefs or behaviour on the fallible evidence of their dreams.

2202. s.d. *Enter a dumb-show:* One may readily compare those featured in *Gorboduc*; Kyd may have intended to parallel the masques at the Spanish court in Act I Scene 4.

2214. s.d. *Exeunt:* This 1592 stage-direction appears strange, given Andrea's words at line 2213; is it a careless copyist's error, or did some brief pause in the performance occur in the action here, contrary to assumptions that Elizabethan playhouse practice was to dispense with intervals? Certainly it is consistent with the characters' departure from the stage at this point that towards the end of the play the Ghost and Revenge apparently return (line 2691, s.d.), but it is utterly inconceivable that they should not be present to witness the culmination of the whole piece. If by 'Exeunt' at line 2214, nothing more is meant than that they retire to the gallery they occupy throughout, why is such a movement not indicated at other points, say after line 91 or line 96? Such stage-directions also affect our sense of the Ghost's and Revenge's positions during the action: the indication of entrances and exits suggests that they did not sit on the platform, the lack of them suggests that they did, yet it also seems needless to note as an 'entrance' the appearance on one of the galleries of characters already visible there. Elizabethan theatre scripts are rarely consistent, but it would be fascinating to have a fuller knowledge of the staging of Kyd's tragedy.

2222. *show:* Craik reads 'shield' here, an attractive alteration, but one perhaps not strictly justified since sense can be made of 'show'.

2223. *With what . . .:* This line in the 1592 text continues 'dishonour, and the hate of men', but most editors accept that these words have been picked up from line 2224, and that something has dropped out; even 'With what' may be an erroneous repetition of the first words of line 2222. B. L. Joseph believes that the repetition is a deliberate figure, but other editors have substituted such words as 'With what weak arguments defend thy name?' or 'With what devices seek thyself to save?' (Boas).

2231–4. *Unhappy mothers* etc.: The sentence beginning here appears to be incomplete, but may not be utterly defective. The sense presumably is 'Mothers of unrevenged children are unhappy, but their fathers by contrast are simply monstrous to forget so quickly children whom they have nurtured, yet now allowed to die without concern.' It may therefore be unnecessary to postulate defective syntax.

2246. *applies our drift:* J. P. Collier substituted 'applauds' for 'applies' here, but the meaning 'guides us to our target' makes the change needless.

2247. *And all the saints* etc.: An overt piece of Christian imagery (cf. note on line 1361).

2280. *motion:* The term used for puppet-shows at this period (*OED*'s first reference being dated 1598), but it may be that here it is used in a less specific sense to indicate any type of stage spectacle.

2283. *Why, then I'll fit you:* Edwards remarks on the double meaning of 'fix you up with a play' and 'pay you back, punish you appropriately as you deserve'.

2289. *too quick:* Lorenzo is clearly intended to butt in and cut Hieronimo's explanation to a minimum, to which the older man responds irritably, but Mulryne suggests that the remark also means 'you are far too much alive', in which case the remark may be an 'aside'.

2300–302. *Why, Nero* etc.: These were the lines, quoted by Thomas Heywood in his *Apology for Actors* (1612) and assigned to 'M. Kid', which identified the previously anonymous author. The Roman Emperor Nero was notorious for his predilection for performing in stage entertainments and devoted much effort to becoming a successful tragic actor during his reign (A.D. 51–4).

2315–17. *could tell what . . . can tell how:* The implication appears to be that the gentlemen and scholars know how to invent the appropriate speeches to improvise (see note on line 2318), while princes and courtiers are skilled in the art of elocution, but Edwards is sceptical, believing that the two sentences mean roughly the same thing.

2318. *country manner:* There seems to be little historical support for its being the Spanish national custom to improvise plays on the basis of an 'argument' (line 2319). Only the 'Italian tragedians' of the *commedia dell'arte* (see note to line 2374) appear to have established such a working-method.

2321. *of a Knight of Rhodes:* The story of Perseda and Soliman outlined here was probably taken from an English translation of Yver's *Printemps d'Iver* (1572); it also forms the main source of *Soliman and Perseda* (*c.* 1599), of which Kyd may well have been the author (see Introduction). A number of the relationships in *The Spanish Tragedy* are of course reflected in the plot details of *Soliman and Perseda.*

2354. *You must provide* etc.: A metrically defective line (among many others); the line might begin 'You must provide yourself . . .'

a Turkish cap: Presumably some early form of fez.

2355. *fauchion:* The word 'falchion' or 'fauchion' derived from the Latin term for a sickle, and refers to a sword with a broad blade with the cutting edge on the convex side.

2356. *a cross:* This is presumably the cross of the Knights of St John of Jerusalem, better known today as 'The Maltese Cross'; the knights of Rhodes settled in Malta following their eviction by the Turks in 1522.

2370. *Tragoedia cothurnata:* The *cothurnus* was the buskin of the ancient classical stage, the thick-soled ankle-boot worn exclusively by tragic actors; Hieronimo's views on the relative dignity of tragedy and comedy reflect those of Renaissance critics.

2374. *The Italian tragedians:* The performers of the *commedia dell'arte*, whose origins go back at least to the later Middle Ages, were famous for their ability to improvise drama on the basis of an agreed synopsis of the action.

2383. *in unknown languages:* Speculation continues as to whether or not 'Hieronimo's play' was presented on stage in a welter of tongues, or whether English was in fact used, despite the pretence that Greek, Latin, Italian and French were actually being uttered. The note at line 2483 implies that the piece really was performed in these languages, and that the reader (unlike the spectator) is favoured with a translation, but the blank-verse format makes that open to question. Whether an Elizabethan audience would have accepted even fifty lines of foreign dialogue even with ample gestural accompaniment is dubious; indeed, Balthazar voices what may be held to be a real objection to the notion in lines 2390–91. Edwards suggests that two alternative versions may have been available; Hattaway (pp. 109–10) believes that Kyd may have been conducting an experiment in audience-response here.

2395–6. *And, with a strange* etc.: These two lines are transposed in the 1592 text and its immediate successors until 1602.

2395. *wond'rous show:* The tableau is, of course, to consist of Horatio's corpse behind a drawn curtain (see line 2562, s.d., below).

2404. *the fall of Babylon:* Almost certainly a reference to the Tower of Babel in Genesis xi, which its builders hoped would reach to heaven, but which was aborted in a confusion of competing languages. Babel was often associated with or confused with the city of Babylon, which in the Book of Revelation xviii stood as archetypically emblematic of sinfulness and corruption, being founded by Cain.

2406. *And if the world* etc.: cf. *Hamlet*, III. 2. 287: 'For if the King like not the comedy . . .'

2412. s.d. *She cuts down the arbour:* Possibly Isabella overthrows the property arbour or a tree forming part of it, or simply strips away some of the leafy branches from it (see note on line 867).

2420. *complot:* The sense of a pun is strong here, but the connotations are serious enough.

2435. *Rhadamant:* See note to line 33.

2441. [–] *to no end:* The sense would seem to require a pause before the sad reflection 'to no end'.

2445. s.d. [*Exit*]: No exit for Isabella is supplied in 1592's text at this point, possibly because there was no room at the foot of the page, but she has either to drag herself off the stage wounded, to be carried off by attendants, or to remain on stage until Hieronimo's 'curtain' can cover her in some way (see next note). 1592 indicates no scene break, but the location clearly changes from garden to palace, and a new scene must begin at that point.

s.d. *he knocks up the curtain:* There is considerable uncertainty as to what precisely Hieronimo is doing at this moment. T. W. Ross assumes that whatever he does is done to conceal Horatio's body hastily from the Duke, who enters hard on Hieronimo's heels, and that the Marshal simultaneously hides Isabella's corpse, whose removal from the stage is certainly not indicated (see preceding note). Part of the problem lies in the words 'knocks up', which might suggest lifting an already positioned curtain with a stick or a staff of office, or hasty concealment, but the latter seems contradicted by the Duke's remark at line 2447 about Hieronimo taking 'all this pain'. It seems more reasonable to assume that Isabella limps off, and that Hieronimo then enters for the new scene carrying the curtain which he proceeds to fit up (with a ladder, hammer, nails?) over one of the open doors in the tiring-house façade at the rear of the stage, behind which the actor playing Horatio can get into position in time for the discovery at line 2562. This would not impair the dramatic excitement at the revelation (as would obviously be the case if spectators saw Hieronimo hastily covering up with a curtain the corpse he had just dragged in). Hieronimo is busily engaged in adjusting his curtain when Castile enters and makes his comment.

2455. *the gallery:* Some editors argue that this is unlikely to refer to the 'upper stage' or 'balcony' of the Elizabethan public playhouse, although it is known that the gallery immediately above and behind the stage platform was sometimes pressed into service for certain scenes staged 'above'. They deem the gallery here to be the imagined gallery of an Elizabethan mansion, the 'long gallery' of such houses as the Vyne in Hampshire or Hardwick Hall in Derbyshire, often used as an alternative to the great chamber when masques and spectacles were to be presented (see note to line 120 of Addition D below). However, throwing *down* the key (see next note) does seem incontrovertible evidence that the gallery of the playhouse was used by the royal party to watch the action from. If this were the case, Andrea and Revenge could scarcely be permitted to use the same gallery, and if they did not sit on the stage itself, perhaps Michael Hattaway's view commends itself, that one of the *side* galleries was used for the royal party in order for them to witness the discovery of Horatio's body, so that the *rear* gallery could have been assigned to Revenge and Andrea's Ghost. If one accepts this, one must also accept that some of the best seating in the theatre would have to be sacrificed.

2456. *throw me down the key:* Hieronimo presumably wishes to delay any rescue attempt for long enough to allow him to hang himself (line 2626, s.d.), by ensuring that he has a literally captive audience. The doors eventually have to be broken open (see line 2630). Hence the instruction must mean 'Throw the key down from the gallery to the stage floor for me', and Hieronimo then 'locks' one tiring-house door as a symbolic gesture that his auditors are in fact prisoners. Frank Ardolino (see Guide to Further Reading) suggests that the device derives from the bull-ring.

2459. s.d. *with a chair:* Edwards assumes that this entry clinches the argument that the royal party watched the play from the stage platform, but Balthazar could well appear in the gallery, placing a chair in a space cleared among the empty benches there, and then retreat as if to the tiring-house proper, to prepare for his entry as Soliman.

2460. *hang up the title:* Presumably Kyd is here following public playhouse practice in having the play's title (or its location) displayed on a board hung up or carried on at the side of the stage; one interesting reference to such a practice occurs in the induction to Beaumont's *The Knight of the Burning Pestle:* 'Down with your title, boy, down with your title' (lines 8–9).

2482. *the book-keeper:* In the playhouse company the book-keeper or book-holder seems to have been responsible not only for prompting the actors and making sure they entered on cue, but for acting as property-master, make-up artist, etc., and seeing that the entire performance proceeded smoothly. He doubtless supervised rehearsals as Peter Quince does in *A Midsummer Night's Dream.*

2483. s.d. *in sundry languages:* See note to line 2383.

2491. *adamant:* The term originally signified a rock of fabled properties, which coalesced into a reputation for impregnable hardness. Because of the word's association with Latin 'adamare' ('to have an inordinate liking for'), it also came to have the sense of 'magnet' or 'loadstone', a mineral which attracted objects to it.

2532. *Perseda:* The 1592 text reads 'Persedaes' but it is clear from the sense that the generally adopted reading must be correct.

2542. *Well said:* Not a compliment on the felicity of Bel-imperia's last speech (ignoring the fiction that the characters are improvising their own dialogue), but rather a compliment on Hieronimo's overall achievement in planning the drama as a whole.

2545. *You would be better to my son* etc.: 'In real life you wouldn't kill my son off quite so cruelly.' The sequence of dramatic ironies which follows is set in train by this apparently jocular remark by the Viceroy; Kyd's gift for 'black' humour is strongly marked at this point.

2554. *The death of Ajax:* A Homeric hero of the Trojan war, second only to Achilles among the Greeks in terms of personal valour.

2558. *The hopeless father* etc.: cf. *The Jew of Malta,* I. 2. 317: 'The hopeless daughter of a hapless Jew' (Boas). It is impossible to say which line has precedence.

2564–9. *Here lay my hope* etc.: Another striking passage of anaphora, culminating in a concluding catalogue, chiefly consisting of mono-syllables.

2570. *breath that gave me life:* A notable paradox which presumably means that Horatio by being born brought new life to his father, but that his death extinguished all the old man's animation.

2582. *He shrieks; I heard:* The abrupt switch of tenses is puzzling, but the sense is clear, and while to read 'shrieked' would be consistent, the emendation is not strictly needed.

2591. *reconciled:* i.e. to Hieronimo (see lines 2138–73).

2592. *March'd in a net:* The common proverb is 'you dance in a net and think nobody sees you' (see Tilley N 130), i.e. to consider oneself free from suspicion when actually exposed to view all the time.

2622. *his latest fortune:* It is tempting to assume that Hieronimo alludes to a concrete object, but he seems to be saying that his ultimate destiny at this point rests firmly in his grasp. There is irony even here; things do not work out precisely as he plans.

2627. *Hold, Hieronimo!:* Editors are unreconciled as to the interpretation of this remark, which is unpunctuated in the 1592 text. It might be seen as a command to the Viceroy to restrain Hieronimo from suicide, or as a plea to the Knight Marshal to postpone his decision to hang himself. The first hypothesis is weak – a shocked Viceroy striving with an elderly official is not only slightly comic, but impossible to stage if the royal party occupies one of the galleries. The second interpretation is more attractive, since other lines indicate that the Viceroy issues orders rather than taking action himself, and in the King's words one can hear a last despairing appeal to his trusty Knight Marshal.

2630. s.d. *[They* [ATTENDANTS] *break in . . .]:* The 1592 text has no stage-directions at this point, the 1602 copy providing the wording inserted here. It seems clear, following Craik, that while this action takes place, the royal party leaves the gallery and re-enters the main stage to confront Hieronimo.

2639. *Why has thou done:* etc.: This and the questions from the Viceroy and the Duke which follow seem to be needless in view of Hieronimo's lengthy exposition in lines 2564–626, but perhaps the nobles were still recovering from the shock of realizing that the murders were actual, not illusory. Edwards argues that lines 2627–75 constitute a variant alternative to the finale, and are intended to replace Hieronimo's long speech in lines 2547–626 with something more pithy and dramatic, and that a few lines of introduction (lines 2639–41) are needful to provide the opportunity for a few facts to emerge before Hieronimo declines to speak further. Certainly Hieronimo's line 'The thing which I have vow'd inviolate' (line 2662) seems peculiar in the light of his long confession earlier, and might point to the presence of unsuppressed matter in the present text, yet it seems equally hard to believe that the exposure of Horatio's corpse was ever excluded from any revised version, or that the actor playing Hieronimo was not allowed a resounding speech of triumphant self-vindication.

2641. *both my children thus:* Here follows Addition E in the 1602 version, which incorporates lines 2650–53, and lines 2642–9 of the 1592 edition (see notes to Addition E below).

2665. s.d. [*He bites out his tongue*]*:* This stage-direction occurs in the 1602 text, 1592 giving no indication of the stage action at this point.

2672. s.d. *mend his pen*: A quill pen required regular sharpening with a knife to retain its fine point.

2674. s.d. *He* [HIERONIMO] *etc.:* This stage-direction clearly needs to precede line 2675 and not succeed it as in the 1592 text.

2675. [KING]*:* 1592 has no speech prefix here, giving line 2676 to the Duke.

2684. *Take up our hapless son:* According to the stage-direction at line 2691 it is the Viceroy who himself carries his son off stage, but perhaps it needed two men to perform this action with any dignity, and so no contradiction need be involved.

2688. *Scylla's:* Scylla, one of a pair of rocks standing between the Italian mainland and Sicily, took its name from the fact that in a cave on the rock nearest Italy lived Scylla, a terrible monster with six heads, who either barked like a dog or was accompanied by barking hounds. On the opposite rock lived Charybdis, who swallowed the ocean three times daily and belched it forth again.

[*reef*]: The 1592 reading retained in 1602 is 'greefe', but most editors adopt the reading 'gulf'. However, the alternative 'reefe' is attractive, and I favour it, since the 'gulf' is more applicable to the whirlpool of Charybdis.

2689. *Acheron:* See note to line 19.

2691. s.d. *a dead march:* A solemn march for a funeral procession, probably played on trumpets.

the [VICEROY]: 1592 and 1602 both read 'the King' or 'the king' (cf. line 1036, s.d., above).

2701. *as Dido fell:* According to Virgil's *Aeneid*, Book IV, Dido killed herself when deserted by Aeneas, who fled from Carthage to follow his destiny in founding Rome. Other sources have her kill herself rather than marry a husband she does not love.

2704. *Proserpine:* See note to line 76.

2705. *her princely doom:* See line 79 above.

2713. *vestal virgins:* Roman maidens often dedicated their lives to the goddess Vesta, the deity of hearth and home, whose sanctuary stood in the Forum where an eternal flame burnt. It was tended by the Vestals, virgin priestesses whose chastity was a by-word.

2714. *Orpheus:* cf. note to line 1950.

2722. *Titius:* See note to line 480 of *Gorboduc.*

2723. *Don Cyprian:* The Duke of Castile, whose punishment may seem somewhat excessive, being stabbed to death by Hieronimo and then doomed to hellish torment; certainly Hieronimo has no personal animus against him, except for being Lorenzo's father. He may be intended to be simply expendable in the final holocaust, unless we adopt the view that he plotted Andrea's death by ensuring his death in battle, in order to rid the family of an unsuitable suitor to Bel-imperia (see note on line 1641). Alternatively, his death may be intended to accentuate Hieronimo's cruel frenzy or the gods' indifference.

2724. *Ixion's wheel:* See note to line 66.

2727. *Chimera's neck:* The Chimera was a fire-breathing creature, one-third lion, one-third goat, and one-third dragon; Bellerophon eventually killed her.

2731. *Sisyphus:* Sisyphus was a corrupt King of Corinth, said to have been punished for his sins by being compelled eternally to roll a huge stone up a steep hill, from the crest of which it rolled to the bottom once more.

2733. *boiling Acheron:* See notes to lines 19, 1017 etc. A certain casualness seems to have crept into Kyd's mythological allusions at this point. Phlegethon was traditionally the river of liquid fire which flowed into the Acheron, which in Greek means 'river of sorrows'.

2736. *haste we down:* Several commentators ingeniously suggest that Revenge and Andrea exit to Hell by way of a trap-door in the platform stage.

ADDITION A

12. *waiting on his cup:* cf. line 513 above.

13. *assure [he]:* The 1602 text reads 'assure me', but the sense seems to demand the meaning 'favours give assurance (or guarantee) that he is not destined for an early grave'. Craik has 'assure me he', which retains the reading of the 1603 quarto, but makes an awkward line to speak and scan.

36. *poor:* Many editors alter the 1602 reading to 'pure' by analogy with 'spotless' and by contrast with 'black', but one need not seek for needless duplication of ideas; 'pure' can regularly mean 'unfortunate' or 'hapless', and this conforms with Hieronimo's picture of his dead son. If this seems unconvincing in conjunction with 'spotless', the sense that Horatio was 'humble' or 'lowly' in his father's eyes might still support the 1602 reading.

50. *Gird in my waist of grief:* The pun on 'waist' and 'waste' is notable.

ADDITION C

8. *nine months':* The original spelling 'monethes' has to be accorded two syllables to maintain the scansion.

13. *Aye, or yet?:* The 1602 text reads 'speake I, or yet', but J. M. Manly's emendation is convincing, i.e. 'Yes, and what more?'

38. *[unto]:* 1602 reads 'us to', which is attractive, but 'unto' is more idiomatic.

39. *That valiant but ignoble Portingale:* Some commentators argue that this line might be more fitly introduced after line 36, but this seems unnecessary: the sense is surely that by sparing Balthazar's life Horatio took the Portuguese Prince to his mercy.

41. *Nemesis:* The Greek embodiment of fortune's capacity to strike down or victimize the presumptuous, or those over-endowed recipients of her gifts or favours.

Furies: See note to line 65.

42. *things call'd whips:* As Edwards says, this line bears a close resemblance to *2 Henry VI*, II. 1. 133–5: 'have you not beadles in your town, and things call'd whips?'

ADDITION D

17. *crevice:* The 1602 text reads 'crevie', which is attractive, but nevertheless a misprint.

30. *we burn daylight:* The phrase became proverbial for any form of time-

wasting (cf. *Romeo and Juliet*, I. 4. 43, 44: 'Come, we burn day-light, ho! . . . We waste our lights in vain – like lights by day'). Yet in several instances the remark is employed literally, as here, to suggest a lack of thrift in using expensive torch-light when day has dawned (see Tilley D 123).

33. [*Hecate*]: The 1602 text spells this name 'Hee-cat', but it is clearly a reference to the goddess whom the Greeks associated with night and the underworld, although the Elizabethans connected her with the moon (cf. *A Midsummer Night's Dream*, V. 1. 373: 'By the triple Hecate's team'). Her three manifestations on earth were as Hecate in Hades, Diana on earth, and Luna or Cynthia in the firmament. Seneca refers to her as Trivia in *Medea* and as Hecate in the *Hippolytus*. She was associated with sorcery (see *Macbeth*, III. 5) and reputedly sent demons and phantoms out into the night from the underworld. The word is usually disyllabic in English.

36. *aggots*: Correctly 'aiglets' or 'aiguillettes', the popular ornate jewelled or metallic tags attached in Tudor times to the ends of laces linking sleeves to doublets, decorating slashed sleeves or adorning hats, etc.

45. *I'll prove it to thee*: i.e. that 'night is a murderous slut' (line 31) etc., for conniving at Horatio's murder.

47. *the book:* The almanac which printed an annual record for the coming year, which included tables showing the phases of the moon (cf. *A Midsummer Night's Dream*, III. 1. 46–51).

75–8. *one knows not* etc.: I take the sense to be 'One does not know what may happen: Good God, that I should plant this tree, for example – but leave that aside. Masters bring up and train servants, who are ungrateful and turn round and injure those who nurtured them.'

105. s.d. *The* PAINTER *and he sits down:* Plural subjects with singular verbs were common in Elizabethan English.

120. *gallery:* Long indoor walkways or galleries came into vogue in many great Tudor houses, where they were chiefly used for taking exercise in inclement weather, the display of portraits, or as supplementary and alternative venues for events more usually held in the great hall (see Mark Girouard, *Life in the English Country House*, New Haven and London, 1978, pp. 100–102). Cf. note to line 2455 above.

matted: *OED* dates the earliest use of 'mat' or 'matt' meaning 'to dull colours' or 'to give a matt finish to' as 1602, but it is hard to discover any other meaning which would fit the sense required here. Boas advocates 'set in a mat or mount' but it seems unnecessarily strained as an interpretation.

142. *Judas ... colour:* It was a long-accepted Christian tradition that Judas Iscariot who betrayed Christ had red hair.

154. *the stars extinct:* cf. line 832 above.

164. *old Priam of Troy:* See note to line 789 of *Gorboduc*.

177. *Hector:* The legendary Trojan champion ultimately slain by Achilles (see note to lines 48–9).

ADDITION E

12–14. *Had I as many lives* etc.: cf. *Dr Faustus*, I. 3. 102–3:

Had I as many souls, as there be stars,
I'd give them all for Mephostophilis.

16–19. *Who were thy confederates* etc.: cf. lines 2650–53.

19–26. *Oh, good words* etc.: cf. lines 2642–9.

APPENDIX

The Sources of *Gorboduc*

There would be little point in reprinting every account of the reign of the
legendary Gorboduc and its aftermath on which Sackville and Norton
may have drawn for their tragedy. There is general agreement that one of
the most influential versions must have been that included in Geoffrey of
Monmouth's *Historia Regum Britanniae*, or the *History of the Kings of Britain*,
completed in 1136. The work, which purports to trace the fortunes of the
British people from the legendary Brutus (believed to have founded
Britain twelve centuries before Christ) down to Cadwallader, who died in
A.D. 689, is in twelve books. The story of Gorboduc and his sons is found
in chapter 16 of the second book, although it is clear that such divisions
are not Geoffrey's own. The whole work has been translated by the late
Lewis Thorpe for Penguin Classics, and the first extract printed below is
reprinted from that version.

Countless retellings of the material selected for his *History* by Geoffrey
appear during the centuries intervening between his day and the first
presentation of Sackville and Norton's drama, in 1561–2; one among
many with a claim to have played some part in shaping the dramatic
narrative is the account given by Robert Fabyan in his *Prima pars
cronecarum*, which appeared anonymously in 1516, and of which chapters
24, 25, and 26 are devoted to the reigns of 'Gorbodio' and his two sons.
Fabyan's work was reprinted several times during the sixteenth century,
and in 1811 it was reissued as *The New Chronicles of England and France* by
Sir Henry Ellis: it is from this edition that the second extract is taken.

The story continued to be popular after the performances of 1561–2
and publication of *Gorboduc* in 1565 and 1570; Edmund Spenser (*c.* 1552–
99) recounts the legend in his romantic epic, *The Faerie Queene* (Book II,
Canto x, 34, 35 and 36), which began to appear in 1590. Although
obviously appearing too late to have influenced Sackville and Norton, the
stanzas are of interest in the light of *Gorboduc*'s ancestry, and they form
the third extract, below.

1. Geoffrey of Monmouth, *Historia Regum Britanniae*, II.16

After the death of Cunedagius, his son Rivallo succeeded him, a peaceful, prosperous young man who ruled the kingdom frugally. In his time it rained blood for three days and men died from the flies which swarmed. Rivallo's son Gurgustius succeeded him. Sisillius came after Gurgustius, then Jago the nephew of Gurgustius, then Kimarcus the son of Sisillius and after him Gorboduc.

Two sons were born to Gorboduc, one called Ferrex and the other Porrex. When their father had become senile, a quarrel arose between these two as to which should succeed the old man on the throne. Porrex was the more grasping of the two and he planned to kill his brother by setting an ambush for him. When Ferrex learned this he escaped from his brother by crossing the sea to Gaul. With the support of Suhard, King of the Franks, Ferrex returned and fought with his brother. Ferrex was killed in the battle between them and so too was all the force which had come over with him. Their mother, whose name was Judon, was greatly distressed when she heard of her son's death. She was consumed with hatred for Porrex, for she had loved Ferrex more than him. Judon became so unbalanced by the anguish which the death of Ferrex had caused her that she made up her mind to avenge the death upon his brother Porrex. She chose a time when Porrex was asleep, set upon him with her maid-servants and hacked him to pieces.

As a result of this the people of Britain were for a long time embroiled in civil war; and the island came into the hands of five kings who kept attacking and massacring each other's men in turn . . .

2. Robert Fabyan, *Prima pars cronecarum*, chapters 24, 25, 26

Gorbodio the sone of [Kinimachus] was made ruler of Brytayne, in the yere of the worlde folowyng the foresayd accompte, iiii.M. CCCCC. & .xlix [i.e. 4549] whiche allso passed his tyme lyke unto the forenamed Dukes or kyngs, without any speciall memory of honoure notyd by wryters. This [king], by most lykelyhode to [brynge] hystories to accorde, shulde reygne over the Brytons the terme of lxiii [63] yeres, which terme endyd, he dyed, and lyeth buryed at new Troy or London, levyinge after hym ii sones named Ferrex [and] Porrex, or after some wryters Ferreus [and] Porreus.

Ferrex with Porrex his brother, sonnes of Gorbodio, were joyntly made governours and dukes of Brytayne, in the yere of the worlde iiii.M. vii C and xi [471[sic], in fact an error for 4611] & contynued in Amytie a certayne tyme: After which tyme being expyrid . . . Porrex being Covetous of lordshyp, gaderyd his people, unwetynge Ferrex his brother, entendynge to distroy hym; whereof he [Ferrex] beyng warned, for lacke of space to assemble his people, For savegarde of his persone fled sodeynly into Gallia or Fraunce, & axyd ayde of a Duke of Gallia, named by Gaufride [i.e. Geoffrey of Monmouth] Gurhardus or [Suardus], the whiche duke hym ayded, & sent hym agayne into Britayne with his hoost of Gallis; after which landyng his brother Porrex with his Brytons hym mette, & gave to hym batayll, in the whiche Batayll Ferrex was slayne with ye more parte of his people.

But here discordyth myn Auctour with some other wryters, and with the Chronycle of Englande, for they testyfye that Porrex was slayne & Ferrex survyved; but whether [i.e. whichever of the two] of them was lyvynge, the moder of thyse ii bretherne named [Widen] settynge aparte all moderly pytie, with helpe of her women entryd the Chambre of hym so lyvynge, by nyght, and hym there slepynge slewe cruelly, and cut into smal peces, and thus dyed the ii foresayd bretherne, after they had thus ruled Bretayn in warre and peas, to thagrement of most wryters v yeres.

Here nowe endyth ye lyne or ofsprynge of Brute, after ye affermaunce of moste wryters, for Gaufride sayth, after the deth of these forenamed bretherne, great discorde arose amonge the Brytons, ye which longe tyme among them contynued; By meane whereof the people and countre was sore vexed & noyed under v kynges. And further sayth Guydo de Columpna [Guido delle Colonne] that ye Brytons abhorred the lynage of Gorbodio, for so moche as firste that one brother slewe ye other, And more for Innaturall disposicion of the moder [that] so cruelly slewe her owne childe.

The Cronycle of Englande sayth, that after ye deth of the two forenamed bretherne, no ryghtfull enheritor was laft on lyve; wherefore ye people were brought in great discorde . . .

3. Edmund Spenser, *The Faerie Queene*, II. X. 34, 35, 36.

> His [Cunhah's] sonne *Rivallo* his dead roome did supply,
>   In whose sad time bloud did from heaven raine:
>   Next great *Gurgustus*, then faire *Caecily*
>   In constant peace their kingdomes did containe,
>   After whom *Lago*, and *Kinmarke* did raine,
>   And *Gorbogud*, till farre in yeares he grew:
>   Till his ambitious sonnes unto them twaine,

Guido delle Colonne: thirteenth-century Sicilian author of a *Historia Destructionis Troiae*, adapted from a poem by Benoît de Sainte-Maure.

Arraught [fashioned] the rule, and from their father
    drew [withdrew],
Stout *Ferrex* and sterne *Porrex* him in prison threw.

But O, the greedy thirst of royall crowne,
    That knowes no kinred, nor regardes no right,
    Stird *Porrex* up to put his brother downe;
    Who unto him assembling forreine might,
    Made warre on him, and fell him selfe in fight:
    Whose death t'avenge, his mother mercilesse,
    Most mercilesse of women, *Wyden* hight,
    Her other sonne fast sleeping did oppresse,
And with most cruell hand him murdred pittilesse.

Here ended *Brutus* sacred progenie,
    Which had seven hundred yeares this scepter borne,
    With high renowme, and great felicitie;
    The noble braunch from th'antique stocke was torne
    Through discord, and the royall throne forlorne:
    Thenceforth this Realme was into factions rent,
    Whilest each of *Brutus* boasted to be borne,
    That in the end was left no moniment
Of *Brutus*, nor of Britons glory auncient.

GLOSSARY

abroad: in the open air, outside

abstracts: plot outlines, synopses

abuse: deceive, delude

accident: event, happening, incident, incidental detail

actions: lawsuits

adamant: hard rock, magnetic stone

adjudge: condemn, sentence

adrad: greatly frightened

advantage: assistance, help, opportunity

advantages: taking advantage

adventure: take risks

advise: consider, ponder well, reflect, take care

aggots: aiglets, shiny lace-tags

airs: vapours, winds

Albany: Scotland

Albion: England

all is one: it doesn't matter

all one: 'neither here nor there'

all only: merely

allow: accept, approve of

ambages: ambiguous remarks

amity: friendship, love

and: if

apparent: evident, undoubted

appease: pacify

appointed to: assigned to

apprehension: comprehension, grasp on the situation

approved: proved

argument: demonstration, indication, manifestation, plot, scenario, subject-matter, token

articles: points, terms

articulated: listed as items

as: so that

as if: so that if

ask: demand, require

aspect: appearance, looks

assay: assail

assuage: appease, calm

assure: make certain

at full: amply, totally, utterly

attend: await

author: agent, causer, instigator, originator, promoter, 'voucher for'

avail: advantage, benefit, help

avowed: pledged, sworn

aye (for): always, for ever

backed with: supported by a background of

bacon: pig

baleful (humours): pernicious (tendencies)

ballace: weigh down

balm: a soothing restorative

band: bond (noun)
bane: agent of ruin, poisoner
banned: cursed
bare: meagre, simple
base: lowly, mean
baseness: contemptible character
Bashaw: officer, Pasha
battle: force, body of troops
bear: accept, put up with
bear (it out): pretend, 'carry it off'
beg at: entreat
behoof: benefit
behove: befit
bend: aim, direct, level, apply, incline
bent: applied, braced, directed
beray: disfigure, soil
berayed: defiled, dirtied
bereave: dispossess, rob, remove
bescratched: very badly scratched
beseemed: was appropriate to, became, befitted
betide: befall
beware: take warning
bewray: disclose, expose, let out, reveal
blandishment: allurement
blasted: blighted by frost
bleared: deceived by blurring, distorted the vision
blood: bloodshed
bode: endured
book (the): the almanac
book-keeper: prompter
boot: compensation (noun): profit (verb)
boot (to): also, as well
bootless: incurable, lacking remedy, useless
boots not: is no good to
bound: frontier, boundary
bow: bend, deflect

bowed: brought low
bower: arbour, leafy recess
braid: start, sudden jerk
brake: bushy thicket
brave: bold, 'smart', splendid
bravely: worthily
break: confess, reveal
breathe abroad: express freely
breathing: breath, breeze
brittle: fragile, perishable
broils: tumults
brook: endure, stand
brought to light: gave birth to
brunt: assault, onslaught
bugs: 'bogies', hobgoblins
burden: musical refrain or theme
burn daylight: waste time
but: anything, except, only
by: through
bye: pay for

caitiff: (adj.) despicable, wretched
Camberland: Cambria, Wales
camp: army, 'host'
cankers: inward malice
carbine: armed and mounted soldier, carabin
care: caution, concern
carefull: full of anxiety, care
careless: lacking care
carrion: dead flesh meat
cast: arranged, devised, effected, planned
catastrophe: dénouement, 'terrible finale'
cause: affair, business, facts of the matter (noun); because (conj.)
cease: bring to a halt
censure: judgement
certain: acknowledged, indubitable
chance: fortune

changeling: child surreptitiously substituted

charge: aim, burden, level, responsibility

charged: enjoined, ordered

chevalier: cavalier, knight

civil: communal

clap up: bundle into custody

cleanly: efficiently

clear: expunge, purge

clepe: call (to witness)

cloaked: concealed

close: contact (noun); agree (verb); hidden (adj.)

close with: 'come to grips with', grapple with

closely: secretly, subtly

coil: rumpus

colour: pretence, pretext, semblance

coloured: counterfeited

commends: compliments, greetings (noun)

commixed: mingled

common: general

common weal: public good

companions: 'low types', 'nobodies'

compare: comparison

compass: bounds, extent (noun); bring about, effect (verb)

complaint: amorous pleading

complaints: expressions of grievance

complot: conspiracy

conceited: formed

conceits: gags, notions, pleasing concepts, quips

conceived: imagined

condiscent: agreement, consent

condition: nature, personality

confederate: accomplice, associate

confirm: strengthen, support

confused: disordered, unruly

confusion: destruction, overthrow, ruin

consent: agree

consort: accompany, escort

constrain: compel, enforce, exert

contemn: despise, disdain, scorn

contend: battle

content: contentment

control: curb, restrain

conveyance: cunning dealing

cornet: company of cavalry

corregidor: advocate

corsive: corrosive, eating substance

countercheck: halt by interposing

counterfeit: imitate, impersonate

countermured: enclosed within double walls

courage: ambitiousness, encouragement, pride, spirits, vigour

courser: war-horse

coy it: pretend to be indifferent

credit: credence, reliability (noun); believe (verb)

cross: encounter, frustrate, match, oppose (verb); sword-hilt (noun)

cunning: skill

cunningly: cleverly, knowingly

dag: a heavy pistol

dainties: dishes, fare

dalliance: amorous play

dally: trifle

dark: darken (verb)

darksome: dark and gloomy

debate: dissension, strife

decay: decline in health and strength

declaration: statement of claim

deed: crime

deep: the ocean (noun); solemn (adj.)

defend: avert, ward off

deferred: prolonged

deflowered: ravished

deign: think fit

demean (him): behave, conduct (himself)

depart: departure

derived down: bequeathed, handed down

descant on: 'give a commentary on', 'go on about'

descended: hereditary

desert: merit, worthiness (noun); desolate (adj.)

deserved: justly carried, was worthy of

despite: contempt, hatred, insult, scornfulness

despiteful: malicious, malignant

determine of: decide on the method of, fix

determined: agreed, decided upon, resolved, settled

detested: detestable, disgusting, hateful, revolting

device: plan, plot, scheme, stratagem, trick, ingenious entertainment

devise: plan, plot, scheme

dewed: damped, moistened

dinged: knocked, smashed

direful: dreadful, terrible

dirge: funeral hymn

discharged: executed

discontent: vexation

discretion: exercise of judgement, prudence

disdain: contempt, indignation

disfurnish: divest, strip

disjoined: 'undone'

disparagement: indignity

dispatch: hurry up, make haste

dispoil: uncover, strip

distain: defile, stain

distract: deranged

distressed: crushed in battle

distressful: anxious, badly distressed, troubled

distrust: breach of trust, treachery

divorce: separation

doom: judgement, sentence (noun); pronounce judgement on (verb)

dote: act madly, love to excess

doubt: anxiety, apprehension, danger, fear

doubtful: uncertain

doubtless: undoubted

draw: bring, put

drawn: drafted, drawn up

dreadful: full of dread

dreary: bloody, gloomy, horrible

duke: leader

during: enduring, lasting

each where: in every place

eager: fierce, keen

ecstasies: rapturous outbursts

effect: be effectual

either: both

ejectione firmae: writ to evict a tenant

eke: also

end: completed, ended

engrossed: concentrated, monopolized

enjoin: impose on, strictly command, engage, join together

enjoyed: possessed

enlarged: set free

entertain: cherish, maintain

entertainment: social exchange

enthralled: enslaved, imprisoned

entreated: behaved towards, treated

entreats: entreaties, supplications

envious: odious, spiteful
envying at: filled with envy towards
equity: fair play, justice
erst: previously
estate: kingdom, rank, state, status, social class
estate (chair of): royal throne, 'state chair'
even: impartial, just
exasperate: exacerbate, increase the severity of, intensify
exclaim against: denounce, protest
exclaims: exclamations, outcries
exempt: debar
expected: anticipated, awaited
experience: trial
expressly: explicitly, positively
expulse: expel
extend to: signify
extinct: extinguished, 'out'
extremes: circumstances, crises, dire circumstances, harshest severity, stringent punishments
extremest: cruellest
extremities: dire straits, deep emotions

fact: action, crime, deed
faggot: bundle
fail: become bankrupt, deceive, let down
fair: 'sweet'
faith: trustworthiness
fall from: abandon
fame: renown, reputation
farder: further
fashion: mere form
fatch: contrivance, trick
fathers: ancestors, forefathers
fauchion: broad curved sword
fault: crime, culpability, offence
favour: love-token

fear: frighten
feature: bodily shape, bearing
feelingly: acutely, with a sense of pain
fell: cruel, deadly
fenced: fortified, protected
fet: drawn, fetched
find: discern, make out
fine (in): at last, finally
fit: behove, fix, satisfy
flattering: beguiling, complimentary
flout: mock
fond: amorously foolish, stupidly diffident
for: because of, since
for why: because
forced: impose on him
foreset (of): intentionally
forged: carried out, devised, feigned
forgery: falsehood
forth: out of
fortune: destiny
forward: eager, presumptuous
forwardness: initiative, zeal
frame: compose, contrive, direct, make up, construct, create
fraud: deception
fraught: filled, laden, weighed down
friend: lover
frolic: full of fun (adj.); 'live it up', make merry, sport (verb)
front: brow, forehead
froward: adverse, awkward, perverse
furnish: provide, set up
furnished: provided, equipped, stocked
fury: fierce emotion

gage (to): as a pledge
gain: obtain agreement
gallery: covered walk

gape for: eagerly desire
gaping: eager
gear: affair, business, 'little matter'
generally: by all
gentle: kind, well-bred
gin: begin
gird in: confine
give back: pull out, reject, withdraw
give over: abandon
give way: allow free scope
go by: keep out of trouble, let it go
grace: countenance, honour (noun); back up, embellish (verb)
gracing: adorning, 'mounting'
grafted: implanted
gramercy!: thank goodness!
grandam: grandmother
graved: buried
graven leaves: engraved writings
gree in one: mutually agree, 'see eye to eye'
greet: honour, salute
griefull: full of sorrow
gripe: vulture
ground: basis (noun); base behaviour on, found (verb)
grudge: scruple, uneasiness
grudging: resentful
guerdon: due recompense, 'medicine', reward
gummed: sticky, stuck tight

habit: clothing
haggard: in a wild state, untamed
hainous: hateful, infamous
halberts: halberdiers
hale: drag
handkercher: handkerchief
hap: chance, happen (verb); (mis)fortune, luck, occurrence (noun)
hapless: ill-luck-bearing, unfortunate, unlucky, void of hope
hardly: harshly, unreasonably, with difficulty
harms: evil acts
hatefull: full of hate
hautboys: oboes
hazard: expose to risk, imperil
heads: leaders
heaps (so many): such a mass
hearken to: attend to
heat: fury, strife
heavy case (in): in a sorry state
here-hence: as a result
helpless: remediless
hereto: to this
hest: command, order, bidding
hie: chase, go, speed
hight: named, was called
hold: adjudge to be, include, stop, work
holp: helped
homely: kindly
homicide: killer, murderer
hour (by the): at fixed times
humane: kindly
humorous: moody, temperamental
humour: fancy whim, strange 'turn', temperament, tendency

ill advised: injudicious
ill-maimed: badly injured
ill-succeeding: turning out badly
ills: evils, harmful acts
image: reflection, symbol
imagines: plans (noun)
imbrued: stained
imperfection: senility
imperial: empyreal, of highest heaven
import: significance, weight
inclined: tended to favour

inclining: downward sloping
incomparable: without precedent
indiscreet: impudent
inevitable: inescapable
inexpected: unexpected, unlooked for
inexplicable: permanently tied
infect: corrupted, diseased, infected
infective: infection-bearing
infernal: hellish, underworldly
infortunate: ill-fortuned, luckless
injurious: wickedly hurtful
insatiate: discontented, unsatisfied
instance: instant, moment, proof
insult for: behave arrogantly over, brag about
insulting: exulting arrogantly
intercept: block, hinder, obstruct
interdicted: forbidden
intimate: proclaim publicly
inured: accustomed, conducted, practised
invade: seize, usurp
invention: contrivance, design
inviolate: impervious to inquiry
ire: anger
ireful: angry

jarring: ticking by
jealous: suspicious, vigilant, watchful, zealous
joined: encountered in conflict
joys: enjoys
jutty: jut out, project

keep: maintain, guard, hold captive
kill: stab
kind: commonsense, natural conduct, kinship, descent, birth, heritage, nature, sex
kindly: familial, natural
kindness: affection

kindship: good will, kindness
knavery: crafty trick

labour: engineer, work hard for
large: ample, broad
large (at): freely, fully, openly
largely (more): more freely, more fully
largesse: bounty, liberality
late: recent
lately: recently
latest: final
league: alliances, friendship
least: lest
leese: lose
leisure: 'a breathing space'
lend: grant, impart
length: lengthen
length (at the): in the fullness of time
let me alone: leave it to me
lewd: base, vile, wicked
lewdly: wickedly
life: lifetime
light: comfort
lights: 'bright glances', gleams, 'rays'
like: please, satisfy
limed: made sticky, smeared, caught, trapped
list: choose, wish
lively: lifelike, living
living: active, glowing
loadstar: 'guiding light'
longs: belongs
looked: anticipated, expected
lotted: allotted
lottery: chance, fortune
lotting: apportioning land
lust: desire, obsessive desire
lustful: cheerful, vigorous, vital

madding: frenzied
make repair: appear
make up: arrange, settle
malice: harmfulness, injurious
  nature
maliced: entertained malice
malign: regard with envy or hate
man-at-arms: armoured horse-
  soldier
map: guidebook
martialist: soldier, warrior
mask: 'cloak', 'cover'
Mass: by the Mass
mass: dense aggregation
massy: solid, weighty
match: encounter
matted: 'matt finish'?
matter: content of significance
mean: agent, instrument, course of
  action, means, method (noun);
  lenient, moderate (adj.)
mean (by ... of): as a result of
mean (in the): in the meantime
meaner: less exalted
measure: recompense, treatment
meditation: preparation time, study
meed: gain, reward
melancholy: depression, state of
  grief
men's-kind: male creatures
mindful: brooding, unforgetting
mining: undermining
minister: agent, executant
minority: while under age
mirror: example, model
mischief: calamity, damage, disaster,
  evil, trouble, wickedness
misconceived: suspected
misconster: misconstrue, 'get me
  wrong'
miscreant: rogue, villain
misdeem: suspect, fear

misdone: acted wrongfully,
  destroyed
misdoubt: distrust, misgiving
mishaps: wretched fortune
mistrust: suspect the existence of
moe: more
moiety of: half share in
mood: fierce spirit
mortal: deathly
motion: impulse, proposal
mought: might
mould: making (i.e. of earth),
  shaping
mount: climb socially
move: impel, prompt
mustachio: moustache
mutable: changeable, fickle
mystery: hidden meaning, unknown
  outcome

nature: affection, natural feelings
ne ... ne: neither ... nor
nearer: more personal, more serious,
  more vital
neck (in his): on his shoulders
neglect: disregard, leave unattended
neighbour-bounding: adjacent
new begun: entered a new phase
next: handiest, nearest
nill: will not
nipped: destroyed with frost,
  'nipped in the bud'
no notice: not kept informed
no way: no form of entrance
nobility: noble status
noblesse: nobility
noisome: noxious, offensive
none: no, nobody
notice: knowledge

occasion: opportunity
of: concerning, provided by

offence: displeasure
only: merely
oppress: crush in battle, overwhelm
or: either
ordnance: artillery
outrage: extravagant behaviour, violent behaviour or outburst
overcloying: excessively satiating
overkindly: abnormally indulgent
overthrew: fell down

painted: dissembled, feigned, superficial
pangs: anguish, keen emotion
parasite: 'sponger'
pass: surpass
passengers: passers-by
passing: exceedingly, utterly
passion: distressed condition, painful suffering, strong feelings, upset state
passport: authorization, letter of safe conduct
pate: head
pattern: 'blueprint, model'
paunched: slit up the belly
pease: appease, pacify
peer: equal
persuade: win over
persuasions: convincing pieces of evidence
pestered: encumbered, plagued
piece: firearm
pinched: was niggardly, stinted
pined: wasted through suffering
pining: tormenting
pins: spangled decorations
pitched: determined, fixed
pitchy: 'deepest', pitch-black
place (give): take your turn
plain me: express my complaint, grief

plaints: lamentations
plausible: pleasing, praiseworthy
pleasure: take pleasure, amuse
plot: scenario
point: culmination, resolution
policy: crafty purpose, stratagem
politic: artful, cunning, scheming, shrewd
poniard: dagger
poor: humble, unfortunate
porch: entrance
possessed: enjoyed sexually
post (in): in haste
posting: hurrying
practice: action, conspiracy, deception, intrigue, plot, scheme, treachery
practise: contrive, plot, scheme, study
preferred: advanced, promoted
prefix: arrange in advance
present: immediate, instant
presently: immediately, straightaway
presumption: assumption
pretence: false purpose
pretended: proffered
prevailance: mastery, predominance
prevent: anticipate, frustrate, forestall
prick forth: inspired
prickle: thorn
pride: 'the pink', the top of my form
prime: 'the prime of life'
privilege: royal prerogative
procrastinating: delaying
procure: care for
professor: creator, practitioner
proffers: proposals
proof: attempt, evidence, experience
propitious: as a good sign

proposed: anticipated, looked forward

prosecute: seek to bring about

protract: delay

puissant: powerful, strong

purge: cleanse, purify

purple: crimson, bloody

purpose to: intention towards

push of pike: hand-to-hand engagement

quaint: cunning, ingenious

quick: importunate, 'quick off the mark', sharp

quill: pipe from a hollow stem

quitall: amends, reparation

rage: rashness, violence

raked: covered up

rampiers: ramparts

ran abroad: circulated freely

random: impetuosity (noun); deviate, stray at liberty (verb)

range: stroll about

rank: crowded, foul, thick

rase: eradicate, erase

rated: reproached, reproved

raw in mind: fresh in thought

razed: destroyed, obliterated

reached: achieved, struck

reaching: far-seeing, shrewd

reave: plunder, rob, bereave, deprive of

reaved: bereft, deprived

reck: heed, regard

recompt: consider, go over, reckon up

record: sing, warble, recall, remember (verb); testimony (noun)

records: witnesses (noun)

recure: recover, restore to life

rede: counsel, prudence

reduced: restored

reft: eradicated, taken away

regard: concern with, have an eye to

regard (in): seeing that

register: set down

regrate: compassion, lament

reign: territory to rule (noun); control (verb)

remain: continue to belong

rent: pull apart, rend, tear

repair: replace, restore

repine: begrudge, resent

repress: restrain, suppress, withstand

reproachful: shameful

requite: avenge, pay back, repay, reward

reserve: keep, preserve for

reserving: rescuing, saving

resolution: confidence, determination, what is resolved upon

resolve on: decide on

resolved: convinced, satisfied

rest: rely, remain, trust

retort: repay, return

reveal: disclose, explain

rigour: strict enforcement

riots (mad): crazy revelry, 'daft pranks'

rolls: historical documents

roots: extirpates, uproots

rounded: whispered

roundly: readily

routs: gangs, hordes, mobs

routs (rascal): good-for-nothing rabble

rude: rough, unpolished

ruder: clumsier, coarser

rue: have pity on

ruth: compassion

ruthfull: grievous, lamentable, pitiful

ruthless: merciless

sable: black

sable weed: black clothing

sadly: pensively, thoughtfully

saffron: 'crocus-yellow', orange-yellow

salute: greet

salve: allay, heal

satisfy: make expiation

scindered: severed

scour: roam vigorously over, skirmish

scurvy: 'dirty', shabby

seated: positioned

secret: circumspect, uncommunicative

Secretary: official entrusted with private business

secretary: confidant

secure: assured, 'cocky', confident

seld: seldom

self: integrated, single

sequestered: isolated, secluded

serve: suffice

settled: established

shamefastness: decency, modesty

show: display, presentation, spectacle, tableau

shift (let me): leave it to me

shifts: 'clever tricks'

shot: firing

silly: defenceless, frail, helpless, pitiful, 'poor', simple, weak

simplicity: apparent naïvety

sit beside: discount, set to one side

sith: since

sithens: since

skilless: ignorant, inept

slaked: extinguished, quenched

slandered: discredited, lowered in esteem

slaves: men beneath contempt, 'scum'

sleep away: sleep through

sleeve: token

sleight: craft, trickery

smooth: flatter, gloss over

soft: 'hang on', wait

solicit: entreat, importune, pester for sexual favours, urge

soliciting: demanding, ensnaring, enticing, entreating, pleading, urging

soonest: quickest

soothe his humours up: humour him, indulge his fancy

soothe me up: back me up

sort: kind of way, manner

sort (in such): in the very condition

sort of (a): 'a bit of a crowd', several

sorted: assigned, arranged, contrived

sound: fathom, understand

sounding to: implying, tending towards

speaking: eloquent, meaningful

spirits: demons

spoil: deprive, destroy, pillage, plunder, sack

spoiled: stripped

spread: cover, overrun

sprite: spirit

squadron form: in a square

staff: lance, spear

stale: stole

standing: confrontation

state: condition, status

stay: abate, arrest, check, detain, halt, hold back, hold off (on), restrain, stabilize, uphold (verb);

equilibrium, impasse, prop, rest, stability, standstill, support (noun)

stay (in): stable, steady

stays: restraints

stern: rudder

still: always, eternally, permanently

stocks: kindred

stoop: plunge, swoop

stop: block, gag

stopped: obstructed, dammed up

store: abundance, resource

straight: immediately

strange: notable, rare, remarkable

strangely: wonderfully

stranger: alien

strives: contends, struggles

strokes: blows

strond: beach, strand, shore

study: apply myself, seek to achieve (verb); library, private room (noun)

suage: alleviate, appease, assuage

substance: estate, means, riches

subvert: overthrown

succeed: come to pass, inherit, succeed to, turn out

success: outcome, result

sudden: abrupt

suffer: allow

sufferance: long suffering, patient endurance

suggestion: false accusation

surcease: cease, come to an end

surcharged: overloaded, weighed down

surprised: taken prisoner

suspect: anything to create suspicion

sustains: submits to

swerving: deviating

ta'en: taken

tempting: provocative

tender: easy-going

tendered: cherished, nurtured

that: in order that, in order to ensure that, with which

thereto: for that purpose, to this

this: these

thorough: through

thought: 'fancy', mind

thoughtfull: anxious

thoughtless: without reflecting carefully

thoughts: imaginings, 'wishful thinking'

through-girt: struck through

tickle: insecure, precarious

tilt: combat on horseback

time (in): at the right moment

title: placard with the location on

to: such as to

toil: fatigue, weary

tolerate: allow to persist

tortures: means of torture

tottering: swaying

towardness: aptitude, promise

toy: a mere trifle, trifle, trivial point

trade: way of life

tragedians: tragic actors

train: company, retinue, suite, deceit, guile, plot

traitor: betrayer

transpose: corrupt, pervert

travail: labour to effect, toil

travailers: labourers, those who travail

treat: negotiate

trial: determination, 'testing'

tribute: money as tribute

trice (with a): immediately

troth: faith, truth, trust

trudge: get going, move on

truss: tight jacket
truss up: hang, 'string up'
trusty: loyal, trustworthy
truth: genuineness
try: ascertain, determine, prove, select
turned off: hanged
twines: threads
twink (with a): in a twinkling

unbevelled: raw, unpolished
unchosen: 'common', undistinguished, unfavoured
undeserving: unjustified
undiscreet: impudent
unfold: explain, reveal
unfortunate: disastrous, miserable, unlucky
unhap: misfortune
unjust: faithless
unkind: cruel, inhuman, unnatural
unknown: dubious, non-native, uncertain, unrevealed
unmanured: uncultivated, unfertilized
unmastered: insubordinate, incontrolled, untamed
unquiet: times of turmoil
unrest: discomfort, anxiety, turmoil
unskilful: inexperienced, inexpert, unaware
untempered: immoderate, uncontrolled
uphold: entertain, sustain
ure: practice
urged: impelled, provoked, stimulated
use: ask support of, employ, maintain, make use of, treat
uttermost: the most extreme penalty

valiancy: courage, valour

valure: merit, worthiness
vantage: advantage, opportunity
vaunting: proudly exhibiting
vented: disclosed, divulged
ventured: risked
vestal: chaste
vild: vile
vouchsafe: deign, graciously consent
vulgar: common folk

wail: bewail
wait: look forward hopefully
want: lack
want for: loss of
wanton: amorously inclined, wayward
wantons: lechers, people of loose behaviour
war: battle
ward: guard, shield
warned: cautioned, ordered
was: caused
waste: devastated, void
watch: guard, tend
watch and ward: guard, patrol
water-breach: an irruption of water, a spate
wealth: good, prosperity, welfare
wearing: wearing out
wedges: metal blocks for splitting timber
weigh: consider, weigh up
weld: govern, rule, wield
welding: carrying
wellnear: almost, virtually
whereof: why
whereto: to what purpose
whether: which of two
which: whichever
while: meantime
whilom: formerly, once
whipstalk: a whip with a handle

wide: wide of the mark

wight: creature, human being, person

wilder: erratic, more passionate

wile: crafty device

wilful mad: obstinately unreasonable

will: wilful attitude

wings (of shot): musketeers on flanks

wit: know (verb); intellect, mind (noun)

withal: as well, besides

withdraw: disperse, divert

wither: dried up

without: outside

wits: skill, talent

woe-begone: grief-stricken, oppressed with misfortune

won: secured

wonted: customary

work it: bring it off, have it agreed

worldlings: mundane beings

wot: know

wrack: wreckage

wrapped: conceded, enclosed, enraptured

wreak: avenge

wreakful: vengeful

writ: document, writing

writhe: deflect

wroke: avenged

wroth: angry

wry: perverted, unjust

yielden: surrendered, yielded